Praise for

A World

Nominated for the CIL.

Longlisted for The Guardian Children's Fiction Prize 2013

Highly Commended for Branford Boase Award 2013

'*A World Between Us* is an outstanding debut novel for teenagers . . . Thoroughly researched and beautifully written.'

The Guardian

'A fantastic historical fiction debut set in the Spanish Civil War, featuring a wonderfully passionate and resourceful heroine.'

The Bookseller, August 2012 (Pick of the Month)

'Carefully-researched and rich with fascinating period detail, *A World Between Us* is a compelling story of politics and passion, bravery and love.'

Booktrust

'A multi-layered story about politics, nationalism and the rose-tinted desire to create a better and more equal world.'

Books For Keeps

'Syson brings history alive through careful detail.'

The Observer

'A gripping romantic adventure.'

TES Magazine

'Well crafted and well written, this novel delivers an attractive mix of romance and rebellion.'

Celia Rees in Armadillo

'Packed full of passion . . . this is a harrowing, thrilling and romantic account of the Spanish Civil War.'

That Burning Summer

'This is only the second novel from an author very much to look out for.'

'A touching evocation of a desperate wartime romance, which evokes a vanished era of hardship and fortitude.'

'Lydia Syson is the kind of writer who lets you know from the outset that you're in safe hands.'

'Syson's beautifully developed characters . . . make the history come vividly to life.'

'Beautifully evoking the atmosphere of a small rural community under threat, it simmers with tension and intensity: readers will be rooting for Peggy and Henryk and captivated by their blossoming romance.'

'Not once did I want to put the book down . . . A beautiful, enchanting and memorable book which captured war perfectly and hooked me within its pages.'

Liberty's Fire

Liberty's Fire

LYDIA SYSON

HOT
KEY
BOOKS

First published in Great Britain in 2015 by Hot Key Books
Northburgh House, 10 Northburgh Street, London EC1V 0AT

A CIP catalogue record for this book is available from the British Library.

ISBN: 978-1-4714-0367-5

1

This book is typeset in 10.5 Berling LT Std using Atomik ePublisher

Printed and bound by Clays Ltd, St Ives Plc

www.hotkeybooks.com

Hot Key Books is part of the Bonnier Publishing Group
www.bonnierpublishing.com

Supported using public funding by
ARTS COUNCIL
ENGLAND
LOTTERY FUNDED

ALSO BY LYDIA SYSON

A World Between Us
That Burning Summer

For Phoebe

Macadam [tarmac]: Has put an end to revolutions; barricades no longer possible. Nonetheless very inconvenient.

Ruins: Something to make you dream. Add poetry to a landscape.

Dictionary of Accepted Ideas,
published 1913 from notes made
by Flaubert in the 1870s

'There's more to love than girl meets boy'
From *Red* by the Communards, 1987

MARCH 1871

This is the story of a revolution, and a city that rose to claim its rights.

In the summer of 1870, Napoleon III, emperor of France, recklessly declared war on Prussia – the most provocative and powerful of the German states. Instead of glory, the emperor met with humiliation. Instead of victory, he found defeat. France became a republic for the third time in a century, and under a troubled makeshift government the war with Prussia intensified.

Soon Paris was under siege. Deprivation and disease killed thousands, yet the citizens who stayed refused to give up. But patriotism doesn't fill an empty belly. Parisians looked for food in the sewers and the zoological gardens: rats, birds, dogs and elephants ended up on plates. Then the bombardment began.

Twenty kilometres away, in the Hall of Mirrors at the French Palace of Versailles, the King of Prussia was crowned German emperor and the Second Reich was born. Nine days later, to the fury of besieged Paris, France surrendered. The Prussian army marched in triumph through a silent city draped in black, and then retreated to camps all along the eastern walls to watch and wait, wait and watch. This armistice had cost the country a great slice of France, and millions of francs, which all had to be paid. The Prussians would not leave without their spoils. It was a bitter, glowering peace.

And the shame of it for Paris! The betrayal! They had been sold, not defeated, said the cabmen. The city was seething. Just one false step, and the barricades would rise again.

1.

Jules stared intently at the image emerging under the sunlight. Blues turning to browns, the tones shifting before his eyes. Trapped behind the glass of the wooden printing frame were the ruins of the emperor's out-of-town palace: scarred columns, gaping roof, sky and rubble, all slowly appearing in their sudden and terrible decay.

This sight was even more shocking than the real thing. Face-to-face with the crumbling shell of a building at Saint-Cloud a few days earlier, halfway between Paris and Versailles, Jules's chief concern had been to get the plate out of the camera and safely developing in his portable darkroom within the ten minutes it took for the collodion to dry. He had managed this not once, but three, four, and finally five times. Three interiors, one view across the water – with some very effective reflections – and this, which you'd hardly know whether to call an interior or an exterior shot. The last plate he had left to print.

This was the point of decision, the moment that always made his heart thud harder. Now. Precisely now. He unclipped the back of the frame, arresting the print at just that fraction of a second when the image was perfect – neither bleached out of recognition nor too shadowy and dark to make it out. He peeled the albumen paper back from the glass-plate negative and there it was. A true representation. A perfect witness. This is what I saw that day.

But there was more work to be done before he could admire the print: washing, toning, washing, fixing, washing again. Finally he laid the glistening image on the workbench and stood back. Once again, Jules Hippolyte Washington Crowfield had successfully performed the miracle that was photography. He felt entitled to some applause.

'Anatole!' he bellowed.

A violin stopped, listened, and into the pause Jules shouted for his friend a second time.

Thunderous feet. Anatole burst in, instrument tucked under his arm, bow waving, bringing a nose-tickling cloud of rosin into the room with him, and a half-grown tabby cat who'd overtaken him in her rush to get up the stairs.

'The dust!' cried Jules. He shooed them both straight out again, slamming the studio door behind them all, and almost caught the nose of the cat. 'I've told you a million times about the dust. How can I be expected to keep my plates clean when you bring in your filth?'

'But you called me,' protested Anatole. 'It sounded very urgent. A fire at the very least. All these chemicals – and that lamp! My God! I never know when you're about to go up in smoke.'

Jules gently took Anatole's violin and bow. He placed them on a side table on the improvised landing that linked the attic staircase to a curious construction perched high on the rooftop. An architectural afterthought, it served as both photographic studio and laboratory. When Jules wasn't curtained in darkness, he had a bird's-eye view of Paris: roofs, chimney pots and grey tiles stretched out forever. Inspecting Anatole's jacket, he brushed it down with his hands to remove every last trace of rosin. Then, with a cryptic smile, he led his friend inside.

The studio smelled of cider orchards in late autumn – a vinegary tang. Anatole's foot crunched on a discarded eggshell. A chair, a dusty pillar pretending to be a ruin, some velvet drapery and a dying potted palm were arranged at the far end of the room, next to a simple folding screen. They had entered at the business end: a workbench, tripods, hoods, shelves. A broken-spined copy of *Rational Photography*, propped next to *The Silver Sunbeam*. Various other manuals in English and French, which, thanks to a Martinique-born mother and a succession of French nursemaids through his childhood in East Liberty, Pennsylvania, Jules spoke perfectly.

Piled up below the bench was a heap of wooden boxes – baths, Jules called them. On top, stacks of glass and plate-holders, and above that, several shelves of stoppered bottles with labels in alphabetical order – collodion, ether, ferrous sulphate, potassium cyanide, rottenstone and silver nitrate. There was a kind of poetry in these words which Anatole enjoyed, though his attention tended to wander when Jules tried to explain each chemical. In the corner was the darkroom cupboard – red-shaded lamp, dripping tap – into which Jules vanished for hours to practise what Anatole called his 'black arts', and where he disappeared now.

'So what exactly did you want to show me?' Anatole asked. He frowned at a series of photographs leaning against the back wall. They were lined up on the floor like a battalion waiting for action. Most were of Anatole. 'Haven't I seen these already?'

He inspected himself critically, unconsciously mirroring his own expression in each. In some he stared straight at the camera, frank and knowing. Other photographs captured the fresh innocence of a young man new to a big city, a sense of possibility. Jules had also recorded every stage of each of Anatole's experiment with his whiskers over the past nine months – sideburns long and short, moustaches of varying degrees of lushness, a neat beard, very briefly – not a success, they both agreed. And a few pictures showed Anatole in his old National Guard uniform, adopting the usual military pose: right arm tucked into jacket, eyes fixed steadily on some invisible victory that lay ahead. A reservist during the recent war, he'd done his share of rampart duty, but never quite made it beyond the city walls. In every portrait, his black hair was equally dishevelled, his dark eyes just as compelling.

'Well?' said Anatole, wondering if Jules would ever look for another sitter for his experiments. Surely he must be tiring of photographing the same face – the same body indeed – for so many months? It would mean a rent rise: when Anatole had joined him in this grand apartment, Jules had generously suggested occasional modelling duties in the studio would do nicely in part-payment – he was only just getting to grips with photography at that point. But the theatres were reopening, and Anatole's income ought to be on the rise soon.

6

'One moment,' called Jules from the darkroom. He reappeared holding the glossy new print by its edges.

'This . . .' he said with uncharacteristic drama, setting it on a music stand he'd borrowed from Anatole. 'This is all that's left of Saint-Cloud now.'

They both stared.

'Incredible,' breathed Anatole.

'Isn't it?' Even Jules's voice wobbled a little.

'It's like . . . it's like . . .' Anatole had no words to describe the image before him. A gaping vista in tones of brown so rich they were almost purple. A roofless hall with twists of ironwork, convulsed as if by a giant's hand.

'It's like Pompeii . . . or Herculaneum, isn't it?' said Jules, twisting one end of his delicately pointed moustache.

'The end of an empire. Who would have dreamed it could come so quickly . . . unimaginable . . .'

'I know. Those are the gardens, through that broken archway.' Jules pointed from a safe distance.

'Oh yes, I can see the remains of the fountains.'

'Damnation . . . what's this?'

They both peered, bending shoulder to shoulder, hands clasped behind backs for fear of fingerprints. Right at the edge of the picture, the faintest of figures could be seen, like a spirit flitting past.

'An apparition!' said Anatole.

'Blast it! I thought I'd got a clear shot. Not quick enough. Never even saw that fellow, whoever he is . . . Hmmm . . . I wonder how I missed him. Yet another ghoul, I suppose, come to stare at horrors.'

'Unlike you, I suppose! Never mind. It all adds to the atmosphere,' Anatole said, trying to console Jules.

'The ghost of an autumnal guest, you mean? A final trace of one of the empress's famous house parties? And I never did get that invitation . . .'

For months, every time he wrote from America, Jules's father had repeated the question. An East Coast industrialist, he'd sent his younger son to Paris the year before to learn to trade on the Bourse – and make some useful connections of course. But almost any young man in the world would have been better suited than Jules to a career in financial speculation. And the timing could hardly have been worse. Barely had Jules arrived in Paris than the city began to ring with the cry of 'To Berlin!' Within a few months, Emperor Napoleon III was writhing in agony on the battlefield at Sedan, crippled by his gallstones, his army half-slaughtered by the Prussians. When the empire fell but the fighting continued, the richest residents of Paris abandoned the capital for their country estates, and Jules discovered his own spoils of war: a photography business and all its equipment, complete with a horse-drawn darkroom, up for sale for a song.

'Too late!' said Anatole. 'And now the Prussians have destroyed the palace completely.'

Jules shook his head. 'Oh no! This wasn't their doing. It was the French army who wrecked the palace, attacking the Prussians when they were occupying the heights of Saint-Cloud.'

'And they say the camera doesn't lie.'

'Nor does it. You're the one jumping to conclusions.'

'True,' said Anatole. 'So you've been round the city outskirts as far as you can now?'

'All the way to Saint-Denis. Where of course I had to stop. Terrible sight.'

Due north of Paris, Saint-Denis marked the beginning of the German zone of occupation, currently half-circling the city to the east.

'I don't suppose the Prussians are showing any signs of leaving?'

'Quite the reverse. They're not going to go without all the billions of francs they're asking for. It does make you wonder though. Is this peace or just a truce?'

'Maybe it's no bad thing the rabble rescued their cannon last month,' suggested Anatole.

It hadn't exactly been planned. But before the Prussian victory march, the 'red' militiamen of the National Guard – the people's army – had raided the gun parks and arsenals of central Paris. With the help of women and children, they'd hauled several hundred cannon to the safety of the heights of Montmartre, Belleville and other radical working-class neighbourhoods. When you can't trust your own government to look after you, you have to take things into your own hands. After all that had happened, they weren't prepared to be left defenceless. Even the poorest had sacrificed what little they had to help pay for these cannon.

'Something's definitely up now,' he continued. 'Every time I look out of the window, there seems to be another troop of militiamen marching by . . . Did you hear the church bells hammering away earlier? As soon as I've got Act II under my belt, I'm going out to see what's happening.'

Jules glanced at the window. From the studio you had to go right out onto the roof to see down into the street below. 'I heard

9

drums when I let the cat out, and I wondered. Well, no doubt you'll get a message from the battalion, if you're really needed.'

'No, I won't,' said Anatole. 'Didn't I tell you? I resigned last week. Handed my uniform back and everything. Didn't seem much point any more. No more thirty sous for me!' He was distracted by the sight of another print, equally melancholic. 'Have I seen this before?'

'No, I went through the Bois on the way to Saint-Cloud.'

This one showed the elegant parkland of the Bois de Boulogne, now looking more like a graveyard than a pleasure garden. Lines of hacked tree stumps stretched out like tombstones. A few bare branches lay on the grass, about to be dragged away for fuel. A couple of ducks swam right in the middle of the lake, where they couldn't be reached to be eaten, but the swans were all gone. Round the edge of the lake wandered a few wraithlike shapes, living shadows. Jules was still experimenting with his exposure times.

'Not one of my better efforts.'

'I like the effect. That blurriness. Almost romantic, which is no bad thing. It's depressing to see the Bois like this. Don't you remember how lovely it was last summer?' said Anatole, draping a friendly arm round Jules's shoulders. The cat, Minou, wound herself round their legs. 'Oh well. Life's getting much brighter now – gas back in the streets, shops opening, boulevards busy again. Paris will soon fill up. And spring's just round the corner – everything will look different then.'

'I hope so.' But Jules's voice sounded ominous. He obviously wasn't thinking about daffodils. 'By the way,' he continued, changing the subject but staying close to Anatole. He pointed to one of the prints that had been leaning against the wall. Anatole was looking over his violin, about to play. 'I was thinking of framing that portrait – you wouldn't mind? We could put it in the dining room.'

Anatole shook his head. Why should he mind? He'd never been very aware of his own beauty before he met Jules. It tickled his vanity to see himself – quite literally – through a photographer's eyes. Whether it was the light, or the angle of the camera, or just the way Jules kept him talking while he set up the shot, he had a trick of making him look good, and he couldn't help feeling good too.

But you couldn't grow up with so many clever, teasing older sisters and take yourself too seriously. Nobody in their hard-working family – all musicians and school teachers in Limoges – was allowed to preen or rest on any imagined laurels for a moment. It was one reason why he'd come to Paris the year before: he wanted to make a go of his career alone. 'Paris isn't going to know what's hit it,' Anatole's sisters had joked at the railway station when he left, straightening his tie for him and spit-polishing his boots. Very funny.

'Good,' said Jules, then held up his hand to listen. Another burst of drumming rose from the street below. 'And whatever the fuss is about now, let's hope everything calms down before any news reaches Philadelphia,' said Jules.

'Or even Limoges.' Anatole also owed his family a letter.

'At least your family approves of what you're doing here. Mine never will. Have you told your father about the new show?'

'Not yet, but I will. Good and distracting. Especially if I mention Marie.'

The muscles in Jules's back hardened.

'Marie?' he said. 'That new soprano? How's she getting on? Do you think she's going to be any good?'

He shrugged Anatole's arm off his shoulders, and began to tidy up the studio. Still in shirtsleeves from his violin practice, Anatole shivered, suddenly colder, so Jules quickly tossed him a jacket of his own, which had been hanging on the coat stand by the door.

'She could be,' said Anatole, pulling on the sack coat with pleasure. The material and the cut were both finer than anything he owned himself. Jules had arrived in Paris with strict orders from his father to buy his shirts and cravats only from Charvet, and it was one of the few instructions he'd carried out to the letter – until the war. He'd promised to take Anatole for a fitting, when the shop reopened. 'But it's never easy going from the chorus to the spotlight. She's feeling the pressure.'

'Is it that obvious?' Jules removed Minou from the top shelf where she was delicately stepping between bottles of chemicals, and placed her on the floor. The cat jumped straight back up onto the workbench.

'It was awkward this morning. I felt for her. First time she'd sung the main Act II aria in front of the whole company, and it was expressive, but far too thin. All pinched and wiry on the long notes, and squeaky at the top. Nerves, I suppose. She was in tears afterwards. Not surprising. It was humiliating. And more to the point, if it happens again, she could lose the part, and she's been lucky to get a chance like this so young.'

'Maybe she doesn't deserve it?' suggested Jules.

'Oh that's harsh. Everyone's on edge at the moment, for one reason or another.'

It was quite true. The depleted performers of the Théâtre Lyrique no longer felt quite like a company. Some musicians had volunteered to fight in the early rush of patriotic fervour after war broke out; quite a few were now dead. Some had vanished to the provinces, and even now others were disappearing. A shift was taking place, movement in the ranks. There were new parts to learn, new partnerships to forge.

'And from what I can gather,' Anatole went on, lowering his voice as though there might be a risk of being overheard, 'she's been abandoned by a rich banker, who ran off to hide in the country with his family before the siege, and now claims to have fallen back in love with his wife. Or something like that.'

'That old story. Maybe he's found a more attractive mistress in the nearest village.'

'Unlikely,' said Anatole.

'Oh? You know this man?'

'Never heard of him. Just know he'd be pushed to find anyone more beautiful than Marie.'

'So she got the part in the show on her looks too?'

'And her voice,' said Anatole reprovingly. 'She's going to be a sensation one day. The audience will adore her. She'll have her pick of new protectors as soon as the show opens. Anyway, I expect she'll be better at the next rehearsal.' Anatole was now straddling a chair back to front. He looked and sounded rather pleased with himself.

Jules stopped sweeping up the broken eggshell and turned to look at him. 'Really?'

'Yes, really. You see the only way I could stop her crying was to suggest that we had an extra practice session before the main run-through. We're meeting on Monday. I'm sure I'll be able to help. It's mostly a matter of confidence. And concentration. She's very worried about her brother. He's been a prisoner of war for months and the Prussians still aren't saying when he's going to be released.'

'Poor girl. I'm sure she was delighted to accept your offer,' said Jules.

'She was, as a matter of fact. Of course she was.'

Anatole jumped up as he spoke, and flung his chair to one side. Taking the dustpan and brush from Jules and chucking them in a corner, he began to waltz him around the room.

2.

20th March

Blurred with grief, Zéphyrine stumbled down the steep Montmartre lanes to the municipal pawnbroker shop, pushing her way through gathered knots of people. She didn't know why the pavements were so busy, and she couldn't make herself care. Why had her grandmother waited to give up now? Now, of all times, when there was finally bread in the shops again, and hope for the future? What was the point of surviving the siege, suffering so much, getting through the whole war, only for this? It was unbelievable. And Zéphyrine had deluded herself for far too long. She was wicked, useless, wretched.

Two days earlier Zéphyrine realised, with creeping horror, that the worst was finally coming: there could be no other explanation. All that shouting and drumming in the lane outside, such a racket with the bells in the early hours, and never a flicker of Gran'mère's papery eyelids? But by then she hadn't been able to risk going to the pharmacist, Monsieur Balard, not with so much commotion outside. She even thought she heard a few gunshots. Anyway, she couldn't pay him, and what if she'd gone and got trapped in the crowds? That's when she should have called the priest of course. But Zéphyrine had done everything wrong. Gran'mère had taken her in when nobody else wanted her – she had done everything right – and this was how she had repaid her.

At least she had not died alone. Her forehead was still warm when Zéphyrine bent to kiss it. You'd hardly have known she was dead. So the girl had gone on sitting by the bed, holding her bird-claw hand. She just kept on watching over her exactly as she had been doing for weeks already. She didn't know what else to do. At first, the changes were so slow and slight that she barely noticed them – skin tightening over teeth, colour fading. By the next morning though, her grandmother looked like a stranger.

Then Zéphyrine realised there were practical things that had to be done. She wished she had started sooner. It was hard to move and clean up a body so stiff and strange, skin and bones though it was. It took hours, and she had to keep stopping, to calm her nausea. Finally, reluctantly, she slipped Gran'mère's wedding ring off her scrawny finger – easy to do when it was so loose – and looked around the bare room. There was only one other thing left to pawn: the thin, ticking mattress, patched and repatched so many times. She hated to leave Gran'mère on the floorboards, but their hardness couldn't hurt her now. Zéphyrine rolled the mattress up and tied it into a bundle, then waited, listening, for Madame Mouton to go out. She wanted to escape before the concierge could remind her again that the rent was due. All the debts built up during the siege suddenly had to be paid. This cowardly government said so. Everyone was furious about it. Except Zéphyrine had a different priority now. She somehow had to find the money to pay for a decent burial too.

It was even busier at the pawnbroker's than usual. Eau de Javelle hung in the air, the tang of bleach prickling her nostrils but failing to mask the stale odour of old clothes. She was rubbed threadbare herself, a wrung-out rag. As she took her place in the queue, she felt herself sinking. Compulsively turning her grandmother's ring on her own finger, she edged bit by bit along a wooden bench polished smooth by endless shuffling and sliding. Walled up in her own misery, she was deaf to the lively discussions taking place all around her. The talk was of cannon, cowardice, capitulation and finally triumph. Two generals had been executed by a mob. The government forces had fled. Paris had been left to govern itself. For the time being, at least. But Zéphyrine took none of this in. She shifted herself and her burden slowly closer to the front.

Eventually, a door opened, and the mattress was prodded, inspected, removed. The ring she had to pass over the counter. She imagined all the piles of abandoned possessions they would be joining: scissors, candlesticks, bedsteads, joiners' tools, linen and watch chains, all left at 'Auntie's' in the hope they would one day be reclaimed.

'Here. Ticket. Money.' The voice came from behind frosted glass, the shadow behind broken into dark squares. The government liked to protect the employees of the mont-de-piété from the public. The invisible speaker grew a little kinder. 'I'd come back and claim it as soon as you can. Can't say what the rules will be by next month. Or who will be in charge, come to that.'

A few francs rattled across the counter towards her, and a yellow ticket.

Zéphyrine gripped the paper voucher in her hand so tightly she nearly tore it. 'Is that all?'

'I don't set the prices, dear. Next please.'

There was no point in arguing. But Zéphyrine couldn't even begin to meet the bills with this pathetic sum. She felt herself beginning to crumble.

'Wait!' The voice was imperious again. 'I need to see your marriage certificate.'

'But . . .'

'Rules are rules.'

A tiny sob leapt from Zéphyrine's mouth, and she clapped her hand over it before another could escape. There was a long silence, while a pair of eyes peered at her from the small gap between the counter and the screen. The woman clicked her tongue, and made a face. 'Go on then. Quick as you can. I'll let it go this time. Times are hard and you're right – that won't go far.'

Zéphyrine pushed her way out, and emerged on the pavement hardly able to see. Without the mattress weighing them down, her arms felt light and floaty, as if they might rise by themselves. She didn't know what to do with her empty hands. That bulky mass had smelled almost comforting. It had taken her back to the nights when she had first arrived in Montmartre: her grandmother would hold her tight in a great big hug and tell her she'd soon get used to Paris and then she wouldn't miss Brittany any more. She always said Brittany. Never mentioned her mother. And Zéphyrine pretended she didn't care, though she still waited and hoped for a letter from home. Nothing ever came. 'Just the two of us now,' Gran'mère would say. 'The Lord he taketh away, and he giveth too. I'll look after you, and you'll look after me.' But now what?

Zéphyrine blinked very hard and shook her head, hoping it would clear her mind as well as her eyes. She'd always been good at putting on a brave face, and she needed money a lot more than she needed comfort. She had to save Gran'mère the shame of a pauper's funeral. Zéphyrine couldn't bear the idea of that communal pit: so many strangers' bones all tumbled together like so much waste, and not a flower in sight.

She thought longingly of the bundles of silk flowers that transformed their rented room in the old days, before the war killed all demand. Pink and mauve, yellow and scarlet, tumbling blossoms, all seasons together, and so real you wanted to smell them, though all you ever got was a sniff of glue. Hours of work in every petal. These flowers never wilted. They were made to bloom for a year or two on a bonnet or ballgown, then fade at the back of a wardrobe. She decided she wanted fresh flowers for her grandmother's grave. Only fresh flowers.

'I don't mind if I do,' said a gruff voice.

Zéphyrine's eyes focused on the brandy-befuddled workman swaying in front of her. He tried to take her arm, but she shook him off. He lurched towards her again, still leering and laughing.

'Get off me!' she shouted. 'I'm not what you think . . .'

He stopped his pawing and burped. Then he straightened his blue cap and frowned at her, eyes settling. 'You what? If you didn't want it, then why were you looking at me like that, you stuck-up bitch . . . ?'

Zéphyrine didn't wait for his anger to explode. She gathered up her skirts and made off as fast as she could, looking back over her shoulder as she ran. There he was, still standing and swaying, face redder than ever, while a group of men outside a café pointed and jeered at his mistake, and whistled after her. Then her foot caught on something hard and she fell, sprawling.

She spat sandy earth from her mouth, cursing the man she'd run from, and all the others too. What had she done? How had she looked at him? Was it his fault or hers? It was only because her grandmother had kept her on such a tight rein till then that Zéphyrine had managed to avoid trouble like this before. She ought to have thanked her for it, instead of resisting all the time. She'd seen it happen to others of course. It was almost impossible for a working girl to make her way through the streets of Paris without being taken for the wrong kind of working girl, a *fille publique* . . . This man was unpleasant, but she'd got away this time. The important thing was that the police didn't make the same mistake. Once they had your name on their files, there was no going back, no rising from the depths.

Wiping away the gritty spit with the back of her hand, she raised her head. Something else was blocking her way: a solid wall across the great open thoroughfare at the bottom of the hill leading up to Montmartre. Two walls, she saw when she looked harder, in parallel, neither of them high, but both rising fast. Blocks of paving stone had been pulled up in a jagged line to make them, and Zéphyrine had fallen into a gap.

'Hup . . . grunt . . . hup . . . grunt . . .' A human chain was passing the stones along from hand to hand, and they had a good rhythm going. In the sandy earth between the broken edge of the paving blocks and the beginning of the barricade, a couple of children sat making mud pies and digging for worms. A dog rooted around them, going quietly wild with the excitement of all the fresh smells set free by the works.

Another man's voice, older, and another hand on her arm. 'Up you get.' She froze. 'It's Zéphyrine, isn't it? Oh yes, I know you. Don't worry. You're all right with me.' He kept talking while she slowly obeyed, scrambling to her feet. 'I used to drink with your grandfather. Years ago. When he first came to Paris. We had some times in the old days, I can tell you, before . . . Ah well.'

The old man gently brushed off her skirt as he spoke, shaking his head and mumbling quietly. 'I remember you from his funeral. Such a comfort to your grandmother, though I've not seen a hair of her since the siege. How is she? Shame he's not here to help now.' His grey beard quivered, and he touched his hat briefly, before bending to retrieve his pick.

'Get a move on, Bertrand! We haven't got all day!' A fierce female face rose from between the two walls ahead, and ducked back down.

'My missus,' he explained, grunting as he began to prise another stone away to add to the barricade.

Zéphyrine smiled thinly, willing him not to say more, willing his wife not to look more closely, and notice what Bertrand hadn't. She would crumble under the weight of too much kindness. She wasn't ready to open her mouth, either to ask or answer questions.

The atmosphere here made it easier to pretend. Everyone was so busy. The Montmartre National Guardsmen had spent

21

weeks sitting around since the armistice, idling away the days with nothing to do but smoke their pipes, play dice and drink, their rifles piled up in pyramids. There was the occasional demonstration in support of the French Republic. Otherwise, just waiting. At last the men were hard at it again and pleased to have a job to do. Their women were even more pleased, and also, it had to be said, a great deal more organised.

There was almost a party feeling in the air, a sense of camaraderie. Zéphyrine couldn't join in. She'd got too used to isolation over the past few weeks of silent vigil. How fast everything moved on while you weren't looking! How quickly the printing presses rolled, and the newspaper headlines changed, and the posters too. 'Save the Republic!' New ones were plastered on every wall and kiosk. 'Citizens!' they called out. 'Citizens! You have the future in your hands!'

The future in her hands? It had never felt less like it. Zéphyrine turned abruptly south, down a street that led to the centre of Paris. It was all too much to take in. She was just so tired, so tired of everything, so tired of worrying about money and food and fuel. Her limbs felt loose, and her eyes kept closing. Each time her lashes fluttered shut, Gran'mère's face reappeared in her mind's eye. She couldn't seem to conjure her how she had been in life. She only saw her frozen in death: a stretched haggard creature, with eyelids like silken petals, dark and crumpled.

Zéphyrine walked faster, forcing her eyes back open. Money, she kept thinking. Where could she get more money? She tried to calculate. A few sous for hot water, so she could go to the laundry to wash her grandmother's shift. And her own, come to that. Rose would help her. She could borrow money for the washing. But how much might the priest cost, or the gravedigger? And would that vulture of a landlord let her stay without her grandmother? She would have to steel herself to ask Madame Mouton. Not without money he wouldn't though. Money. Money. Everything always came back to money.

Feathers dancing on their splendid hats, two girls jiggled across a passageway, and knocked on the door opposite. They still had a bit of a wait before getting to work. Better to pass the time with friends. In side streets all around, in building after building, up staircase after staircase, in tiny rented rooms where chairs were strewn with underclothes, and water steamed in jugs and basins, young women were getting up, yawning, stretching. Downing drinks in preparation for the long night ahead. Shuffling packs of cards. Tightening corsets.

Zéphyrine watched. With much giggling and laughter, the girls waiting in the street were let in by three others, also rouge-cheeked and bright-lipped. They looked happy enough, she thought with a shock. They could afford nice clothes. Underwear too. (An upstairs shutter opened, and another girl leaned out and called down.) They seemed to be able to do exactly what they wanted. Of course there was still a way to make money. There was always a way for a girl to make money in Paris, day or night.

No. She mustn't think like this. There was one other alternative. Keep on walking, and you'll get to the river. Once she had thought of it, the waters of the Seine kept swirling before her, drawing her on. Zéphyrine pictured herself on the parapet of a bridge. She thought about plunging into nothingness, and the thought didn't seem frightening. She used to love diving off the rocks at Le Cabellou years ago, twisting in the air, showing off to her small half-brothers. She remembered the roar in her ears, the rush of bubbles, the silence. And then the gasp, as she burst back into another element, and her lungs filled with air again. It was no good throwing herself into the filthy Seine. She couldn't be sure of sinking.

The first time she heard the gulls in Paris – screeching, mournful, wheeling overhead near the river or the canal – she imagined they were calling her back to Brittany. Their voices had a way of sounding human. Where she came from, they called them soul birds. Drowned sailors, like her father, or so she used to think. But the truth was that nobody was calling Zéphyrine. Her brothers might miss her a bit, and maybe the dog, but her mother and stepfather certainly didn't want her back. They'd be happy to forget she'd ever existed. It was Gran'mère who told Zéphyrine the reason why. Her father had been a sailor – that was true enough – but her mother hadn't even known his name. That was why she'd left her bastard daughter in Paris, so she could finally be rid of her shame.

Gran'mère had wanted to warn her, to protect her. She was worried it would happen again. But shame was part of Zéphyrine's inheritance. What was the point now of pretending she didn't know shame already?

She tugged off her cap to reveal her hair, combing out the tangles with her fingers. She let her shawl fall a little from her shoulders, and pulled open her blouse to show some flesh. Then she ducked her head and raised her arm and had a quick sniff. Could be worse. Don't think about it, she told herself, not quite believing what she was about to do, reaching inside herself for a bit of the old bravado, the spirit that made her grandmother shake her head and tut. It was hard to find. She felt so numb.

Nothing mattered now except the money. Up ahead she saw a church, its curved back turned towards her: the Notre-Dame-de-Lorette. It's too late for you, the building seemed to say. Too late. You're falling already. You've got nothing, and nothing to lose. Three more prostitutes passed, red petticoats flashing, ribbons at their necks. They stared right through Zéphyrine. They didn't even see her as competition.

On she walked, her footsteps mechanical, without direction. She barely knew she was moving her legs. They took her towards the vast cross so recently carved from the city's ancient alleyways, towards its axis, its meeting point. Its stomach. Without realising it, she made for the biggest marketplace in France, to put herself up for sale.

3.

Anatole was heading in the very same direction. He strode along pavements so clean and well swept that in this part of town you'd never guess there was no government in Paris. He hurried past gilded restaurants whose tables were all but vacant, and food shops spilling out delicacies that no one was buying, where shopkeepers stood ready to pull down the shutters at the slightest alarm. Anatole was not far behind Zéphyrine, though neither knew this.

Quietly, under his breath, he whistled the dancing violin theme of the overture, and his step became lighter. *If I Were King* was a perfect choice for the reopening: the opera had always been one of their most popular shows. Everyone loved the elaborate jewels, that exotic scenery. After so many months of freezing candlelit concerts in front of a lowered curtain, breath frozen on singers' lips and audiences huddled in greatcoats, how glorious it would be to have all the costumes out again, the stage itself open at last! Soon they would set the theatre ablaze again with light and colour and warmth and song. Thawed at last, Anatole's fingers wouldn't let him down. He allowed himself to look forward to the distant buzz and chatter of an audience taking its seats as the orchestra tuned up, feeling the heat of the lights, and breathing in the mingled drift of scent and tobacco. He couldn't wait to hear again the imperfect silence that always fell when the conductor made his appearance and prepared to raise his baton.

Anatole glanced around, suddenly unnerved. An equally bewitching, waiting quality hung over these near empty streets right now. You'd think a wicked fairy had enchanted Paris and nobody had discovered how to break the spell.

When he passed Zéphyrine a few minutes later, close to the gothic buttresses of Saint-Eustache, Anatole didn't look at her twice. There wasn't much to notice to be honest. Just another grisette plying her trade, and rather early in the day. What exactly was it that made him turn and look back? A sudden change in atmosphere perhaps, a tightening in air already taut with expectation. Something about to turn nasty.

Two men, dapper in dark frock coats and top hats, jostled each other on the pavement.

'What do you mean, you scoundrel? You did not see her first. We had just agreed a price, hadn't we, my dear?'

The taller gentleman tried to kiss the girl's hand, but she stood as still as a statue. She wasn't making a very good fist of it, thought Anatole. Why didn't she say something? You have to be decisive in life. Make your mind up quickly or you'll lose them both, he urged her in his head. But her eyes just kept darting from one man to the other.

She was a skinny little thing. When Anatole looked more closely though, it was clear she'd have more to offer, if she'd had more to eat. She seemed to be pouting, but this was

27

deceptive too: she had closed her mouth into a tight fake smile, and her lower lip was so full it stuck out despite itself. She stood half-turned, hand on tilted hip, skirt lifted to reveal a pretty ankle, yet there was nothing seductive in her clothes or her posture. A kind of horror was gathering in her gaunt face. Anatole wondered if she was about to make a run for it.

Luckily for her, neither of her customers seemed to notice. They were staring at each other instead, aggressively brushing their lapels and rolling up their sleeves. They began to prance a little on the pavement. Tap, tap went their boots, echoing more loudly than they should in this strange new Paris, so free of its usual hustle and bustle. Shoulder to shoulder they circled, eyes smouldering and waxed whiskers quivering. One knocked roughly against Zéphyrine, and she let out a cry of alarm.

She's frightened, Anatole saw. She's not used to this. He slowed his pace almost to a standstill, and went on watching.

'Stop!' she said in a shaky voice. 'Stop, I'll . . . I'll . . .'

And before he could think twice about whether it was wise to intervene in a dispute between strangers, Anatole was in the middle of them all, grabbing the girl's wrist. He marched her out of reach of the fists about to flail, talking loudly and familiarly all the while. 'Ah, there you are at last! And about time too. We have an appointment, I believe. Hurry up, now!' And he muttered under his breath, 'Don't for God's sake turn round, and please could you walk quickly, as I'm a little late. They can do what they like to each other, but I see no reason for you to get involved. Do you think I'm overdoing it?'

Zéphyrine was too taken aback to reply or resist. He had swooped her away so quickly. Then she recovered herself, and promptly tried to pull away from his grip. 'Oh for God's sake let me go! What do you think you're doing?'

'I'm rescuing you of course. What does it look like?'

'Well, don't! What even makes you think I need rescuing?' she spat at him, still struggling.

Anatole glanced behind him. The two men were staring after them in fury.

'The look on your face,' he whispered. 'And now the look on theirs. Quickly. Walk faster. Look up into my eyes, and laugh prettily.'

'Laugh?!' She glared at him, though kept hold of his arm. 'What the hell have I got to laugh about?'

He kept them both going at a brisk pace. 'Surely you can act better than that. And if you can't, well . . .' No need to finish the sentence. He felt her shiver. He slowed down a little.

'But I need the money,' she protested. 'The second gentleman had promised me five francs.'

'I'll give you six,' Anatole assured her, silently cursing himself. Now he'd have to borrow again from Jules.

'You'd bloody better,' she said. 'You owe me now. I'd been walking for nearly an hour, and then along you come and I lose two customers at once. How dare you?'

It was Anatole's turn to be lost for words. Such ingratitude. She was probably one of those Belleville girls, just the type his mother had warned him against. Not that – far enough away in Limoges – she had ever exchanged a word with anyone from Belleville of course. She probably didn't even know where it was. Somewhere on the outskirts, she'd once said vaguely. One of the new arrondissements. And his mother called them 'scum', not girls. Thanks to the newspapers, everyone knew that type. Anatole would have abandoned this one then and there if she hadn't looked back across the square one more time, and let out a whimper. 'Hurry! They're still following us.'

An even bigger building loomed ahead: the vast glass cathedral of the marketplace, Les Halles.

'In here.'

Anatole whisked Zéphyrine in through the elegant opening ahead of them, and everything changed. The air was different in here. The light was different. Voices sounded different. It was another world, made by some magnificent god of order who had put a dome over the streets and caught up all the little creatures running around below to watch at leisure. The stallholders were close to packing up. Shouts and bangs and the crash of trolleys rang around the high glass covering. An hour later and the huge gates would be firmly closed.

Zéphyrine stopped.

'Where now?' said Anatole, but she didn't hear him.

She was staring up at the roof, which didn't block the sky but let it through. Cast-iron pillars rose almost forever, blossoming into garlands.

'This way.' Anatole dragged her along a passageway to the butchery area, and then into the first small alleyway leading off that. For a few minutes, they didn't stop moving. Fast past displays of entire beasts: whole pigs and flayed lambs. A right turn down another walkway. More slowly past stalls hung with yellow-skinned plucked chickens, and geese suspended by outstretched necks, naked but for tail and wing feathers. Rabbits and hares up-ended, ears drooping, still in their furs;

coils of sausage and blood pudding; glistening steaks; gleaming kidneys. Hearts and lungs darkest of all. Red against white aprons. Sawdust, but not enough, and knives flashing silver as they sliced through flesh. Carcass blood ran along the gutters, trickled into the drains. The smell of it here was overwhelming, its odour too rank this late in the day for Zéphyrine's empty stomach to bear. Holding the back of her hand across her mouth, unable to speak, she pulled Anatole to another halt.

'What? What is it?'

She shook her head. If she'd been blindfolded and spun round, she couldn't have been less certain which way to stagger next.

He was beginning to get annoyed, at himself as much as her. Then he looked at her closely for the first time. Such dark circles. And red swollen rims. She looked as if she'd been crying for days.

'You're hungry,' he said bluntly. 'And when did you last shut your eyes?'

'None of your business,' Zéphyrine snapped back, when her breath had returned and she'd pushed back the bile. 'And it's not what you think.'

She hoicked up her shawl, holding it tightly round her neck.

Raising his eyebrows, he replied, 'You don't know what I think.'

Neither did he exactly. She'd be hard to shake off now, in this state. He should never have picked her up. He didn't know what had come over him. But she had seemed so lost. And look at her now, shivering as though she'd never stop. He'd better feed her at least, and get her warm, before he sent her packing.

'I need something to eat myself . . .' He turned away, and she followed.

Anatole knew his way around the market like a stallholder and often took this shortcut to the theatre. Before long he'd picked up bread and cheese and a bottle of wine, and they were weaving their way between fruit and vegetable stalls, out in the open on the other side.

Anatole looked around one last time to be sure they hadn't been pursued. 'Come on. This way.'

'Where are we going now?' Zéphyrine asked. 'And what's that? What's going on?'

She pointed towards the Hôtel de Ville. You could only see its grey slate roof from here, but right at the top of the City Hall, just where the three-coloured flag of the Republic usually flew, a bright red banner was streaming in the March breeze.

He laughed. 'Very funny.'

She frowned.

'You don't know?' Anatole shook his head, disbelieving. 'Where on earth have you been?'

Zéphyrine couldn't tell him. 'I – I –'

But it didn't matter. The news was so remarkable that Anatole rushed on. 'The Central Committee has taken over the Hôtel de Ville.'

'The National Guard? In charge of the whole of Paris?' said Zéphyrine. She looked dizzy. Ordinary working men had only been recruited to the Paris militia, as fédérés, since the war with Prussia. They served in neighbourhood units for thirty sous a day, and the radical battalions, of which there were many, even elected their officers. These were the men now running the City Hall?

'That's right. For the time being anyway. And keeping things in remarkably good order, for the most part, as it happens. The government abandoned the place without a fight. Completely scarpered! And the army with it. If that's not cowardly . . .'

'Where to?'

'Oh not far . . . to Versailles.' Barely twenty kilometres away, south-west of the city.

'They just went? Just like that?' Maybe she wouldn't have to pay the rent backlog after all.

'The Central Committee has announced elections of course. And then we'll see. Paris will decide. As it should do. If I'm honest, anything's got to be better than that bunch of tyrants.'

'And are you honest?' she asked, suddenly suspicious, hanging back. Zéphyrine was on the very edge of flight.

'As the day is long. Come on, this way.'

'Can't you just tell me where we are going?'

The street opened onto another broad square: two wide grand buildings with golden arches mirroring each other, a fountain in the middle and, on the far side, a bridge over the river.

'I don't suppose you've ever been inside a theatre?' he said.

4.

Zéphyrine drew herself up with every last morsel of dignity, and made for the main entrance of the Théâtre Lyrique. Then she felt a pull on her arm.

'Not that way, I'm afraid. It's the stage door for us.' Anatole raised his violin case in explanation.

She would never have noticed the unassuming wooden door at the side of the building. It led into a small lobby, where a scattering of cane-seated chairs bore the imprint of a great many waiting bottoms. Some vases of long dead flowers. An actual bottom, clad in black, waggled back and forth in slow, steady rhythm: a woman on her knees scrubbing the floor, ready for the new season. The doorkeeper, asleep under a newspaper, didn't so much as grunt as they dashed past.

Anatole wiped his brow theatrically, and flicked his wrist as if to show what a narrow escape they'd had, and then tiptoed exaggeratedly up the stairs.

How odd that this man could almost make her laugh at a time like this. For a moment, Zéphyrine felt a kind of reprieve. His charm made her feel less of a whore. Even when he wasn't smiling, you could see that was where his face wanted to go. And there was something so healthy about him: his skin seemed to glow.

'We got away with it,' he said, smiling again. 'Come on.'

And then the hollow drag in the pit of Zéphyrine's stomach quickly returned. It wasn't just hunger now, but fear. She had no idea what she'd got herself into, and no idea how to get out of it. He had promised to pay her though, and the thought of her grandmother – cold, still, waiting, not even a candle for company – kept her going.

The inside of the theatre was disappointing. Zéphyrine thought the whole place could do with a good clean. A dirty streak curved up the wall of the winding staircase, smeared by a thousand nervous and sweaty hands. By the time they reached the top, her face was hot and glowing, toasted by gaslights. They plunged into a warren of dark and dusty passages and shadowy doorways. Distant, slightly alarming sounds came from all sides: the squawk of a clarinet, a burst of laughter behind a thin wall, a warbling high-pitched song going relentlessly up and down the same five notes of a scale.

It would be easy to get lost here. Concentrate, Zéphyrine told herself: you might need to know your own way out. On they wound, up some flights of wooden stairs, and down others, and finally up some more. The corridor twisted through one door, and then another. The tantalising smell of the freshly baked baguette tucked under Anatole's arm made her salivate.

The dressing-room doors were numbered like a furnished boarding house. One, half-open, let out a stale, greasy odour, but revealed racks of gorgeously shiny clothing, glittering and bright. Zéphyrine glimpsed a hare's paw, white-powdered, lying abandoned on a dressing table. Behind another door, an argument was raging.

Anatole looked round to see if she was keeping up. Her hunger looked a lot like wide-eyed wonder. It flattered him. 'I could show you the stage from the wings, if you like. They've probably finished setting it up now.' Sun-drenched beach scenery and waving palm fronds. He pulled a watch from his waistcoat pocket and checked the time. 'Hmm. Maybe later. Come on.'

A cloth-covered door ahead marked the limit of backstage life. All at once, bare wooden floorboards gave way to carpets, and yellowing paint to green silk wallpaper. Zéphyrine couldn't keep herself from stroking it as they passed. She had barely begun to take in the sudden change when Anatole peeped through a frosted-glass window, round like a porthole, and led her through yet another numbered door. They emerged into eye-watering gaslit brilliance.

Zéphyrine gasped. It was another world again, this time made of crimson velvet and gold brocade, illuminated by glittering crystal chandeliers. They were in a box, a luxurious loge set high in the elaborate gilt-covered arch that framed the curtained stage, and which looked out into the vast expanse of the auditorium.

'Well?' said Anatole proudly. 'It's usually brighter than this of course. At least it always used to be. I'm sure they'll turn the gas back on full when the season starts again. Not long now!'

'Isn't it?'

'No – we open on the sixth of April. And, even now, it's not as bad as it was during the war. Of course the theatres were shut for quite a while, and then we were down to candles and oil lamps – very dreary – and you can't imagine how cold it was. Well, perhaps you can . . .' He looked away.

All this luxury, thought Zéphyrine as she stepped forward, yet you'd struggle to see much more than half the show. She had a better view of the seating than the stage. Steadying herself on the soft velvet-covered balustrade, she looked out into the auditorium. It was vast, its circling balconies rising layer upon layer to an airy cloud-painted dome of a ceiling. So many empty seats below, all tipped up – waves in a crimson sea. You could pack thousands in here. Pairs of golden angels flew around the main arch, garlands of flowers looped between them. If Gran'mère saw this, she'd think she'd arrived in heaven.

'That's where I sit.' Anatole pointed down towards the orchestra pit, immediately below. It was dark and workmanlike, scattered with chairs and music stands and sheets of paper, and felt a very long way down. Zéphyrine staggered dizzily backwards and sat down rather more suddenly than she'd intended on a soft padded chair.

'Sorry,' she muttered, blushing, and looked around the inside. The space of the box was not much bigger than the room in which she'd eaten, slept and worked for the past two years with Gran'mère, though it had a sight more furniture. The carpet was soft as moss, and there were even curtains, though she couldn't see how they could close. How you'd imagine a smart tart's bedroom, she supposed, without the bed. Did that mean she'd soon be lying on her back on that soft mossy carpet with her skirts pushed up to her neck? She hoped it would be quick. She hoped it wouldn't hurt. She just wanted to get this whole business over and done with. She shuddered.

'Are you cold?' Anatole asked. 'Can I —'

'No, no.'

'I thought —'

'It's nothing.'

He stood just behind her, suddenly formal, staring straight ahead of him, hands clasped behind his back. She could hear him breathing; it was slightly uneven. When would he touch her then, or was she supposed to start the whole thing off? Zéphyrine sat bolt upright, gripping the seat of her chair. This was worse than waiting on the bench at school to say catechism for the nuns. From force of habit, her hands crept under her thighs: if she sat on them, perhaps it might stop her doing the wrong thing. He seemed to be waiting for something, but she hadn't a clue what for. Why didn't he make it more obvious? If he wanted his money's worth, it was a funny way to show it.

She didn't think she could stand much more. 'I've changed my mind,' she wanted to say. She needed to get . . . home. It still counted as home, as long as Gran'mère was still there. But she should never have run away. What was she thinking, to leave Gran'mère alone? People shouldn't be alone when they're dead. It's not right. She wanted to earn her francs as quickly as she should and get back to make all the arrangements. Zéphyrine glanced behind her.

Anatole shuffled his feet.

Go on, then, she kept thinking. Just do what you have to do. Or tell me what to do. Let's get it over with.

Anatole coughed. 'I'm Anatole, by the way. Anatole Clément. And you're . . . ?'

'Zéphyrine. My name's Zéphyrine.'

38

Names! Who needs names at a time like this?

'Well, here we are,' he said, his voice artificially bright, like the gas lamp's flare. He tucked his violin case between his legs, put the bread and wine on one upholstered chair, and took off his jacket to hang on another. 'It's a bit like a picnic, isn't it?'

She didn't answer. Her eyes jittered over every gold fringe and tassel the box boasted, every carved leaf on the elaborate candlesticks, every scratch on the mahogany sideboard. Anything rather than meet his eye. And then Zéphyrine caught sight of a pile of bloody bandages shoved behind the door, and her mouth went dry. A broom was leaning across them casually, as if someone had thought of clearing up properly, but had been called away in the middle of things.

'Stage props?' she asked, her voice squeaking. Her knees had begun to shake. Why had she come here? She'd obviously fallen into the hands of a murderer: a young man with easy charm who picked up young girls, only to get rid of them in all sorts of horrible ways in the dark chambers of an empty theatre. Maybe there wasn't a violin at all in that case he gripped so tightly between his legs, but something sharp and gleaming. Maybe that was why he'd taken her through the meat market. Perhaps that was where he collected his instruments of torture.

Anatole took out a small pocketknife, and tested the blade absent-mindedly against his thumb.

'Props? Good Lord, no! The real thing, I'm afraid. This theatre was turned into a hospital during the siege.' He opened the bottle of wine and set it on the side table at the back of the box. 'You wouldn't believe the mess they left behind. All those actresses pretending to be nurses.'

Anatole gave the pile of rags a half-hearted kick, then consulted his watch again, and frowned. He was late to meet Marie. She probably wouldn't be very happy about that. She didn't strike him as a waiting-around kind of girl, especially not for the likes of him. Oh well, it was too late now. He'd done it again. It would be something to make Jules laugh when he told him about it later. He always mocked Anatole's habit of taking pity on waifs and strays. Though he had rather fallen for the half-grown kitten Anatole saved from the casserole during the siege. (A few seconds later, and Minou would have been strangled and skinned.) And what about Jules himself? When Anatole first ran into him last summer, Jules had been attracting the wrong sort of attention from a suspicious restaurateur in the Passage des Panoramas, one of the glass-covered passages that ran through Paris. Jules had lost his sense of direction, wandered back and forth too many times in front of one establishment. The police hadn't actually been summoned, and of course Jules would never admit Anatole had rescued him. But Anatole knew better.

'Would you mind waiting a little?' He couldn't just throw her out now, still so hungry and exhausted. He really had mistimed things, but he didn't fancy letting Marie down either. And he'd been looking forward to their private rehearsal, a chance to get the measure of her away from the company. When he came back he'd make sure this Zéphyrine – pretty name, if it really was hers – he'd make sure she was fed and then see her safely onto an omnibus. Duty discharged. She could stay here and rest and eat until then, and nobody need ever know. 'I'm afraid I've got an urgent appointment just now. But I'll only be an hour, at the most.'

She shook her head.

"I don't mind."

'Make yourself at home here,' he said. 'You won't be disturbed, I promise. Don't move!'

Zéphyrine couldn't seem to take her eyes off the bread.

'And for heaven's sake don't wait for me to eat.'

The door whispered shut behind him and Zéphyrine listened intently. To her relief, no key turned. The carpet outside was too thick for her to hear his retreating footsteps, but he had gone back to his whistling, and that seemed to be dying away. She jumped to her feet. How she needed that bread. Stuffing a large chunk of it into her mouth, she ripped away the greaseproof paper folded round the cheese, and shoved that in too. She chewed steadily, pressing herself into the shadows at the back of the box. Anyone might be watching.

Anatole had left his coat. She eyed the garment warily, and went on swallowing down the bread and cheese, mouthful by determined mouthful. Hiccups threatened, so she reached for the bottle and gulped down a little red wine. It didn't stop her heart beating so fast, or the pain in her stomach, but it gave her a bit more courage. It wouldn't hurt to look, she decided. She might as well. After all, he had promised to pay her. She brushed her hands against each other to get rid of the crumbs, then wiped them on her skirt. The jacket felt well made, in a good flannel, though its green silk lining was fraying at the seams. A cleanish handkerchief and a receipt for some violin strings from a shop called Voirin in one pocket. She put them both back, and listened again. The sound of a piano came from somewhere behind the stage.

A new doubt entered her mind. An hour would be plenty of time for Anatole to get the police. Was that his so-called 'appointment'? Her skin felt clammy and her stomach began to churn in a different way. Maybe he was an agent, on the lookout for girls just like her. Arrest would mean inspection, at the police station, for disease. Everyone knew that. Worst of all, her name would go on the police register, and it would be there forever. If the police said you were a prostitute, that was it; it was official. You'd be a *fille publique* for the rest of your life.

It was time to go.

But still Zéphyrine hesitated. She had come too far to trudge back to Montmartre empty-handed now. Steal an egg, steal a cow. How could pinching a few francs to pay for her grandmother's funeral be any worse a sin than selling herself? If the Heavenly Father did exist, he ought to forgive her. She crossed herself, just in case, and shook Anatole's jacket until she heard the jingle of coins. Then she took the lot.

5.

Marie, waiting in a practice room on an upper floor of the Théâtre Lyrique, had just cast on the ribbing for a second sock when she heard Anatole coming. She quickly thrust her knitting out of sight just as he burst in.

'Sorry I'm late,' he said.

'Are you?' she said. 'I hadn't noticed.' An obvious lie, but it had the right effect and he smiled. Her eyes followed his as he bent to pick up the ball of grey wool that had rolled off her lap and under the piano. Smiling even more as he wound it up, he presented it to her with a bow.

First she blushed and then she smiled, mock-prim. 'You caught me at it.'

'The darning diva,' he said. 'Not what I was expecting.'

'I wasn't darning,' she replied. 'I was knitting, if you must know.'

'Making something for —' Anatole stopped himself. Best not to ask about her brother. She was looking so much brighter than she had a few days earlier, and he wanted her to stay that way. 'Let's get started then. No point in wasting any more time,' he tried again. 'Not that you have of course. Just me. Sorry.'

He occupied himself with opening and propping up the lid of the baby grand. Alone with Marie in the practice room, Anatole found himself unnerved by her newfound poise. He couldn't remember what she had been wearing before, but he noticed it now: a black silk afternoon gown, very fashionable, and well suited to her golden hair and ivory complexion. The bodice was low-cut, but modestly veiled in the same sheer black material that had been used to make the long sleeves – some kind of gauze, Anatole supposed. Very effective. If the story going round the orchestra was true, that disappearing banker must have been a real fool to let her go.

'You've got the music?'

Marie nodded, and straightened the sheets of paper on the music stand above the keyboard, before stepping away so that Anatole could push back the stool and sit down. He wished she would say something. She'd been easy to talk to when she was upset a few days earlier. You'd hardly think she was the same person this afternoon. He stretched his hands, waggled his fingers, and set off on a series of arpeggios, major first, then minor. Heat rose from his body, and sweat beaded on his forehead. He couldn't play like this, but he couldn't find his handkerchief to wipe it away either.

He shrugged apologetically when she offered him hers. 'Warm up?' he joked.

Anatole relaxed a little as she began to sing. Up and down, up and down. Her voice rose and fell with his notes. Eventually they were ready to start work.

'Now, you'll have to tell me what kind of speed you think we should take the opening . . . does this sound about right?' Anatole played the introduction, and stopped, questioningly.

Marie nodded. 'Almost. Just a little more slowly . . . at least that's how I've been practising . . . and Léon – you know, the new répétiteur we've been rehearsing with – he seemed happy enough with it at first.'

'Fine . . . we'll go from the top then.'

But when Marie came in with the first few lines – 'Your noble ancestors . . .' – Anatole shook his head. 'I think I'd better take it more slowly – you're bringing the whole tempo down too suddenly.'

Marie bit her lip. 'Sorry. Let's try again.'

'No, don't apologise. That's why we're here, remember.'

'Yes, of course. Thank you.'

The next attempt was more successful. Anatole nodded encouragement, and they made it to the end with just a few hiccups.

'To my ear, you're making too much of the breath before you sing "*esprit*" . . . Look, just here . . . I don't want to hear any inhalation there . . . How does that line feel to you?'

'Yes, I think I know what you mean . . .' said Marie. 'I feel as though I'm almost swallowing the word. Let's just take this section. And then could we work on some of the transitions, like here?' she pointed. 'I find that part very tricky.'

'I'm not surprised,' Anatole reassured her. 'All that ornamentation. Nobody could find that section easy. We could slow it right down a few times, and make sure you're getting those bars quite accurate?'

'I think that would help a great deal.'

It was indeed a demanding aria. But Marie had been trained to perform with her lips forming a smile, and before long they were both smiling. Her voice returned true and strong and clear. Anatole could believe Marie was Princess Néméa in her Indian palace, singing of love to a dreamy fisherman.

'Excellent!' cried Anatole, and she bowed her head. 'The coloratura was superb that time, didn't you feel?'

'Thank you. Yes. It felt much better. Let me just have a sip of water, and perhaps we could go through it just one more time. I wasn't completely happy with the breathing in this bar . . .' Marie sang the notes, and then leaned over his shoulder to show him the place on the score. She smelled of jasmine.

Anatole almost wished he hadn't noticed. He knew Marie had no great reason to set her sights on him. What did he have to offer an up-and-coming soprano who'd probably soon have Paris eating out of her hand, apart from a reliable accompaniment and a bit of company? But then again, how much did it matter what Marie thought of him? A flirtation would be fun – it was impossible to be completely immune to her – but she didn't quite make his heart surge. That was what he was still waiting for. Anatole knew exactly how the throb of passion should feel – a swooping, tremulous mass of strings, soaring and sinking, catching you unawares and loosening reason. Hadn't he recreated it often enough?

'No, I agree,' he said, slowing his own breathing. 'Tell me when you're ready.'

They began again. This time the first section went very well. Then they reached a short interlude, during which Anatole played the part taken by the cello. Suddenly he stopped. 'That was your entrance . . .' he said. 'You missed it! Do listen. I'll start again.'

'Oh dear. I'm so sorry.'

'Look, I'll take it from here.'

Marie missed her entrance again.

'Don't worry. We'll sort it out by tonight.' Anatole twisted to look at her over his shoulder. 'Are you feeling quite well? Why don't you sit down for a moment . . . or have another glass of water?'

He stood up, eyes flicking towards the door.

'No, no. I'm just a bit distracted. Please, let's try again.'

'Of course. Whatever you prefer.'

One last look at the door – he didn't realise he was doing it – and Anatole settled back at the piano to play. Again, her first section was fine. His eyes and mouth widened as he neared the point Marie needed to come in for the second time. He even began to nod his head . . . but too late. He stopped. Silence.

'Sorry,' she said. 'Sorry. I don't know why I can't concentrate all of a sudden. So much for third time lucky.'

'Fourth time instead perhaps?'

'No . . . I don't think it would help. I've just got too many things on my mind. I need to clear my head. And anyway, I'm sure you've got things you need to do.' That was a little prickly. Surely she hadn't seen him come in with that girl, Zéphyrine? But then Marie leaned across to gather up her music from the piano, perhaps slightly closer to Anatole than she strictly needed to, just for a moment, before rustling away. He stretched his hands out again, closed the piano lid and drummed his fingers briefly on the polished wood. He couldn't think what to say.

'No more word from your brother?' Anatole spoke over his shoulder.

'The prisoners of war are only allowed to write once a week,' she reminded him.

'Of course. You did tell me. Well, at least there was last week's letter. And he is reasonably well cared for in Bavaria, you think . . . ?'

'I suppose so. He's not going hungry certainly. There seem to be rules. But how much longer will I have to wait to see him again?'

'It's the trains, I believe,' Anatole offered. 'They don't have enough carriages for so many prisoners.'

'Oh yes. I know that's what they say. But it was agreed, wasn't it? They promised. The armistice has been declared. The Prussians have had their victory march. And they had enough trains to bring their own troops here to defeat us. What are they waiting for? It's just so unfair.' Her words thickened in her throat.

Anatole stood up. 'Yes, very unfair,' he agreed.

'I just want all this to be over, and everything to get back to normal.'

'Hmmmm.' What did she mean by normal? Anatole wondered. The bright lights of the empire? Comings and goings and parties till dawn and plenty of people with plenty of money to spend? 'I'm sure everything will settle down again after the elections.'

'I hope so. But what if the government supporters are defeated? Can you imagine what might happen if the Reds get in? Or if they don't, and then there's a repeat of the bloodshed of '48? Another revolution?'

'Surely you're not old enough to remember 1848?' Anatole said tactlessly, looking at her more closely.

'No, no, of course not – I wasn't even born. But my parents often spoke of it.'

Spoke, Anatole registered. Then he remembered the only other thing he knew for certain about Marie – that both her parents had been killed in a famous railway disaster a few years earlier. That might explain the banker.

'Sorry . . . yes, of course.'

Marie seemed to forgive him. Suddenly unguarded, she began to gabble out her worries. 'I really thought this nightmare was over.'

Anatole was a sympathetic listener, usually the perfect audience for anyone wanting to pour out their heart. Maybe it came of having so many older sisters. Today he was distracted. He kept thinking of that girl in the box, Zéphyrine, and wishing she had been a bit more ready to talk. It would have made it far easier to help her. Silence made everything so much more awkward. She was out of her depth, he supposed, and he had to admit that he was too. He really must get back and see her off the premises as soon as he could. The last thing he needed now was for Marie to run into her. Marie was still talking, her voice ever more breathless and uneven.

'I thought everything was going to be all right again after the armistice. It was bad enough during the siege, just dragging on and on, and hardly knowing what was happening outside Paris, or when it would ever end.'

Anatole nodded guiltily, and tried to concentrate. Thanks to Jules he couldn't really claim to have starved while Paris was besieged – if you had the money to pay for it, there was always something to be had, and Jules always had enough. Although

Anatole kept expecting to be summoned any moment by his battalion for a great sortie against the Prussians ('Foolhardy!' according to Jules), the call had never come. He hadn't even had to worry much about his own family, all safe in the middle of France, no brothers threatening to volunteer. The freedom of not having to account for his every movement in letters home had been positively liberating.

'Very difficult,' he said. 'Awful.'

'Impossible!' Marie contradicted. 'And now I just can't bear it . . . so much uncertainty, going on and on and on . . . It's hateful. All I wanted was for Emile to hear me sing again.' Her eyes were shining more than ever. Tears were clearly threatening. 'Was that so much to ask?'

'Emile is your brother?' Anatole thought he had better clarify.

'Yes, yes, that's right. My only brother. My only relative in fact. And I had hoped so much he would be back for the first night.'

'And maybe he will. There's still plenty of time. But right now, the most important thing is that you don't ruin your voice for this evening.' A hiccup made Anatole realise he still had her handkerchief. He wasn't sure whether to return it or not. 'In fact, don't you think it would be a good idea to let your voice rest completely until six o'clock?'

She glanced at him sharply, and reached for her shawl. 'Yes, you're probably right. I've taken up too much of your time already.'

'No, not at all . . . I've enjoyed our rehearsal.'

A slightly tight smile. 'Yes, so have I.'

Marie seemed to be waiting for something else.

'I tell you what . . .' said Anatole, suddenly inspired. 'Why don't you come and hear the election results at the City Hall with me next week? I'm going with my friend Jules – Mr Crowfield. It's bound to be interesting, and then you won't have to wait a moment to find out the news. Whatever it turns out to be.'

'Crowfield?'

'American.'

'Oh, how interesting.'

Marie agreed to meet them, and Anatole walked her back to her dressing room. For just a few minutes he even managed to forget about the girl he'd left in the second-best box. When he finally pulled open the door again, she'd vanished, and he realised he'd been an idiot. His coat was still there, but his money certainly wasn't.

6.

Night had fallen good and proper by the time Zéphyrine got back to Montmartre. From the half-open door of the church a roar of voices came, stopping her in her tracks. It didn't sound much like Vespers. A cluster of black-clad widows were on their way in, deep in conversation. Passing the basin of holy water at the entrance, they crossed themselves as usual. Zéphyrine followed them inside, and did likewise from force of habit.

Everything smelled more or less the same. Cold stone and old incense, the waxy smell of a hundred lighted candles. At first the congregation didn't seem very different either, although Zéphyrine had never before seen so many crowded into the pews on a Monday evening, nor fancy bonnets among the white caps. Instead of incense, wreaths of tobacco smoke drifted towards the ceiling, twisting up from the pipes of men who sat with their hats firmly on their heads. Some of the women were smoking too. Zéphyrine was glad Gran'mère couldn't see this, or hear the way the people whooped and whistled in response to the speaker.

It wasn't Père Ambroise in the pulpit. Instead of his soporific nasal drone, a woman's voice came ringing out over the heads of this noisy congregation. It was followed by another wave of cheering. As soon as the applause died away, the woman spoke again.

'No more weakness!' she commanded, and Zéphyrine instantly felt her backbone stiffen. 'No more uncertainty!'

Another roar hit the rafters.

'Here in Paris beats the very heart of France! Don't listen to the monarchists who'd drag us back to the days of Empire! Don't trust the so-called Republicans of Versailles! We must demand our rights! The Republic must be guaranteed, and with it the liberty of our beloved city, and our freedom from the chains of slavery! Your children's future depends on you. The future of Paris depends on you!'

The speaker wore a red-striped jacket over a plain black dress. Her immense brow furrowed over a strong Roman nose – the kind of nose Gran'mère used to call clever, on a man. One arm was raised above her head, and her hand was outstretched as if reaching for freedom. The distant look in her eyes made Zéphyrine wonder if this woman could see something she couldn't. How did she dare to step up to the pulpit like that? How could she? What was she thinking of, standing there behind the eagle-carved book rest? Not that she was reading her speech.

'Citizens! *Citoyens and citoyennes!* It is up to us, the workers, to declare ourselves free of the old ways at last! It is up to me, and it is up to you! We must be ready to take this opportunity for self-determination. We must seize the future in both hands!'

Zéphyrine was unbalanced by another huge roar of agreement. Like a great wave, it caught her at her chest, and she came out of her trance. Coins hot and clinking in her palm,

53

she cast about for someone she knew. Arguments kept breaking out in the pews, all jabbing fingers and wide-stretched eyes. Still no sign of the priest.

At last! A familiar face. Creeping up to the end of one of the back benches, she nudged the girl sitting at the end. Rose Lenoir lived a few streets away, where her mother ran the local laundry. Before the war, Zéphyrine always looked forward to seeing Rose. They'd chew the fat as they pounded the linen, and her grandmother always chided her for taking so long over it. 'I was just helping Rose with her deliveries,' Zéphyrine would explain, and then she would be forgiven, for a fever in childhood had left Rose's foot paralysed, and she'd been lame ever since. Everyone knew how heavy her baskets could be.

At the sight of Zéphyrine, Rose instantly shuffled up and got all her neighbours to do the same. She patted the empty space left on the bench, reaching up to pull Zéphyrine down into it. Rose smelled of soap, as usual, her skin as well scrubbed as her clothes, and her eyes shone.

'Where have you been?' asked Rose. 'Why didn't you come up to the Butte on Saturday morning with everyone else when the soldiers came to take our cannon? I was sure I'd see you. Everyone was there . . . and she —' nodding at the speaker in the pulpit — 'she was so wonderful! She always is.'

'I couldn't,' Zéphyrine hissed, resisting. 'You see —'

Her words were drowned out by another cry for action. A mother across the aisle raised her head and fist to agree; the baby who had just been feeding at her breast, kicking his legs in concentrated bliss, stared round in surprise at the sudden disturbance. There was a ripple of laughter, and his mother clapped her hand over her bare breast. But the child just gurgled happily at all the smiling faces, and went back to his supper.

'I can't stay, Rose. I've got to go.'

Rose didn't take her eyes off the pulpit. Zéphyrine sighed, and returned to her hunt for the missing priest.

A neatly bearded man in a side pew looked up from his notes and met her searching eyes with his. His eyebrows lifted enquiringly, and he beckoned her over. She hesitated before taking a step towards him, pointing at her chest as if to say, 'You want to talk to me?' He nodded. A silk top hat rested on the man's knees. His jaw was set, and his nostrils seemed to be struggling with some disgusting smell. Just in time, one of the black-shawled widows bustled over with her collection box, shaking her head, and drew Zéphyrine away to the light of the open door.

'Who is he? What does he want with me?' Zéphyrine asked.

'He keeps trying to interview people. Just ignore him. He says he's a journalist. Maybe he is. Maybe he isn't. We think he must be a spy from Versailles. Best leave him alone.'

Zéphyrine turned to glare at him. He frowned – as if he had a sour taste in his mouth – and bent back to his writing.

'Do you know, he asked if the speakers here – what did he call them again? That's right – the orators – he asked if the orators were paid to speak here . . . No, to "perform" he said!' The widow spat out the word 'perform'.

'Can you tell me something else?'

'If I know the answer, dearie, I'll tell you anything you like.'

Her kindness brought Zéphyrine close to the edge again. *No more weakness*, she told herself again. Just say it out loud.

The widow jingled her collection box absent-mindedly while she waited for Zéphyrine to speak, happy to catch anyone coming and going.

'Help for the wounded of the siege!' she called. 'Help the poor orphans!' She had to shake quite hard to be heard in all the racket. It sounded more like a marketplace than a church.

Zéphyrine choked back the tightness rising in her throat. She wasn't an orphan. She could stand on her own two feet. Somehow. She had to start somewhere.

'I'm looking for the priest. For a funeral. Do you know what I have to do? How much it will cost? Gran'mère, you see, my grandmother I mean . . . Gran'mère is dead.'

And then, despite the bread she'd eaten, or maybe because of the wine or perhaps because it was the first time Zéphyrine had said those words out loud, the windows of the church began to ripple and spin, and she collapsed in a heap on the flagstones.

7.

Rose picked Zéphyrine up from the church steps. She took her back to the house behind the laundry, and Madame Lenoir immediately sent her own mother to watch over Gran'mère's body. Then she set several pans of water to heat on the stove and dispatched her sister to summon the undertaker. The younger children were shooed like chickens from the kitchen, the tin bath lifted down from its hook on the yard wall, and a screen was arranged round it. Meanwhile Rose went and found clean clothes for Zéphyrine – a cotton dress and shawl, and a nightgown and petticoat and underthings too, all perfectly pressed. 'We're lucky, running the laundry,' Rose whispered. 'People leave things behind sometimes, and don't come back. Stuff gets lost.'

When the bath was ready, Zéphyrine needed to hold on to Rose's arm to climb into it. Just lifting a foot seemed an effort by then, and she couldn't stop shivering. She tried to make herself as small as she could, hugging her knees. She felt like an empty milk churn, sour and curdled inside: if she knocked against anything, she would surely clang and then everyone would hear how hollow she was.

Rose pretended not to notice, and distracted her with the neighbourhood news between jugfuls of hot water.

'Best day since before the war, and you missed everything. What timing. The soldiers of the line came right past here on their way up. We knew straight away something was wrong. Didn't you hear it?'

'Yes, I heard it.' Of course she had. You could hear everything from that attic. But it didn't mean you could do anything about it.

'I woke up first!' chipped in the youngest girl, Hortense, from behind the screen.

'No, you didn't, I did!' said Laure, and the screen wobbled as she gave her sister a shove.

The children had all crept in to hear the tale told again. Nobody in Montmartre could hear it often enough.

'Well, I was out on the street first,' said their brother proudly.

'Shut up and let me tell the story,' called Rose, flicking water at them over the screen. 'Or I'll send you all outside.'

Zéphyrine wiggled a soapy finger in her ear so she could hear properly. It did sound exciting, the way Rose told it. Boots quietly tramping in the earliest hours of the morning. Waking to the scrape of steel on stone and under-the-breath swearing, as the government soldiers came sneaking up the hill to steal Montmartre's cannon and disarm the people of Paris. But the army's call for horses – too late – went unanswered, and suddenly, from the houses all around, came the cry of treason. Before long, the infantrymen were confronted with a troop of furious women and children.

'Weren't you scared?' Zéphyrine asked.

'We weren't!' yelled the children, lying, while Rose nodded.
'Tell her what happened then,' came a solemn voice.

'We weren't there. We didn't see that,' said Rose sharply
'Anyway. That's enough. Out you go. Zéphyrine has to dress,
and we need to put her to bed. Up you get.' She wrapped
Zéphyrine in a stove-warmed towel, and whispered in her
ear. 'Things got nasty later. Out of hand, you know. There
were deaths. It wasn't meant to happen. It wasn't good. But
sometimes these things can't be helped.'

Then Madame Lenoir's sister came back and said, 'It's all
arranged. They can do it tomorrow.'

The funeral was very quiet. Not many mourners this time. Not
like her grandfather's, with its hearse and plumes, and half
the neighbourhood following behind. That was the first time
Zéphyrine had ever come to Paris, two years earlier, getting the
bus, and the train, and the bus again with her mother, and never
dreaming that she wouldn't be going home with her afterwards.
Nobody had told her she'd be left behind with Gran'mère, so
she'd never had a chance to say goodbye to her half-brothers.
It was a trick, she realised later. She was never quite sure who
had planned it, but she could guess. Her stepfather had made
his hatred of her clear from the day he'd moved in.

At Papi's funeral everything had impressed her, from the
moment the procession had left the church, chanting of
Paradise. This time the priest's words went through her like
air, and left no trace. She wouldn't care if she never saw Père
Ambroise again in her life, never again heard him murmur
'my dear child' or 'I'll pray for you'. They returned from the

cemetery, with all its new graves, and Zéphyrine slept at the Lenoirs' for a whole night and most of the rest of the day too, only getting up for a supper of broth and bread, before sleeping again. It was good to feel nothing. She was too tired even to dream.

The next morning, Rose took her to see the Montmartre Women's Vigilance Committee. The women there could organise water into wine, she said. They'd help her.

By this time, Zéphyrine could begin to argue. 'But I can't take charity . . . I don't . . . I'm not . . .' She tried again. She didn't know she already had – that Hortense had taken a collection in the neighbourhood to make up the money needed for the funeral. 'Gran'mère would . . .' At a glance from Rose, trudging doggedly, unevenly, beside her, her voice trailed off. They both knew her grandmother's thoughts about charity were no longer relevant, any more than her favourite proverb: 'A goat must graze where it's tethered.'

'In any case,' said Rose, breathing harder from the steep climb. 'It's not charity. It's redistribution. It's making things fair for once. What on earth is wrong with that?'

'Nothing. Nothing at all.' *And a goat may wander where it will*, Zéphyrine added in her head.

She was awed by the silence that greeted them when they walked into the committee room. She'd been expecting discussion, discord – the kind of raucous debate she'd heard at the political meeting in the church. Everyone here was so hard at work that they didn't even look up at first. A big trestle table in the middle, hard wooden chairs round it, and women's heads down, pens in hand, papers piled high, working away.

'What are they doing?' she whispered.

Rose looked vague, and waved an unhelpful hand. 'Paperwork.'

'Oh.'

The quiet scrape of nib on paper continued, and Rose gently cleared her throat. The first worker looked up, and Zéphyrine caught her breath. That woman from the church. But now she seemed less godlike and more human. Definitely still clever. Zéphyrine found herself blushing under her careful scrutiny.

'Yes?'

Faint lines at the corners of her eyes – she wasn't young – suggested that she wasn't always so serious.

Zéphyrine swallowed, and let Rose do the talking.

'Someone else who needs our help, *citoyenne*.'

The woman smiled slightly. 'You are so good at finding them. I sometimes wish you were equally good at finding the men who are shirking from their duties to defend Paris. But I daresay they'll show themselves in time. Once they realise what's at stake.'

Her mouth straightened, forming a great line across her wide, open face.

Rose nodded. 'Zéphyrine has just lost her grandmother.'

'I'm sorry to hear that. Did I know her? Was she one of ours?'

Zéphyrine shook her head quickly, and felt herself going even redder. She couldn't possibly reveal Gran'mère's views on committee women. 'You wouldn't have met her.'

She was sure this woman spent no time on her knees. She might be at home in a pulpit, but she didn't look the praying sort.

'No matter. How can I help you now? You are looking for work, I take it?'

'Yes. Yes, I am.'

'Can you nurse?'

'Of course, she can!' Rose interrupted enthusiastically. 'She's just been nursing her own grandmother, haven't you, Zéph?

'I – I . . . no, I really can't.' Zéphyrine hung her head. How could she explain how much she hated a sickroom? That blood and vomit and excrement made her heave and turn away? How could she admit to her impatience and incompetence? 'I'm no good at all at that kind of thing. I did it because I had to. And anyway, I didn't make her better. She died.'

Rose gulped. 'But that wasn't your fault . . .'

The Vigilance Committee woman moved swiftly on. 'Any factory experience? Ever worked in munitions?'

'No,' Zéphyrine whispered, ever more wretched. 'I used to make . . . I used to make flowers.'

A half-smile, lowered eyes.

'I see. Then I'm sure you are good with your hands. We are setting up sewing workshops —'

'I'm not experienced in fine work,' said Zéphyrine quickly.

'Oh dear. You don't seem to have a very high opinion of yourself.'

Zéphyrine didn't feel she could argue with that.

'Plain sewing, I can do,' she said quietly. 'And I can cook. I'm good at that. When I have something to put in the pot.'

'Excellent.' The woman was already leafing through her files. 'Then I think I have just the right position for you.'

8.

23rd March

There was still an odd expectant silence on the pavements a few days later when Anatole and Jules set off for an evening drink. The stillness was broken from time to time by the hoarse cries of the newspaper boys, their voices raised by the drama of the coming election. '*Le Cri du Peuple!*' shouted one. 'The People's Voice!' On the next corner, politics came in a slightly different shade: '*La Vérité!* The Truth! *Le Vengeur!* The Avenger!'

As they strolled to their usual café, Jules bought a selection of papers, saying that he preferred to see all sides of a situation before coming to a decision.

'How very sensible,' said Anatole.

'Very dull, is what you mean,' said Jules. 'But I'd rather be dull than ill-informed. By the way, you haven't told me why you need to borrow more money,' he said, holding the door open.

'I —'

'Not that I grudge it,' Jules added hastily. 'My father will hardly miss it. And his cheques seem to be getting through again now, which is just as well.'

'That's good to hear. I may have been a bit of a fool, I'm afraid. Long story. I'll tell you over a beer.'

Jules knew how to be patient. 'Billiards first?'

Anatole nodded, and followed him upstairs. As they played, the talk inevitably turned towards the elections.

'Thiers has dug his own grave, abandoning the city to the Reds like this,' said Anatole, chalking his cue. 'I don't understand it. If he was so scared of the radicals and the workers and the socialists, never mind the mutualists and the trade unionists, or the International Workingmen's Association come to that . . .' Anatole paused to think whether he might have missed anyone out. 'Oh yes, and the women and children of course! If he was so bloody worried that he had to try to steal the National Guard's cannon, why on earth didn't he stand his ground when there was resistance? What exactly did he expect to happen?'

'He obviously wants to stay head of the provisional government and he expected his army to follow orders, however unnatural . . .' Jules pocketed another ball with his usual grace.

'Well it didn't. Perhaps it never will again,' said Anatole. 'We'll just have to see how the National Assembly reacts to the Paris elections, I suppose.'

'Have you heard of any of the men standing? Who on earth are they all?'

'Fair question. I think one's meant to be an acrobat of some kind – a circus sword-swallower. A few journalists of course. A shoemaker, I think, believe it or not. But we'll find out soon enough. Just because nobody's ever heard of the fellows, it doesn't mean they're no good. They just haven't had a chance before. Damn.' Anatole had misfired again. 'The table's yours.'

Jules leaned across the green baize to set up his shot. Anatole watched as one long check-trousered leg rose lightly from the floor. Jules's quiet elegance and precision infuriated Anatole as much as it intrigued him, and he knew exactly what would happen next. Sure enough, Jules's ball hit Anatole's with a crack, bounced off the red with another satisfying thunk, and rolled against the rail. A breath of a smile, but Jules never gloated.

Anatole laid down his cue, held up his hands and bowed his head in mock-surrender. 'Your game, sir . . . I think drinks are on me. After a fashion.'

They made their way downstairs to the bar. Cloth in hand, the white-aproned proprietor was quietly polishing glasses while keeping his ear on as many conversations as he could. Monsieur Louvet had built up his business from nothing. Now he had a place to be proud of, he didn't want it collectivised, or whatever it was the workers were planning. But nor did he want his widowed sister over in Belleville evicted because she couldn't come up with the rent. If only Paris could just get back to business as usual.

'It'll blow over,' he said out loud, wiping up a few drops of crimson from the marble bar-top before they could stain. His movements were precise, and oddly soothing.

In the mirror behind Monsieur Louvet, Jules watched Anatole. Hesitant at first, he finally confessed what had happened with Zéphyrine.

'. . . and when I got back to the box, she was gone, and so was my money. Oh, and all the food of course. She must have been starving.'

Jules raised an eyebrow. 'Picking up a street girl. You can do better than that. I suppose she's the type that thinks property is theft.'

'Very funny,' said Anatole.

Jules ran a finger round the edge of his wine glass, sounding a high thin hum. 'I don't know what possessed you,' he said.

'I'm not sure I know either,' admitted Anatole. 'I just felt sorry for her, I think. She looked so desperate. Not any more though.'

'Sounds as if you've had a lucky escape.'

'Maybe. Maybe not.' Anatole took another swig of beer.

'What is this urge you have to rescue complete strangers? Always playing the hero.' Jules looked at him sternly. 'Very odd. Too long in the orchestra pit, I reckon.'

'Oh, really? Is that your diagnosis?'

'Let me see now. We need to look at the symptoms.' Jules pretended to consult a notebook. 'Prone to grand gestures, speedy seductions, sudden overflowings of passion. Occasional confusions of identity. Yes, everything seems to be there. I think what you're suffering from is an inability to tell the difference between opera and real life.'

'Oh, doctor . . . will I live?' Anatole feigned a swoon. 'Is there a cure?'

Jules caught him before he tipped off his stool, and set him upright. 'It's possible. I believe I can do something for you. But it's unlikely to be overnight.'

At that very moment, a couple of elaborately costumed National Guard officers strolled into the bar, gold braid glittering, boots polished to a high sheen.

'Oh look,' said Anatole. 'It must be catching. There seems to be an epidemic. You'd better take my pulse.'

He pushed up his sleeve, and offered Jules his wrist. Three cool fingers on his skin. Eyes quickly meeting.

'Far too fast,' Jules said briskly. 'I think you need another drink. Don't worry, I'll get this.'

But it took some time to attract Monsieur Louvet's attention. At the other end of the bar a stack of saucers had mounted up, another round just ordered, and the discussion was getting very heated. The patron leaned over towards his customers and gently observed that not everybody who lived in Belleville was filthy scum.

In the sudden silence this produced, Jules signalled their order. 'Your health!' he said when it arrived.

'And yours. Thanks.'

Their glasses chinked – Anatole's beer against Jules's wine – they drank and shifted on their stools.

'You've got beer froth on your moustache,' Jules told Anatole, on the point of leaning forward to wipe it away.

Anatole checked himself in the mirror behind the bar. 'Oh yes . . . so I have.'

When he pulled out a handkerchief to clean himself up, he realised it was Marie's. He'd forgotten to tell Jules. 'By the way, I've invited that soprano to come with us to hear the election results. I thought you should see her. She'd make a wonderful model for you – and heaven knows you need a change.'

9.

26th March

A few days later, when votes had been cast and counted, the crowds gathered in front of the Hôtel de Ville. It was like a sea at sunset, rippling with red. Red sashes across shoulders, red rosettes pinned to lapels, red hair ribbons and liberty caps, and red lapels too of course. A red banner still billowed out over the City Hall itself, and many more now fluttered from handheld flagpoles and open windows. Warm and bright, the sun caught the brass muzzles of the Guardsmen's rifles and made them glow. It brought out the heady scent of spring flowers stuffed down gun barrels, shedding fragrant petals. Violets. Baby daffodils. Vivid blue *Muscari*. A radical new governing body had been elected for Paris, by Paris – by those who had been prepared to vote, at any rate, and were the right sex to do so: it was called the Commune, just as it was in 1789, after the storming of the Bastille. Another new dawn for the city of Paris, and independence from the rest of France.

Marie felt every drumbeat vibrate in her bones. She clung to Anatole's arm and tried not to show her nervousness. Everyone else seemed to be having such fun, leaning out of windows, throwing hats in the air, basking in the warmth. Anatole's head was thrown back, and he was pointing. 'Look over there!'

Bread held aloft on bayonets. Marie thought it was absurd, and a waste of good food. She was on the point of repeating what she'd overheard on her way here: that with half of Paris still in the countryside, and frightened to return, it was an easy victory for the Commune. But she held her tongue. Rifles were pricking up like a field of corn, endless battalions of the National Guard filing into the huge square. *Cantinières* stood around in jaunty Tyrolean hats, braided jackets and pert skirts with red striped hems, painted casks slung across their shoulders ready to administer to the troops from golden taps. Marie looked at them acidly. The women in uniform were certainly enjoying the attention their presence always attracted. She felt invisible, and even Anatole barely seemed to notice she was there.

'Will it be long now?' asked Marie, leaning in so Anatole could hear. It was very aggravating. He might not have much money, but he did make a very handsome escort, and behaved more like a gentlemen than the real thing ever did. He'd certainly do for the time being. Yet he seemed almost immune to her charms.

He didn't even turn round to reply. 'I don't think so – look!'

Anatole was right. There must have been some sign from inside the City Hall, for the men perched on the surrounding windowsills began to wave their flags with even greater passion. A platform had been constructed in front of the building. More drapery and red banners were arranged like the curtains of a stage, a backdrop to the proceedings. At their centre was a statue of Liberty herself – fair Marianne.

'At last,' shouted Marie through a deafening volley on the drums.

The air shivered and the ground trembled, and a troop of red-sashed deputies strode onto the dais. A great many beards. Gold tassels, silver fringing, rosettes and ribbons galore. The new government of Paris stood before the people in all its glory. The Commune.

'Here we go. Let's hope he can keep it short. Can you see?' asked Jules.

'Yes – just about. What a shame you can't photograph this,' said Marie helpfully.

'You read my mind.'

One of the men in the front row was shuffling papers.

'Who's that, I wonder?' asked Anatole.

The answer came from a stranger standing nearby, a man with a pencil in his hand, taking notes. He could have been a journalist or a spy.

'Ranvier. Mayor of Belleville. Used to paint plates, I believe.'

Marie just caught the word 'Belleville' and shuddered automatically. These people. Why, when she was growing up, working-class Belleville hadn't even been part of Paris proper! Hearing the name, Marie imagined filthy streets swarming with cut-throats and revolutionaries, anarchists and pickpockets, society's outcasts all plotting and scheming and planning the downfall of anyone with a sous to their name. Could people like that actually be running Paris now?

The plate-painter on stage began to speak. 'Citizens! My heart is too full of joy to make a speech. Permit me only to thank the people of Paris for the great example they have given the entire world . . . In the name of the people . . . the Commune is proclaimed!'

He was drowned out by an answering cry from the surging crowd.

'Long live the Commune! *Vive la Commune!*'

A military band struck up 'La Marseillaise'.

'*Le jour de gloire est arrivé!* The day of glory has arrived!'

Marie winced at the sound of several thousand voices singing a song they loved in six or seven different keys. But the spectacle of so many fluttering handkerchiefs was charming. From the river came the repeated boom of cannon, sounding in triumph for a change. Gunpowder hung in the air. Men wept. '*Aux armes, citoyens!* To arms, citizens!' they chorused.

'What could go wrong?' Jules murmured. 'The people have pronounced.'

Anatole was grinning like a child on his birthday. 'This is exciting, you've got to admit . . .' He turned from Marie to Jules, who stood on either side of him, and they saw his eyes were brimming over too. 'What more could you ask? A peaceful revolution! Democracy! Justice! This'll make up for the last few decades, surely. We must be on the right track now.'

Marie looked away.

Jules shrugged. 'The royalists won't stand for this,' he said. 'Never mind the Bonapartists.' The National Assembly at Versailles was made up of as many political shades as the newly elected leaders in Paris, but it was united in its opposition to the Commune.

'Too bad! Paris will never give up its municipal rights now. I'll put money on it.'

'You'll need money to put money on it,' Jules pointed out in a low voice, right into Anatole's ear.

'Shhh.' Anatole shook his head quickly, and glanced at Marie.

'Are the Commune leaders really all foreigners?' she asked suddenly. 'They don't look it, do they?'

Anatole was puzzled. 'What did you say?'

'Why would you think that?' asked Jules.

'I heard . . .' She hesitated. What had she heard? 'I heard they were all international, or internationalists, or something . . .'

They didn't quite laugh at her.

'Oh, you mean the International Workingmen's Association?' said Anatole, understanding. 'No, they're not foreign. They just all believe in socialism, and things like that.'

'Socialism? I didn't know . . .' she said to nobody in particular, and nobody heard.

'Will you give me a leg up here?' Anatole asked Jules, pointing at a newly vacated lamp post. 'I just want to get a bit higher. I'll tell you what I can see. Do you mind, Marie?'

She shook her head and withdrew her arm to free his. 'These crowds are very exhausting, aren't they?'

If Anatole didn't offer to take her home, perhaps his expensively-dressed friend would get the hint.

'You'll get a fresh wind soon!' said Anatole cheerfully, swinging himself up by a cast-iron curlicue, with the help of a reluctant heave from Jules. 'Or come and have a look from up here – you can see much better! How many thousands of people do you think there can be here . . . ? The rue de Rivoli looks completely jammed too . . . It's unbelievable. Everyone left in Paris must have turned out to see this.'

Another song started up, a stirring anthem about tyrants going down to graves, and the Republic's summons. From his new vantage point, Anatole scanned the faces of the singers. They were rough and ready, but sang with as much feeling as any musician at the Théâtre Lyrique. That's what was needed, he thought. Pure emotion. How could he explain this to Marie? How could you capture a spirit like this, and recreate it evening after evening? Perhaps you couldn't. He loved watching it all though, and being part of it. Anatole could hardly tear himself away. He looked one last time across the sea of smiling faces, before he offered to walk Marie home. But something caught his eye. He stared, and his expression turned to anger.

'What is it?' Marie called up, alarmed.

'Watch out – he may be about to fall!' Jules shouted. A person could be trampled to death in a crowd like this.

But Anatole felt anything but faint. He jumped down from his lamp post and vanished.

10.

A few moments later, Zéphyrine felt a firm hand on her shoulder.

'Hey!' She shook it off and spun round indignantly. At least she tried to. With so many people jostling around, pressing in on all sides, and such a racket going on, it was hard to make the dramatic gesture she'd intended.

'Hey,' echoed Rose, who'd made Zéphyrine come to the celebrations, thinking it would cheer her up, and inspire her with a bit of revolutionary spirit into the bargain.

'You stole my money!' hissed Anatole, wanting to make a scene without actually making a scene.

'Me?' said Zéphyrine, hands moving to hips.

A shiver of doubt crossed Anatole's face. Her white, ribboned cap was spotless, her dress neat and crisp.

Rose frowned. 'You stole his money?'

Anatole stared at Zéphyrine and glimpsed, just for a moment, a reflection of his own uncertainty. A flicker in her eyes that told him she knew exactly who he was. 'I want it back.'

Zéphyrine had admitted nothing yet. Another chorus of 'Le Chant du Départ' broke out. 'The Republic is calling us,' everybody sang.

'Now.' Anatole raised his voice another notch, keeping up the pressure, enjoying the prospect of reporting the incident to Jules. Surely he would approve this time.

'I – I've spent it.' She tossed back her head, half-closing her eyes. Defiant, or buying time?

Of course she'd spent it, probably on that dress, which actually suited her better than the drab skirt and buttoned blouse she'd been wearing before. Anatole looked around for a policeman. Then he remembered that he wouldn't find one: the National Guard was in charge of law and order now. There was no shortage of Guardsmen in the square. So what should he do? Grab the nearest militiaman and ask him to arrest her?

'Hoy!' he shouted, to no effect.

'Do you want to make a run for it?' Rose whispered a little obviously. 'I can move faster than you think when I have to, you know.'

Anatole grabbed Zéphyrine's arm to stop her vanishing again, but she was already shaking her head, and shaking him off. 'No.'

He looked at her cheeks, already less cadaverous than he remembered. He watched as she tucked a straggle of hair back under her cap, and straightened her shawl. With her feet neatly together again, and her eyes lowered, she suddenly looked a very different kind of girl.

'Well, "Zéphyrine" . . . or whatever your name is . . .' he began.

'It is Zéphyrine. I'm not a liar,' she said as yet another person pushed past her and knocked her askew.

'I can't hear you!' said Anatole, leaning in closer. The bugles were sounding again. The crowd was on the move, all the battalions getting ready to file past the stage.

'I said I'm not a liar,' she shouted, and shot an angry glance at Rose, who was giggling behind her. 'And I'm sorry I took your money. I needed it.'

Rose couldn't stop herself then. Zéphyrine had confessed that part of her encounter with Anatole.

'It was for her grandmother. She had to pay for her funeral.' And she ducked back behind Zéphyrine, who gave her a furious shove. She didn't want Anatole's pity.

His mouth dropped open, and he struggled for words.

'It's true. She's buried now,' Zéphyrine muttered. In Anatole's silence some of her earlier defiance returned. 'So thank you.'

Anatole mumbled some acknowledgement, and let go of her arm. She didn't move away though.

'I didn't know what else to do,' she said. 'And then when you suddenly disappeared, how was I to know who you might come back with? You could have had me arrested. You must have known I wasn't registered with the police. It was obvious I was breaking the law when you found me.'

'I hadn't thought that far,' Anatole admitted. The endless, degrading rules that governed every woman trying to make a living from her own body had never been his problem. 'I . . . never mind.'

Zéphyrine blushed again. There was one obvious way to make good her debt, and they all knew it. A surge in the crowd pushed Anatole right up against her, closer than they'd ever been. Then it was his turn to flush. They steadied themselves, apologised, and lurched simultaneously into speech.

'Do you want —' she began to ask.

'Look, why don't you . . . ?'

'Sorry . . . what were you going to say?'

'No, I interrupted you.'

'I just . . .'

'I tell you what. Forget the money.'

'What?'

'I was going to give it to you anyway.'

It was difficult to talk, still crushed together like flotsam twisting in a tide. Rose detached herself. She had seen the way they were looking at each other.

'I think I'll leave you two to sort this out,' she said quietly. 'See you at the club later?'

The girls kissed cheeks, then Zéphyrine faced Anatole again.

'Thank you, but I don't want to forget the money. I shouldn't have taken it. I'm not a beggar. It was a mistake and I want to give it back.'

'If you insist . . .' said Anatole, though he didn't hold out his hand.

'I haven't got it now, but I will get it for you, I promise. You'll have your . . . seven francs . . . soon.'

'Seven francs and twenty-three centimes.'

Anatole's face came close to Zéphyrine's, too close for her to see he was beginning to smile. Then their halting conversation was drowned out by a fresh outburst of singing, even more wild than before.

'Anyway,' said Zéphyrine sharply, proudly, 'I've got a job now.'

'Good. I'm glad to hear it.'

'So I will pay you back. It won't be long.'

It was a matter of dignity.

'Well, you know where to find me. If you insist,' said Anatole.

Zéphyrine hesitated. She knew her way round every lane and alley in Montmartre, but this part of Paris confused her still. She remembered Les Halles of course, and she could get herself back there – it was more or less a straight line. But after that?

'The Théâtre Lyrique,' he reminded her. 'Near the Île de la Cité – you know, the island in the river. You really can't miss it.'

'That's good. Though I don't know when . . .' She met his eye, and looked away.

'I'm in no hurry,' he said, although suddenly he was. Anatole was tempted for a moment to do something he might regret. They parted quickly, and when Zéphyrine looked back, she saw no sign of the young violinist.

APRIL 1871

And then April arrived, with all its uncertain glory. Almost as soon as the sun had brightened the streets, the rain returned. But at last Paris was free to decide how it would run itself. The city would take no more orders from monarchists, or empire-lovers or even peasants, come to that. Committees met, policies were argued, decisions made, decrees declared. The church was separated from the state, salaries were fixed, newspapers multiplied. The leaders were wary though, and careful not to take things too far. They ignored the calls from the clubs to take over empty property. They even left the Bank alone. Caution was the watchword, despite what the foreign newspapers would have had their readers believe.

But who would have thought intransigence could turn so quickly to civil war? Who would have imagined the soldiers of the line would actually be prepared to fire on their brothers in the citizen's army, the National Guard? Outside the city walls, between Paris and Versailles, fighting began. Elsewhere in France, other rebellions were put down, distant communes dying almost before they had lived.

Inside Paris, life carried on. In some parts of the city, you'd be forgiven for wondering exactly what had changed.

11.

3rd April

Zéphyrine's knife thudded against the wooden board faster than machine-gun fire. She was chopping carrots, under pressure, in a hot, noisy kitchen. This was a workers' canteen, and making food instead of flowers felt altogether more useful, and more permanent. People always needed feeding.

She liked having her sleeves rolled up again. Zéphyrine enveloped herself in the smell of softening onions and marrowbones, savoury steam and a sense of purpose. Everyone working together, and everyone talking too, about the latest decrees, the latest threats, last night's debate. There were so many opinions flying around all the time: you had to keep talking, and listening hard, to keep up with it all. So many changes, all at once, and best of all, the rent cancelled again. Well! Wasn't that the point of the elections? At last Paris had a government who was on the side of the tenants instead of the landlords. The Commune was really something to be proud of.

'Who wants to go up to the Butte this evening, to watch the fireworks?' called out one of the cooks, banging down the lid of the slop bucket. There was plenty of laughter at that, and disapproval from some, but plenty of volunteers too. Zéphyrine was tempted. It wasn't far from home, and you got such a view of the battlefield from the top of Montmartre, over the windmills' sails.

The biggest cauldron of soup she'd ever seen was on the range, bubbling and spitting with a life of its own. A gigantic dipper hung on a nearby hook. It took two strong arms to stir with it, and this was usually left to the woman in charge of the canteen, a great tall ageless creature known as the Ladle. Zéphyrine tipped her carrots into the cauldron, sweat prickling on her forehead as she bent over the heat. In a few hours the children would be lining up with their bowls in the dining hall, the orphans of the siege hungry for their lunch. Hurry, hurry. So much to be done. So good to be part of it, right there in the stew of life. The thoughts that plagued her at night could easily be kept at bay by day.

There was such a hubbub inside that at first nobody noticed the change outside.

Then:

'Listen!'

The talking stopped and the screaming began. They already knew the noise of cannon fire of course. In the distance, that is. Prussian shells had fallen on many parts of Paris in January, but never here. Anyway, this was completely different. In January they had been at war. But now – to be shelled by your own countrymen? It was incomprehensible that Versailles should attack like this. Barbarous. Impossible. A few women rushed to the roof, to see for themselves, and came running back to report. It was true. It was terrible. Out of a blue sky, shells were falling on Paris. Thiers's government was trying to bomb the rebellious capital into submission.

'Get in the cellar!'

One or two ran down the stairs to crouch, head in arms, among sacks of potatoes. Others refused to be budged. Zéphyrine froze, uncertain. Then she retied her apron, and went back to her chopping. What would happen would happen.

After the children had eaten, their lessons were abandoned. They spent the afternoon in the courtyard filling sandbags for new barricades, supervised by schoolmistresses in black wearing red cockades. Through the steamed-up window, Zéphyrine could just make out their heaving shadows. When the last pot had been cleaned, and the knives put away, the floor swept and the fire damped down, she hung up her apron and hesitated in the doorway.

Anatole had been in Zéphyrine's mind all that day. After the celebrations, Rose had come round – rent debts wiped out, Zéphyrine was back in her room at Madame Mouton's – and she'd quizzed Zéphyrine about Anatole for hours. She had nothing to tell her. Eventually Rose turned up her nose with a sniff and declared she had no time for men anyway, and nor should Zéphyrine, not in the middle of a revolution. Better that she stopped talking about them then, in Zéphyrine's opinion. But she would have found Anatole hard to forget even without Rose's regular reminders that he had awfully dark eyes, something sparky about him when he spoke, and hadn't he seemed very determined to find her again? He looked so different from the Breton boys – all ruddy and windswept – or the pale young workers of Montmartre, always so hungry for one thing or another, their eyes constantly looking for something she couldn't give them. Next to them, Anatole seemed golden.

It was either now or never. Anatole could be leaving Paris at any moment, in uniform to fight, or in disguise to flee. Zéphyrine had money in her pocket again. If she didn't make good her debt to him right away, it might be too late. She decided to take her chance, and head south into the centre of the city, to the Théatre Lyrique.

'Ils ont attaqué, ils ont attaqué, ils ont attaqué!' Versailles had attacked. Skirmishes had turned suddenly into vicious warfare. The new proclamation was already on every poster. The printing presses worked overtime, spreading the terrible news right through the city in just a few short hours:

'Not content with cutting off all communications with the provinces, and making vain efforts to defeat us through famine, these furies are following the Prussian example to the letter and bombarding the capital . . . But we have been elected by the population of Paris, and our duty is to defend this great city. With your help, we will defend her. The Executive Committee of the National Guard.'

All through the streets, the cry rang out. 'To arms, to arms.' Drums and bugle calls sounded, and everywhere you turned a new barricade had miraculously sprung up. Passers-by were stopped with shouts for help, or just a quiet, pointed word: 'Your paving stone, citizen.' And another solid block of stone would be offered, and usually taken, and laid with modest ceremony, sometimes with enthusiasm, sometimes reluctance.

Cross-currents of marching battalions came from every neighbourhood, wave after wave of men tramping along the boulevards, heading south-west towards Issy. Zéphyrine darted from pavement to pavement, judging her moment as best she could. She narrowly escaped a galloping horse, a skitter of hooves flashing as it swerved, and then horse and red-shirted rider clattered out of sight. From the battlefield, the ambulance wagons had already begun to arrive. The wounded were returning from the front, and the dead with them.

Zéphyrine reached the big square by the river. She remembered the fountain and column, and stood by its fantastical gushing creatures, staring in panic at one theatre and then another. Which was Anatole's? Then she recognised the posters outside the Théâtre Lyrique. But they had all been stamped over. 'CANCELLED. CANCELLED. CANCELLED.' One frame after another repeated the message. The building looked completely dead.

Zéphyrine had no idea how or when these people worked. She supposed it counted as work. She looked for that entrance at the side marked 'Stage Door', and pushed it cautiously, certain it would be locked.

It wasn't, and she remembered the lobby with the chairs as soon as she saw it again. No charwoman this time. Once again, a newspaper fluttered on the face of the porter, who lay back in an upholstered chair, a few rows of empty pigeonholes behind him. Voices – raised voices in fact – could be heard coming from one of the many mysterious rooms beyond. The theatre wasn't as empty as it had looked.

She rapped her knuckles on the wooden counter.

'Excuse me!' she said firmly, and stepped quickly back as the man she'd just woken up sprang to his feet with limbs all over the place. He shook himself like a dog coming out of a pond, and then slowly collected the scattered sheets of his newspaper. Only when they were back in a neat pile, and folded on the counter, did he finally acknowledge Zéphyrine's presence.

'Yes?'

She stared at a scar on his nose, but could not quite meet the narrowed eyes just above it.

'Please could you tell me where I can find Monsieur Clément?'

'Come to pick up his washing, have you?'

'It's none of your business what I've come for,' she replied. 'I asked where I could find him.'

They had a brief staring competition, which Zéphyrine won. The nose indicated the staircase. Up she went.

The building's strange, distorting acoustics made it hard to work out exactly where the shouting was coming from, but at least there were no other noises to distract her, for everyone in the building seemed to be gathered in one place this time. Higher and higher she climbed, until she had to stop and catch her breath. At the top of the final flight she reached a door that was half open. Hundreds seemed crammed into the room beyond, an effect of all the mirrors lining the walls, offering infinite and deceptive reflections of the gathered meeting. She pushed the door a little wider, and every one of those faces seemed to turn at once.

12.

Anatole looked too and saw Zéphyrine's eyes flitting from face to face. Grabbing the barre that ran at waist-height round the room, he pulled himself to his feet. He hadn't dared dream he would see her again.

'All those in favour, raise your hands.' Dr Rousselle, who had called the meeting, began to count out loud.

One arm held above his head, Anatole threaded his way through chairs and instruments and musicians and singers. He could not get to the door quickly enough, could not take his eyes off her. She might fade away like one of Jules's creations, he thought. So he kept his gaze fixed on her, like a camera lens, and she stood there, exposed.

'And all those against?'

A shifting of bodies, and a resistant murmur. Fewer hands. Anatole didn't look round. 'Sorry,' he mumbled as his foot caught on a pair of outstretched legs, but his eyes did not leave Zéphyrine's. A ripple of laughter circulated behind him, and Marie reddened slightly on his behalf.

'Any abstentions? The motion is carried. This company is hereby declared a cooperative association. Now, fundraising . . .'

Anatole shut the door on the discussion. He had reached her at last, and there she was, living and breathing before his eyes. Heavily, in fact: her cheeks were glowing.

'Those stairs!' she said. And sat herself down on the top step to recover. The long shadows of her eyelashes fell on her face. Anatole sat next to her, close enough to imagine he could feel the warmth rising from her skin. She fanned her face with her apron. The fringe of her shawl trailed near enough to touch.

'If I'd known you were coming . . .' he started. Nobody in the world had ever given him such difficulty in finishing his sentences. It was ridiculous. In the usual run of things, he was the kind of person who sometimes finished other people's sentences.

'Then what?' she asked him, genuinely curious.

'I – I don't know. I suppose I could have met you downstairs. Told you what time I'd be free. Made an arrangement.' Maybe she couldn't tell the time. He had no idea what a girl like her might know.

'Oh I see. It's one of those polite things some people say. Gentlemen.'

'I suppose so,' he admitted.

'But it doesn't really mean anything?'

Was she flirting? It was hard to tell. She was very direct.

'No, no, I'd never say anything to you I didn't mean,' he found himself confessing, and was delighted when she smiled but didn't lower her eyes. 'Anyway, I'm not exactly a gentleman. I never was and now I don't suppose I ever will be. We're all citizens now, aren't we? *Citoyens* and *citoyennes*?'

He moved a little closer. And she shuffled away.

'And now the *citoyennes* are showing what they're made of,' said Zéphyrine, reaching into her skirt pocket. 'Here. I said I'd return the money I took. I'm sorry. But we're even now.'

Anatole held out his hand for the francs she was offering. She took it in one of hers, and firmly pressed the coins into his palm with the other, counting each one out, then closed his fingers over them, as though she were entrusting money to a small child.

'There. That's done,' she said, and patted his fist.

The movement was so quick, her skin rough but so warm and alive. Anatole sat with his hand still extended, silently wishing she hadn't let go. He opened his tingling fingers, and looked at the coins in his palm.

'What's the matter?' Zéphyrine asked quickly. 'Isn't it enough? I'll count it again.'

And just so that he could feel her fingers on his again, he let her.

'That's right,' they said together, and then a roar of laughter from the meeting across the landing made them look at each other in alarm. It was quickly followed by scattered applause and the scrape of chair legs on parquet. Flustered, Zéphyrine stood up, seemed on the verge of speech, and then started down the stairs, her wooden soles clattering.

Anatole rushed after her, almost falling into her in his haste. 'Please wait,' he called. 'Stop. Where are you going? Don't go. Please.'

He hadn't rehearsed this at all. He didn't have a clue what to do to keep Zéphyrine from disappearing. She stopped and looked back up at him, with a gaze that didn't seem to want to let go. The turn of her bare neck caught his eye, and he wanted to touch that too, and take her cap off so he could see the colour of her hair better. What did it mean, the way she kept on looking at him? It made his skin shiver. It felt familiar and yet completely strange. He ran down and caught up with her.

'What is it?' she asked.

'I wondered . . . that is to say . . .' He was about to ask if she was hungry, invite her to have supper with him, but suddenly he was afraid she'd be insulted. 'Are you busy this evening? Might you —' And then he looked down at his empty hands and remembered. 'Oh no! I've left my violin. I've got to go and get it.' He had messed everything up. He would have to let her go, and that would be that.

But she just leaned against the curve of the wall, gripping the banister behind her back, and looked him straight in the eye. 'I can wait.'

The voices from the landing above grew louder again. The meeting was definitely breaking up. Zéphyrine continued to stare at him, and he didn't move until he realised her gaze had shifted slightly. She was looking at Marie, who was now standing at the top of the staircase, holding the fiddle case, her face unreadable.

'You forgot this,' she said, holding it out to him, just as everybody else came sweeping out of the meeting room, all arguing and singing and shouting. Voices and shoe leather banged and clattered down into the lobby and out onto the pavement. Other singers and musicians came out discussing the meeting and were now parting, calling farewells and arranging rendezvous across the square. Zéphyrine stood by the stage door, her arm suddenly in Anatole's tight grasp.

He looked at his hand as if it belonged to someone else, and immediately removed it. 'So many people . . . all the excitement . . . I was worried that . . . but of course, I know perfectly well you don't need my help to get down a staircase. Please don't think I make a habit of . . .'

Nobody had ever taken Zéphyrine's arm in that way before, a way that made her feel alive with something that wasn't anger. Nobody had ever looked at her quite like that. He made it hard to look away. She wished he hadn't let go.

'A habit?' she asked. His earnestness made her want to laugh, but also cry. It was very confusing. His hands were beautiful, with their long, strong fingers. She had touched them. 'Now, let me see . . . I think you've grabbed hold of me every time we've met so far.'

Anatole looked quite forlorn. 'You're right. How strange. That does look like a habit, doesn't it? But I only seem to do it with you.'

'Which means . . . ?'

Before he could answer, Marie was there again. 'I might have to start asking for tips,' she said lightly, handing Anatole his violin. 'You seem to be confusing me with a porter.'

Then, utterly gracious, she held out her hand to Zéphyrine. 'Good evening,' she said.

It was a bit like being introduced to a princess, Zéphyrine thought later. There was something so perfect about Marie: the way she held herself, her hair, her beautiful dress. All she needed was a glittering coronet.

Zéphyrine nodded. 'Pleased to meet you.' She'd never expected someone like this might ever talk to someone like her, let alone shake her hand.

'I beg your pardon, both of you,' said Anatole, more flustered than ever. 'Please allow me. Mademoiselle Le Gall, may I introduce —'

'Le Gall?' interrupted Zéphyrine, her face bright with recognition. 'You're not from Brittany, are you?'

'My grandparents were. I was born in Paris.'

'And I am from a village near Concarneau. My name is Zéphyrine.' Citoyenne Zéphyrine, she almost said. 'But I've been a Parisian too these last few years. Still, you're the first opera singer I've ever met. You *are* a singer, aren't you? You must be.'

Marie laughed politely, musically, delightfully.

'Yes, I am. And I hope I won't be the last you meet. You must come to our concert, mustn't she?' she said, turning towards Anatole, who frowned.

'What concert?'

'Oh, I'm sorry . . . I forgot that you missed the end of the meeting. Doctor Rousselle is organising some public concerts to raise money for the ambulance stations, and for the widows and orphans of . . . the Commune.' The last word seemed to stick a little in her throat. 'So our work together may not be wasted after all, Anatole.'

'I hope not,' he returned stoutly. 'Is there a date for it?'

'Not yet, nor a place. I daresay both will be decided soon enough.' She shuddered. 'The situation seems to be becoming more urgent by the day.'

'Well, I've never been to a concert,' said Zéphyrine. 'I'd like to come. If I'm not working of course.'

'Naturally. I hope we will see Mister Crowfield at the concert too. What do you think, Anatole? It was such a pleasure to meet him last week. You must know Mister Crowfield too . . . ?'

Zéphyrine shook her head. 'No. I've no idea who you're talking about.'

'Really? I assumed . . . So you and Monsieur Clément . . . Do tell me where you met . . .'

Zéphyrine was struggling to know what to make of Mlle Le Gall. She and Anatole obviously worked together. But were they familiar in other ways? Zéphyrine decided that if she made herself quite clear, perhaps the singer would too. It was best to be clear. And the discussions at the club had made her bold, far bolder than she ever used to be. She narrowed her eyes and spoke in a hard, matter-of-fact kind of way.

'He picked me up near the market about ten days ago. He thought I was a tart, a *fille publique*. Can't really blame him. I thought I was about to become a whore myself. Well, you know how it is . . . a girl's got to live.' She shrugged, as if she didn't care how close she'd come to falling. And then she worried that Anatole would think worse of her for talking like that, and wished she hadn't.

Marie began to twist and turn the tassel of her little bag. Of course she knew how it was. There was barely a woman in Paris who didn't, who wasn't making such calculations to survive, day after day, at one level or another – whether she admitted it or not.

'I wonder . . .' started Anatole, but another troop of marching men was coming over the bridge and getting closer. It was hard to speak through the noise, and impossible not to turn and stare. Nobody could ignore that heart-twisting bugle call.

'So. Are you going to help defend the barricades?' asked Zéphyrine, following his gaze. 'If the Versailles army gets any closer?'

'I hope not!' said Marie, before Anatole could answer, turning away from them both, all composure gone. 'I must go now,' she said. 'This city . . . this war . . . I can't . . .' She hurried off.

'Wait . . .!' Anatole called after her, but far too quietly. As he watched her go, he ran a hand through his hair as if it might straighten his thoughts too. But Zéphyrine was reassured. If they cared for each other in the way she had feared, Mlle Le Gall would not have gone, and he would not have let her go.

'Her brother was captured by the Prussians – he's still a prisoner of war,' he explained. 'She has no other family living . . .'

'How awful for her.' Zéphyrine was instantly sympathetic. At least some of her family were alive, even if they wanted nothing to do with her. And her little brothers – half-brothers – they were still too young to fight. Zéphyrine could afford to feel sorry for Marie.

'They say Thiers is negotiating to get the prisoners released more quickly, so maybe he'll be back soon,' Anatole continued.

'Of course he is!' said Zéphyrine. 'He's going to need them to defeat the forces of the Commune.'

'True,' said Anatole. 'But that doesn't make things any easier for Marie, knowing Emile might be back to fight another war, and a civil war too.' Another thunderous roll of cannon fire had begun to sound in the west.

Zéphyrine repeated something she'd heard Rose say. 'It's a shame Thiers is so much better at negotiating with the Prussians than he is with his own people.'

Anatole looked impressed. 'I don't understand it. It's all getting out of hand so fast. I thought there would surely be talks, discussion, something sensible to resolve the crisis. But the Versailles government seems so quick to fire —'

'That's because they're scared,' interrupted Zéphyrine, getting into her stride. She loved the way he drank in her angry words, feasted on her face. 'Afraid of us. Democracy's a dirty word for them. They think it just means poor people taking their things. They don't understand. But they have to understand. And they should be afraid. This is a battle Paris cannot lose. It's our last chance to make life fair.'

Anatole nodded, and gripped his violin case more tightly. 'Let's walk,' he said suddenly, 'while we still can walk.'

'Just walk? Why? Where to?'

Anatole waved his hand towards the river, the bridge, the pale towers and turrets of the Conciergerie, the building that held the royal prisoners in the first revolution. 'It doesn't matter, does it? Wherever we can.'

They walked a long way, wandering westward along the river.

Little by little, the awkwardness dissolved. Within half an hour, they couldn't stop talking. They took it in turns to interrogate each other, to find out as much as they possibly could, as quickly as they possibly could. There seemed no time to waste. Zéphyrine told Anatole about her grandmother. How she had loved and feared her, how she had struggled against her tight rein, yet would have done anything for her. She relived the dizzy despair she had felt at her death and the moment of utter panic as the last shovel of earth had covered the rough wood of her cheap coffin. How would she have got through those first few days without Rose, and the Lenoir family? What would she have done if Madame Mouton had not kept her room? And now she had her comrades at the canteen, and a whole new life.

When they reached the gardens on the far side of the Tuileries Palace, you could almost smell the rising sap. They pointed out to each other the buds on the trees, swollen almost to bursting. Soon it really would be spring, and about time too.

Then Anatole spoke of his bossy sisters, and of the excitement of arriving alone in Paris the year before. Nobody to tell him what to do any more. Everything had been new and glamorous to him. The city itself seemed to glitter and sparkle then – not like now – and at times Anatole had felt quite dazzled.

So they'd both arrived as innocents from the provinces, they agreed. But they were Parisians now, through and through. Living in the greatest city in the world, a city like no other.

'But it's not really one city, is it?' said Zéphyrine suddenly. 'It never has been, I don't suppose.'

Anatole stopped. 'What do you mean?'

'I mean there are lots of different worlds in Paris. It's just most of the time they never meet. The poor and the rich. Me and you.'

'Oh, I'm not rich,' said Anatole quickly. 'Not at all. What gave you that idea?'

'That's what you think. Maybe you still have to earn a living. You don't have a country estate, or servants. But you can't really

96

imagine what it is to have nothing. Really nothing. Nothing at all. To hang on to life by the skin of your teeth. Can you?'

'No, but . . .'

Zéphyrine smiled, and touched him to make him look at her again. 'It's not your fault. I'm not blaming you. And you're nothing like the speculators and the developers and the landlords and the aristocrats. I know that. Those people – the ones who hate us – I can't imagine their lives and they can't imagine mine. But they never try, do they? Because they don't care. As long as other people are working to make their money, and they don't have to see them.'

'But not everybody's like that, surely?' said Anatole uncomfortably.

'How would I know? It's not as if I ever get the chance to ask them. Take you and me, we'd never be talking now, if it hadn't been for the war and the siege. And the Commune, come to that. Unless . . .' Zéphyrine shook her head. Of course there were times that girls like her used to talk to men like him.

'Well . . .' Anatole couldn't deny it.

'You know my grandmother hardly let me out of Montmartre before the war. Every day was the same: cutting, and shaping, and glueing. You don't think I ever saw the flowers I made again? We'd take them to the back doors of the milliners and the dressmakers and get what we could for them. I used to peep through, and wish so much I could see the shops, and what became of our roses, and our lilies, and our violets. But that wouldn't have "done" would it? Of course, they were always trying to lower the price, finding something to complain about, saying the nuns made them better, and cheaper too.'

'I wonder if any of your flowers ended up on stage at our theatre . . . or in the audience,' said Anatole. 'They must have. Imagine that.'

'Maybe. But then of course nobody wanted bright flowers during the war. Too frivolous. We kept lowering and lowering our price, but then we'd go into town and find the shops all shuttered up, and the hatmakers and couturiers gone. And then we had to pawn our tools. And then sell our pawn tickets, so we had no hope of getting them back, no hope of working again. It's so easy to fall. You just get dragged lower and lower until there's no getting back up, you see. You think you're hanging on and then one day it just happens.'

Anatole was beginning to see.

'Where do you live?' asked Zéphyrine.

Then Anatole told her how he had stayed at first with an old cello teacher of his father's on the other side of the river, in the Latin Quarter, and how much a friendly face had helped at first, and what a difference it had made to have a few introductions at the opera houses. But the couple really were very old, and it was a small apartment and altogether very awkward, and he had just been looking for a room of his own when he had run into Jules.

'Jules?' said Zéphyrine.

'Mister Crowfield, as Marie called him. It's her joke. Because he's American, and Monsieur Crowfield sounds odd to her.'

And Anatole told Zéphyrine of the luck of that chance meeting. How generous, how sophisticated Jules had seemed . . . what good company he was, and so kind. How much easier city life was with a friend to share it with.

Zéphyrine nodded, thinking of Rose. 'Jules is a photographer now,' Anatole told her. 'He works very hard at it. Portraits mostly, and buildings. You have to keep extremely still. It's scientific but quite magical too. Very precise, but also sometimes just a matter of luck.'

Zéphyrine was never quite sure about luck, she admitted. What was the difference between luck and chance and fate? Maybe all chance meetings were fate, Anatole said. Or just the ones you remember, suggested Zéphyrine. And they talked about their own good fortune in meeting, and finally Anatole convinced Zéphyrine that the money she had taken didn't matter to him at all, and that his intentions really had been pure, if not entirely clear, even to himself. She thought she probably believed him.

They walked arm in arm, both careful to keep a respectable distance, one from the other. Neither wanted to make assumptions. But in the small space between their bodies, the air seemed to hum and crackle.

As the gas lamps began to roar, Anatole and Zéphyrine came to a halt. They were in front of another barricade, but this one was vast. It would have been hard to imagine, unbelievable really, if you weren't standing there right in front of it, and it wasn't even finished. What a triumph of engineering! What shocking grandeur. And it blocked the grandest of streets. There was no need for anyone here to threaten or cajole passers-by for help. There were no semi-circles of iron grating in this great building work, or bits of wood, or benches, or children fingering the dirt. Workers had been paid to raise this barricade. They had stopped and started at set times.

Somebody had consulted a plan, and told others what to do. Tomorrow they would start again. Wheelbarrows were lined up, waiting, beside a huge mound of earth. This was a barricade that really meant business.

On the stone rampart above the line of cannon, Guardsmen marched with lanterns. Up and down, up and down they went, cocky as hell, shadows swinging.

Anatole felt Zéphyrine stiffen. He didn't guess it was pride that straightened her spine. He imagined she was afraid.

'Will they let us pass, do you think?' murmured Anatole. Jules always said you mustn't let people intimidate you. But it was hard not to feel cowed by quite so many sandbags, a ditch so deep, and everything around so neat and orderly. He longed for a strip of braid himself, and wondered what had happened to his old battalion. The smarter the neighbourhood, the less likely its National Guard unit was to be in sympathy with the Commune. He ought to go and find out.

'Of course they'll let us,' said Zéphyrine. With a flick of her head, she strode forward, pulling him with her.

There was a flurry of movement above, and Anatole was startled by the click of rifles being cocked.

Zéphyrine didn't flinch. 'Good evening, *citoyens*!' she called up. 'This is going to be the finest barricade in all Paris! And what a grand job you're doing of guarding it. Long live the Commune! *Vive la Commune!*'

'*Vive la Commune!*' came the cheerful reply. 'Would you like to see the view from here?'

'Of course we would,' shouted Zéphyrine. 'But how do we get up?'

More Guardsmen emerged from the shadows. 'Here. Step down over here, and then come up this way. Just don't tell the boss.'

Zéphyrine turned back to Anatole, her eyes gleaming in the shadows. 'Ready?'

She jumped down into the ditch, as instructed, then turned and held up her hand for him to join her. Their feet sank into the sand. It smelled cool and damp, like seaside without salt. The looming barricade looked higher than ever. Undaunted, Zéphyrine gathered up her skirts and began the ascent, a foot on a cannon wheel, fingers scrabbling against stone, then hessian and sand, then stone again.

Anatole looked at the violin case in this hand, and decided to take the risk. He glanced around to be sure nobody was watching, and tucked it into the shadows, hiding it well under a tarpaulin. A moment later he scrambled up too, close behind Zéphyrine. It was easier to find toeholes than he'd imagined. Towards the top, strangers' hands heaved them both up, and then Zéphyrine reached out for Anatole.

He swayed a moment as he found his feet. 'You were very quick,' he said to her.

'Practice,' she said. 'I grew up on the coast of Brittany, remember? All sorts of good reasons to get quick at climbing rocks by the sea.'

'And isn't it worth the climb to get a view like this, citizens?' said one of the guards. 'Just wait till it's finished.'

It was worth it. Anatole began to feel giddy, but not because of the height, or the ditch below. It was the thought of where he might or might not be heading. It made his head spin to think of being tipped into a future without Zéphyrine now, that if he put a foot wrong she might walk away from him. But the alternative was equally unnerving. It felt alluring, and dangerous, and he realised there was no refusing her. Looking out across Paris, and then back at Zéphyrine, who was standing on tiptoe, Anatole lost his balance. His hands flew up as he tried to right himself.

'Oi! What's he doing?' A shout. At the far end of the barricade, another sentinel was getting edgy. He raised his weapon aggressively. 'Stop him. He's signalling!'

'Arrest him!' shouted another, turning likewise. 'He's sending a message to Versailles!'

Several more men grabbed Anatole from behind. Their breath felt hot on the back of his neck as they gripped his wrists, jerking his arms nearly out of their sockets.

'Oh stop it! Shut up! You're being ridiculous!' Zéphyrine waved her own arms to calm the lot of them. 'Be quiet and listen. He's just a bit unsteady on his feet, isn't he?'

The men were surprised into letting go, leaving Anatole rubbing his wrists.

'Yes, that's right. I lost my balance.' His knees felt so weak he feared he might again. But Zéphyrine steadied him again with a broad smile.

'Sorry about that, citizen,' said a fédéré. 'No hard feelings?' A biff to the upper arm this time.

'Indeed not.'

'We'll drink to that.'

Hands were shaken and a flask was passed from hand to hand and mouth to mouth, though Zéphyrine shook her head when it came her way. It was rough stuff, but very warming, and it went straight to Anatole's head. He leaned daringly against Zéphyrine, and she leaned back, balancing him. How hard it was to know what was happening.

From this unfamiliar perspective, as they looked out across the Place de la Concorde, it seemed enchanted. The huge square was brilliantly lit, its fountains sparkling. The obelisk in the centre rose proud and tall, and you could almost forget that barely a month ago the Prussians had marched right through here in their spiked helmets. Almost. Flap, flap. The noise was as mournful as an idle sail. A rising wind had begun to catch the black crêpe de Chine still wrapped round the statue of Strasbourg, a stone woman in mourning for the loss of Alsace-Lorraine. And somewhere, not far off, yet another battalion was on the move. A hundred tramping feet echoed off the facades of the buildings that lined the boulevards. In the north-west, thin columns of white smoke rose into the darkening sky.

'I hope we're getting the best of it,' said Zéphyrine.

The grumbling thunder was continuous now. The Guardsman raised his flask again. 'Course we are. It makes all the difference in the world, doesn't it, protecting what's yours?'

From the length of the half-built barricade came a murmur of assent.

'We're not like them. We believe in what we're fighting. They're paid to kill their brothers.'

Zéphyrine nodded. 'We're defending what's right,' she said firmly.

Keen to keep the peace, Anatole told the men about his photographer friend, how good he was at taking portraits.

He promised to send Jules to the barricade the very next day. There was much excitement at that idea.

'Will he really come?' whispered Zéphyrine. 'Here?'

'I'm sure he'll come if I ask him,' said Anatole. 'And he's very good. A real talent. You should see what he can do.'

'I'd like to.'

Then Zéphyrine smiled at the thought of all the extra polishing of belts and shining of brass buttons that would take place later that night, the waxing of moustaches in the morning. Imagine! A picture of yourself that you could keep forever. Maybe everyone in Paris would have their own photographic visiting card soon enough. Wasn't that equality?

All over the city, church bells began to ring the hour.

'It's eight o'clock,' she said. 'Do you want to come?'

'Come where?' he asked.

'To the club of course.'

13.

Jules spent that evening reading in the drawing room, Minou purring on his lap. He found himself skating over the same poem over and over again: something about a terrible dream landscape, with staircases, palaces and waterfalls. He couldn't take it in at all. At one point the noise of the bombardment made him so anxious that he went upstairs and right out onto the rooftop beyond the studio, in an effort to work out exactly where the shells were landing. Of course it didn't set his mind at ease, as he had no way of knowing what had become of Anatole, nor why he hadn't yet come home, and he was glad to retreat.

Finally he caught the faint ring of the outer bell on the ground floor.

At last, thought Jules. He's safe. Any moment now he would hear his elastic-sided boots on the stairs. And then, in another few minutes, Anatole would be perched once more in his usual place on the other side of the hearth, knees up, heels balancing on the seat of the chair in that slightly rakish way he had, absent-mindedly playing with the cat. With hands clasped in front of him and arms slightly hugging his knees, Anatole would begin his report on the day's dramas, and Jules would reply with his own, such as they were.

Minou jumped down and ran to the door of the apartment, and Jules put his book face down on the carpet and rose from his armchair. It was ridiculous to worry so much, he told himself. Of course Anatole was safe. But the door didn't open. Instead, there came a gentle knock.

When he answered it, Marie was standing on the landing.

'Mademoiselle . . .' he began, 'how kind of you to call. Please, let me take your coat.'

She took it off without speaking.

'Would you like to come through to the drawing room?'

'Anatole . . . ?'

'I'm afraid he's not here. I thought he might be with you in fact.'

'Oh. No, he's not. He was at the meeting at the theatre earlier, but it finished a few hours ago, and I just thought perhaps by now . . . sorry.'

'It's quite late,' they both said at once. And then Marie murmured, almost to herself: 'I shouldn't have come. I'm not sure why I did. He's probably . . . I just wanted to check . . .'

Jules's manners got the better of his disappointment. Anyway, he could do with the company. And he was curious about Marie.

'I'm expecting him back any time. Would you like to wait?'

Marie nodded, following him. She was obviously curious about him too, or Anatole. Jules wasn't quite sure. Her eyes roved over the marble fireplace, the gilt clock. They stopped briefly at the two closed doors leading to the study and the bedrooms, and then fell on a little set of inlaid drawers on a side table, and an unusual vase, cream with angular blue and gold leaf patterns, and two funny handles like indignant arms.

'Japanese?' she asked.

Jules was impressed. 'Yes, that's right. Do you like it?'

'Very much. It reminds me of something that belonged to someone I . . . I used to know.'

She suddenly seemed less certain of herself again.

'Please . . . sit down.'

Jules turned his back on her, busying himself with the fire. He wondered if they should start rationing the coal again. He decided to speak to the concierge about it in the morning. Or perhaps he would simply check the cellars himself. It would be good to know exactly how they were supplied just now, in every respect. He was aware that Marie had turned to the photographs now: framed on the wall, and leaning on the mantelpiece waiting to be hung up. So many of Anatole.

'You've got a very good eye,' she said quietly. 'These are beautiful.'

He stood up. 'Thank you.'

At last Marie sat down. She picked up the volume of poetry he'd just been reading and frowned at the strange image on the cover: a grinning, cross-legged skeleton, with tree trunks for arm bones, hovering over a bed of richly coloured flowers. The thought of her opening the book slightly alarmed Jules. If only she'd picked up the cat instead. But Minou was in the hallway, chasing a feather that had fallen from Marie's bonnet.

'Can I offer you anything . . . ?' he said at last. 'A glass of wine?'

'No. Nothing.'

A brandy might fortify him though. He moved towards the cabinet. Marie suddenly dropped the book and sank her face into her hands.

'I'm so sorry,' said Jules, appalled, picking up the book and quickly putting it away in the bookcase. Jules had always thought of opera singers as worldly sort of women. Anatole certainly hadn't given him the impression that Marie was an innocent. 'You're not fond of poetry.'

She shook her head with a grim smile. 'It's not the book.'

He hovered delicately at the back of her chair, and waited for her to elaborate. All this black silk, he thought. In Paris, unlike Pennsylvania, it was hard to tell if a person was in mourning or at the height of fashion. Jules contemplated Marie's exposed neck, perfectly white against the dark taffeta. By art or accident, a delicate tendril of golden hair curled at the point of her hairline, just below the chignon, which was tied with black lace. Anatole had been right. He really ought to photograph her, he decided. Would she take it the wrong way if he asked her this evening? It was quite hard to judge.

'You've had bad news? Is it your brother?'

Marie looked up, handkerchief pressed to her mouth. 'No . . . that's exactly the problem.' She gulped, but did not weep. 'No more news of Emile at all, and I simply don't know where to go to find out. Anatole has been very kind to me, you know. I thought perhaps he might be able to help again. Or that maybe you would have an idea what I should do now?'

She gazed at him imploringly. Neck turned, a three-quarter profile, looking slightly upwards. A long exposure. Jules had recently seen some very successful English portraits taken from exactly the same angle. Very strong lighting, that was the trick. He forced himself to think about her problem. He had no idea how communication with the Versailles army could possibly be operating now. Presumably she would have to persuade them to let her go to Versailles, and that would need some kind of passport.

'Have you asked at the City Hall?' said Jules, walking up and down as he pondered the question.

'Oh no! I'm much too frightened to go to the Commune. They terrify me, these revolutionary types. So ruthless and bloodthirsty.'

'But what could they have against you? You hardly look like an enemy of the revolution.'

'No! Of course not. But if my brother is a soldier of the line . . . ?'

'Oh, I see what you mean. And I have heard —' Jules quickly stopped himself. This wasn't the moment for rationality and reason.

'What? What have you heard?' said Marie, looking even more worried.

'Oh, not a great deal. There have been a few arrests.'

'Arrests . . . ? What kind of arrests?'

'You can guess the type . . . some priests, of course . . . and informers – police spies from the old regime —'

Marie jumped to her feet indignantly. 'I'm not a spy! Why should they think me a spy?'

'No, no, of course you're not,' soothed Jules. 'And I'm quite sure they won't think that. Why indeed should they?'

If you weren't for the Commune, did that mean you were against it? He hoped not. Luckily, Marie seemed reassured by his words. It was as if simply by being spoken out loud, with his calm male authority, they became true. He was beginning to work her out a little more. She seemed to be the kind of person who liked to map out her life, to plot a course that would take her where she wanted to go. The war had driven her off course, understandably; she was fogged by uncertainty. Perhaps she just needed some help in drawing up a new chart.

'If I could just find out where Emile is now, if he has even left Bavaria . . . Oh, why do we have to be trapped like this again? This is worse than the last siege.'

'There probably is a way. If you're prepared to —'

She sat down again, and leaned forward. 'Tell me what you think I should do.'

14.

Anatole was not on his way home of course. In fact he had completely forgotten he'd told Jules he would be. He and Zéphyrine had stopped at a church.

'Well? Shall we go in?' she said, watching him carefully.

'Yes, of course. I'd like to,' he said quickly. 'After you.'

'It's not where I usually go, with my friend Rose – you know – you met her that day at the Hôtel de Ville. This is quite a new club,' said Zéphyrine. 'But I've heard the debates here are very lively. You can learn a lot.'

She pushed open the door, and he followed her in. There were fewer men here than at Saint-Pierre, but Anatole didn't stand out too much. It was hard for anybody to stand out really, when everybody was so different. Zéphyrine pointed out an empty pew halfway up the church where they could sit together. 'I'll explain later.'

'But there is work more urgent still, which is calling the women of Paris today,' the speaker was warning. Her accent was Russian. 'Our country is in danger. Not just our country – the ideals of the revolution itself are in danger. The Versailles army is massing as I speak. Thiers is building a new army, the prisoners of war returning to bulk its force. But the men of the National Guard cannot fight alone. The time has come when it is no longer enough simply to offer our support as *cantinières* and *ambulancières*. Food and nursing is vital, of course, but I have a question for you . . .'

A fire-stoking pause.

'Is your heart not as stout as your brothers, fellow *citoyennes*? Can you bear to stand by when your sons and fathers are dying for your sake?'

'No! No! We must do more!' shouted a young working woman with a red cockade pinned to her shawl. 'We must fight too!'

The woman in the pulpit suddenly flashed a sword, and the church erupted. Some cheered, while some shook their heads or roared disapproval.

'Can anyone just say what they like here?' Anatole whispered.

Zéphyrine shrugged and nodded, as though she were an old hand at all this. 'That's what the clubs are for.'

Anatole raised his eyebrows, settled back in the pew and continued to listen. Someone was listing the steps taken already by the Women's Vigilance Committee. Organisation. That was women's work. And with each day's fighting, there would be more orphanages to organise, more innocent mouths to feed. Another argued that fighting was not the point: it was not too late, there was still time for reconciliation with Versailles and women should march to Thiers with their demands. Then somebody else shook out the day's newspaper and began to read out the latest declaration made by the National Guard's Central Committee.

Zéphyrine yawned despite herself. Her eyes slowly closed, and her mind began to drift. She awoke with a jerk, forced them to open again and did her utmost to concentrate. The discussion moved to prostitution – how best to ban it. How could such a horror exist under the Commune? It had to be wiped out.

Yes, yes, thought Zéphyrine, feeling sick as she remembered how close she had come, how different everything might have been. Maybe Anatole was right. It had been fate.

Then her eyelids began to droop again. The voices all around her merged into a single murmur, each speaker indistinguishable, a kind of rushing wind in her ears like a late summer breeze in the pines near the seashore. Or the rise and fall of a shell as you hold it to your ear. Her head floated, sank and tilted, coming to rest on Anatole's shoulder.

He shifted slightly, to make her more comfortable. His arm moved round her, and, without her awareness, her body instinctively absorbed the warmth and ease offered by his. She began to dream.

A single strand of dark hair hung loose over Zéphyrine's face, not quite black. Anatole twisted his neck to watch as it gently rose and fell, fluttering like a miniature banner with every breath. Tiny sighs, almost inaudible. Somehow, even in the middle of all this, he felt alone with her. The voices around them seemed to blur and recede. He had to seize this moment: it might last only minutes. But for those few minutes he wanted to concentrate.

He gazed at Zéphyrine's face long and hard. It was the kind of face you had to keep looking at: it was so hard to tell whether it was strange, or beautiful, or both at once, and until she slept, it never quite stopped changing. This was his chance to see it still.

The curve of her cheek was less pronounced from this angle, and the smoky lamplight softened everything. When she was awake, smiling broadly – and her smile was broad indeed – her cheeks turned into hard little apples. Delicate lids and dark eyelashes now shielded her darting eyes, and made her look quite different. Her mouth still curved up a little, her top lip slightly wider and also thinner than her bottom lip, which was plump and full; it seemed to Anatole that her mouth had no choice but to tilt up at the corners, simply to fit her lips together. For the first time he noticed a tiny mole, just to the left of her left nostril. And also that her ears, which stuck out a little, were pierced, but she wore no earrings. He guessed they had gone to Auntie's during the siege, along with the flower-making tools, and never been reclaimed.

Her bony shoulder dug into his chest, but it was worth the discomfort to have her settle deeper. He imagined her exhaled breath entering his own nostrils, and breathed her in, light-headed with the surprise of it all. The last few hours had been like tumbling down a grassy slope, turning over and over. Now he had stopped, his thoughts spinning, the world unsteady around him.

Anatole's urge to protect Zéphyrine didn't seem to want to leave him. He'd have to fight it. He imagined confessing his feelings about Zéphyrine to Jules, but he wasn't sure if he could ever find words that would work. How could he describe the effect she had on him, this girl he hardly knew?

She's real, he wanted to say. He dipped his head towards hers. Woodsmoke and lavender water. Yes, real. All flesh and blood, and nothing else. A voice in his head told him how ridiculous that was. Aren't all women real? He wasn't quite sure. It was sometimes hard to tell. He wanted her to wake up, and ask her what she thought, but he also wanted to stay like that forever.

Would she let him walk her home?

Someone muttered something about the boudoir of Europe. They were talking about Paris, he supposed.

A sharp poke in his back made him turn with a start. Zéphyrine was jerked awake too, rolling limbs stiffening in shock. A winking, chest-rattling old lady, barely a tooth in her head, was shoving them both from the pew behind. It was time to vote, she urged them, a dark dusting of snuff dancing on the bristles on her upper lip. In the nave, opposite the pulpit, where the club's officers sat at a table with papers and notebooks, the chairman had risen.

'So, *citoyens, citoyennes*, you have heard the arguments. Are you for or against? All those in favour of outlawing prostitution in the Paris Commune – raise your hands now!'

Zéphyrine's arm shot up, and Anatole's followed almost as quickly, and she grinned at him. No prostitutes in Paris? A revolution indeed.

The motion was carried. Zéphyrine seized Anatole's hand in both of hers, and unexpectedly kissed the back of it. 'Let's go to the Gingerbread Fair on Sunday.'

15.

6th April

Three days later the funerals began and thousands turned out on the boulevards to see the procession go by. Jules held his hat in his hands and stood among the watchers, mourning the fact that, slow-moving as it was, he could never capture this extraordinary cortège on glass. He found himself inexplicably moved by the sight: six men of the Commune, heads bare and bowed, walking in front of three enormous hearses, each one piled high with coffins and draped in black velvet. They were slowly followed by a weeping crowd, its pace measured by a muffled drumbeat. The red cross of Geneva flashed on the nurses' armbands as they marched alongside. Red-dyed flowers sprouted in buttonholes – *immortelles* – the flowers that would never die.

A fierce hissing sound broke out on the pavement ahead. A man had refused to bare his head in tribute, but his hat was soon removed for him. Jules was glad not to have made the same mistake.

Sobbing came from the spectators, though the widows walking behind the coffins were too shocked for tears. Such sudden slaughter. The news had blown through Paris like a fire catching hold. Versailles had executed prisoners on the battlefield. Corpses were coming back with rope burns on their wrists and crimson holes in their backs. Their backs! It was against the rules of warfare. Even the Prussians had never shown brutality like this.

At the cemetery of Père Lachaise, the bodies were buried in a common grave. A neighbourhood away, a local battalion dragged the wooden guillotine from the prison house. It was burned at the foot of Voltaire's statue. 'Down with the death penalty!' the people cried.

Just a few days later, the weather alone made defeat impossible to imagine. By Sunday morning, blossom had broken out all over Paris, and petals drifted against barricades. The smell of the fair reached Zéphyrine from streets away, for the air was spiced and sweet, and the song of the barrel organ made it sweeter still, putting a dancing spring in her step.

And despite everything, the Gingerbread Fair didn't look so very different from the year before. Almost as many booths brightened the square, still with row after row of deliciously scented pig-shaped biscuits, and men in aprons spooling white icing onto their brown backs as fast as they could. Here was the same fat lady Zéphyrine had seen with Gran'mère, and over there a conjurer she didn't remember was drumming up trade outside his tent. As she passed him, a small round-eyed boy stood transfixed by a speckled hen's egg that had just appeared from his ear. He didn't look as if he'd seen an egg in months. His face fell as the magician whisked it away again.

Zéphyrine spotted Anatole before he saw her. He was standing by the swingboats as they'd arranged, hands clasped behind his back, eyes searching for her. She smiled. Perhaps she could tiptoe up to him from behind and cup her cool hands round his eyes? That would surprise him. Changing her course, she noticed Anatole turn too. He was speaking to someone: a taller man wearing a top hat and a tight slim-waisted frock coat. A bit of a dandy. His moustache was perfectly horizontal and neatly waxed into two fine points, and when he tipped his hat to her, she noticed chestnut hair. So that was Jules.

'But we . . .' Zéphyrine was about to protest out loud. Then she shook her head at herself and strode on. They had a rendezvous. She wasn't turning back now.

'Ah, there you are! Here she is!' said Anatole. 'I told you we wouldn't have to wait long. This is Jules, Monsieur Crowfield, from America. I told you about him, remember?'

She nodded. Jules bowed low, and she bobbed a kind of curtsey.

'Anatole has not stopped talking about you,' said Jules. 'I'm sorry to intrude, but I could not miss this opportunity to meet you.'

'It was my idea,' Anatole added.

Zéphyrine took the hand Jules offered. She felt him look her up and down – just a quick glance, but enough to take her in.

'How do you do?' she said. Then, because she wanted to be sure: 'So, now you have met me, will you stay?'

They both laughed, and she blushed. She hadn't meant to be rude.

'For a while, I think. I love a fair.'

Anatole's eyebrows lifted a little. 'Are you hungry?' he asked her.

'Always.'

'Then I will buy you a gingerbread pig.'

'The pigs look delicious,' said Jules.

'I'll buy you both a pig,' said Anatole. 'Which do you think are the best ones?'

'We'll have to have a look,' said Jules. 'Find the fattest.'

They wandered around the stalls, inspecting the gingerbread livestock. The pigs were fierce little animals, stuck together in layers with sugar – piped curly tails and chevrons of icing on their flanks. Zéphyrine eventually spotted one with a friendly expression.

'Aren't you going to eat it?' asked Anatole, snapping a leg off his own fat biscuit.

'I want to save it,' she said. 'Gingerbread lasts a good long time.'

Anatole snapped off another leg and held it out to her. She was about to open her mouth so he could put it straight in. When she noticed Jules was watching, she took it in her own hand, and then let it dissolve on her tongue. 'Delicious. Thank you.'

'Have his head too . . . it's a bit sweet for me.'

Another snap, which Zéphyrine felt somewhere behind her collarbone. Steadily, delicately, Jules ate his own pig. Zéphyrine thought he wasn't much used to eating outside. His chaperoning presence made her feel fizzy, as if she had a million tiny bubbles inside, just waiting to explode. She hoped it didn't show.

Anatole was singing along with an organ grinder. "'He doesn't have an umbrella. And that's all right when it is fine . . . *Il n'a pas de parapluie. Ça va bien quand il fait beau . . .*'"

Zéphyrine began to join in.

'But here's a big umbrella,' said Jules.

It was indeed a giant one. On the rickety table beneath, a wooden wheel of fortune spun. It whirred and clanked, wooden toys whizzing round while children held their breath. Of course the stallholder feigned surprise at where it came to rest. Anatole, Zéphyrine and Jules moved on, pausing to hear a patent-medicine seller promise half his takings for the war-wounded. Quite a crowd was forming a little further off, just beyond the acrobats' small stage, drawn by a loud patter that cut through the organ music and the laughter and the food hawkers' cries.

'What is it?' asked Zéphyrine. 'What has he got in there? I can't hear what he's saying.'

Jules hung back. 'Neither can I. I'm not sure.'

'Let's go and see.'

Anatole seemed infected by the excitement, and took both their arms at once.

They let themselves be swept and pulled along by the other gawpers. At the entrance to the tent a Russian took their money, and pushed them through. They reeled back, hands over noses. It was smelly inside: animal, overpowering. Fur and shit, caught in a canvas prison.

'A bear,' said Zéphyrine, but couldn't turn away.

'At least it's not a freak,' murmured Jules. 'I can't bear to see the people they call monsters.'

'Is it going to dance?' said Anatole.

You couldn't tell, because it was slumped in the corner like a discarded coat. Except coats don't need chains. From a flap at the back, a man appeared, bare-chested. He wore soft white breeches, almost like underwear, and a pair of torn boxing gloves strung round his neck. At first he ignored the bear: he was more interested in showing off his muscles, flexing his arms and turning from side to side, winking at the ladies. When someone threw him a staff, he poked the animal, pulling at its rattling tether at the same time. The bear growled through its studded muzzle just as it was meant to, staggered to its feet and swayed. The animal was wearing boxing gloves too, tied tightly round its paws, with the cotton padding coming out in places where the leather had been gnawed.

The Russian rang a bell, and the fight began. For a few seconds, man and bear circled each other, the man making strange grunting noises, which should have been threatening but weren't. The bear roared. A soft groan more than a roar really. A sudden, brief flurry of blows followed and the bear slumped on the ground again. Dust from its coat clouded in the air like smoke; the sun streamed through the pale canvas.

Zéphyrine turned away, tugging at Anatole's sleeve. Jules was already pushing his way out of the tent. Behind them rose the complaints of a crowd that felt cheated.

'No point in hanging around here,' said Anatole, without looking round. 'Let's go on the swingboats. That should be a lot more fun.'

A few steps in front, Jules's shoulders twitched.

'Sorry,' said Anatole, catching up with him. 'That was a mistake.'

'Why do they do that?' Jules said quietly. 'Make an animal what it is not.'

Zéphyrine couldn't answer. She ran ahead, overtaking them both. Luckily there wasn't a queue, and she had enough money to pay, though of course the swingboats seated only two. She waited, rope in hand, while the boat gently rocked.

'Go on,' said Anatole, gesturing towards the steps. 'I'll take the next one that's free.'

But he couldn't persuade Jules to join Zéphyrine. He said he had things to do at home. He'd see Anatole later. He tipped his hat at Zéphyrine, and bowed briefly. She waved, with the gingerbread pig in her lap, lying in state on the pink paisley dress Rose had lent her that morning.

She caught one last glimpse of Jules, weaving his way westward. And then she forgot to look again, for the swing was moving higher and faster. Eyes locked, she and Anatole smiled at each other fiercely, taking it in turn to pull down on their ropes, as hard as they could, one after the other. The place du Trône tilted, back and forth, back and forth, back and forth. Zéphyrine heard the air rush in her ears, and felt her forehead prickle with heat. Only their toes were touching. Sky and ground flashed by. The whole structure creaked. She had to stop herself from shrieking. When their time was up, they would get off and then they would kiss. They both knew that.

16.

She broke all the rules, this one. Anatole had never kissed a girl before who kept her eyes wide open. He shut his own again, and surrendered briefly to pure sensation. He felt enveloped in warmth, inside and out, the dark cloth of his jacket absorbing the sun's rays just as his mouth was warmed by hers. With his eyes closed, he felt drunk with the pleasure of the moment. But when he opened them, and met that steady open gaze again, he felt anchored by it. That was better still. He was finding it hard to stand.

'I feel as if I'm falling . . .'

His lips continued to brush hers as he spoke. Their feet zigzagged.

'It's the swings. It's the same when you get off a boat,' she murmured, breath hot and uneven, but still looking straight at him. 'Your body thinks you're still moving. It's confused.'

'Yes . . . but no,' he said, holding her more tightly, grounding himself against her, still feeling a plunging sensation. 'I don't mean that. That is, I don't think it's just that.'

He began to kiss her again, watching her all the while, seeing the smile in her eye as she kissed him back. He gazed at her pupils, wondering at this circle of darkness. How could it really be a hole, like the shutter of a camera? That's what Jules had told him. So he was looking right into Zéphyrine now, actually right inside her. He noticed that her eyelashes (he remembered their shadow) were longer than they looked, because they were dark at first and then grew lighter, almost invisible, and he saw a tiny scar in her right eyebrow, which made a little gap among the hairs. He began to smooth it over with one finger. Afraid she would be worried that he had noticed an imperfection, because she must have seen his eyes stop and start again in their looking, he stroked her other eyebrow too.

She didn't seem to mind his scrutiny. She was happy to be looked at, and happy to look too, and to keep kissing.

It was another miracle to discover just how many different colours there could be in a single iris. Like shards of glass, more intricate than a Venetian paperweight, and in among the greens and greys there were chips of brown like a nutshell, and one tiny fleck the colour of a conker. He drew back further, his own eyes like a metronome, swinging from one side to the other.

'They're not the same colour!' he said, and looked again. 'How can that be?'

She opened them even wider, and nodded, not smiling.

'The left is darker, isn't it?' he said. 'And greyer, I'm sure. Here, turn this way. Let me see in a different light. I'm not imagining it, am I?'

'No. You're not imagining it.'

He laughed out loud with delight. 'I didn't think it was possible. You're extraordinary. Quite extraordinary.'

This time she shook her head. 'They've always been like this. I think it's a curse. My stepfather thought I was a witch.'

Anatole's smile hung on his face. 'He was joking?' Clearly not.

'He said it so often he even got my mother thinking that way. He thought I knew things I shouldn't know. Thought I had some special power, or something.' She rolled her eyes.

'It's not true. Is it?'

'Of course it's not true. He was just such an oaf. I only said what I saw. And I saw things he didn't want me to see. But he said he wouldn't have a witch bastard in the house.'

She looked at him to see if she had shocked him. She had, but he was quick to reassure her.

'Oh, my darling,' he said, and kissed the top of her head.

But she wasn't going to let it go at that, and jerked her head back to look him straight in the eye as she continued.

'That's why they left me here in Paris. To get me away from the other children. They said it was to help Gran'mère after Papi was killed. But he didn't care about her. He just didn't want me to have anything to do with my little brothers and sisters. He thought I'd turn them against him, with witchcraft. When he saw me writing, he thought I was writing spells.' Zéphyrine gave a bark of laughter, and then her mouth clamped shut.

'Well, I'm glad. I'd never have met you if they hadn't,' said Anatole, his voice cracking slightly, which wasn't like him at all. He was used to being bright and charming and kind, and making everyone happy. He loved to be loved. But he wasn't used to letting so much escape. Could she tell how much he meant it? It wasn't just something to say. She looked very serious. Maybe she could tell.

125

'What are you thinking?' he asked straight out, because he couldn't help himself. He wanted to know everything.

'Oh, just about my mother. With me gone, she could be properly respectable, you see. That must have been what she was thinking, not that she'd tell me. And that maybe my stepfather would shut up with his "*telle mère, telle fille*" . . .'

Like mother, like daughter.

Anatole thought of his own family, safely in Limoges all this time. Thought about his father setting off each evening to play the cello at the theatre, while his mother sat down with a pile of exercise books and worked her way through the marking. Two of his sisters were training to be teachers too, and the third gave singing lessons. Not a grand family, by any means – nothing like the Crowfields of East Liberty – but 'respectable', as Zéphyrine put it, or near enough. And rich enough, by her standards.

'And your grandmother . . . ?'

'What about her?'

'Was she . . . ?' How could he put this?

'A *fille-mère* too?'

Suddenly the hard challenge was back in her eyes. Just for a moment. 'Of course not. She couldn't have been stricter with me. She nearly disowned my mother when I was born. Once she had me in her charge, she did everything she could to stop me from going the same way.'

She rubbed her eyes with the heels of her hands, and then shook her head, and smiled brightly. 'You're thinking about how we first met, aren't you? You're still wondering how bad I really am?'

Anatole tried to protest. But she put her arms round him again, and the hunger he'd never felt during the siege flooded his body.

'I'm not telling you,' she mumbled through kisses. 'Because it's a stupid way to think.'

He didn't want to be thinking anyway. Eventually they separated, and he kissed her eyes again, first with his lips and then with his eyelashes, which he brushed against hers, left to left, right to right.

Zéphyrine smiled, returned his fluttering touch, then broke away. 'An eye for an eye.' She looked at the ground, suddenly sombre.

'What?' Anatole reached for her with both hands, and cupped her face and kissed each eye again until he had her attention.

'An eye for an eye, a tooth for a tooth,' she said. 'That's what the Commune is saying now. There must be reprisals.'

Now he understood. She was talking about the latest decree: the Commune's threat to shoot their own hostages, even the archbishop, if Versailles killed one more prisoner in cold blood.

'Do you think they really will?' he asked.

Her eyebrows came together. 'I don't know . . .' she said slowly. 'But I think perhaps they should.'

And then like a shadow in the sky on a bright windy day – eyes screwed up, you look up, but already the sun is back – the darkness quickly passed. Just at that moment it was easy to pretend. You didn't have to think about hostages, or prisoners, or executions when the leaves were green and bright and fresh, and the air was warm on your skin.

Anatole and Zéphyrine held hands and wandered among the booths, through the spiralling music, the bursts of laughter and applause, and the sweet, sweet smell of gingerbread and blossom and roasting nuts. Other couples were courting too, and kissing in the dappled shade of the trees round the edge of the square. Today the world was indulgent and everything delightful. This year, of all years, the Gingerbread Fair was set to run for an entire week: a week of endless unclouded festivity, like a promise.

17.

Late that night, Anatole came whistling up the stairs, his arrival breaking the building's silence. Luckily there weren't many left here to be disturbed by his good humour. Just a few maids, who wouldn't bother to open doors and shush him now that their masters and mistresses weren't around to complain. The last removal wagon had come and gone: the neighbourhood seemed almost deserted except for the servants.

He grinned in the dark. Tomorrow evening Zéphyrine had agreed to meet him again. Late, after the canteen was shut, and when she'd got her committee work done. But she'd agreed. It was incredible. His whole life had been turned upside down.

He reached the top landing, closed the door behind him and immediately crashed into the side table in the hallway. Feeling his way into the drawing room, suppressing a curse, he scrabbled for a match to light the gas.

A hand closed tightly on his wrist and Anatole bellowed.

'Is this what you're looking for?' Jules pressed his silver Vesta case into Anatole's palm.

'Oh it's you,' said Anatole. 'Obviously.' His heart was thumping harder than he was prepared to admit. 'Thank you.'

He lit the gas in silence, without looking at Jules, who leaned against the wall, watching him.

'Well?' said Anatole eventually, shaking the match out and walking through to the dark drawing room, where he flicked it into the grate. A few embers in white ash.

'Well, what?'

'Was that meant to be a joke of some kind?'

'No.'

'Then what were you doing alone here in pitch-blackness? Why didn't you say anything when I came in?'

No reaction.

'Why aren't you saying anything now?' Anatole persisted.

'Why should I?'

Anatole sighed. He felt himself going hot. Partly with anger, but also with guilt. Some part of him knew that he hadn't behaved well, but he wasn't prepared to admit it, not even to himself.

'Be like that, if you really want to. I'm going to bed.'

'Good idea. It's very late. Goodnight.'

But neither of them moved.

'Look,' said Anatole, in what he hoped were measured tones. 'You'd better just tell me what the matter is.'

'It's nothing,' Jules replied. 'Nothing important.'

Anatole had just had a perfect day. He'd been hoping that Jules would be fast asleep by the time he got back. He wanted to slip into bed, without a word to anyone, and lie in the dark and rehearse every last moment of the past twelve hours in his head. He had calculated that the pleasure of that would keep him going for the next . . . nineteen and a half. How could he have thought he knew what it would be like? Nobody could know, before it happened. To be so close, to be able to say anything, to be caught in someone else's eyes and breath like that. And you could kiss a girl under a tree, without shame, and nobody even notice. There was no confusion.

But the day would be tainted if it ended like this. Everything would be tainted. Anatole made himself try again. At least he made it seem as if he was trying again.

'Well, you're quite clearly angry about something. Something I've done, presumably . . . is it dust again? Did I get dust on your plates or your negatives or something the other day?'

'No. You didn't.'

His voice suggested that Anatole knew perfectly well it was nothing like that. But Jules was the sophisticated one, the one who knew everything, who was so good at explaining the way the world worked. Wasn't it up to him to put this thing into words, whatever exactly it was? Anatole had never quite understood that.

'If you don't tell me, I'll never know,' he said. 'Which means you'll probably go on being angry. Which will be no fun for either of us.'

He spoke lightly, much more lightly than he felt, and waited for a reply. Some invisible line had been crossed, but what? There was a chance that his instincts were wrong. Anatole and Jules had spent so many months together – touching, and not touching, talking, and not talking. Drifting happily, because they could. They never said anything out loud, not anything important, and it seemed stupid, almost dangerous, to change that now. Actually, to Anatole, it felt impossible. The silver matchbox was heating up in his hands. He looked at the engraved letters – JHWC, all intertwined – and leaned forward to slip it back into Jules's pocket. Jules seemed to freeze as he did so. And then he sighed, and put the case on the side table between them both, as if he did not want it to burn him.

'It's not important.'

Anatole was driven to sarcasm. 'Obviously not.'

He picked up the silver matchbox, and tossed it gently in the palm of his hand, producing a soft, rhythmic rattle. Then walked over to the uncurtained window and stared out. The panorama in the west was impossible to ignore any more. Every night another volcanic display started up, flashes and sound effects and coloured smoke so remotely beautiful it was hard to believe that beneath them buildings were burning, women and children cowering, and men dying. Anatole pulled himself away from the sight, back towards Jules. 'Except . . . oh!' He pretended to understand. 'You were waiting for me. Waiting up for me. Oh for God's sake, you're turning into my father!'

Jules, still leaning against the wall, the gas roaring gently in his ears, closed his eyes. He spoke very quietly, almost despairingly. 'Your father . . . ? Of course I'm not. That's ridiculous.'

Anatole remembered other nights Jules had waited up for him, nights when he had been late back from performances, and they had stayed up talking for hours. Birdsong had interrupted them. And he remembered bright mornings modelling in the studio in early autumn, sunlight warming bare skin under the camera's gaze. Of course Jules was nothing like his father.

'I think you're being ridiculous,' he said, hearing how feeble he sounded. Then his anger returned. 'No, I know what's bothering you. You thought I might bring Zéphyrine back?'

'I – I —'

132

'For God's sake. How dare you?' Anatole hurled the Vesta case across the room at him. It bounced off the wall a few feet from his head. Suddenly he had the upper hand. Suddenly he felt in the right again, and not in the wrong. 'How dare you?'

Jules flinched again.

'You think she's a common tart, don't you? That's what all this is about.' Anatole slammed his fist against the mantelpiece. 'You think she's a *fille publique* who just wants to get me into her clutches so she can screw me for all I've got. Which isn't much anyway . . .' His fists clenched and unclenched.

'Calm down,' said Jules. 'It's not about money.'

'I was calm . . . until you started all this. You were the one who wasn't calm when I came home.'

Jules seemed almost relieved at Anatole's anger. Having provoked it, he remained annoyingly in control of his own emotions. Perhaps the relief came from finding something they could argue about, something that could be said.

'Well, let's both be calm now,' he said.

'I don't want to be calm any more. I don't feel calm.' Anatole sat down. Elbows out, his hands kneaded the upholstered arms of the chair, as if he might spring up again at any moment.

'Look, it's not for me to judge . . . Zéphyrine . . .' Jules spoke her name as if trying out a foreign language. 'But —'

'No, you're right,' snapped Anatole. 'It's not for you to judge. So don't. You don't know anything about her.'

'But I do know she's not . . . Well, you told me yourself.'

Anatole wished he'd never said anything about that first encounter. But it was too late now. 'What exactly are you afraid of?'

Jules swallowed and shook his head. Still Anatole refused to admit to himself that he had not been kind to Jules. He persuaded himself that if nothing had been said, nothing could have happened. Guilt made him angrier, and more cruel still.

'You don't think she might simply have fallen in love with me?' Anatole said.

He might just as well have hit him. Jules looked down, tracing the pattern of the carpet's golden scrolling with a bare toe. It looked completely out of place, completely vulnerable. Anatole even noticed a shirt tail hanging from beneath a waistcoat. He realised Jules must have gone to bed and then got up again, unable to sleep. Meanwhile, Jules opened and closed his mouth, and finally spoke to the carpet.

'I'm sure she's happy to let you think you've seduced her. It's how most tarts operate, the clever ones. Haven't you ever noticed? One minute you're both in love, without a care in the world. The next minute you're paying her rent and God knows who else she's entertaining at your expense.'

'I bought her a gingerbread pig. I didn't buy her a château on the Loire.'

'I'm just saying —'

'What?' snapped Anatole.

'That you've got to be careful. I'm not sure that you know what you're doing. When you get mixed up in . . .'

'I understand. You think she's going to "infect" me. That because she's poor she must be diseased?'

'I didn't say that,' backtracked Jules.

Anatole glared at him, eyes narrowed, thinking.

'You're talking about her as if she wasn't a proper human being, and you don't even realise it,' he said.

Jules shrugged. Something happened inside Anatole. It was like the moment an E string unexpectedly snaps and spirals away from a bow. But it's not so unexpected. It had already been coming. There'd been a false note, a subtle variation in pitch that demanded attention, which was easier to ignore than fix. Until the string actually broke. Suddenly Anatole was fed up with all the toing and froing with Jules, so thrilling, uncertain and surprising in the early days of their friendship. Perhaps something to do with the fact that his friend was a little older, wiser, more worldly – certainly a great deal richer. But now he wanted something different. A different kind of excitement altogether. Zéphyrine offered him admission into a world he knew nothing about.

'Oh, I see. It's another kind of infection you're worried about. You think her politics are contagious?'

Jules didn't answer at first. The silence between them felt explosive. Then he muttered, 'Who knows? But if you're going to turn yourself into a hero of the people, you'd better get back into uniform as soon as you can.'

Anatole was still breathing heavily. 'I damn well will.'

'It won't be long before you're arrested if you don't,' said Jules.

'Feel free to join me. The battalions round here need all the help they can get, Zéphyrine says.'

Jules didn't rise to that. He declined with a brief dip of his head, as if refusing a second cup of coffee.

'Something tells me I'll be more valuable as a photographer than a fusilier.'

It was true that his reputation was spreading. Officers sidled up when he set up his tripod these days, with mumbled queries about the cost of an illustrated visiting card. Up in the studio, Jules had a whole collection of barricade pictures. He'd taken them all over Paris. He never charged.

'Probably,' said Anatole.

They both shifted uneasily, feeling the argument was at an end, if not resolved, but unsure how to disperse the remaining heat. Then they were both drawn back to the window by the sound of distant crackling, no louder than paper being crumpled in a fist. Side by side, Anatole and Jules stood and watched the flashing sky.

'I'd never seen you as a revolutionary before,' said Jules quietly.

'I'd never seen you as an artist.'

'I'm not sure if I am one.'

'I think you are,' said Anatole. He smiled. Jules's face was untightening at last, his eyes softening. That was more like it. Jules didn't drop his guard for many people, but Anatole was one of them, and that fact made him happy. He could see Jules was more pleased than he wanted to admit. 'A real artist. And anyway, you are still serving the cause, however you might feel about it. There will be much more freedom for artists in the Commune, Zéphyrine says. There's talk of a new federation. All sorts of ideas, apparently.'

'I look forward to hearing about it,' said Jules.

Anatole decided to make the request he'd been mulling over on the way home. Jules could always say no. 'I was wondering . . . I was thinking . . . this isn't for the cause, though . . . it's just for me.'

'What were you wondering?'

'I thought perhaps . . . not that I've told her—'

Maybe he shouldn't ask. Maybe it was too much to ask.

'A photograph of Zéphyrine?'

'Yes . . . that's right. How did you know?'

'Just an idea.' Jules hid his face as he bent to pick up the matchcase. 'Of course. She'll be interesting to photograph. A challenge . . . Oh don't take that the wrong way. I just mean to capture all that life, and energy, and keep it still. As it happens, I've arranged for Marie to come here for a portrait session the day after tomorrow – I told you she called for you a few nights ago, didn't I?'

Anatole thought he probably had.

'She's very interesting. More complicated than I realised. Anyway, why doesn't Zéphyrine come here at the same time? They would make an interesting contrast, wouldn't they? Visually, I mean?'

Anatole hesitated. Having urged Jules to look for new models to photograph, he could hardly object, but he felt very uneasy at the prospect of Zéphyrine and Marie posing side by side. He couldn't think how either would react.

'I don't know. They've only met once. I think individual portraits would be better.'

'Yes, you're probably right.'

Jules was suddenly so reasonable.

'But you still want Zéphyrine to come at the same time?' asked Anatole.

'It would certainly make things easier for me. I'll have everything set up, you see.'

'Yes. Thank you, Jules. You're very generous. I'll ask her tomorrow.'

'Let me know, so I can prepare the plates.'

'Yes, I will, but I won't tell her why I'm bringing her here. I want it to be a surprise..'

'Really? If you think that would be best.'

Anatole decided it would. He felt very grateful to Jules, and it made him want to hug his friend, but he stopped himself.

'I wasn't going to ask,' he admitted. 'You seemed so angry.'

'Sorry.'

'It's wonderful,' said Anatole happily. He didn't think to apologise himself. 'Thank you. Thank you so much. She'll be amazed. I hope I can persuade her to come. I wonder if she'll have time. She's so busy, you see. So much to do, isn't there? I'll ask her tomorrow. What should I tell her? Oh, I'll think of something. Thank you, Jules.'

The dreamy grin Anatole had worn in the dark on the landing was back.

'No need to rush things,' said Jules gently. 'We could do it next week instead.'

'But I want to rush things,' said Anatole. 'I want to.'

'Evidently.' A half-smile from Jules.

'Oh, I know it seems odd, to have fallen like this, so suddenly, so hard. I can't explain it myself. Can you ever really explain something like this?'

'No,' agreed Jules quietly. 'Probably not.' He pulled a chair to the fireplace, and picked up the poker. He glanced down at his bare feet, as if surprised to see them himself, then wriggled his toes and began to prod the embers.

Anatole came over to join him. 'You didn't really get a chance to talk to her at the fair, that's the problem. But please trust me. She has a friend, too, Rose, and she wants me, us, to meet. She's the one who helped her after her grandmother died – did I tell you her grandmother died?'

Jules nodded.

'And I was also thinking . . .'

'You can be such an innocent, can't you?' Jules said, shaking his head.

'What?'

'Nothing. Never mind.'

Anatole stood up again, and stretched. His head was still buzzing. 'I'm worn out, but I still don't think I'll sleep yet. Would you mind if I practised for a while? Would it disturb you? I'll shut the door of course.'

'It wouldn't disturb me. You know I like to hear you play.'

'Oh. Good. But put some slippers on if you're going to stay in here. And listen . . . you mustn't fret about me and Zéphyrine.'

Anatole wanted to smooth away every last bit of tension between them. He had persuaded himself that he could, that everybody could be happy.

Jules was accommodating. 'I'll try not to,' he said. Then, just as Anatole was leaving, he added: 'It's just that . . . falling too deeply, too quickly . . . it can be like an addiction. And once you're obsessed, well, you're trapped, aren't you?'

'Stop, Jules, there's nothing to worry about. Nothing at all.'

18.

10th April

For the first time in ages, Zéphyrine did not feel the emptiness of her room. She actually forgot to fear for the future. The gingerbread pig was propped up on the beam of the attic, just missing a few bristles of icing, knocked off in her pocket on the journey home. The mice hadn't found it yet, and Zéphyrine certainly wasn't tempted to nibble. For once she felt light-headed with something that wasn't hunger.

Outside, she could hear brooms sweeping steps, and the soft, repetitive thud of dust being thumped out of a rug. Madame Mouton, probably. With all pressure from the landlord now removed thanks to the latest decrees of the Commune, and the faint tension that had always persisted between Gran'mère and the concierge gone too, Madame Mouton couldn't be friendlier. As Zéphyrine left for work, the concierge broke off her cheerful singing to tell her the latest. Two of the Montmartre battalions had made a surprise attack on the Versailles forces in the night, and even beaten them back a little way. A cork in a bottle, said Madame Mouton, that's what this would be.

Just you wait. They wouldn't be hemmed in like this much longer. You couldn't mess with Paris and expect to get away with it. The National Guard would show Versailles what real fighting was.

Zéphyrine went off singing too. So much to sing about today, she thought cheerfully. She was on an early shift and had told Anatole she would meet him after work. Not right away, she had warned him, though she'd be as quick as she could. There was something else she had to do first. His face had clouded when she told him.

It wasn't easy to find real flowers to take to the grave. Every branch of blossom she spotted was just out of reach, so all she managed was a sprig of pink, brought down by shaking. On the way to the cemetery, Zéphyrine began to panic, as if Gran'mère could somehow still tell her off for being late. In her head, Zéphyrine explained her long absence – explained, not excused, she tried to remind herself; Gran'mère just seemed to shake her head. 'It's not been easy. I was going to come before. I wanted to. It's just, just, just . . .'

Just that everything seemed to have gone out of her head these past few days. Even with a queue of children waiting with bowls in hand, her thoughts kept drifting. She'd find herself standing like a statue, her ladle poised but not pouring, until someone jogged her elbow, and she splashed the soup. At the Vigilance Committee her sewing slowed to a halt. Her needle rested motionless between her fingers, for seconds on end, only brought back to life when Rose, or one of the other girls, clapped their hands in front of her face, and made her blink and splutter out apologies. At the slightest excuse, Anatole seemed to sneak into her thoughts. Everything made her think about him. What would he say to this? She must tell him about that.

She reached the cemetery gates, and stopped. Coming here for the first time since the funeral was bound to be hard. Then it would get easier. Soon she'd be visiting every week, looking after things as she was supposed to. As Gran'mère would have expected. As she used to look after Papi's grave, until she became too ill herself. So that meant the sooner Zéphyrine got it over with, the easier it would be the next time. She took a deep breath. Then she heard her name, and her heart danced. She turned to see Anatole jumping down from a cab, one arm behind his back. But he couldn't reach up to pay the driver without revealing what he was trying to hide. The fiacre drove off with a crack of the whip, and Anatole walked towards her holding out a huge bouquet of hothouse flowers. She ran up to take them.

'These aren't for you – they're for your grandmother!' He pretended to whisk them out of her way for just a second, so that she had to grab his hands in her own to hold them still, to sink her face into their intensity. When she looked up, grinning, he reached a finger out to wipe a speck of lily pollen from her nose. They gazed at each other, suddenly becalmed, and the gatekeeper stared at them suspiciously, and sucked on his pipe. A group of children had been playing prisoner's base, until their game was interrupted by the arrival of Anatole's cab. Now they formed a semi-circle and watched intently to see what the couple would do next. One of the boys whistled. Zéphyrine whisked round to scowl at him, put an arm through Anatole's, and then flounced into the cemetery and past the mortuary house.

'Where did you get them?' she asked as soon as they were out of earshot. She sniffed the flowers again and sighed, almost queasy with the heavy smell of them, so sweet and sickly. Her grandmother had taught her to make flowers just like these. She knew exactly how each stamen fitted together, how to curl every silken petal and sepal. 'They're so . . . grand.'

'I stole them. Well, not quite. One of the singers at the theatre has an admirer with more money than sense, luckily for us. He's besotted and simply won't believe that she left Paris weeks ago.' He shook his head in despair at the idiocy of some people. 'So every day he brings her more flowers, and every day the doorkeeper winks and says she isn't there but takes them anyway and sells them as soon as he can. Today I managed to intercept the flowers before he got his hands on them.'

'Thank you.'

Anatole smiled, then frowned. 'But are they too grand? And would you prefer to visit your grandmother on your own? I can wait for you. I'm quite happy to wait here for you.'

'No, of course you mustn't,' said Zéphyrine quickly, walking faster and pulling him with her. 'I'm glad you're here now. It means I can introduce you to Gran'mère. In a way. Sort of.' Then she admitted how little she had wanted to come by herself, and that she had begged Rose to keep her company but Rose was late for a meeting.

Anatole shivered sympathetically. They turned left at the grand circle and headed down the hill. Tall family sepulchres rose like sentry boxes on either side. Their shadows cut across the path, alternating with blinding shafts of sunlight which shot out between monument after monument.

Zéphyrine shaded her eyes, and hopped over a shadow. 'It feels as if you're walking over a grave,' she said. 'I really don't like it here.'

'All these doorways,' agreed Anatole, holding her arm a little more tightly.

'Yes. They look as if they must lead somewhere.'

A Gothic arch followed a vast flat tomb and then another upright one, with a pointed roof. They passed metal doors and wooden ones, and even some stained-glass windows. Behind the formal avenues, graves were heaped haphazardly, tightly packed and tumbling down the hillside, an overcrowded stone city. 'I'm not so silly as to think anything's about to come out of one,' she said firmly. 'But they do make me feel . . .'

Her voice trailed away. Zéphyrine didn't want to admit it. They made her feel angry, and jealous. Even in death, it was different for some people. Some families had a home waiting for them, and some didn't. Famille Grandjean. Famille Chardon. Famille Maigne. How did it change your life to know that your name had been carved on stone before you were born and would be there long after you were dead?

'Some of these look neglected.'

'Their families have run away from Paris,' said Zéphyrine, glancing at him, then back at the scrambling ivy, shiny and pale from the recent warm weeks. 'It doesn't take long for the creepers to take over.'

It was a reasonable walk right down to the lower section of the cemetery, where the poor were buried. The bouquet felt heavier and heavier, and more and more out of place. They left the solid stone tombs and paved walkways behind them, and

144

moved onto a wide dirt track, and Anatole fell silent. Zéphyrine suddenly realised why. He thought her grandmother was buried in the paupers' pit. He thought that was where those grand flowers were heading.

'Gran'mère is over there, look!'

They stopped at a gap in the middle of a row of plain wooden crosses, and stood looking down at a pile of earth. It was bare and raw, like a scar on the grass, and you could see roots and bits of rock, she supposed.

'It will sink down soon, they say. In about six months.'

'In six months?' he echoed.

'And then we can put the cross back. Do you know, after all my worries, it turned out that she had already bought the plot for Papi? Maybe she knew she'd be following him soon. I wish she'd told me.'

Zéphyrine looked at the grave and thought of her grandfather. She had thought of him the day she first met Anatole, the moment she had looked up at the glass roofs of Les Halles, and realised he had brought her to the very place where Papi had lost his life. She pictured again those tiny ladders that led to upper rooftops so high it made your neck ache and your head spin just to look at them. She imagined a man up there, a man like a bird, working on the roof. Zinc flashings, slippery in a sudden shower of rain. And once you started to fall, there was little to catch hold of. If you had been inside, looking up, at just that moment, could you have seen him? Had anyone caught a glimpse of her grandfather's startled face – shock turning to horror, hands scrabbling on smoothness, eyes wild – sliding through rain-smeared glass? You could think you had dreamed a sight like that. Yet if Papi had not slipped, she would not be here with Anatole now. So that was the moment that had changed Zéphyrine's life forever too.

She knelt down, and gently laid the flowers on the earth. They would wither without water of course, but it couldn't be helped now. She tried to concentrate on what lay beneath, under the petals and the earth and the wooden coffin lid. She ought to say a prayer, she supposed. '*In nomine Patris, et Filii, et Spiritus Sancti,*' she mumbled at last, feeling the dampness of the ground seeping into the knees of her stockings. It was so quiet she could hear Anatole breathing, and then swallowing awkwardly, almost in a gulp. He moved his feet slightly. She should have come alone. It was too difficult to think about her grandmother in the right way with him there beside her. Old bones and shrivelled flesh so close to his warm skin and pumping heart, all that rushing blood that made her blood run faster too.

19.

Marie decided to take Jules's advice. She would go the following Monday, waste no more time. But there were things you had to do before paying a visit to one of the most powerful men in the Commune. Getting ready for somebody as important as the head of the police would take a while.

After several hours in front of the mirror, Marie looked around at the chaos in her rented room. Stockings and petticoats overflowed from pulled-out drawers, and discarded gowns covered the bed. The half-hoops of her second-best crinolette writhed like a defeated sea monster on the floor, and seemed about to gobble up a pile of rejected shoes she had hurled into the corner. Marie found it hard to contain her clothes since moving to this place, so much darker and pokier than the last. But with nobody paying her visits these days – nobody who would care – the mess didn't bother her much. As long as she looked the part when she left the building.

She didn't miss the banker's visits: the constant requirement to make oneself available at all times, no matter how late, or how tired she was from a performance. Always having to put on another act. There had been a price for that apartment.

But as Zéphyrine had said the first time they met, and she had pretended to ignore, a girl's got to live. Though the eviction notice had come as a shock, there were certainly advantages to living within your means, and paying your own rent. Of course Marie missed the little luxuries, but she could eke out what was left if she had to. She planned to take her time before rushing under the wing of a second 'protector'.

Marie examined herself in the mirror again. She was determined to make exactly the right impression today. The problem was that she couldn't work out what that might be. Was it better to dress up to the nines and act the coquette? Or should she opt for her oldest, plainest, most workmanlike cotton, and play the serious supporter of the revolution? Eventually she opted for something in between. A final glance in the glass reminded her to remove the delicate gold crucifix round her neck. Then, just as she picked up her shawl, yet another thought struck her, and she dashed to her sewing basket for the embroidery scissors. It was a shame to ruin a good bonnet, but she'd had no desire to wear this one since the Commune took over. A single red rose pinned to her bosom – an immortal red rose – that should prove her loyalty to Monsieur Rigault most decisively . . . shouldn't it?

After a half-hour walk, she arrived in sight of the spiked railings that sealed the dark cul-de-sac leading to the Prefecture of Police. Even to reach that huge fence she had to get through a mass of loitering soldiers. Marie's courage wavered. Did they have nothing better to do? They seemed such a ragged bunch, these Guardsmen, leaning against walls, idly hurling stones down into the river. Marie sniffed, expecting to smell brandy fumes, and wondered what Emile would have had to say about their down-at-heel boots and torn jackets. All the time he'd been a prisoner of war, she'd been imagining him in his usual gleaming uniform, leather and brass all polished to a sheen. But how could that be true, she suddenly wondered, in a prison camp? What did captives wear?

A metallic crash behind her made her clutch her throat.

A clumsy young Guardsman had dropped his rifle. He grinned at her as he bent to pick it up, and then began to inspect it for damage. 'Didn't mean to scare you, mam'selle.'

Marie smiled feebly, and turned away from him to press her face between the bars. How on earth were you supposed to get through?

'Just a minute.' He was calling her back. 'Your pass. I'm meant to ask for your pass. Then I can let you in here.'

'I don't have one,' said Marie, pulse racing. 'That's what I've come for. I need to see Monsieur Rigault.'

He looked her up and down. Not quite unpleasantly. She froze.

'I'm sure he'd be very pleased to see you,' he said at last. 'It's this way.'

He opened a small gate next to a large iron one, and Marie found herself in a narrow courtyard filled with yet more soldiers. All staring at her.

'Where do I go now?' she whispered to the Guardsman who had let her in. He seemed about to abandon her, his duty done. He gestured towards a sentinel guarding a large door on the far side of the courtyard with wall lanterns on either side. Marie kept walking. Some signal must have been exchanged between them. The door swung open and her footsteps echoed down an immensely long corridor, which she hoped was leading her to the chief of police's office, though she couldn't be sure. Yet another guard stood at the far end of this passage. Each one seemed better dressed than the last, she noted.

'I don't have a pass, not yet,' she quickly explained. 'I need to see the prefect. Himself.' Best to be insistent. You can act, she reminded herself. 'I have an appointment,' she lied.

'Wait here.'

The waiting must be part of the trial, Marie decided. Fifteen minutes went by, and nobody returned. There was nowhere to sit. Her mouth felt coated in cobwebs when she tried to swallow. She thought of Emile and she thought of Anatole. She clenched her jaw and stood her ground. She must think of it as an audition, she decided. A part she had to win, no matter what.

Distant doors continued to open and shut in the bowels in the building. This time the banging noises sounded closer. The door right in front of her finally opened again, and she was confronted by another new guard.

'This way.'

Seven more doors opened and shut behind her, watched by seven more guards, before Marie finally reached the sanctuary of Citizen Raoul Rigault. In a large, nearly empty room, the prefect of police sat writing at the only table. A pair of yellow gloves lay neatly folded on the green leather surface. His jacket, fringed with scarlet and gold, was nothing less than spectacular.

Two gendarmes stood behind his chair, clearly waiting for orders. Another man – young, clean-shaven – was leaning against the mantelpiece at the far side of the room. Rigault did not look up.

Marie stared at his dark bushy beard and wondered if this was what it had been like to stand before Robespierre during the Reign of Terror. It was impossible to forget the first revolution, how violently virtue had turned to bloodshed. Rigault was the man who boasted of having invented a guillotine that could cut three hundred heads off in an hour. Secret agents were his speciality. He was obsessive about hunting down the spies from Versailles, who seemed able to carry back to Thiers, within hours, every decision the Commune made. This was Rigault's revenge perhaps, for the secret police who'd plagued his revolutionary activities for several years. He even bragged of having issued a warrant for God's arrest.

Marie braced her knees to stop them trembling, breathed deeply, and tried to imagine she was overcoming stage fright. She knew how to do that. She took a tentative step forward, feeling the gaze of the room hot on her face. Except for Rigault's. His pen, monotonously scratching, continued to fill the silence. Marie held up her head and walked right up to the table, so that her shadow fell over his papers. She coughed.

The scratching continued.

'Monsieur Rigault?' she said at last in little more than a whisper. Then she added, '*Citoyen?*'

At last he raised his head. He stared at Marie intently and in silence through a small oval pince-nez, attached to his lapel by a fine chain. The eyes behind the glass were younger than she'd expected, not much older than Emile's perhaps. Rigault looked her up and down, eyes pausing for a moment at the red rose. Then he smiled, his fleshy lips glistening. '*Citoyenne*. Is there some way in which I can be of assistance?'

Was he being sarcastic?

'Yes, please, I need to get a pass. I need to leave Paris, for a short while.'

He let her words settle before responding to them.

'How strange, to wish to desert the Commune at our hour of need!'

'Yes, indeed, and of course I am very anxious not to miss any rehearsals. But you see —'

'Rehearsals?' he interrupted. 'Now let me guess . . .' He leaned back in his hard chair, twiddling his pen in one hand as though it would help him think. His gaze ran up and down her, and made her feel he could assess her measurements through her clothing with the precision of a dressmaker.

She stood up straighter. He wouldn't intimidate her. She was used to being stared at. It was her profession. She'd been trained to be stared at, hadn't she?

'You are an actress . . . a dancer perhaps . . . ? No, of course, I have it – with that lovely melodious voice, you must surely be a singer. Am I right?'

Marie held his gaze. There was no point in denying it. Perhaps she could turn it to her advantage. She tilted her head, and simpered a little. 'Yes you are! How clever of you! And we are preparing even now for some fundraising concerts – at the theatre and also at the Tuileries Palace.'

'Very important,' he said. 'Music can lift the public's spirits so effectively at a time like this. We rely on good spirits.'

'Oh yes, indeed . . .' she agreed warmly. She had got him on her side. It had almost been too easy. 'Music is so very valuable in that respect.'

'And so, my dearest diva . . .'

'Yes?' She leaned forward too eagerly, then quickly mumbled that she really wasn't a diva; she wasn't important at all. She had only just left the chorus, she explained – since the siege – and naturally there were plenty of other eager singers who'd be more than happy to take her place if need be.

'So you must be very desperate to leave if you are prepared to sacrifice your opportunity for stardom?'

'We are a cooperative company now. Nobody is indispensable.' A heroic stance would be good here. Liberty leading the people. She gazed into the middle distance.

'Still, I cannot let you go.'

Marie's shoulders collapsed. He was deliberately twisting her words. 'But please, I just need a few days.'

He teased her with more silence. A trap?

'Why?'

'I need to . . . I need to . . . My brother, you see, he is a prisoner.'

He sat up straight now, all attention. 'One of ours? What's his name?'

'No, no . . . He is a prisoner of the Prussians. He has been for months.'

Rigault frowned. 'Sedan?'

'No, Metz.'

'I see.' A hundred and forty thousand had surrendered at Metz in October. An entire army. 'So where is he now?'

'I think . . . I think . . .' Marie was indeed thinking, as fast as she could. She was tempted to lie, to tell Rigault that Emile was already back in France. It might strengthen her case. But she had no proof. And she was certain this man, who seemed to know and see everything, would find out somehow that she had lied. 'I'm not entirely sure. He was in a hospital in Bavaria after Metz. And then in a camp at a place called Ingolstadt.'

He didn't seem to recognise the name. Perhaps she had mispronounced it.

'But the prisoners are being released, even now,' he pointed out. 'Thousands are returning. The Versailles army is strengthening every day, damn it. So, your brother will be back soon. And I'm sure he will try to rescue you.'

They stared at each other. At first Marie thought they had reached a stalemate. Then, through his round glasses, his eyes narrowed. She decided it was time to ratchet up her performance.

'Precisely. And, you see, I cannot bear . . . I cannot bear . . .' Marie began to sob. He sighed noisily and gestured for one of the subordinates to supply a handkerchief, which Marie of course rejected, fumbling instead for her own. She was about to reach the turning point of this scene, but worried she was in danger of losing his attention. 'You see, I cannot bear for him to fight against us, as an officer of the Versailles army. I believe I can persuade him to desert. And join the National Guard.'

At this Rigault stood up so suddenly that the man behind him had to catch his chair to stop it crashing to the floor. Rigault leaned across the table. Short and stocky, he was slightly less imposing on his feet than he had appeared when seated. Still, Marie had to force herself not to back away.

'I'm sure you can be very persuasive, my dear *citoyenne*,' he said. Leaning on one hand, he reached across with the other, and fingered the red rose pinned to her bodice. 'Gaston!'

The young man at the mantelpiece straightened.

'Shall we let her leave?'

The other man opened his mouth, and shut it again without replying. Marie felt like a funambulist, a tightrope walker, balanced between the Commune and Versailles. One slip . . .

'Or should we first check the informants' register we are working our way through? All the sneaking toadies of the Second Empire. And all those who applied to be. Oh you'd be amazed how many there were.' Rigault continued to look at her steadily. 'Is it possible that this young lady is on our list of *mouchards*? Does she have "form"? A history of telling tales?'

He let the questions hang. Everyone except for Marie seemed to understand that they were rhetorical. She didn't realise she was shaking her head.

'No? Really? I suppose I should take your word for it?'

She nodded, but Rigault wasn't interested in her word. He had already turned to the fellow at his left shoulder. 'As a matter of fact, I have a feeling she could be useful to us. The passport papers, please.'

Marie felt a rush of gratitude. She almost called him 'sir' again. Instead, she closed her eyes and held on to the table.

'A few questions, naturally,' Rigault continued, taking up his pen again. 'First things first.'

With a theatrical swipe, he crossed out the word 'Empire' at the top of the form, and wrote 'République' in its place. Then he smiled his wet smile at her again. 'Still the same forms, I'm afraid. Clearly the Government of National Defence didn't think it worth its while to print fresh ones. It was only ever going to be a matter of time for those traitors. Which sadly leaves us with so many more things to organise. So much work still to do.'

Marie didn't dare reply. She couldn't risk a word that might jeopardise this pass.

'Let me see now. Eyes.' Rigault took the opportunity to stand up and inspect her eyes so closely that she could feel his breath on her face. She held her own breath, and tried to keep her nostrils from flaring too obviously with disgust.

'A lovely shade of blue,' he said. She closed her eyes. 'However, I think I'll just write "blue".'

Then he turned to the man by the fireplace. 'How would you describe this *citoyenne*'s hair, Gaston?'

'Oh, golden. Quite definitely golden.'

'Golden it is.' He scribbled some more, and moved his finger down the list. What an excruciatingly slow business this was. 'Nose? Medium, I think. Beard? None, I'm happy to say.' He laughed at his own weak joke. The others laughed politely too, except for the one called Gaston. 'Chin? Quite round, I'd say. Face? Oval, certainly. Perfectly oval. But, oh dear, what's this? Complexion?'

Rigault's gaze became even more lingering.

'Your complexion is very pale. This is a matter of some concern. Are you feeling quite all right? I think I should have someone get you a glass of water.'

Only water? Marie had always been convinced that radical types like Rigault survived entirely on absinthe and brandy. These men seemed sober as camels. Still, you could slip all sorts of things into a drink of water. She wouldn't touch a drop, she decided, but she just managed to choke out a reply.

'No, no thank you. I'm quite well, thank you very much, *citoyen.*'

There was another silence, while Rigault read through what he had written, still smiling, and again insisted on checking each distinguishing feature on the list against its original, as if it might have changed in the long minutes that had passed.

'Do forgive me if this is taking up too much of your time. It's not every day we strike quite this lucky, I'm sorry to say . . . Ah, look, citizens . . . how delightful . . . see how rosy her complexion has become now? Charming.' Her blush deepened. 'Now . . . all you need to do is sign here.'

He pointed, and held out a pen still warm from his fingers. Stubby, grubby fingers, thought Marie. He used one to show where she had to sign, keeping it pressed down so that she was forced to brush against it as she wrote.

She pushed the paper back towards him, and he picked it up with a flourish.

At last she dared to smile. Any minute now her passport would be safely in her purse and she'd be gone, escaping through all those doors and corridors, past all those guards, and back out to the relative freedom of the quai des Orfèvres. She couldn't wait to tell Jules and Anatole what she'd managed entirely on her own. How impressed they would both be. And in another few days she'd be at Versailles, and if, as she feared, her brother was still waiting to be released by the Prussians, at least somebody there would have news of him.

Rigault smiled back. For just a moment, Marie could almost have kissed him. Then he folded the paper neatly and tucked it into his own breast pocket.

'I'll keep this safe until we get word of your brother's return to Versailles. Don't worry. We'll know where to find you, and then you can get to work on him. I hope I'll be seeing you again very soon.'

20.

11th April

Anatole kept his secret for two long days, and almost all the way up the stairs too. Zéphyrine's arms flailed in front of her, as, sightless, she tried to make sense of her new surroundings.

'Where are you taking me?' She tried to push off her blindfold, but Anatole simply batted her hands away from her eyes.

'I told you. It's a surprise.' A hand at her waist continued to steer her upwards. She swung her hip against its pressure. They were both out of breath.

'But how long will it take?' She didn't like this kind of darkness. She was tiring of the joke.

'Nearly there now.'

Zéphyrine stopped dead to listen. The walls gave nothing away.

'I'll smell it out.' She sniffed, and made an even more determined effort to get her blindfold off, but Anatole caught hold of her hands, and covered them with kisses, and then couldn't stop himself from kissing her mouth too while it was so open and exposed.

She stopped resisting, and they came to a halt on the landing. Anatole made her forget everything except for the here and now. It was only later that she wondered what she was doing. When they were together, he was so very hard to resist. Up to a point. Just as they reached that point, a voice echoed down the staircase.

'Hurry up! We're going to lose the light if you take much longer —'

'Coming!' Anatole quickly shouted back, but it was too late. Zéphyrine had recognised Jules's voice.

'Oh, I'm going to see your apartment at last!' she said triumphantly, imagining a meal, and wrenching the silk cravat from her mismatched eyes. Her hair fell down in the process. 'No, stop, Anatole. Wait.'

'What is it? We need to hurry.'

'I can't walk in looking like this.'

'You look beautiful.' He pulled her up a few more steps, and then into him again. He ran his hands through her loose hair while they kissed again.

'Ow!' Zéphyrine detached his trapped fingers from her tangles, and tried to repin it. 'Stop. What's Mister Crowfield going to think?'

Of course he had heard. He was already waiting for them at the open door, on the next landing up.

'I'm going to think that if we don't get a move on, we'll have to rearrange it for another day. Marie is already here.'

'Rearrange it?' said Zéphyrine. Then what would happen to the food?

'Very good to see you again.' Jules bowed politely and kissed Zéphyrine's hand. 'Do come in.'

Moth wings fluttered in her chest as she walked in. How many Montmartre families could you fit in a place this size? How many shacks from Le Maquis, the shanty town on the other side of the hill? She didn't belong here. Jules knew that. She could tell, despite his perfect manners. Wasn't it obvious to Anatole too? Apparently not.

'And this is Minou,' said Anatole, swooping up the cat as she raced towards him, miaowing, and presenting her upside down, like a baby, to Zéphyrine.

She backed away. 'A cat!' she said. She hadn't seen a cat for months. 'Where on earth did you get it? Why didn't you eat it?'

Jules looked at Anatole. Minou squirmed in his arms and jumped to the floor.

'She . . . she was very frightened when I found her. Some boys were . . . never mind.'

'Hungry?' said Zéphyrine.

'Yes,' said Anatole, ashamed.

Jules intervened. 'Now, let's go upstairs. I'm sure I can find a brush for your hair up in the studio. If you don't mind . . . Follow me.' His voice was matter-of-fact, not unkind. Perhaps she had imagined his disapproval at the Gingerbread Fair. Anatole had told her that Americans didn't stand on ceremony, nor were they very concerned how many centuries back you could trace your name.

'It's surprising what the last occupant didn't pack,' continued Jules.

'He left Paris in a hurry, like all the other cowards,' said Anatole.

'And I have a feeling that he'd been living beyond his means for some time. Our gain, however. And mine in particular, as you'll see in just a moment.'

So many doorways invited exploration. She wanted to stroke the wallpaper, to test with her fingertips if it was really silk. She wanted to try out the rose-damask upholstered chairs one after another, and sit at the glowing walnut dining table she'd glimpsed through a half-open door. But Jules led the way straight down the corridor to a spiral staircase that led up to another floor. Behind his back, Zéphyrine twisted round to look at Anatole, with a cross, questioning face. What was this all about?

'You'll see,' he mouthed.

'Ladies first,' said Jules at the top, waving Zéphyrine towards the studio.

She stopped dead at the doorway. Marie was already standing beside the 'antique' column, leaning forward, an elbow on the column top, one finger to her chin. The other arm was horizontal, hand drooping gracefully, as if barely aware of the single silk rose it held. A small bribe had secured the loan of a costume from the *Sleeping Beauty* ballet, and the help of the wardrobe mistress in smuggling it out of the theatre. The dress was gauzy pale pink, the veil even more transparent and it floated from a garlanded headdress.

Zéphyrine was entranced. 'Oh. How lovely,' she sighed.

Marie stepped down, extending both hands. 'You're here. That's good.' And then, seeing Zéphyrine's confusion, she said, 'We met outside the theatre. Do you remember? Mademoiselle Le Gall – Marie – I sing in the same company as Anatole.'

'Yes, yes, I do remember, of course,' said Zéphyrine. 'You look different today.'

'So do you,' said Marie.

Zéphyrine pinched her upper arm. 'A little fatter each day.' She joined in with their polite laughter.

'Can I look?' she asked, walking right up to Marie to inspect the details: the embroidery on the bodice, the shoes with their satin rosettes. The artificial flowers on her headdress were exquisitely made, the curve and settle of their petals utterly convincing. Zéphyrine was impressed.

Jules began to fiddle with his tripod. Zéphyrine edged round until she was facing the huge brass lens of his camera.

'Anatole told me you took photographs, but I didn't know what it would be like . . . This is enormous! Just like a little cannon, isn't it?'

'Its shots are less dangerous, I hope,' said Jules.

'This is the studio camera, for portraits. Much bigger than the one you take out on your travels, isn't it, Jules?' Anatole was eager to explain everything to Zéphyrine.

'That's right. The other one is over there.' Jules pointed it out.

Anatole tried to demonstrate the tripod. 'And the stand is adjustable, here, you see.'

'Please don't move it,' said Jules. 'I'd just got it perfect – no, you stay there too, Marie. Thank you.'

Anatole retreated and Zéphyrine started to look for somewhere to sit, somewhere out of the way, a corner where she wouldn't disturb proceedings. But then she noticed the view from the window, and couldn't help remarking on that, and the rooftops and the distant smoke. Then she darted over to the table where there was a collection of flat rings laid out, each with a tab attached to it.

'Can I see?' she asked, picking one up and peering through it, mystified, and then putting it down and picking up another. 'Why do you need so many? What are they for?'

Jules took it out of her hand, and explained, without explaining anything. 'Waterhouse stops.'

Zéphyrine nodded, baffled, and turned back to Marie, who had rearranged herself again.

'I think you look beautiful,' said Zéphyrine. 'I hope Jules can do you justice.'

Anatole shook his head. 'Zéphyrine!'

'Oh I don't mean to be rude. But you won't do one like that, will you?' She pointed at a blurred and shadowy image of Anatole. 'You can't really see what he looks like, can you?'

Anatole laughed. 'Oh that was when Jules was obsessed with his "theory of sacrifices" – wasn't that what you called it?'

Jules nodded, smiling faintly. 'That's right. It's a matter of light and shade,' he said. 'And letting go of the idea of focus as your goal. I think it gives a photograph more soul if you simplify. Sometimes – to capture the inner likeness – you need to sacrifice. It's a case of trying to eliminate external detail.'

'Oh. I think I see what you mean. But I like detail,' said Zéphyrine firmly. 'It's more truthful, isn't it? This makes him look like . . . like an angel or something.'

'It was an experiment,' said Jules.

'Something to do with how much you screw the lens?' said Anatole. 'I like that one. It makes me look more ethereal than I'm used to. The violin helps.'

'Ethereal?'

'He means not quite of this world. Celestial you might say,' said Jules.

'I think he looks like a Greek statue,' added Marie. 'Except for the violin.'

'Or just plain dead,' said Zéphyrine. 'I won't be in your way here, will I?' She went to sit on a chair in the corner, on her hands, as usual. 'No more questions now, I promise. But how long does it all take? Will I be able to see the photograph right away?'

'You'll be able to see the negative quite soon. The print takes a little longer.' Jules was patient, but he also made it clear that he needed to get on with things.

Zéphyrine tried to shrink herself. But then she saw the pile of flat wooden boxes waiting beside the big camera stand. 'And what do you do with those? No, no, tell me afterwards. I'll shut up now, I really will. You won't know I'm here.'

'What do you mean, we won't know you're here?' said Anatole, shaking his head. 'Don't you understand?'

'Oh sorry . . . I think I'd better go now then, right away.' She leapt up. 'It was lovely to see everything. Very interesting. Thank you so much for showing me,' she said again, looking around. 'But, Anatole, what have you done with my shawl?'

'Oh for goodness' sake, Zéphyrine. Stop!' Anatole blocked the doorway. 'I didn't bring you here simply to watch. Jules is going to take your likeness, too.'

That did shut her up.

'Mine?' she whispered. 'Really? A photograph of me?'

'Yes. You.' He took her hand, but she pulled away.

'But he can't . . . look at me . . . if only I'd known. Why didn't you tell me? I could have . . . I would have . . .' She clutched at her hair, then her skirt.

'You see,' Jules said quietly to Anatole. 'You have to be careful with surprises. I did warn you.' He coughed. 'I've got three plates ready to prepare for each of you. If you're lucky, and keep still, you'll even have a choice.'

Marie glared at both men, and swiftly detached herself from the column.

'Don't worry,' she said. 'It won't matter what you're wearing. Head and shoulders. That's what's important. I'll fix your hair for you, and I've another shawl here too, a good one . . . if you don't want to use your own, that is.'

'You don't mind?' said Zéphyrine.

'If it's clothes you're worried about, have a look in that trunk,' said Anatole still not understanding Zéphyrine's dismay. 'All sorts of things in there, aren't there, Jules? Have you ever even been through them all?'

Anatole opened the lid and Marie began pulling things out. Brocade curtains and satin cloaks. A black-and-white Pierrot costume. A military jacket, with a row of brass buttons forming a V in front.

At the other end of the studio, Jules was opening and shutting drawers. 'Eureka!' he said, waving the promised hairbrush, and striding over.

'Thank you,' said Marie. 'Now, this is going to be fun.' She pulled out the last pin, tucked it into her bodice, and began to brush Zéphyrine's hair with vigour. Her scalp tingled delightfully and the air crackled with electricity. Nobody had brushed Zéphyrine's hair for her since she was tiny.

Anatole seemed dazed.

'What about this?' Marie held up a length of black organza. 'Drape it round your shoulders – that's right – slip the dress down a little more – and you'll look just like —'

'No. Stop. This is ridiculous. I want you to take her portrait just as she is. A Communarde, and proud of it,' said Anatole. 'Why should you have to pretend to be someone else? You're a citizen of Paris, and anyone's equal. Anyone's.' He took her by the shoulders and stared into her face. 'Aren't you?'

Zéphyrine let the silk slide from her shoulders and float to the floorboards.

'Aren't you?' repeated Anatole. Minou came out of the shadows to catch it. A cat-eating Communarde, thought Zéphyrine.

'Yes . . . yes, of course you're right,' she said.

'Look,' he said, snatching up a newspaper from a chair. It was the *Journal Officiel*, the Commune's daily, containing every new decree. 'Hold this. For posterity. Will you be able to see the date, Jules?'

Jules looked from one to the other, and back to the window, still checking the light, the lenses.

'I doubt it. You'll probably see the title though.'

'That'll do. Well? It's up to you.'

Zéphyrine straightened her back. 'Yes . . . just as I am then. Take me as I am.'

'Good,' said Anatole proudly. Zéphyrine was glad he hadn't kissed her in front of the others. He stepped back a pace.

Jules went under the hood. 'Ready now?' he asked Marie in a muffled voice.

'Yes. What do you think?' A different kind of smile had appeared on her face. A stage smile, realised Zéphyrine. She thought it looked charming. But it was no good her trying anything like that.

'Almost ready,' said Jules. 'Could you just open that blind please, there, just a little more, Anatole? Yes, that will be perfect. Don't move now.'

Marie held her smile while Jules vanished into the darkroom. They heard the clink of glass, a bottle unstoppering, and he returned a few minutes later with a large dark square in his hand and a greater sense of urgency. Zéphyrine held her breath while he slid the plate-holder into the back of the camera, then slid out the dark slide that protected it.

'Ready?' he called. 'But don't answer! Now!'

He removed the lens cap. Every one of them stood as still as they possibly could while the seconds ticked by. And at last it was over. Jules raced back to the darkroom with his plate. Zéphyrine, Marie and Anatole laughed with relief.

'Don't disturb him now,' Anatole warned. 'This is the moment that matters most.' And he told the girls about the early days, when he'd nosily drawn back the curtain to see what Jules was up to with his mysterious light and all that pouring water, and ruined everything.

Three plates for Marie, then three for Zéphyrine.

The first time she closed her eyes at the wrong moment.

'Now you look dead,' said Jules bluntly. 'Let's try again.'

The second time, her trembling fingers dropped the newspaper, and she bent to pick it up. She knew the plate must be ruined even before Jules disappeared into the darkroom.

'This is terrible. Such a waste. I don't think I'm any good at this,' said Zéphyrine, holding out her hands. 'Look how it makes me shake.'

Marie glanced at Anatole, who had taken her hands, and was trying to still them.

'That won't help,' she said. 'You're making things worse.'

She took Zéphyrine aside, away from Anatole, and taught her how to breathe, slowly, steadily, from a place deep inside. 'Here,' she said, laying a hand just above Zéphyrine's stomach. 'Breathe from here. Let me feel you breathing. That's right. In. And out. And when he says "Ready" don't move, but take in most of a breath and just hold it, and that will keep you still.'

Zéphyrine nodded, hardly daring to look at Jules, who was setting up the camera again.

'This time, it will be fine,' said Marie. 'Won't it?'

Anatole gave Zéphyrine the newspaper again, and squeezed her hand.

'It's just a photograph,' he whispered. 'Not a death sentence. Don't look so grim.'

'I'm ready,' she replied. 'I won't move. I promise I won't spoil it this time. Is this right?'

'Now!' called Jules, and again, whisked off the lens cap.

She stared, unblinking and defiant, at her own reflection in the lens.

Even after she had changed into her ordinary clothes, the glow of performance clung to Marie, and her eyes stayed bright. 'Thank you!' she called to Jules. 'Emile will be so delighted.'

It wasn't a good moment to answer, so he didn't.

'If you send the print to his regimental headquarters, I expect he will get it, eventually,' Anatole said.

'I wonder if it's worth the risk,' said Marie. 'It would be dreadful if a photograph got lost. And perhaps they read the letters . . . ?'

'Who?' asked Zéphyrine.

Marie fluttered her fingers vaguely. 'Oh, you know . . . "them".'

Zéphyrine picked up the newspaper. She wasn't a very fast reader, but the nuns had done their job, and she was competent enough.

'Have you seen this, Marie? They're calling here for the "active collaboration of all the women of Paris who realise . . . that the present social order bears in itself the seeds of poverty and the death of Freedom and Justice." It says we must "conquer or perish".'

'"Conquer or perish'?" Jules's voice cut in from behind the thin walls of the darkroom.

'Everything seems to be happening so quickly,' said Anatole quietly. 'How active, do you think?'

Zéphyrine didn't answer.

'Look, Marie!' She waved the newspaper at her. 'They are talking to us. "Mothers, wives, sisters of the French people". Is it a meeting? Why don't we go? See what they say?'

'Oh, I'm not sure. I don't much like meetings,' said Marie, taking the journal and scanning it uneasily. 'There are quite enough at the theatre, if you ask me, with all this cooperative business. And this one sounds as if it might get violent.'

Zéphyrine continued to read over Marie's shoulder. 'It sounds splendid to me,' she said. 'They want a march of women to Versailles. Imagine! If the Versailles army were to fire on a crowd of unarmed mothers. The world couldn't ignore us then!'

Marie went white. 'The army would never do that,' she said. 'Do you think the men are monsters?'

Zéphyrine realised she'd been tactless.

'We're probably too late anyway,' she said. 'There'll be another meeting.'

'There's always another meeting,' agreed Anatole. 'See what happens.'

'Yes,' said Marie slowly. 'We'll see what happens.'

Jules emerged from the darkroom and declared the success of the final plate.

'I'll make some prints tomorrow,' he said. 'But you can see the negative now. Don't touch – I haven't varnished it yet of course.'

They kept a careful distance. It was a fine portrait, even in reverse. You could read the name of the newspaper quite clearly – in mirror writing – and somehow, despite the necessary stillness, Zéphyrine looked full of life, proud and purposeful. Jules was pleased, Anatole even more so.

'Oh yes,' said Anatole. 'It's extraordinary how well you've caught her. Look at those fierce eyes!'

Zéphyrine pretended to toss her head.

'Blazing,' agreed Jules. 'You'll have to sign it when I've done the print.'

'Will I?' said Zéphyrine.

'Yes,' said Marie. 'Citizen Zéphyrine.'

21.

A week later, Montmartre was still preparing to conquer or perish. There had been no let up in the bombardment and the newspapers were reporting heavy casualties among the National Guard battalions fighting in the green suburb of Asnières, on the banks of the Seine eight kilometres from Paris. In the vestry of the church, sitting in a semi-circle round the stove, Rose's aunt read aloud from *The People's Voice* while Zéphyrine, Rose, the Ladle and some fifteen other women recruited by the neighbourhood committee got on with their sewing. The more experienced seamstresses worked on uniforms; the rest made sandbags, ready to be filled.

Zéphyrine looked at the pile of hessian on her left, and her heart sank. So many sacks still to sew. She would never get away. The only answer was to speed up her stitching. Hunched over her work, she began stabbing furiously with her needle.

Rose, who noticed everything, said, 'Is there a prize now?'

'What are you talking about?' said Zéphyrine, without looking up.

'I thought they must have announced a reward for whoever makes the most. You'll put the rest of us to shame if you keep going like that.'

'I'll sew as fast as anyone likes,' said the enormously tall woman they called the Sleepwalker, who was working through her own pile at a great rate. 'Makes sense to get more money.'

'That's if we ever get it,' her neighbour mumbled, and went back to sucking on her pipe.

That stopped a few needles in their tracks.

'What? Not more delays?'

'It's the bank. Monsieur Whatshisname won't release the money to the Commune. So the Commune can't give it to the Women's Union.'

'Men!' Rose tutted. 'They've got to stop all this shilly-shallying. Time to apply some pressure. Show who's in charge.'

'They're scared, I reckon,' the woman next to her said, shaking her head. 'The men of the Commune are scared of going too far. But it's too late for that.'

'Anyway, it's ridiculous. How can we get things done without money?' agreed the Ladle.

'I'll show them how to put pressure on the bank,' said the Sleepwalker. She rolled back her sleeve and flexed an impressive arm. Someone whistled, and a few others put down their sewing to clap. 'Never too late for the Commune to take over the Bank of Paris.'

'I'm sure we'll get what we're owed in the end. And at least it's a fair wage,' said Zéphyrine. She wasn't used to being so optimistic. It was a good feeling. She had never realised before that having something to look forward to was a pleasure in itself.

She dropped a finished sack on the pile on her right, licked the end of a new length of thread, and squinted at her needle.

'And an equal one,' agreed another woman.

'Thank heaven there are no convents round the corner any more, doing the same job for less!' added Rose's aunt. This provoked laughter and a cheer of solidarity from the other women, and, of course, a song. It would be all right, they chorused: 'Ça ira, ça ira.'

Zéphyrine joined in. The singing slowed down the sewing, but it felt good. She felt part of things here as she never had all those months working away alone with just her grandmother. Times like this always made her worry about what could happen if the Commune failed. She had nothing to go back to.

'What time do you think it is now?' she asked Rose, who puffed out her lips and said she reckoned she'd heard the bells for the hour about ten minutes earlier.

'I can stay later and finish your lot if you like,' she offered. 'Got nothing better to do. No fancy man to meet, any rate.'

'How did you know . . . ?' Zéphyrine stopped, and shrugged. She supposed it was obvious.

Rose looked at her sideways. 'You've not said a word about Anatole since the Gingerbread Fair.'

Zéphyrine's needle hesitated for a fraction of a second, and then kept moving.

Rose persisted. 'Nothing wrong?'

'I've hardly seen you.' Zéphyrine sounded defensive.

'Not my fault. You know where to find me.'

'I know. Sorry.'

'Well?'

'Well, what?'

Zéphyrine didn't want to talk about Anatole any more. Before anything had happened between them, Anatole was like an idea, a thought to play with. She didn't mind sharing a thought. Things had changed.

'I suppose he's different from anyone you've ever met before? Hey! Are you even listening to me?'

'Yes, yes, I am . . . sorry. I've been busy.' She couldn't even quite bring herself to tell Rose about the photographs. Sitting next to her, Rose hard at work as usual, Zéphyrine was ashamed. How vain she had been. Rose was interested in more important things. Maybe Zéphyrine would tell her another day, when the print was ready. 'I'm a bit tired.'

'I'm sure you are,' said Rose. 'Not getting enough sleep?'

Her arch look maddened Zéphyrine. 'Shut your filthy mouth!' She pretended to laugh, pretended to be equally knowing. 'Get back to your sewing.'

So much for asking Rose for the advice she needed so badly. Zéphyrine stitched a final knot and bared her teeth as she bit the thread off. The moment she'd spoken, she knew she'd made a mistake. Once you'd suggested a thing like that, let someone imagine you were a woman of the world, you couldn't go back on your tracks. You couldn't admit there was stuff you had no idea about. Now she didn't know who else she could talk to. As far as Gran'mère was concerned, there was only one way for a girl to stay out of trouble: stay out of reach. That was how Zéphyrine had been brought up, constantly reminded that she only had to look at herself to see what happened if you didn't. But how could Zéphyrine make herself stay out of reach of Anatole? Just the thought of him, even when he was

175

nowhere near – the memory of one moment, or the anticipation of another – it could do strange things to her body. It alarmed her the way he made her burn up inside.

She realised Rose was speaking again, and returned to the room with a jolt, determined to concentrate. When Zéphyrine had pieced together the floating fragments of words, her mouth fell open.

'Work at an ambulance station? On the battlefields? You could be killed!'

'I know,' said Rose in a low voice, glancing at her aunt, who was locked in heated argument with the Ladle and not listening to them. 'My mother won't let me go to the front line so you don't need to worry. It's too dangerous, she says, and anyway, she needs my help with the little ones at night.'

'You're not going to run away?' Zéphyrine put a hand on Rose's arm. 'You will be careful?'

Rose shook her off. 'Oh, you're as bad as my mother. Nobody changed the world by being careful.'

Zéphyrine supposed not.

'Anyway, I don't think they'd want me, with my gammy foot. But it's all right. I don't need to leave Paris to be an *ambulancière*,' said Rose. 'They've just opened a new ambulance station here in Montmartre. The Women's Union keep calling for new nurses.'

'I know.'

'All those grand ladies who helped during the siege are nowhere to be seen now. And I'll be good at looking after the laundry.'

'You're very good at looking after people,' said Zéphyrine, trying not to think of blood-stained sheets and bandages. She had a horrible feeling she knew exactly what Rose was thinking.

'Much better than me,' she added firmly. She'd done all the nursing she could bear to while her grandmother was dying.

Rose narrowed her eyes. '"From each according to her abilities, to each according to her needs,"' she quoted at Zéphyrine. 'Louis Blanc. Sort of.'

How did Rose always remember the names of all the different politicians?

'I'll stick to soup and sandbags then.'

'At least you're taking care of one Guardsman, even if he's only lovesick.' She smirked, and then looked harder at Zéphyrine. 'Anatole is in the National Guard, isn't he?'

'He was, during the siege of course. But you know what it's like round where they live. His battalion's just melted away. Or joined the party of order. And he can hardly walk into a Montmartre unit, can he? It just doesn't work like that. You know that.'

'Hmm.' Rose went back to her sewing, tight-lipped.

Zéphyrine reached the café, windswept and breathless, hoping they would all still be there. She saw Jules and Marie right away, sitting at a table near the window. A fédéré sat between them, only his back visible, and Zéphyrine was tempted to retreat. But Marie had seen her, and was waving, and she supposed Jules would know where she could find Anatole. Then the stranger stood up and looked round, following Marie's gaze, and of course it wasn't a stranger at all.

Zéphyrine stood for a moment with a grin on her face.

'Look at you!' she said stupidly, since he could hardly look at himself. She adjusted his kepi, and fingered the button on a cuff. She had to run a finger and thumb down her nose to clear the tears unexpectedly gathering in the corners of her eyes.

Jules pulled a chair out for her, and summoned the waiter. 'Another glass, please.'

The others had already eaten, and their plates been cleared away. Arriving hungry, Zéphyrine didn't want to admit she hadn't eaten. She'd find something later, in Montmartre, where suppers came cheaper.

'You didn't know?' said Marie.

'No!' admitted Zéphyrine.

'Anatole does like his surprises,' Jules said, and Anatole shrugged.

'I wanted to see your face.' He reached out to stroke it.

'Speaking of which . . .' said Jules, tapping Anatole's arm with a meaningful look.

'Don't worry,' said Anatole. 'I was coming to that. I hadn't forgotten.'

He reached in his breast pocket and produced three plain-backed cards, two white and one red. He held them out to Zéphyrine, face down in a fan, like a gambler, and they all watched her hesitate.

He nodded. 'Go on, take one.'

She took the middle one, and turned it over.

'It's me,' she said, incredulous. You really could see everything. The little gap in her eyebrow. The buttonhole of her blouse. The title of the newspaper was perfectly clear – *Journal Officiel* – and Zéphyrine held it up with obvious pride. Every hair on her head was there, and you could even see two dots of light reflected from her fierce eyes, as well as the dark shadows beneath them. Zéphyrine put a finger to her face, almost expecting the girl in the photograph to do the same, like a girl in a mirror.

'How clever and quick you are!' she said to Jules. 'And how kind.'

'Thank you. That one is for you to keep,' he told her. 'And I can print more, if you want. Anatole has one already of course.'

'And I want you to sign it. He's done a wonderful job, hasn't he?' said Anatole, turning the other two cards over to show her.

The photograph of Marie impressed Zéphyrine even more.

'Beautiful, of course,' she sighed, and Marie closed her eyes like a cat in acknowledgement. 'So beautiful. And what's this?' Zéphyrine tilted the red card towards the light to read the words.

'Oh that's from my new battalion – the Fédération Artistique. It's just for musicians and actors. That's an exemption card.' Anatole put it safely away again. 'We've all got one to use when we have rehearsals, or performances, or something.'

'Oh.'

'I have my first rampart duty tomorrow evening.'

'Oh,' Zéphyrine said again, pleased and sorry at the same time.

'I do hope you'll be careful,' said Marie. 'The bombardment's getting worse every day. You'll be so exposed on the ramparts.'

'You can't change the world by being careful,' said Zéphyrine. She gazed at Anatole, picturing his fine fingers curling round a trigger rather than a violin neck. She found she didn't like the idea at all.

Marie and Jules exchanged glances.

'The weather's only going to get worse,' said Marie, looking out at the flapping awning. 'I'm going home before it pours. Goodnight, everyone.'

Jules rose too. He plucked his hat from the coat stand, buttoned his jacket and offered her his arm. 'I'll walk with you. I've got a good umbrella.'

As soon as they were gone, Anatole took Zéphyrine's hands in his own. 'I've missed you,' he said. 'I always miss you.'

'I know. I can feel it. All the time.'

'All I ever think about is when I'm going to see you again.'

'I know,' she said, putting her palms against his palms, measuring her fingers against his fingers.

The waiter returned to clear the table, white apron gleaming. 'Anything else, sir? Mademoiselle?'

His expression was blank, completely professional. It made her as uncomfortable as the wink of a man in a wine shop, because she couldn't tell what he was thinking, and she hated that. He'd have her down as a tart, she was sure. Why else would a man of Anatole's class mix with a woman of hers? She shouldn't care, but she did: it was hard to shake yourself free of ideas drummed into you since you could walk.

'Are you sure?' asked Anatole. 'Something to warm you up? A bite to eat?'

The waiter hovered.

'Nothing, thank you,' she insisted.

'I'll have a coffee,' said Anatole, and then they were alone again. Only the clink of porcelain on white marble and the smell of coffee took them out of their trance. Anatole stirred in a few sugar lumps.

'Just a sip?' she said, unable to resist.

'Here.'

Nothing could have made Anatole happier than the thought

of her lips touching the cup where his lips had just been. He drank in the sight of her drinking, the movement in her throat, a glimpse of her tidying-tongue on her lips as she set the cup down.

'Do you know it's nearly a month since I first met you?' he said.

'Already?'

'I wanted to buy you a present . . .' Anatole hesitated.

'Another surprise?' said Zéphyrine.

'Of course . . . except . . . I didn't want . . . that is to say . . . I couldn't think . . .'

'What?' she said.

'Well, I didn't want you to take it in the wrong way.'

There could always be a wrong way. Every present could be taken as a transaction, and they both knew that. But how could you tell the difference between a love token and a payment for services? Anatole wanted to be clear, absolutely clear, to himself, to Jules, and most of all to Zéphyrine. He wasn't like other men. He didn't want a mistress to dress up and show off. He didn't want to give her delightful trinkets with strings attached, to buy her love. Surely it was possible? Something for nothing, nothing for something.

'I won't. I'll try not to. I'm sure I won't.'

'It's not much.'

He put his hand in his pocket and opened it for her to see. A scrap of silk. She untied the thread that kept the tiny parcel together. Two little black daisies, made of glass. Without thinking, she pinched her empty earlobes.

'You noticed?' she said. 'You knew.'

He nodded, still uncertain of her response. With great concentration, she took first one, and then the other, and fixed them in each ear, then held back her hair so he could see them. He nodded again, and she put her arms round his neck and hugged him fiercely.

'Thank you,' she whispered into his skin. 'I love them.'

'I love you,' he whispered back, so quietly that she might not have heard.

They left the café, and, as usual, Anatole began to walk up the hill with her, keeping his arm firmly round Zéphyrine. The wind was gathering strength, sending twigs skittering across the pavement and tearing posters loose from walls. It lifted skirts and tugged at shawls. A few hundred feet from the square where they always said goodbye, a violent gust snatched Zéphyrine's cap from her head, blowing it out like a pig's bladder ball, and bowling it across the street. At just the same moment there was a great crack of thunder, as loud as a cannon shot, and the rain started to fall down in sheets. Zéphyrine grabbed Anatole's hand and they gave chase. The cap put up a good fight, zigzagging across the square, stopping and starting again as soon as they got close. They splashed through puddles, and crashed into lamp posts, dragging each other on. At last they caught up with it, all life lost. Anatole picked the cap dripping from the gutter, picked off a wet leaf and held it out to Zéphyrine.

'I believe this is yours, *citoyenne*.'

She took it from him and began to wring out the sodden mass of cotton. Then she pulled him into a doorway, gently wiped the rain off his face with her cap, and kissed him goodnight. The wind and rain kept buffeting them, but neither very much cared. This was where they always parted, just here, before the road got steep.

MAY 1871

In May the pavements were polka-dotted with fallen blossom, and one song was on everyone's lips: they sang of the cherry season, *le temps des cerises*, just round the corner now. Soon young men would be hanging the shining fruit on lovers' ears like drops of blood. How merrily the blackbird would sing by day. How mournfully the nightingale by night.

On the boulevards, the carefully constructed ramparts continued to rise. Just as quickly, those ramshackle barricades thrown up in the poor quarters of Paris back in March began to bloom, greening over where urchins had planted tufts of grass. Determined flowers suddenly appeared, and passers-by caught their breath at the sight of them. Laughter came easily in the first weeks of May. Wild speeches, brilliant colours, cheerful bravado.

For Anatole and Zéphyrine, *le temp des cerises* had come early. The pair met whenever they could, sometimes late at night at the café with Jules and Marie, just occasionally alone. Their time together was snatched from practising and patrolling, from cooking at the canteen and stitching sandbags and recruiting for the ramparts and barricades. It was stolen from sleep itself.

If she ever let him, Anatole would have happily watched over Zéphyrine's breathing until dawn. Instead he spent sleepless nights imagining the possibility. Every day seemed more golden.

The sun shone, but the sky was no longer blue. Smoke from burning villages to the west of the city formed a haze that never quite lifted. There was always the faint smell of carbon in the air. It had become normal.

But the crisis was coming to a head. Elected representatives gave way to a Committee of Public Safety, a dictatorship, set up to defend the Commune by decree, in the name of 'freedom'. There could be little debate now. One by one, hostile newspapers were suppressed. It had happened before, less than a hundred years earlier. Paris remembered the Reign of Terror, after the first revolution, and shuddered.

22.

4th May

A Thursday evening, still early in the month. A crash from the studio above made Zéphyrine jump and Anatole's bow freeze. He dashed to the bottom of the staircase and called up. 'Everything all right, Jules?'

The answer was reassuring.

'Just dropped some glass plates, blast it. Damned waste, as I'm running low, but I know where I can get more. I didn't mean to alarm you. Don't stop practising on my account, for God's sake – you've only got a few more days till the concert, haven't you?'

Zéphyrine was curled up on the chaise longue with Minou. 'He's right,' she said when Anatole returned. 'Don't stop.'

'Aren't you bored of hearing the same bit over and over again?'

'Of course not. Anyway, it's not exactly the same, is it? That's the whole point. Or you wouldn't have to keep at it.'

Anatole raised the violin to start the section again, and stopped without playing a note, bow hand hanging at his side, his eyes once more on Zéphyrine.

'What is it?' she said, edging herself upright. The cat resettled herself, and increased the volume of her purring. 'Are we putting you off? Shhh . . . Minou. You must be quiet.'

'Don't blame Minou.'

'No, of course not.' Zéphyrine nuzzled her face in the cat's fur and squeaked through pursed lips: 'You're completely innocent, aren't you?'

She found Anatole's adoration of the animal endearing and shocking at the same time. It still made her head reel to think that while he'd been keeping Minou alive all through the siege, Gran'mère was starving to death, and Zéphyrine herself queuing in the hope of a portion of rat meat. But she supposed that wasn't Anatole's fault.

He was still looking at her. Nobody ever looked with more intensity. Most of the time she liked it. Sometimes it made her feel uncomfortable. What if this thing was like a storm, the kind that came on strong and suddenly and then blew itself out just as fast?

'So what is it?' she persisted. The force of his gaze made her tucked-under toes glow and tingle. Even her hair seemed to crackle. He sat down next to her, and immediately made everything worse. Zéphyrine felt out of control. She thought of her mother. Was this how it happened?

'You know I'd do anything for you, don't you?' he said so earnestly she didn't quite want to hear or see, so instead she pulled him towards her and kissed him, eyes shut. The cat slid away, unnoticed, and he sighed and moved closer. She untucked her legs and felt the weight of him, his bones and muscles, a button that dug into her. There was a shifting of furniture from the studio above, and footsteps.

'Come on,' she said, wriggling away. 'Keep playing. I love listening.'

'If I must.' Anatole slowly stood up.

'You haven't got long.'

'Wait until you hear it with the whole orchestra. I'm just a tiny part of the machine.'

'Not a machine,' she corrected. 'You could never be anything like a machine. Anyway, I'll always be able to hear your bits, won't I?'

'No, not really,' he said. 'You shouldn't. Everything has to work together seamlessly. Maybe not like a machine . . . like a union, or a committee?'

She nodded. Zéphyrine liked that idea, except for the way it made her feel guilty. She wasn't doing much work now.

The melody soared and danced. She lay back and listened, closing her eyes so that she was floating in pure sound, helpless in its current.

Later that evening Zéphyrine went to Marie's room to borrow a dress for the concert. She could have worn Rose's pink paisley again, but Rose was getting harder and harder to find. Anyway, Zéphyrine was about to go to a palace for the first time in her life – a people's palace now – and it would have been rude to turn down such a generous offer.

'You really don't mind?' Zéphyrine said when she arrived.

'I've got clothes here I haven't worn in months,' Marie said. 'Look at the size of that trunk! My insurance, it was meant to be. I was saving the best dresses to sell, in case things got tight, but the fashions have changed so much already. I think I'm too late.'

'You might not get as much for them as before the war, but things can be altered. There'll always be someone who'll buy a good dress that's going cheap.'

'Of course. You're right. Well, come and see what you think.' Marie had already laid out three or four gowns on the bed for Zéphyrine to choose from. Other possibilities too: a muff, some gloves, a pair of delicate shoes. All presents the banker had bought her before he vanished from Paris and cancelled her lease without warning. All lovely things, beautifully made. 'I know you are a little thinner than me, but we are about the same height, aren't we?' She slipped off her mules and they stood for a moment eye-to-eye, a horizontal hand to each forehead.

'Doesn't it make you scared, to sing in front of so many people?' Zéphyrine suddenly asked.

Marie was about to laugh prettily. But faced with a gaze so serious, so curious, she found herself answering just as seriously.

'Yes, nearly always. Terrified. But I don't know if I could sing if I wasn't frightened. It's just part of the whole thing, part of what I do, and how I am.'

'But even so, it's what you want to do?'

'Yes. More than anything.'

Zéphyrine looked at her thoughtfully, and nodded.

'I see.' She turned her attention to the pile of clothes. 'This is very grand,' she said wistfully, fingering a slightly showy afternoon dress in silk with a broad green-and-black stripe.

'Too grand? I think you're right. Not such a good idea now I come to think about it,' Marie said, quickly whisking it away. 'I forgot you'd need a corset for that one.' She didn't want to draw attention to the fact that Zéphyrine had so little to

188

hold in. She'd soon plump out, Marie thought, if she'd only let Anatole take better care of her.

She pulled another dress from the pile. 'Better?'

'Oh yes! That's very pretty!' Zéphyrine held it against herself: a simple, summery affair in white muslin with blue spots.

'I think it will be perfect. Let me find my black sash. It goes with the ribbons at the wrist and neckline – do you see? Then we can see how it looks on.'

'Thank you!' Zéphyrine began to unbutton her blouse, turning her back for modesty.

Marie was happy to be of use, and not just because clothes always took her mind off things. Over the last weeks she had discovered – slightly to her surprise – that she liked Zéphyrine a great deal. The girl was straightforward. Quick and sharp. Marie could see exactly why Anatole – so charming, and so impressionable – had fallen for her. And she and Zéphyrine weren't as different from each other as they looked. Just one foot wrong, and any woman on her own in the world could find herself in the gutter in no time.

'Lovely. Look in the mirror. And stand still while I tie the sash.'

'You really don't mind lending this? I'll bring it back laundered of course.'

Zéphyrine plucked at the muslin. It was a little bunched at the waist, but not obviously too big.

'Not at all. It suits you beautifully, much better than it does me. Now, you'll need finer stockings than those . . .'

Marie had other reasons to be kind to Zéphyrine. An ally like her could be very useful. She was still worried that Rigault really had set his spies on her. Increasingly frightened to turn round when she heard footsteps on the pavement behind her, she found herself pathetically suspicious when she noticed anyone standing for too long under one lamp post. It could be no bad thing to be seen at a women's meeting, rallying to the cause. She needed to cement her Commune credentials.

Marie had given up hoping Rigault would ever send news of her brother. How could she have believed for a moment that he might? She thought she understood his game, but nothing would induce her to trade herself for the sake of that passport. It was also getting harder to believe that abandoning her work was the right thing to do at the moment. With new musical projects announced each week by the Artistic Federation, Marie's ambitions felt suddenly within reach. If she left Paris now, she might never have the chance to sing at the Opéra. But if she stayed, any on-stage triumph would be sour without Emile there to witness it. She felt hopelessly torn. For the moment, her only option was to hedge her bets.

'I hope Anatole likes the dress,' said Zéphyrine uncertainly. Marie registered the doubt in her voice, and wondered if she still saw her as competition.

'I'm certain he will.'

Although Marie had briefly been tempted to fall into Anatole's arms – they were so lovely, and she had been so lonely – her approach to love was firmly practical. Her intention was to go up, not down, in the world. And he certainly didn't need any more admirers. Poor Jules, thought Marie, looking at Zéphyrine and noticing her new earrings. Poor Mister Crowfield.

* * *

At the final rehearsal the next day, Anatole looked up to see Marie coming down into the orchestra pit, music in hand, her face unreadable.

'I came to tell you: I've done it,' she said, and paused to see his reaction.

Anatole looked at her, and continued to rosin his bow. 'You want me to guess?' he asked.

'Has Zéphyrine told you already?'

'Not that I know of . . .'

She lowered her voice. 'I've registered with the Women's Union.'

'Bravo! That's splendid news.'

Marie didn't react to his enthusiasm.

'Isn't it?' he said.

'Perhaps.' She shuffled the pages of her music. 'But it does make me frightened. I couldn't decide what to do for ages. What if the Commune is defeated, and my name is on their list? What if the Commune triumphs, and I haven't declared my loyalty?'

'Well, since you have now declared your loyalty, the point surely is to make sure the Commune does triumph. So you should do all you can to help it.' An oboe began to sound an A, and Anatole tucked his violin under his chin, ready to tune up. But Marie still stood there.

'It's easy for you to say that.' She looked around to make sure nobody was listening. 'You believe in all this, you and Zéphyrine.' She didn't say the other thing they were both thinking: 'and you don't have a brother in the Versailles army.'

Anatole couldn't argue, and nor did he want to tell Marie what to believe. She and Jules could both be so stubborn, so cynical. He didn't want to hear their doubts. He didn't want the certainties Zéphyrine had given him to be undermined.

'And what if they make me fight?' Marie asked.

'I don't think any *citoyenne* will be forced to fight.' He hoped he was right about this. He couldn't imagine Marie with a rifle on her shoulder, any more than he could bear to think of Zéphyrine as a target for the enemy's machine guns, the merciless *mitrailleuses* you heard grating the skies every evening outside the city walls when the wind was in the right direction. Whatever he said out loud, in his heart he did feel it was different for men.

'But some of the money for the union is to be used to buy petroleum and weapons.' Her clear blue eyes were steady. 'And haven't you seen the notices?'

The conductor rapped his baton on the music stand. 'Five minutes!' he called.

'Should you go back to your place?' said Anatole.

'I've got five minutes.'

'The notices, you said?' Whatever it was, he had a feeling he didn't want to hear.

'Thiers's notices. Saying what will happen when Versailles attacks. What they will do to the Communards.'

'Oh those.' Anatole was dismissive. 'Nobody believes empty threats like that. If Versaille was going to attack Paris, why haven't they done it yet? Anyway, people like us have nothing to worry about – we're just rank and file. It's the leadership they'll be after. The men at the top. Why on earth should they bother with the likes of us? For goodness' sake, they can hardly send half of Paris into exile. Devil's Island wouldn't hold us all!'

'We'll see,' said Marie, which was something she said a lot these days.

23.

6th May

So the grand doors of the Tuileries Palace were thrown open for the first concert, and everyone was astonished at how many people turned up. Some came to gloat, some to despair. A few held their heads up high, and went in chattering. Others just couldn't shake off the old habits of submission, and still bowed and scraped, keen to mind their manners in so much splendour. And then there were those who came to judge and sneer, mocking not the building but its new occupants. Zéphyrine watched Jules noticing them all, and, as usual, she could not decide what he was thinking.

Anatole had warned that they would need to arrive early, if they wanted time enough to look around the imperial apartments, and to secure seats too. Even so, there was a river of hopeful concertgoers ahead of them in the queue.

'Do you think we're too late, already?' said Zéphyrine. She tugged at the cuffs of the white gloves Marie had given her, pulling out the wrinkles on her fingers. Not a bad fit. Quite transforming.

Jules looked unperturbed. 'Wait until you see the size of the palace.'

'Shall we go then?' asked Zéphyrine.

'Without Rose?' Jules was curious about the washerwoman's daughter.

'She couldn't come. Too much committee work, she says. And she's taking a petition round the clubs after her shift at the ambulance station. Still trying to get Versailles to release Blanqui from prison – in exchange for the archbishop.'

'Good luck to her.' Jules looked grim. Blanqui – black-clad, uncompromising – had been at the heart of every revolutionary uprising that century. He'd already spent half his life in prison. 'I think I'd rather have the archbishop.'

'Shhhhh. Don't say that here.'

It was just as the posters had promised. At last the palace was being 'rendered useful to the people'. For fifty centimes you could wander through and gawp at the actual rooms once occupied by 'the tyrant' emperor and his wife. Citizens stood in uniforms at the entrance selling tickets, and making the usual collections for widows and orphans.

Jules handed over a generous donation and was rewarded with a red rosette with a little copper liberty cap in its centre. He examined it, without a word, then pinned it onto Zéphyrine's shawl.

'Thank you,' she said.

'This way,' he simply replied.

'So you've been here before?' Zéphyrine didn't know whether to be impressed or disgusted. 'To a party?'

'I'm not that grand,' Jules said with a faint smile. 'And

certainly not that important. No, an English journalist I used to know brought me here – to help translate – on the night of the empress's flight. You know, after the surrender at Sedan.' Some heads turned, and he lowered his voice. 'He couldn't understand the kind of French the soldiers spoke.'

Gutter French, he meant. They shuffled on a few paces, and Zéphyrine waited him to elaborate. When he didn't, she poked him.

'Ouch.'

'You can't just stop there. What was it like?'

'You'll see for yourself soon enough.'

'But that very night . . . ?'

Unusually, Jules reddened slightly, and coughed. 'I'm sure you can imagine. She left in a hurry.'

'A mess?'

'Somewhat. Bedclothes on the floor. Gloves . . . and . . . whatnot . . .'

Zéphyrine laughed, delighted. 'Oh . . . underwear you mean! You saw Eugénie's corsets!'

'No, no . . . not those.' Jules put a finger on his lips, and shook his head.

'Her drawers!' Zéphyrine said, even more loudly. 'Or just her shift? No! You saw the empress's drawers! What were they like?'

He shushed her quite angrily, and she knew she'd gone too far. She ducked her head away, and smiled only at her own feet, looking forward to telling Anatole later.

They finally reached the foot of the grand staircase. It was decorated with cooking pots and tin plates. A battalion of

National Guardsmen, some now sitting around on benches, some more obviously on duty, had clearly been quartered there for some time. There were mattresses and blankets pushed to the corners, and even shirts and stockings hanging up to dry. Clothing was draped on marble statues and hung from railings supported by gilded banisters, candy-cane twisted. On the first landing, a pair of retired soldiers who'd served the empire for decades, sat recovering from their climb. Their lips were tight and lined. They stared accusingly at the National Guard soldiers now treating the emperor's old palace with such disrespect.

Zéphyrine's fingers trailed along the wall-panelling, hesitating at holes made by nails where fédérés' marching orders had been pinned up. A few still fluttered. Names were scrawled and scratched in the woodwork, like Lovers' Lane promises. Jules shook his head, and kept walking.

Upstairs were the staterooms, bare of furniture but swarming with people, echoing with endless feet.

'Where is everything?' The question was on everybody's lips. Not a chair, not a door handle was left. 'Where's it all gone?' Nobody seemed to know. Some drapery still buzzed with imperial bees, each golden insect hand-stitched by an unknown female hand. And crystal chandeliers still glittered, luminous and complicated and symmetrical. So much red velvet and brocade. It reminded Zéphyrine of the theatre. In the Throne Room they stopped in front of a new poster signed by Dr Rousselle.

'"The gold that drapes these walls is your sweat and toil . . ."' Jules read the words aloud. '". . . Now your Revolution has made you free, and you return to possess your wealth . . . here you are at home."'

'I don't feel at home,' she admitted.

'This way to the empress's bedroom!' called a guide. No bed now of course, but Zéphyrine and Jules watched a party of dressmakers cry out with delight at looking glasses that sprang down from the walls on all sides.

'Oh, we must have something like this in the shop, when Paris is Paris again!' they said. 'Take a note, quick, so we remember how it works.'

They left in a fluttering flock, the last woman poking some faded drapery with her parasol, as if to check it wasn't alive.

'Extraordinary . . .' murmured Jules, as they stood in front of a sign beside a secret recess. It seemed that a whole garment workshop had been kept permanently at work above here, unseen women stitching endlessly at gowns, which then descended by some elaborate mechanism straight into the bedroom. Zéphyrine imagined this faceless army dedicated to keeping the empress in new clothes, ruining their eyes for a pittance. She shuddered. An old lady standing next to her suddenly shook her head, and sighed. 'So foolish of them, really . . .'

'What do you mean?' asked Zéphyrine, curious.

'They could be living here still, in this paradise, couldn't they? It didn't have to be like this. If only they had done just a little for us. Just a little. But what did they care?' She moved away.

'The concert is in that great hall we passed earlier,' said Jules. 'Shall we go and sit down?'

Zéphyrine nodded, too overwhelmed to speak. She couldn't have explained how she felt. Triumph, perhaps, but also churning horror and confusion. Jules was more silent even than usual in her presence. What he was actually thinking, she still had no idea.

Ghosts greeted them all along the corridors: statues swathed and bound in white linen.

'Why don't they want us to see them?' asked Zéphyrine, wondering what obscenity these sheets could be concealing.

Jules licked his lips, trying to choose his words. 'They are probably . . .'

Zéphyrine hurried on into the vast domed ballroom, not wanting to press him again. Workmen were still setting out the seating for the concert audience, and clambering up and down ladders to drape red silk over picture frames. She hardly dared look. And then one screen slipped, and all she saw was a portrait of a general with a helmet, and fierce staring eyes.

'War heroes,' confirmed Jules. 'Admirals, field marshals . . . battlefields. But there can be no pride now in the triumph of Empire.'

'And nor should there be,' said Zéphyrine with indignation. 'Those pointless, cruel wars. That savagery. Surely, you can't think —'

'No, no,' Jules interrupted her. 'I see no glory in any of that. I just wonder . . . never mind. Look, there are a couple of empty spaces left on the bench over there. A bit squashed. Perhaps those ladies wouldn't mind moving up a little.'

White-capped, baskets on knees, the old women wore masks of fortitude, their worn and wrinkled faces set firm. Zéphyrine knew the type so well: they had queued uncomplainingly in frost and rain all through the siege. They must have sat here already for hours today, all through these busy preparations.

'They are here to do their civic duty,' she whispered to Jules. 'They're not expecting to like the music. Let me sit by them.'

Space was made, and they shuffled along, trying not to tread on toes and hems. Soon Jules was flipping the tails of his frock coat over the back of a velvet-upholstered bench. Squeezed so close together, it was impossible not to be aware of each neighbour's body and breathing, but they were the lucky ones. Cigar smoke and hundreds more voices drifted in from the gardens below – an ever-growing, good-natured crowd who laughed and waved their useless tickets at the open windows, and joked about their outcast state.

As the ballroom filled up, it became stuffier and hotter. Zéphyrine's face prickled. She hoped the little droplets of sweat she could feel forming on her nose were not too obvious. Inspecting her gloves again, she was dismayed to see a mark on the fingertip. Perhaps a bit of spit would get it out? She bent her head, and licked her finger quickly, and tried to rub the grubbiness off on her shawl without Jules noticing. But of course he did. He noticed everything. She quickly folded her hands in her lap again, and hid the stain.

'You're nervous,' he said. 'Don't be.'

Zéphyrine winced. 'I can't help it. I don't think I could be more scared if I was on stage myself.'

'I know. I used to feel like that when Anatole performed in public.'

'Did you?' Zéphyrine couldn't imagine it.

'I made the mistake of imagining how I would feel, in his place. Then I would think of all the things that could go wrong. It always ruined the evening of course. I think I understand better now. Musicians are different. They live for performances, even if they do get nervous.'

Jules seemed to come alive when he spoke about Anatole.

'I suppose so,' said Zéphyrine, turning back to the stage. A thought had entered her head that she didn't want to pursue. 'I wonder what they're doing now. Warming up, I suppose.' She had learned that much now. She loved listening to Anatole playing, even just climbing up and down scales, or leaping through arpeggios. She knew exactly what expression he would have on his face right now: slightly cross, though he wasn't at all. It was just his practising face. 'We've still got hours to kill.'

'No – look. Here comes the orchestra now, though I can't see Anatole . . . and here's the chorus too – look – there's Marie.'

Zéphyrine leapt to her feet to peer over the heads of the people sitting in front of them, and waved her hand frantically. Jules gently pulled her back to the bench before the chorus of complaints behind them became too loud.

'Don't worry. They're just tuning up,' he whispered, seeing her dismay at the low cacophony.

Silence fell as the conductor appeared, and a few moments later Zéphyrine nearly jumped out of her skin. Crashing cymbals, fast and furious violins. Heads nodding, eyes widening. A sudden blast of brass and everything calmed down. Her nerves calmed too, and she began to enjoy herself, concentrating with all her might on the dancing violin bows – all she could see of the string section – and persuading herself that she could identify Anatole's. She refused to talk to Jules during the interval, for the orchestra continued to play, and they were both able to catch a glimpse of Anatole's face, though he didn't see them. The programme was long, and varied – patriotic poetry, a piano solo, the violin professor from the conservatoire. From time to time the performances were overwhelmed by competition from a National Guard band playing in the room next door, cheered on by the overflow audience.

The concert came to a climax with the appearance of a star everybody knew. She strolled onto the stage, fleshy arms outstretched, white dress trailing behind her and a scarlet sash at her wide waist. Instantly her name rang out from all around the hall.

'It's la Bordas! It's la Bordas!' Bordas was the revolution, in flesh and blood. She was the voice of France herself. It said so on the posters. The singer smiled and her hair sparkled. Zéphyrine glowed. Bordas was looking at her. Right at her! Then she realised that every man and woman in the room was equally convinced that the singer was gazing directly into their eyes. Having captured the entire audience, Bordas raised a hand, lifted up her eyes and the orchestra began to play. Every heart in the room felt itself beating in time, expecting, knowing exactly what was coming next. By the time Rosa Bordas reached the chorus, all were in song together.

'It's the rabble – the scum of the earth! Oh well! I'm one of them!'

'*C'est la canaille! Eh bien! J'en suis!*'

What spectacle! What an apparition! What glory! And it only got better. Gold braid glistening, a fédéré officer appeared suddenly from the corridor with a huge red flag, which he handed to the singer. Without a break in her song, she seized the pole, slowly unfurled the banner, and enveloped herself in the sign of the Commune. The audience was delirious, intoxicated, ecstatic.

'Bravo! Encore!'

'Isn't she incredible?' Zéphyrine turned to Jules.

Lips firmly pressed together, he replied with a tight nod.

Into the hopeful silence that followed the applause, the distant sound of cannon fire erupted. The outcasts on the steps of the terrace turned their eyes from the lit windows of the palace to the flashes illuminating the sky beyond the Arc de Triomphe.

24.

12th May

The best part of a week went by before Zéphyrine managed to see Rose again. She came into the canteen for breakfast one morning and explained that she'd been working nights. It was early enough still for most of the tables to be empty. On a nod from the Ladle, Zéphyrine wiped her hands on her apron and slid herself onto the bench beside Rose to keep her company while she ate.

'What's it like, then?'

Head lowered over a steaming bowl of milky coffee, Rose nodded vigorously. The ribbon that always tied the long plait up in a loop at the back of her head was drooping. 'Busy,' she mumbled through a large mouthful of bread. 'Very busy.'

She had dark circles under her eyes, and smelled of sweat and disinfectant rather than soap. There was a splash of blood on the hem of her apron. Either she hadn't noticed, or there had been no time to wash it out.

'You'd better go straight home and get some sleep,' said Zéphyrine.

Rose pushed back her bowl, and braced herself with both hands against the table, looking for the energy to stand.

'I'll try, but I must get the little ones off to school first. And it's so busy at the laundry. We're taking the overflow of linen and bandages from the ambulance station now, and it's all we can do to keep up. My mother's depending on me.'

'Tell her I'll come by when I'm done here.' If she couldn't bring herself to tend to the wounded herself, at least she could help look after the nurses. It meant disappointing Anatole but he would have to understand.

'Would you?' said Rose, giving her a quick hug. 'That would be a big help.' She held Zéphyrine at arm's length and inspected her. 'Do you know, I thought we were losing you?'

'What on earth do you mean?'

Rose waved a dismissive hand. 'Oh . . . all your gallivanting in town. Operas. Concerts. Photographers. More important things to do than help the Commune. You're getting so grand, aren't you?'

Zéphyrine was indignant. 'No, I'm not.'

'I thought you might be leaving us soon, to lead the high life. Isn't that man – Anatole, or whatever his name is – shouldn't he be setting you up with an apartment by now? Buying you a little lapdog? A carriage? A diamond necklace?'

Zéphyrine couldn't quite tell if she was joking or not. Rose knew Anatole's name well enough. She flushed lightly, and thought of Minou. She was glad her cap covered her ears and Rose hadn't noticed her new earrings.

'Don't be ridiculous. He's not like that. And he's only a musician. He couldn't afford anything like that even if he – or I – wanted it.'

205

'So what does he want?' said Rose more gently, and took Zéphyrine's hand, making a show of examining it for a ring. 'What do you want?'

'I don't know.'

All the discussions at the club confused Zéphyrine. The speakers she most admired sneered at marriage contracts. (Contracts! Of course they're called contracts. Just another capitalist financial transaction. Legalised slavery. Women bought and sold, from father to husband. It was time to put an end to marriage.) But what if you thought you did want to be with someone for ever and ever? Did you need to have something to show for a promise like that? And then again, what if you weren't so sure? She wished she had time to talk to Rose properly about everything. Or even Marie.

'You're going to have to decide. Everyone needs to know where their loyalties lie.'

'But I do know,' said Zéphyrine. 'Of course I know. I want to help the Commune.' She liked working with the committee – recently they'd been visiting vacant workshops, making a list of buildings that could be turned over to cooperative use. They were going to change things so it would be different for everyone, always. Equal pay for equal work. A proper education for girls, for this life, not the next, which was all the nuns ever seemed to care about. It was hard fighting for all this, and keeping Versailles at bay too. It took commitment. Maybe she wasn't showing enough commitment. 'Don't worry – I've not been completely swept off my feet, you know. I'm not an idiot. I know what's important.'

'I just wish the Commune didn't make it so difficult. You know they've completely banned women from the battlefield now? By order of the Committee of Public Safety.'

'Oh, Rose, but you promised me you weren't going to go to the front.'

'I'm not. I can't. I really can't.' She looked down and shook her head at her foot. 'I wouldn't be able to run away with the men, would I?'

Zéphyrine gave her a mock punch. There had indeed been a great many chaotic retreats. The National Guard – always resistant to orders – was running out of military commanders. The latest to be appointed was not even an army man, but a journalist.

'Rose. Stop that talk.'

'Really, you don't know what it's like. If you saw the state of the men by the time they get back here – so much blood lost, and their wounds stinking. Nothing you can do to stop them dying.'

Zéphyrine put a hand to her mouth.

'They need help so much sooner than we can give it,' Rose said. 'And so often they've got separated from the rest of their company – or the rest of them have run away – and nobody even knows who they are. Oh, Zéph – the coffins! It's pitiful.'

'But you won't go, will you, Rose? Promise you won't? Didn't you hear?'

Rose nodded grimly. 'About the nurse who was raped and killed? By the Versailles soldiers? I know. Horrible. Inhuman.'

Zéphyrine's mouth fell open. 'No, I didn't mean that . . . I hadn't heard,' she said. 'I was just talking about our own lot, who seem quite bad enough.'

Nine brave women had gone out to nurse a few weeks earlier: they were insulted, humiliated and sent back to the city as if they'd come to get in the way, instead of helping.

'Oh yes, it makes your blood boil. I'm sick of these men acting as if they don't need us. As if we don't matter, and what we do doesn't count. And all this stuff about emergency powers. That's not what they were voted in for. That's not democratic. It's one form of tyranny for another.'

The Ladle was calling Zéphyrine.

'Go on.' Rose gave her a kiss and a quick push back towards the kitchens. 'You'd better get back to work.'

Zéphyrine returned the kiss. 'And you'd better get some sleep.'

'I'll do my best.'

25.

16th May.

Four days later, the Commune organised another enthralling distraction from the horror outside the city walls. At the Place Vendôme, the grandest of squares – it was barely a stone's throw from the Tuileries Palace – Paris gathered for a spectacle that promised to be greater even than the concert. People waited, penned behind barriers in all the surrounding streets, beside themselves with excitement. After weeks of debate, the huge, hated column at the centre of the square was coming down. The statue at the top, the emperor of the First Empire, would be sent crashing to the ground. But what else could be expected to fall?

The slates were a worry: suppose they came shearing off the roofs to slice the heads beneath? Whole balconies might tumble down with the shock of the demolition. Or the vast column itself could crash right through the road, burying its outdated triumph in the muck of the sewers below. And if the sewers themselves burst, what then? Every window in the square was criss-crossed with paper strips in anticipation, every forehead lined with worry.

Jules had applied for permission to photograph the event, giving him admission inside the barriers. There he was now, *laisser-passer* in his coat pocket, Anatole at his side, acting as his assistant for the day. They had even had a private guard to get them and the mobile darkroom into the square early that morning.

'It looks as if they've been digging a grave for a giant,' said Anatole, when they had first arrived. Within a few hours, a long bed of branches lay on top. The fall of the emperor was to be cushioned by an eiderdown of twigs and brushwood, a mattress of sand and dung. All morning men had been stripping off the bronze, and chipping away at the stonework just above the square base.

'Will your camera be safe? Supposing the lens shatters?' Anatole asked Jules.

No reply. Jules must have seen some signal, some movement. He had retreated again beneath the black velvet in readiness. So Anatole lifted the edge, and asked the questions again.

'Just have to see,' came the snappy reply. 'It should survive. Certainly hope so.' Jules emerged again, blinking, and looked around. He was less immaculate than usual today. The repeated delays and false starts were fraying his temper as well as his moustache. Might there be some punishment if he failed to capture the occasion to the Commune's satisfaction? 'But I wish they'd get on with it.'

'Shall I ask someone what's happening?' Anatole gestured towards the trio of Guardsmen who stood a few feet away, protecting Jules's darkroom. 'It must be nearly three.'

Jules consulted his fob watch again and nodded. He ran a finger along the back of his neck, unsticking his stiff collar.

Across the square, the conductor of a small brass band raised his baton, sending Jules ducking back beneath the camera hood, and just at that moment the ropes stretching from a wooden windlass and anchor in the square to the emperor's feet high above began to tauten. Every voice was stilled. Just a faint creaking could be heard. The red flag continued to flutter in the breeze. Then the first few trumpets sounded.

Five or six members of the Commune leadership were standing in the square holding themselves as taut as the ropes. Anatole glanced at them, then searched the mass of faces being kept back at the rue de la Paix. Somewhere among them was Zéphyrine, who had been given a day off work for the occasion. He couldn't see her, but he felt an invisible rope tightening between them, something between pain and pleasure.

The wooden machinery began to groan under the pressure, and the men to grunt. They strained at the bar for several minutes to no effect. A sudden crash, and the ropes hung slack. The capstan, springing back, had catapulted six or seven workers into the air and onto their backs. But the column stood as tall and firm as ever. There was a collective sigh of disappointment. A few murmured treason.

Anatole did not know what to wish for. He'd learned to hate the glorification of the empire this column stood for. But somebody had made that statue, those reliefs. Couldn't you dismantle an idea without taking apart everything connected with it?

'At least I didn't waste a plate on that.' Jules emerged again, unfolding a gleaming white handkerchief to wipe his face. 'I suppose it's back to the waiting game now.'

'It looks as though it will be a while, doesn't it? Do you think you need me?' asked Anatole. 'I could get you a drink? They'll let me back in with my pass.'

'Go on then. Nothing will happen in a hurry. I can manage alone for a short time.'

Jules watched as Anatole skirted the mound of earth and branches, his bouncing stride speeding up nearer the half-built barricade. A brief discussion with a sentry – he would charm him, of course – and then he disappeared. Jules had a feeling that Anatole would not remember why he said he had gone. He sighed. He was thirsty, and hungry too, after all these hours of waiting around. But a different kind of emptiness, an unfamiliar void, was settling inside him.

That was it then. All those months of gently teasing, prodding and tempting Anatole. All the wondering while the silver sunbeam danced a little harder in Jules's heart, and Anatole had seemed to waver, and Jules had kept patience. The only comfort he had left was his own failure. So many times, on the very brink, he had drawn back, waited and watched, sensing the moment was not right – almost, if he was honest, enjoying the unsaidness of it all. There was a certain pleasure in uncertainty, after all. But he had spun things out for too long.

At first, Zéphyrine had confused Jules. Analytical as ever, he tried to frame Anatole's response to her, and looking for parallels he found a few. He knew, after all, that Anatole was already inclined to flirt with the unknown. He had witnessed his joy in plunging into an unfamiliar world, how difference and a certain kind of disobedience excited him. It made a strange kind of sense. Patience, Jules had counselled himself, as he waited and hoped for Anatole's attention to turn again.

That day in the Place Vendôme, Jules resigned himself to the fact that it wasn't going to. Under the light Zéphyrine cast, Jules would go on watching Anatole's love for her take shape like a heliograph in sunshine. Perhaps, he reflected, perhaps he should take one other consolation. He might have been incompetent in its execution, but when it came to his own feelings, Jules had never before loved longer, nor more deeply.

He mounted the steps of his portable darkroom and double-checked the developing baths. They were filled to the right level. There was plenty of water in the tank. He had forgotten nothing. But the activity failed to distract him. He sat on the wooden steps and waited, numbly, for something at last to happen. After a few minutes, a movement right at the top of the column caught his eye. An officer had suddenly appeared up there. What was he doing? Madness! No. He was removing the red flag. Nobody wants to see the red flag fall. Symbols were everything. The man climbed slowly down the inner staircase and the column seemed to sway as Jules watched. But still nothing happened.

Eventually a second winch was rolled into the square. Looking up from his perch, Jules lined the column up against a tall chimney pot, ready to spot the slightest deviation. At half past five he realised the angle between chimney and statue was slowly growing, and he slipped into the darkroom to prepare the first plate. You couldn't hurry this. The viscous liquid slid gleamingly, at its own pace, in its own time, from edge to edge of the glass, until the whole plate was covered. Outside, little by little at first, then with stronger movements, the whole column started to sway, to and fro, to and fro, the stone shifting with the gentlest of groans. As if it could hardly believe its own demise, the whole vast structure seemed to fall in slow motion, its shadow moving with it. It broke up in the air as it descended, inner organs spewing. Slowly, almost silently, clouds of dust spurted up and outwards, and as the haze thickened to a fog, there came a wild roar of jubilation.

When Jules emerged, ready to slot the plate quickly in place, the emperor was already lying on his back at the end of a trail of pale and broken boulders. His outstretched arm was broken off, his robes were cracked, and bare toes in Roman sandals pointed delicately skywards. And his laurelled head? It had snapped at the neck and turned aside.

The crowd streamed into the square. A young sailor got there first, and leapt over the body with a jubilant cry, his foot brushing the emperor's nose. 'Long live the Commune!' he yelled, his words echoing around the square. The statue averted its bronze eyes.

There were speeches of course. Red flags on the pedestal. Soon they would remember Jules and call for him. They shuffled into lines, jostling to be included in the photographs, sporting top hats and kepis, buttons and boots. So many staring at the lens, so steady and so serious. Everyone wanted their moment with the fallen emperor. Plenty wanted to spit in his stony face.

It didn't take long, out in the open, on a sunny day like this. All Jules needed was a few seconds of strong light. But in those few seconds how much could change. There was always a child who suddenly moved. A mother who looked down. An officer who glanced behind him at the wrong moment. It was so hard to get everyone looking in the right direction, doing the right thing, all at once.

Jules was a watcher. He didn't like to shout out, to tell people what to do or where to stand. That was meant to have been Anatole's job for the day. Luckily, one of the officers who had been guarding the darkroom volunteered to convey his instructions. Happy to help, he said, on such a glorious day as this. *Vive la Révolution*.

26.

17th May

A day later, Marie stood in the backstage lobby, and studied the envelope for clues.

'Aren't you going to open it then?' the doorkeeper said, over the top of his newspaper.

Not in front of you, she thought, holding the letter defensively against her chest, but she wasn't so stupid as to get on the wrong side of him.

'When did it arrive?' she asked. 'Today?'

He stuck out his lower lip as he pondered the question. You would think she'd asked him to draft a peace treaty with Versailles.

'No, I believe it was . . .' He got to his feet with a groan, and began to sift through a pile of papers and envelopes. Marie tried not to tap her toe. It was all very aggravating. 'Oh yes, it must have been yesterday.'

'Yesterday?' Marie was horrified.

'The messenger said it was urgent. I wonder who it's from,' he said.

You wonder, thought Marie, taking the envelope. Wonder away. You're not going to find out from me.

'Thank you so much . . .'

She skipped upstairs and found an empty dressing room. A few unused costumes for *If I Were King* hung lifeless on their pegs. Marie sat down in front of a mirror, made a space on the table among the jars of pearl powder and pomade, and laid down the envelope. She knew exactly who had sent it. She recognised the writing from the note that had summoned her to an audition a few days earlier. The Opéra. The most prestigious stage in Paris. It was almost too terrifying and thrilling to bear. How many times had she imagined a moment like this? She told herself not to rush. If it was the news she was hoping for, she ought to savour it.

Perhaps her luck was changing. Or perhaps she should make it change, she corrected herself, suddenly grim. If there was still no word from her brother by Monday week, she decided to grit her teeth and go back to the Prefecture. Her mouth crimped in disgust at the thought of Rigault's wet lips hiding in that repulsive beard. Next week she would decide. Now, with a deep, calming breath, she turned her attention back to the letter in her hand.

Marie could hardly bring herself to take the next step, but she knew she couldn't put it off any longer. She used a pair of tweezers to slice open the envelope. Scrambling down the page, her eyes struggled at first to read the lines in order. The first words she recognised were 'so sorry not to be able'. And then she understood. She had not been rejected . . . Monsieur Melchissédec had agreed to sing after all. Ah, that was a calculation Marie understood. The baritone's father, a police commissioner in the old regime, had just been arrested. Cooperation with the Commune was clearly the best strategy for his son at this point. But then she wondered if she had misjudged the Commune. Could it be so very terrible if it was prepared to open doors like this to people like her – doors that had for years been so very firmly and so very unfairly shut?

She went back to the letter. There had been a change of plan, it seemed. Unforeseeable circumstances. (Resignations?) And there wasn't much time – the first rehearsal was due to take place the following day. Could Mademoiselle Le Gall please confirm as quickly as possible that she was already familiar with the part of Leonora in Verdi's *Il Trovatore*? Unfortunately, they would only perform the final act on 22nd May – the execution scene – but this was the most demanding in the opera for any soprano. Marie was to understudy Madame Lacaze.

She knew it would have been unrealistic to hope for a solo. But even to be asked to understudy was more than enough for Marie: it kept hope alive, right to the very last moment. Any singer could catch a chill overnight and ruin her voice. She could trip and twist an ankle between the dressing room and the stage. The important thing for Marie was to be ready for anything.

She knew every note. And more importantly, she had already thought long and hard about how she would play Leonora, if she ever got the chance. Not as a wilting wallflower, but bold and brave, impetuous and passionate. After all, she had to be ready to lay down her life for her lover.

'"Wrapped in this dark night",' she began to sing to the mirror, '"you do not know that I am close to you."' This had long been her favourite aria. She would make an audience swoon with the smoothest legato, trilling crescendos, crystalline pianissimo. She would be so sweet and sad that no eye in the house could remain dry. Her thoughts rushed ahead. Perhaps, in rehearsal, she would sing so beautifully, so convincingly, that once he realised her talents, the director would find an excuse to demote Madame Lacaze. '"On the rosy wings of love . . ."'

She would have to see. But this made up for so much. Really, *Trovatore* was more than Marie could have hoped for: gypsies, disguise, civil war, love . . . destiny of course. And vengeance, terrible vengeance.

Just before six that evening, as if in retribution for the felling of the Vendôme column, a vast, thunderous boom resounded through Paris. Every building in the city seemed to rock. Marie was hard at work in a practice room in the attics of the Théâtre Lyrique with a young baritone also recently elevated from the chorus; she grabbed hold of the piano, and found herself gabbling a prayer. Anatole, hurrying to meet Zéphyrine, wondering whether this might be the evening she finally let him accompany her up the hill and into her room, hoping it would be, steadied himself on the nearest lamp post. Zéphyrine herself was just a few streets away. She stopped dead with her hands over her ears, crushing her black glass earrings so their spikes dug into her neck. Abandoning his printing, Jules rushed to throw open the studio window:

it was like being caught in the roar of an express train as it rushes through a country station. He gasped for breath. His ears sang.

But a train passes quickly, and is gone. This grew louder, as if the skies themselves contained an army. Above the southern rooftops, a towering, roaring cloud, hundreds of feet high, appeared from nowhere. It was like an evil genie. From deep within the clouding smoke, the endless firing continued, a violent crick-cracking like musketry, but deeper. Or the hammer blows of an almighty anvil, only quicker. From this distance, lit by the sun's glow, the cloud had a capricious, uncapturable beauty: innumerable silvery ostrich plumes, continually unfurling, whirling, twisting in the air, revolving round themselves and others, endlessly and speedily rolling in and out of one another. White and black and grey and yellow, the colours kept changing places as Jules watched. The metallic rattle and ringing continued. And from the sky fell burning timber, molten lead, empty bullet cases and human remains.

It was only a matter of minutes, but it seemed forever. Finally the monster softened into mere smoke and dispersed. The noise died down and elements drifted away to spread the news around the city. Just a few wispy shreds hovered above the empty space on the avenue Rapp where once a cartridge factory had stood, where hundreds of women and girls used to work. Nobody knew who was to blame.

27.

21st May

The applause died down in the Tuileries Garden and the musicians of the National Guard's brass band put away their instruments, their minds on a cooling drink.

'Citizens!' A staff officer spoke from the conductor's platform. 'Yesterday Monsieur Thiers promised to enter Paris. Still he is not here. We say he will never enter our city. So you are cordially invited to rejoin us in the gardens next Sunday, right here, to enjoy the second of our concerts for the benefit of the widows and orphans of the Commune. We look forward to seeing you then.'

Under the trees, the four friends parted. Marie was the first to bid her farewells.

'Sleep well! You must look your best tomorrow night!' Anatole called after her.

'I hope I will. See you at the Opéra.' She hurried off, still hoping some mishap might strike Madame Lacaze in the night.

A glimpse of a face in a crowd soon unsettled her. It was so much like Emile's that she diverted her course through the lime trees, about to run right up to the young man. Of course it wasn't him. She realised just in time. How could it have been? A trick of the light, and too much wishing, too hard and for too long. His resemblance to her brother had been uncannily close and Marie could not shake off the feeling that Emile was close now too. Her nerves must be getting the better of her.

Jules waited for Anatole in the shade of a tree, and looked away. Anatole was making one last effort to persuade Zéphyrine to let him walk her home. He was thoughtful enough to glance quickly round to check Jules wasn't watching before he slid his fingers round the nape of her neck, lightly stroking the soft short hairs hidden beneath her cap in a way which he knew would make her arch her back. She did of course, pushing towards him and bending away at the same time.

'Let me come home with you,' he begged again.

Her head was light as spindrift, her body melting like tar in the sun. If Anatole came even as far as the bottom of her lane, she didn't think she could send him home tonight. She thought she could trust him now. He had convinced her that he wouldn't disappear overnight like Marie's banker. Better than that, over the sewing and the chopping and the stirring, women had been talking. They argued a lot: was it right for a bastard child to have the same rights as a legitimate one? They compared notes too: how much easier it was to walk down the street these days without a man trying to take advantage. And they discussed other stuff too – important, secret stuff – in lowered voices. Zéphyrine had picked up a thing or two at last. Despite what Gran'mère had always said, Zéphyrine had worked out for herself there didn't always have to be a baby. There were ways of stopping it, things you could do.

But the next day was Monday. At six in the morning she was due in the kitchens, by six that evening at the Opéra. This wasn't something to rush. They had all the time in the world. They could wait a little longer.

'Tomorrow's too big a night! I don't want to be falling asleep, do I? Nor you either.'

He kissed her evasive eyes. 'I won't stay. Just to the bottom of the hill?'

'It'll be another long walk for you for nothing,' she said firmly.

'Not nothing. More time with you.'

'Go home with Jules. Who could blame him for turning you out altogether, when you leave him alone so long? Then where would you be?' She raised her voice deliberately.

'I'm not that hard-hearted,' Jules called back. 'But I am going home now myself. See you later. Goodnight.'

They heard his footsteps on the gravel. Zéphyrine couldn't find it in herself to push Anatole after him, and he made no effort to go. Instead, he kissed the back of her neck.

'Come on then,' she said, twisting with pleasure. 'I'll show you where I live. It's about time. But you mustn't stay for long. You know you've got to get a decent night's sleep tonight.'

It was a long walk up the hill, and they had almost given up on words by the time they reached the house. There was no sign of Madame Mouton, or any of the other lodgers, but they were silent on the stairs. Once the door was safely shut behind them, and Zéphyrine had lit a candle, the first thing Anatole noticed was the gingerbread pig on the beam.

They had come too close, too many times, to be very shy with one other now. There was awkwardness of course. Moments like this are rarely perfect. Bodies have to work things out. At one point Zéphyrine's eyes filled with tears and she closed them, and Anatole kissed them. Saying goodbye was very hard.

There was a sticky heat to the night, which felt more like August than May. Back in his own bed, Anatole lay with a sheet tangled round his legs, his body still aching with tenderness and lust. He had got home at midnight, true to his word, but his mind would not let him sleep. He had thought it would never happen, and finally it had. It made him want even more from Zéphyrine.

He loved her independence, though perhaps she wasn't quite as independent as she liked to make out. Certainly not of Rose and her influence. Equal pay for equal work was one thing of course. Fair enough. But all this talk in the clubs of marriage as slavery . . . Did Zéphyrine really believe that? He hoped not. He would go mad if they didn't discuss their future soon, if he couldn't persuade her.

Something changed in the quality of the bombardment's rumble, which put sleep out of reach entirely. He might as well get up and see what he could see, instead of lying there alone, listening and worrying. Anatole wrapped the sheet round himself and stumbled, yawning, into the drawing room.

Jules was still up, watching from the balcony. 'Something's happening. I'm not sure what. Over towards the Arc de Triomphe, I think. It's hard to tell exactly where.'

Anatole grunted, and joined him at the window. Nothing outside could be more important than what was going on in his head. He had to talk about it. Except for that one terrible argument, Jules had always been so understanding about Zéphyrine. Surprisingly so, really – you couldn't ask for a better friend. He ought to be the first to know. It would be wrong not to tell him first. After a few minutes, Anatole blurted it out.

'I've decided, Jules. I've got to do it, as soon as possible. It's easy now anyway. You don't even have to go to a church. They'll do it in the City Hall, under a red flag.'

Jules glanced at him: bare-shouldered and sweaty and dishevelled. There was nothing to say. He turned his attention back to the sky.

'She can always say no,' Anatole continued. 'I'll understand. There are lots of good reasons why she might. But I think it's right to ask. I think the time has come.'

Jules sighed, so quietly that perhaps Anatole didn't notice.

'So you're going to propose,' he said.

28.

22nd May

Monday. Zéphyrine almost overslept. Anatole hadn't wanted her to put her clothes on again just to see him out. He would be careful, he promised. After a last lingering look at her, he took the candle, and she must have fallen asleep before he finished tiptoeing from the building. How strange it was to wake up naked. She quickly washed and dressed, and headed down from the attic. Just as she reached the second landing, the funereal booming ring of the church bell began to sound. The alarm peal caught her like bad news, in the pit of her stomach. Almost simultaneously, fists began to hammer on the door below, and a scream reached her ears.

'The Versailles troops are here!'

Zéphyrine's muscles refused to obey orders. She had to grab the rickety banister to stop herself hurtling down to the flagstones at the bottom. Madame Mouton seemed to have collapsed already, from shock, in the doorway.

'They're here! They're in Paris.'

A small ragged boy with a red armband, not more than

ten years old, stood on the doorstep. He repeated the words mechanically, as if saying them enough times would make them believable. There had been false alarms before.

Zéphyrine pushed past Madame Mouton, took the boy's shoulders and shook him hard. 'It's impossible,' she said. 'It can't be true. There's been no warning.'

He wriggled out of her grip, and screamed into her face. 'It's true! It's true! The Versailles troops are here! The Versailles troops are in Paris!'

'Who sent you?'

'Rose. Rose Lenoir. I'm her cousin. She's at the town hall. She says to come right away.'

Zéphyrine turned to the concierge. 'Take the children to the cellar. Keep them safe.'

This brought Madame Mouton back to life. She pulled herself back to her feet and planted her hands on her hips. 'You must be joking. Do you think I'm hiding them now?' she said, elbows like indignant wings. 'They'll do their share, don't worry.'

Zéphyrine hugged Madame Mouton, eyes tightly closed. They squeezed each other with all their strength, and then Zéphyrine rushed off down the hill, almost immediately running into a fédéré who was buckling on his ammunition belt as he came out of his own doorway.

'What are the orders?' she shouted.

'I don't know,' he shouted back.

And everywhere it was the same, until they realised that there were no orders. There wasn't a plan. Every neighbourhood had to fight for itself.

The throng outside their town hall was muted and scared. Everyone wanted someone else to tell them what to do. From the garrison up at the windmill came urgent drumming – the call to arms. Zéphyrine waited for people to pour into the streets in their hundreds, all ready and willing to defend Montmartre to the bitter end. Two months earlier, when the cannon were being stolen, everyone had rushed out without a backward glance. But half the men here weren't even in uniform. It was if they were scared to be seen in their kepis.

And still not a sound from the heights of Montmartre, from the guns they had risked so much to save. When the whisper of rumour began, it was hard to know what to believe. People said the Communard general had arrived up there in the early hours and found a rusting abandoned mess of artillery, that nobody had thought to take care of Montmartre's precious gun park. Surely that couldn't be true? Surely, after all these weeks, Montmartre was better prepared than this?

At first, Zéphyrine couldn't find Rose anywhere. She was about to go and look at the ambulance station when the door of the town hall opened, and there she was, limping awkwardly but determinedly down the steps. Zéphyrine called and waved, and Rose saw her, and changed direction.

'What's the news?'

'They've taken Trocadéro. That's where the shells are coming from – listen! There's fighting on the streets on the Right Bank. And the station at Saint-Lazare has fallen already!'

So close. What could that mean for Anatole? The drumming thumped through Zéphyrine's head. She couldn't think. But she knew her duty was to her neighbourhood.

'And here?'

'Hard to tell. Something's happening in the cemetery.'

'Fighting?' Hand-to-hand, above her grandparents' grave?

'Yes. Barricades, everyone is saying. That's the first thing. We need more barricades. We've got to get building again, right away! But there doesn't seem any strategy. No more gold braid, they keep saying inside. No more golden words, I say.'

'The generals can't abandon us!'

No answer.

'Let's go to the boulevard de Clichy, and see if we can help there.' Rose began to push her way through the milling men.

'I'm coming,' said Zéphyrine, her voice rising.

Paris woke to find a third of the city already taken. The troops had swarmed in during the warm night, thousands pouring through the gates of Passy and Auteuil, Saint-Cloud and Sèvres. Doorway to doorway, they had crept through the streets. The outer suburbs fell first, quickly and easily, and there was no struggle either in the wealthy western neighbourhoods that were next on the soldiers' route. A straggle of Commune volunteers fled east, defeated. By two in the morning, Versailles forces had already seized the grassy heights of Trocadéro while another government column pushed on down the vast avenue des Champs-Élysées. By morning, sympathetic residents were getting blue, white and red armbands out of hiding, arming themselves with the tricolour of the invaders.

All along the Grands Boulevards, well-dressed crowds came out to cheer on the red-breeched troops. They clapped their hands, as if they were at the opera, and called 'Bravo!', as if a battle had been won. Above the marching soldiers, coins showered down from the windows and jingled on the pavements. In this part of Paris, the stones had stayed firmly in place. The people here sat tight, mostly, waiting to be saved, playing cards to pass the time. As soon as they knew they were safe, out they rushed, wine bottles waving. Gentlemen stood smiling while their wives' arms opened, smothering sweaty necks with silk and satin, sowing kisses under kepis.

'How many fédérés have you killed?' they asked.

A young soldier posed with a rifle he had yet to fire, and pretended to pick off a Communard sniper from an attic window. He bowed to laughter and applause. Salvation was sweet, so painlessly delivered.

Jules did his best to block the way.

'You can't stop me,' Anatole said through his teeth. He tried to wrench his friend's wrist from the doorframe, pushing and pulling shoulder against shoulder. They wrestled cheek to cheek, and Jules's breath was in his face, hot and sweet and familiar. 'You can't honestly expect me to stay here and cower.'

'Why not? Why not, for God's sake? It's all over now. Look how quickly the government troops reached Trocadéro.' Unlike Anatole, Jules had stayed awake for the rest of the night, watching from the studio, trying to decide what to do. 'They'll be here in a matter of hours. So surrender now. Better not to be captured in arms.'

'Better for who?' Anatole finally broke through the human barricade, a scar of broken stitches on his chest from a ripped-off pocket. He turned round. Jules stood in the doorway, hands hanging uselessly by his side. 'What do you know? This isn't your fight. You've never understood it.'

Jules didn't deny it. 'At least don't wear your uniform,' he said, his voice cracking. 'Please. It's madness. They'll pick you out like this.' He tried to snap his fingers, to show how fast, but they slid past each other without a sound. 'You won't even make it to the barracks, not from here.'

Jules had a point. Paris was a strange battlefield, and there had been no love for the Commune in this bourgeois neighbourhood at the best of times. It seemed all wrong to Anatole, after all this, to set off to fight without his uniform. But if Jules would worry less . . . Anatole shook his head, and hurried back to his room to change. When he set out again, Jules was still standing on the landing. Anatole kissed him goodbye, once on each cheek. They hesitated for a moment, forehead to hot, bowed forehead, and then Anatole hammered down the stairs.

Marie scalded her tongue and dropped her cup when she heard the news. The spilled coffee left an ugly spattering of brown on the bodice of her dress, and puddled on the counter. Annalise, on the morning shift behind the bar and none too sure how long that shift would now last, was quick to help.

'Here, use this.' A damp cloth, with a sour milk smell. The barmaid folded her arms, and glanced at the café owner resentfully. 'I think we should shut up now. It's going to turn nasty. And I'm not staying here if it does.'

'I heard that, young lady. And don't you roll your eyes at me. We'll shut up when I say so. There are workers still to be fed and watered. You can't guard a city on an empty stomach.'

As he spoke, a crowd of fédérés swarmed in, calling for brandy.

'We are betrayed,' they said. 'Betrayed again. Let's drink to the Commune while we can. The Commune or Death!'

Marie pushed her way out, eyes staring straight ahead. If Versailles could only have waited one more day. Just one more day. That was her first thought. When all the other thoughts came crowding into her mind, pushing and shoving each other out of the way, she wished it could be her only one.

No wonder these neighbourhoods were falling so quickly. Anatole passed a few hastily assembled barricades, already quite abandoned. When he reached the headquarters of his old battalion, he found the door bolted, just as Jules had predicted.

He had run all the way, and sweat began to stream from his face as soon as he stopped, salt stinging his eyes. He leaned against the wall, sliding down to a despairing crouch, hands in his sticky hair. Anatole waited for his pulse to stop galloping, then looked up and down the street, to check that it was definitely as deserted as it seemed. Picking himself up, he brushed off his trousers, tidied himself up. In his rush, he'd missed a collar stud: the back of his neck gaped. He found a spare stud in his pocket, and quickly fastened it. He should have thanked Jules properly for his advice. It was the right decision. Anatole was glad to be in civilian clothes, and unremarkable.

No sound of footsteps. Every shopfront was shuttered, and most of the windows above them too, nobody prepared to stir until they knew what was happening. Perhaps a mile away now, the rattle of gunfire and thunder of shells continued, but the stillness of this street was overpowering.

Zéphyrine had always thought her fingers pretty tough, but it wasn't long before her hands were blistered and bleeding, and Rose's too.

Just after nine, the first cannon on the hillside behind them began finally to fire half-heartedly. Of course they were quickly answered, perhaps from Trocadéro. One shell landed somewhere on the hillside immediately above them, and Zéphyrine braced herself against the wall as the whole street shuddered. Then she went back to her heaving: she was trying to unroot a reluctant fan of iron that had once protected a lime tree. The tree itself had been burned for fuel in the siege. At last the metal came out of the earth, and, bit by bit, with the help of Madame Mouton and her daughter, Zéphyrine dragged it towards the rising pile in the middle of the street. The barricade was still so low at either end that a child playing could have jumped it at a gallop. But it was rising steadily, and there were no children playing here. Everyone was helping, and the strongest had managed to haul a small cannon into the middle of the barricade, wedging it in with a good solid bedstead on one side and a ladder on the other. The praying hands of a stone madonna poked through its rungs.

A muffled cheer went up as a mattress came tumbling down from an upstairs window a little way up the street. A group of women were going from house to house to beg for more.

'The wine merchants!' cried Rose. 'They'll give up their casks for us, won't they?'

'They must. Tell them it's by order of the Commune!' said Zéphyrine.

The shopkeepers didn't need orders, and their customers were happy enough to keep emptying more. Before long, wooden barrels came rolling hollowly down the hill like eggs on Easter Sunday. Women and children crouched at the bottom, ready to intercept the careering, clattering creatures and pack them with stones and cobbles and earth. Earth! Earth! That was the thing, everyone agreed. Beware of ricochet, said the white-haired veterans of '48. Heap the earth up in front too, absorb every bullet.

Towards noon, a messenger on horseback came clattering by, briefly interrupting the fiery sparks of mattock, spade and pickaxe. He brought leaflets from the leadership, printed already. 'Let Paris bristle with barricades,' they shouted. Rose and Zéphyrine looked at their barricade. It was a foot or two higher, but you couldn't say it bristled. They redoubled their efforts.

Marie retreated to her room, feeling cold and sick. It was over. Everything was over. She might never have another chance to sing on the stage of the Opéra, and she was trapped, in every way. Just as she had anticipated, she would be forever tainted by her association with the Commune – having her name in tonight's programme would see to that, no matter that the performance would never take place. The situation felt too enormous to comprehend. Marie had no idea what might happen next or what she could hope for. Survival, she supposed. She was good at that. As for the others, she only hoped that Jules had been able to make Anatole and Zéphyrine see sense

234

that morning, that they had all been together when the news broke. Something seemed to have shifted a little the night before. It wasn't impossible. Surely Jules would have managed to talk them both out of rushing off to the barricades? Anyone could see that the time for heroics was over. Surrender was the Commune's best hope with the army inside the city walls. If ever there was a time to lie low, this was it.

Then a note arrived that turned Marie white. She ran out into the street after its ragged messenger.

'Wait!' she shouted. 'Who gave you this? How did he look? What did he say? Come back!'

But the child did not stop or answer. He had done what he'd been paid for, and there was plenty more money to be earned on a day like this if you were sharp about it.

Almost unable to believe the handwriting on this scrap of paper, Marie went through every word again, and then again.

'I am in Paris,' it read. 'My unit is stationed at the Luxembourg Garden. As soon as I can, I will come to you. Meanwhile, courage! Emile.'

She looked at the date. Today was Emile's name day. It was a sign, wasn't it? She wanted to believe in destiny. It must mean that they would see each other soon. All she had to do was sit it out and be patient for a little longer. At the end of her street she could see a new barricade rising. On the walls were new posters, wet and glistening with fresh paste, a message from the Commune for the soldiers of Versailles urging them to break ranks now, for the last time.

'*Brothers!*' it said. '*The hour of the battle of the people against their oppressors has arrived. Do not abandon the workers' cause!*

Do as your brothers did on March the eighteenth! Unite with the people who are your people. Long live the Republic! Long live the Commune!'

Marie shook her head. Emile was a professional soldier through and through. He would never be persuaded to desert. It was a lost cause.

Down in the cellar, barely able to breathe, Jules could not know what was happening above his head. The darkness made the colours of his imaginings more lurid, and his knotted guts felt as heavy as iron. He tortured himself with elaborate precision. He pictured Anatole lying in a gutter, a bullet wound, a pool of blood collecting round his skull. He wondered if there was anything else he could have said to stop him leaving, and why, at the very last, he had left so much unsaid. In the deep shadows by the coal mound, a couple of maids invisibly wept.

Deciding he would prefer to know the worst, Jules eventually dragged himself back upstairs. He emerged into a silent, deserted building, bricks and mortar holding their breath while the sounds of battle crashed and whined outside. As he opened the main door, confused by the latch – the concierge usually appeared from the shadows, just when she was needed, key in hand, pipe in mouth – Jules had no idea who held this street.

The pavement was still intact at least, he noted. Jules crossed the road to try to get a better sense of things and a cascade of broken glass instantly tumbled from somewhere high above, shattering into smaller pieces at his feet. An unidentifiable rifle muzzle emerged from the window of the corner house, and the crack of firing began.

'Get back inside, you fool!' The scream came from a storey down. A fédéré at different window was half-hidden in thick puffs of drifting smoke. 'They'll be here any minute. You're right in the middle of it.'

Jules froze on the pavement. His eardrums were fluttering from the screaming of the machine guns – they sounded so unimaginably close – and he could barely make out the man's words.

'Get back inside, I said!'

Then a hand reached out from the building behind him and snatched him backwards and inside. He lost his balance and landed in an ungainly heap on the floor. The porter who had pulled him in stood staring down at him, ready to throw him out again if necessary.

'Thank you,' said Jules, sitting up and rubbing the back of his neck. The porter's wife nudged her husband, and he offered Jules a hand up.

'Come in here,' she said, leading the way through a door at the back of the porter's office and into a simple sitting room. Jules's heart began to beat faster again. 'Whose side are you on?' he asked.

'Nobody's,' replied the man quickly, glancing at his wife, who nodded.

'We just want peace, and our children safe,' she agreed, elbowing her husband in the ribs. 'But I recognised you,' she said. 'You're the American photographer, aren't you? You live opposite? I've seen you, with your camera and all that stuff, your cart, always coming and going.'

Jules didn't think he'd ever seen either of them before, but he supposed they must always have been here. He nodded, and then a cry came from right under his feet, making him jump.

'Mama! Mama! What's happening? Who's there?'

The woman stamped on the floorboards and bellowed out: 'Nothing. It's all right. Nothing to worry about. Now keep quiet like I told you, and for pity's sake don't come out unless we say . . .'

Husband and wife exchanged a worried glance.

'They told us we've got to keep the shutters open upstairs.' The man rolled his eyes up to the ceiling.

There was a loud rattle of gunfire outside. Hard to know where it came from.

'Who told you?'

'There are National Guardsmen taking shelter up there. We couldn't stop them. We didn't know if we should. We didn't know what to do.'

Jules nodded. So this was street-fighting. He'd imagined swords flashing outside on cobbles, elaborate oaths, men leaping fantastically from balcony to balcony. Something like *The Three Musketeers*. Absurd really, in this day and age. Street-fighting wasn't really street-fighting, he realised, but house-fighting. All over Paris men were on rooftops and window ledges, hollowing through walls and between cellars, moving unseen from house to house, bursting in on trembling families. Barricades were useless. All you had to do is get above them.

The building began to shake. Not with an explosion, but a series of blows. Every wall shivered. Jules and his new companions dropped to the floor, just as a tremendous crash sounded immediately above them.

'My God,' said the woman, clutching her husband, wiping her eyes, coughing. A blizzard of dust and plaster was still hurtling down. 'They've broken through upstairs. The *Versaillais* are in this house.'

Firing followed instantly. Three shots, two muffled thuds, and another scattering of snowy dust on the listeners below. They gazed at each other like ghosts. Several pairs of boots pounded down the stairs and the door burst open. It banged against the wall so hard that in the hallway a glass-framed picture smashed to the ground with a pathetic high-pitched tinkle.

Three soldiers came in with rifles raised, ready to fire. The men seemed huge in this little room, with their weapons and boots and savage energy. They towered over the tiny concierge and his wife, both backed against the far wall, chests rising and falling uncontrollably. Wild eyes stared through floating dust. Jules, to his shame, had dropped behind a faded armchair. He slowly rose to his feet, speaking in English first, and deliberately exaggerating his Americanisms, forcing each sentence to rise in an unspoken question. Then he repeated himself in French.

'No need for that, gentlemen.' He braced himself and stepped forward with a hand extended to shake the nearest soldier's hand. All three muzzles instantly turned on him. He battled a flinch and held up both hands instead, half-placating, half-surrendering. 'Calm down. Take it easy.'

Two pairs of eyes slid towards their officer's, who shook his head slightly, but did not lower his gun.

'He's a foreigner. They're the troublemakers, they say. The International. They mustn't be spared.'

Panic geysered up inside him. He took a deep breath, and locked his stomach. 'Do I look like a member of the International Workingmen's Association, gentlemen?'

What did a member of the International look like? Everyone in the room was wondering the same thing. Jules remembered Marie's confusion on the day the Commune was declared, and Anatole's easy answer. Weight shifted.

'The rubbish of every nation in Europe has come to destroy Paris,' muttered one soldier, like an obedient parrot.

'I'm not from Europe. I'm an American citizen. Take me to the embassy and check my credentials if you wish. But first I'd be obliged if you would put your weapons down.'

Nobody did.

'They were harbouring Communards,' said the soldier on the left. This one was sandy-haired. Well-scrubbed. Anxious to do the right thing, and follow every order to the letter. 'That's a crime.'

He stepped forward and his gun swung towards the concierge's wife. She dropped to her knees, her fists clasped in appeal, and began to moan. 'We've done nothing.'

'No, no, please, stop,' said her husband. 'They forced their way in here. We couldn't stop them.'

'That's what they all say.'

When nobody spoke, comprehension dawned, and she began to whimper. This strange high-pitched noise penetrated to the cellars below, where her unseen children shifted audibly in alarm. Straight away, the men trained their guns on the floor, and the woman's whimper turned into a scream. 'No! Be quiet! Shut your mouths! I told you to be quiet!'

One soldier panicked and fired into the wooden boards. There was more screaming and scuffling, and Jules, without thinking, grabbed two of the three gun muzzles and forced them upwards.

'They're children, not Communards. Children. But what are you? Do you now kill children in cold blood?'

A terrible silence, in which a distant thud of cannon could be heard, and a timid voice, calling out, 'Mama?'

Finally the officer relented, his decision hastened by the fall of shell, and another shower of plaster, as the engineers upstairs broke through the next wall.

'Get them up here,' he ordered the sandy-coloured fellow, brushing off his own epaulettes. 'But we must see them for ourselves. And be careful. Even children can be armed.'

They edged in at gunpoint, all six of them. Their coal-dusted hands were raised, except for the oldest boy's. He had the youngest on his hip, and was using his own free hand to try to persuade the baby to hold his up too. But the baby squirmed and resisted, and the concierge had to stop his wife from rushing towards them, without making it too obvious that he was holding her back.

The officer stared at the children appraisingly. They looked back discreetly, through lowered lashes, or gazed at their feet, all except for a curly-haired girl of about seven, who was missing her front teeth. Mouth slightly open, she stared back without blinking. When the silence continued, she lowered her arms, and folded them across her scrawny chest. That was enough.

'Take them away. The whole family. Scum. Red scum.'

There was nothing Jules could do to stop them.

As resistance increased, the invading army slowed its pace. It was steady. It was systematic. The generals took no unnecessary risks. It wasn't just the wide straight arteries of Second-Empire

Paris they had to deal with. There was a secret city below, an underground Paris, its labyrinthine reflection. Beneath Haussmann's drawing board, a network of cellars and crypts and quarries wound for mile after complicated mile. No general could possibly know what might be happening there. If the Versailles army didn't take care, they might find the ground opening beneath their feet without the slightest warning.

Hadn't the Communards mined the sewers and filled the catacombs with gunpowder? They had a chain of electricity, didn't they, to set it alight? Or something more devious still: something else that could ignite all of Paris at once. This Commune would die on its feet rather than surrender, everyone said. They were animals, weren't they, after all? Rabid beasts. None more than the women – bitches on heat. You don't take any chances with wild animals, do you?

Anyway, these makeshift barricades were easy to manage. Once you had possession of the buildings above, it couldn't be simpler for a sniper to pick off the Communard defenders below. Foolhardy types in trousers or in skirts, the ones who stood upright and sang and shouted and waved their red flags in half-crazed defiance – these were the quickest of all to kill. The *Versaillais* stalked them like cats in trees, getting rid of fledglings in a nest without even a scratch. They didn't think twice about taking down the children. *Les Enfants Perdus*, they were called – the lost kids – ragamuffins who couldn't lose faith in the Commune now, not after it had put food in their bellies and a pencil between their fingers, when nobody else had cared. The Students of the Commune, another band of fighters called themselves. *Les Pupilles de la Commune.*

At the Place de la Concorde, Thiers's army came to an uneasy halt, waiting to be certain it was quite safe to attack. It was hard to believe that the Commune's Committee of Defence could be quite this unprepared. Surely they had something up their sleeve?

It wasn't long before Anatole ran into a National Guard battalion that took him in. Its temporary leader looked him up and down, and decided he could be trusted. It hardly mattered that he was a stranger – anyone prepared to take up arms against the invaders was a brother. Anyone who understood the urgency, and hadn't already slunk away.

'Here.' A dented musket, and a belt of cartridges, almost full. Not every bit of abandoned weaponry had been seized by the enemy yet. Anatole had time to sling them across his shoulder, and then they were in retreat, darting from doorway to doorway, eyes alive to the slightest movement down the street. The houses were so tall and pale. There were so many windows to watch at once. He didn't want to be alone here. He made sure to keep up with his new companions, though it was hard to run while you were looking over your shoulder. Anatole thought he knew these streets better than any other part of Paris. But they had a way of looking unfamiliar now. You could lose yourself if you didn't keep up. Once, when his back and skull were pressed against the iron hinges of a double door, as he flattened himself out of sight, Anatole heard breathing that was not his own. The skin on his face and neck crawled with the realisation that there was just a thin panel of wood between him and an unseen stranger. He waited for the head-high hatch to slide open, to expose him. A shot at that range would be the end of everything.

A hissed order saved him. Telltale red trousers were glimpsed in the distance. The zing and ping of bullets fell short. His guts unclamped and the men escaped into a side street, and kept on retreating until they finally reached something they could defend.

That mountainous barricade, built high on the Tuileries terrace, stone and sand and plans and foresight – surely that would be another matter altogether? Anatole collapsed into the ditch behind it, shoulder bruised and aching. No need to keep retreating. His breath moaned out of him, between his knees, and his eyes slowly focused on the flask of brandy a hand had thrust before his face.

'Your health.' He pressed the cold metal against his cheek, then swigged until his throat burned. There were more men here, in uniform even, and still plenty of gold braid. Someone must know what to do. Even better, these militiamen seemed happy to ignore the new arrivals until they had recovered themselves.

Anatole put his head back and closed his eyes. He wished he had thought to bring Zéphyrine's photograph. More than ever he wanted to see her face, to draw inspiration from her fierce pride. He had stared at it so often – every time he took out or put away his violin. He held a perfect memory of the image in his mind. But the image was beginning to feel fragile. He had to keep thinking about every detail, to remember the precise tilt of her chin, the look in her eyes, the crackle of her hair and the faint scratch on the print. If he could just keep holding it, Anatole thought, if he could cradle the image in his head, like an egg nestling in the palm of his hand, it would not crack. And wherever she was, with luck, she would not break either.

29.

23rd May

Tuesday. The sun rose again, bright and implacable, sucking the colour from the streets. A menacing shuttered emptiness hung between the houses. It would be the last time the Commune leaders met at the Hôtel de Ville: there were tears and drama but no useful decisions. A few hours later, west of Montmartre, Batignolles fell. As each neighbourhood collapsed into the hands of the National Government, the house searches started in earnest. The once outlawed military police force was back at work, and primed for revenge.

Before the army could advance, every area had to be cleared. The denunciations began, and also the arrests, and the reprisals.

On the Left Bank, the military school filled up with prisoners. On the right, the accused were herded into public parks planned ten years earlier so the city could breathe. Behind elaborate iron gates, on dappled lawns, shots rang out over and over again. And still Montmartre waited for the attack.

* * *

Jules went out to look for bread, and ducked his head at the sight of police officers banging on doors. He calculated the number of houses that lay between them. He reckoned he had an hour or two, and hurried back.

Until that day, he had always respected Anatole's privacy, never entering his bedroom without knocking, though God knows he'd longed to. Force of habit made him knock now, and listen before pushing open the door. The shutters were still closed. Staring into shadows, Jules could, for a moment, persuade himself that Anatole was still there, asleep. But as his eyes began to work in the half-light he saw the bed was empty and unmade, a white ocean of sheets. And there it was, flung over a chair at the end of the bed, buttons gently gleaming, the uniform he had to destroy, to save his own skin and Anatole's too, with luck.

Jules looked at it with venom. He should have imposed his will. Issued ultimatums. But if he'd threatened Anatole, told him to clear off, he might have believed Jules meant it. Anatole would have been just as happy slumming it in Montmartre or with the students in the Latin Quarter as he was in their smart part of town. Jules would have lost him entirely.

He gathered up the jacket and trousers, and, catching a faint familiar fragrance, buried his face in the stiff wool. Bergamot and orange blossom. The scent of English tea. It was the eau de cologne he'd bought for Anatole to celebrate the end of the siege. Anatole had looked at him thoughtfully, then put the cut-glass bottle on his shaving stand. Jules said nothing when

Anatole finally began to slap it on in the mornings a few days after meeting Zéphyrine.

Stupid to indulge in sentiment now. Bundling the clothing in his arms as best he could, he ran up to the studio two steps at a time, dumped Anatole's uniform on the floor, and threw back the darkroom curtain. Calm down, he told himself. He shouldn't have run. He was out of breath and shaky. Or was that how fear worked? Was it simply the thought of being caught in the act?

A few days earlier he'd noticed that he was reaching the end of his supply of collodion, and spent a careful hour making up a new batch, mixing up alcohol, ether, zinc bromide and nitric acid. Then the silver nitrate solution. His hands still bore trace of black.

Jules' stained fingers reached for the new bottle, neatly labelled, deliberately unmistakable. He unstoppered it and sniffed, just to be quite sure. It smelled of bleach and almost rotten pears.

Opening the window, Jules leaned out and lowered Anatole's uniform onto the tiles, piling up jacket, trousers and cap, as far away as he could manage. He thought of funeral pyres. He hoped he had not miscalculated. No, this would surely work. He had studied the reports in the photographic journals so many times: devastating accidental explosions, studios blown up in London, Paris, Birmingham, New York. This ought to do the trick, though it was hard to predict the force of such an experiment. To be on the safe side, he moved his cameras and tripods, heaving them down the stairs, one after another. Then he rescued all the unused plates, and wooden baths. As soon as he had finished up here, he would take the lot down to the courtyard, where his mobile darkroom was waiting.

Back on the roof, his calmness deserted him. He had always been so good at calculating time, to the very second, and now he was running out of it. He had to hurry.

A flash of sun on glass as he sloshed the chemicals out onto the heap of clothes. He tossed the bottle aside; it rattled into the gutter without breaking. Jules climbed back through the window, washed his hands with soap and water – rubbing distractedly at the black stains – struck a match and lit a candle. This he chucked on top of the soaked bundle of clothing, throwing himself to the ground on the far side of the studio in almost the same movement. His hands clutched his head. Whiteness streaked red, then black. A bright shriek in his ears. Another four panes of shattered glass fell from their frame.

Proclamations came thick and fast.

'Let good citizens arise! The enemy is within our walls!'

'To arms! To arms! Paris is impregnable.'

Zéphyrine squatted beside the trouser legs of a young Montmartre fédéré. His machine gun was trained on the empty street ahead. The thunder of artillery and the repeated crack of rifle fire kept mounting, and it seemed to come from everywhere at once, echoing off stone walls and inside your own head so you couldn't begin to make out where the enemy was hiding. The air seemed thicker, and when you breathed, it was like inhaling fireworks. At the back of her throat, Zéphyrine tasted gunpowder: gritty, sulphurous. And suddenly, she couldn't stop swallowing. It was as if her body imagined you could be rid of fear by devouring it. But back it came, sour and sharp. Forehead bowed against the grubby canvas of a split mattress already spilling its woollen guts out, elbows locked round knees, she braced herself. We are rats in a trap, she thought, our tails entangled. Part of her longed to slink off into a sewer, slide between the cracks of life and disappear silently, so she would never have to face what she knew to be coming. But how could she drag herself away from the others?

In one hand she held a cardboard box, in the other a cartridge, ready, waiting. She was aware of a faint rustling, like the movement of a bird or rodent. The box was shaking. The paper cartridges were whispering against each other, as her hand steadily shook.

'What is it?' muttered the fédéré. She had nudged his leg by accident.

'Nothing. Nothing. Can you see anything now?'

'Nothing.'

Another shell fell somewhere. There was screaming too, anger and terror shrilling out. But here, still, jammed in this street, not a single attacker was yet in sight.

More time passed. The young man's leg was trembling too, she realised, the cloth of his trousers quivering like the loose flap of a sail before a boat turns back into the wind. His knees. His knees must be the problem. How could you fire straight if your knees won't serve you? She imagined Anatole standing behind another barricade, somewhere in Paris, waiting for the onslaught, and quickly put the cartridge back in the box. She placed a firm hand on the thick dark wool, just above the

250

fédéré's calf, warm where the cloth had soaked up the sun. She straightened his crooked leg for him, giving it strength. He said nothing, but she could feel the muscles harden and grow steady. So she picked up the cartridges again, to be ready once more. That was her task. She had to concentrate, always prepared. She couldn't make a mistake. As soon as he needed her, she'd be there. He would have to reload so fast. She would be ready for him. She swallowed again, and again. They were all prepared, ready for anything.

The next moment he was falling, not backwards, but against her, so that she toppled sideways too. The sound of the sea was in her ears, gusting wind, a popping gale. His body was slumped over hers, such a dead weight that she couldn't escape. Cherry red and shining, blood soaked into her dress. She couldn't feel any pain though. It must be his blood. She looked up and saw a rifle muzzle coming from an upstairs window, behind the barricade. But it was aiming at her. How could that be? It was aiming straight at her. Her legs scrabbled and kicked. She unpinned herself and edged backwards.

The cartridges! The cartridges! Scattered on bare earth, brown paper, string-ringed, like cigars or dismembered thumbs. Zéphyrine groped for them on hands and knees, fingers like fins or flippers, refusing to cooperate. Another hand. Rose's hand. Rose's voice through the waves and roaring. So much braver than Zéphyrine, always.

'Get up. Get up. We must keep fighting.'

Rose had seized the dead boy's gun and she was reloading. A clunk, and then a second, as she pulled back the bolts. Flash and deafness and clouds of grey. Ostrich feathers. Gossamer.

A cry.

'*Vive la Commune!* Long live the Commune!'

Zéphyrine's fingers closed on a cartridge. This one was smeared with mud, half-crushed by a staggering boot. She found another, gave it to Rose, and refilled her box as best she could, looking wildly around for more. A red flag lay crumpled on the ground. Three more fédérés had fallen, and most of the others in their group – a few men, but mostly women – had disappeared. Zéphyrine crawled towards the cannon, their only hope. But she had no idea how to fire it, and by that time, it was pointing in the wrong direction. Their citadel, Montmartre, had left its back door open. Red trousers blazing, polished buttons sparkling, the soldiers from Versailles attacked from behind, from the side, from every angle but the one they'd been prepared for. A moving wall of bayonets came clashing towards them. Fear made it hard for eyes to focus. There was a sound like silk endlessly ripping.

'Rose, Rose!' screamed Zéphyrine. 'I can't . . . What shall I do?'

'Defend the —'

Then Rose fell too, frozen like a photograph, eyes like glass. Zéphyrine ran.

Jules was shaving when they came. He stood at the washstand, blade at his cheek, and saw his own eyes shift in the circular mirror. Wood against wood he heard, not the gentle rap of knuckles. They were banging at the door with rifle butts or batons. The noise reverberated through the building, and the scum on the surface of the water trembled mildly. Jules

252

removed a final strip of shadow from his jaw, laid the razor – a cut-throat – on the dove-grey marble stand, but decided not to snap it shut. He wiped his fingertips on the white linen towel, and then his face, and checked the cloth for the mark of cuts. None. His hand had been steady. He was determined it would remain steady.

A fresh shirt hung on the towel rail: it cooled his cheeks as it rustled over his ears. Tucking it in carefully, Jules pulled up his braces with a snap. He had already brushed his sack coat free of ash. He fed an arm into each silk-lined sleeve. The banging threatened to splinter the panels at any moment. It was so impatient that Jules decided to forgo his cravat.

He was quick to step aside in the hallway, ready for the soldiers to push past as soon as he let them in. Again, there were three of them. Did they always move in threes? Not men of the line this time, but the other militiamen of Paris, men from the party of order, who had sided with the National Government against the Commune. Now they were ready to deliver retribution.

Two began to search the apartment. The third, their leader, started the interrogation.

'You are sheltering a Communard. We have been informed.'

Jules's eyebrows rose. If he stiffened his face into disdain, he could make a mask of it. Masks were, after all, one of his strengths.

'How interesting,' he said lightly. 'I wonder who told you that. And I wonder who they could possibly mean?'

The officer was used to this already. 'That's confidential, and none of your business.'

'Perhaps not,' said Jules and shut his mouth. Bluff and quick to colour, this man was possibly a drinker, certainly volatile. He must be careful not to push him. But it was difficult.

'Of course, you are most welcome to root out this putative Communard,' he continued. 'And I'm very touched at your concern for my safety. I hope you'll make yourself at home. An aperitif, meanwhile, perhaps?' Jules made a faint bow.

The eyes opposite narrowed. The man didn't understand the word 'putative'. He thought he was being mocked. 'Certainly not.'

He joined the corridor-stalkers, listening for evidence. Only Anatole's door was closed. The leader banged his stick against it.

'What's in here?'

Jules ignored the dent. A pulse in his neck started to throb, and his hand brushed against it. It felt as if a trapped frog were trying to break free. Surely they could see its movement?

'I'll show you,' he said.

At that moment there was a call from the sitting room.

'Something in here, sir, quick.'

They both hurried in, and Jules saw the two other men staring at one of the curtains, not quite daring to approach it. The heavy lined velvet was trembling, first at the top, then the bottom. Another moment, and the ripple raced up to the top again. Jules knew exactly what was going on.

'Come out of there, whoever you are!' shouted the officer, and the movement stopped. 'I told you —' He strode furiously forward, and pulled back the curtain with a dramatic sweep. Fur on end, yellow eyes practically flashing, Minou clung to the top of the lining, all four sets of claws dug in to the cloth. The officer flung her to the floor, and she yowled and skittered away.

'A cat,' he said disgustedly. And led the way straight back to Anatole's door.

The bedroom was tidy now, the bed neatly made, Anatole's clothes folded and packed in the trunk. Jules had even considered blowing dust around the place, but realised he couldn't make such squalor convincing. What did this room say about Anatole? What could Jules say about him? Stay away now, he told him, wishing he believed in telepathy. Even more than he'd been longing to hear Anatole's clumping feet and reassuring whistle coming up the stairs, he wanted not to hear them now.

'Who sleeps here?' The man opened a drawer. It was more dangerous to deny Anatole's existence than confirm it.

'His name is Anatole Clément.'

By then the invader had pulled Anatole's violin case out from under the bed, and was pawing at the catches. Jules winced as he pulled at the silk cloth in which the instrument was shrouded. They seemed almost disappointed that it was just a violin.

'He's a musician,' he said. 'At the Théâtre Lyrique.'

'Heavy fighting round there now. Is that where he is?' The officer waited. His harsh breathing seemed to rob the room of oxygen. Down the corridor, Jules heard the other men shifting furniture, opening windows and banging them shut. Noises echoed in the walls of the well down which he'd very nearly dropped Anatole's uniform. They were all taking their duties very seriously.

'No,' said Jules, trying to keep his eyes still and steady – the hardest thing in the world, he decided. He looked at his shoes very intently, and tried to work out what to say next.

'So where is he?'

Down the corridor, a discordant shimmer of sound, muffled. They were rummaging in the piano. It was possible, in theory, to hide a man in a piano. Jules felt alternately hot and clammy. He wondered how long he could keep up this breezy act.

'Oh, he left Paris about a week ago. It was quite a palaver getting him out, I can tell you.' Just in time, he remembered Marie, and the dress she'd borrowed for her portrait. 'Luckily the wardrobe mistress – from the theatre, you know? – she was able to lend a hand. Monsieur Clément made a very fetching young lady.'

'Did he indeed? Somehow you don't surprise me. And who exactly is this Anatole to you, that you should go to so much trouble for him?'

'A friend. Just a friend.'

It was the officer's turn to raise his eyebrows, and curl his lip. Veined nostrils opened. Jules had been on the receiving end of looks like that before.

'A friend,' the man said with heavy sarcasm. 'Really. That kind of friend, I suppose.' He took a step backwards, as if, for all his bluster, he was suddenly afraid of infection.

Jules stepped forward, and held out his hand for the violin. The man was gripping it too hard, holding it like a shield. The bridge would snap if he wasn't careful. Jules's foot knocked against the violin case, which was still open on the floor between them. At exactly the same time, two pairs of eyes noticed something neither had spotted before.

Jules hadn't been able to bring himself to burn his photographs – burning was harder to hide. Anyway, he couldn't bear to destroy them. So the ones he didn't want found, he'd hidden. They were flattened under carpets and rugs, taped behind pictures, walled up behind books and tucked between pages. Guardsmen and barricades. The fallen column. Zéphyrine and Anatole. Anatole. So many that could prove incriminating. Almost every single one, one way or another. But he hadn't thought to check the violin case.

A photograph of Zéphyrine, the carte de visite Jules had made, was tucked into the green baize lid of the violin case, wedged behind the two bows, and faintly filmed with rosin dust. Before Jules knew quite what had happened, Anatole's violin was in his own hands, and the photograph in the officer's. The man inspected it very closely. He seemed to take in every detail: the newspaper, the hair, the clothes, the defiance. With an ever-growing look of disgust, he turned it over once – the reverse was blank, but Zéphyrine's name was on the front – and back again.

'Or maybe not,' he sneered.

A shout came from upstairs – from the studio. The photograph was tucked inside a jacket. There was nothing Jules could do to retrieve it.

'Follow me,' came the order.

Cradling the fiddle, Jules obeyed. The pulse in his neck still throbbed. The studio looked worse than he remembered.

'What the hell has been going on here? This mess can't be the work of a shell.'

Jules supposed it couldn't.

'Terrible, isn't it?' he said. 'I think I'm going to have to give up photography. It's so damnably dangerous. The chemicals, you know . . . and just look at my hands!'

He held them out. It was nearly impossible to remove every last trace of silver nitrate. He wasn't going to risk these idiots mistaking its shadowy stains for gunpowder marks. He thought about Anatole's left fingertips, very faintly hardened from a lifetime of pressing down on strings. The men poked around in the chaos, boots on broken glass like chips of ice. Jules felt his nostrils prickling. A new smell was drifting into the studio, a different kind of acridity. He looked out across the rooftops, and the others followed his gaze. Smoke was creeping into the sky, as buildings began to burn.

'Scum!' The youngest invader spat, a shining tobacco-stained globule that glistened on the studio floor. His companion kept staring at the sky, disbelieving.

'Who'd credit such a thing?'

'They'd rather be buried in the rubble of Paris than surrender.'

Jules wondered how you could tell who was responsible for what. Faced with a flaming projectile, a building could hardly choose its loyalty.

'Where is it, do you think?'

'Hard to tell from here.'

'Near the river?'

'We'll find out soon enough.'

Yes. Go. Go and find out, thought Jules. Get out before you see anything else you shouldn't.

As if they'd overheard, the three men turned and stared at him. He disgusted them in every way; they were happy to make this plain.

'Let's move on.'

* * *

At two o'clock Anatole was lying on his stomach, wedged between sandbags, trying to get a crick out of his neck. A shot zinged into the hessian, and sand spurted out in a steady hiss, sounding like rain. He wished it would stop. Eventually it petered out, stopping less suddenly than it had begun. Then came the news that Montmartre had fallen.

His own face echoed the chorus around him – stunned disbelief.

'Already?'

'How?'

Everyone mouthed the same question. Montmartre, of all places in Paris. How could it have crumbled so quickly? Montmartre was meant to be unconquerable, unassailable. The people of Montmartre would never let their neighbourhood be taken. Yet it had fallen in a matter of hours, humiliation arriving with devastating speed and efficiency. So what had happened to the people?

The fédérés here shook their heads at the shame of it: blue, white and red flying over the heights of Montmartre. They wondered if the Commune might end where it had begun. Vengeance for March's triumph had been precise, they heard. In the rue des Rosiers, at the very wall where the two generals had been shot in March, over forty men were made to kneel. Three women and four children were rounded up with them. One mother, her child in her arms, refused to get to her knees: she preferred to be executed on her feet.

Anatole thought only of Zéphyrine. Where could she be? How could he possibly find out? She had to be safe somewhere, didn't she? She had to be.

Preoccupied with these thoughts, he didn't notice that the ranks around him were thinning, and not by death. One by one, white-faced men slunk away. They slid off to find a bolthole, a safe spot where they could scrub the powder stains from their hands. Somewhere to stash a uniform, cast away a rifle or cartridges. Sewers and cesspits were filling up. Men wandered away from the barricades to crawl into anonymous workers' smocks, ready to get back to work, all innocence. Who, me?

Safe in her room in the cité Bergère, Marie knitted with the shutters closed, and her heart and ears shuttered too. It was too much. She didn't want to know what was happening out there.

In through the front door
Around the back
Out through the window
And off jumps Jack.

Montmartre taken, another column marched south to the crossroads of Paris, down the long road that led to Les Halles.

Later, different men came to the barricade. Anatole looked over his shoulder and saw them wiping their hands, looking for water, refusing to pick up weapons until they were clean again. They smelled of petrol. Their hair was singed. Their cans were empty. What had they done?

Anatole didn't want to ask, but soon he didn't have to. Smoke, then flames, and finally swirling ashes. The rue Royale was burning in a single sheet of fire. It was the only hope left, the only way the Commune could stop the Versailles troops from hollowing through the houses, or gunning down the fédérés from above and behind and outflanking them. The fire began to spread, from street to street, until all around the barricade the air was dense and dark. Anatole felt hot with outrage, but remained mute. This was no time for protest.

'Brunel says to keep going. Orders. There's more petrol at the garrison. Any volunteers?'

Anatole shook his head, and went back to squinting at the enemy.

Artillery duelled across the huge empty space all afternoon. By then, the Place de la Concorde was strewn with chunks of fountain, twisted lamp posts. The statue of Lille had lost her head. With thirty cannon ranged in front of the Tuileries Palace, returning fire for fire with vigour, the fédérés seemed to have a chance. But as the afternoon shadows lengthened, making it ever harder to hit your mark, Anatole realised that this was just a postponement. Retreat was muttered.

On the other side of the gardens, invisible through trees that had sheltered concertgoers two days earlier, something else was escaping. Oil and turpentine gurgled free, arcs of liquid sluicing out, darkening velvet and brocade, drapes, hangings, embroidered imperial bees, dust sheets. All drenched without discrimination. Boots skidded and slipped on parquet mother-of-pearled with paraffin. At the foot of the grand staircase, and in the courtyard, barrels of gunpowder were rolled into place, fuses laid.

By the time they had been lit, most of the Guardsmen were gone. Protected by the gunboats on the Seine, ignorant of the conflagration still to come, the fédérés were sent along the riverbanks, past the empty theatres, and ordered to rendezvous at the Hôtel de Ville. At their backs, an east wind fanned the flames. Soon crackling thunder rolled through gilded corridors, spitting and crashing and creaking, consuming the last vestiges of Empire.

30.

24th May

Wednesday was the worst. Black bats escaped across the dirty sky in streams, shiny, flimsy wings disintegrating as they flew. Fragments of black silk attached themselves to Anatole's salt-sticky face as they retreated eastward. Moths in mourning, edge-crinkled. Where had this dark blizzard come from? Who had fashioned these grim funereal petals, which crumbled to the touch? What was all this stuff?

Not silk, but paper, so much paper: all the records from the Hôtel de Ville, released to roam through Paris, undoing births and deaths and marriages and deeds of ownership in a moment and forever. The documents of generations – families of shopkeepers, aristocrats, orphans, beggars – were dispersed within hours. Not a trace would remain. As the Palais de Justice burned too, every name of every criminal, every record of every revolutionary, every Second-Empire denunciation blackened and took to the air.

Zéphyrine spent the night huddled under the roof beams of an abandoned house. She couldn't sleep, but nor could she keep moving. Her knees were bleeding, her dress torn. On all fours she had crawled out of Montmartre through attics, led in her escape by a roofer who knew the secret spaces of the neighbourhood, an old workmate of her grandfather. There was more safety in height, he persuaded her. Better a bird than a rat. And then he'd left her here. She had no idea where here might be.

Each time she closed her eyes, the image of Rose's dead face ground into the corners of her mind. She hated herself for leaving her there. And what had become of Madame Mouton? What of her little girl? There seemed so little chance of survival for anyone in Montmartre. Your crime was simply to live there. From one attic window, she had glimpsed a dog licking the blood from the face of its dead owner. Licking and whining, and then giving up and simply howling.

Now she rolled herself into a ball, knees up, fists clenched. She shivered uncontrollably until dawn, her teeth clattering against each other so loudly that the noise in her head drowned out the rattle of machine guns outside.

At first light, she returned to the ground. Zéphyrine kept herself out of sight as much as possible, sliding into doorways and courtyards at the slightest sign of people. Her smoke-stained, ragged clothes would betray her in an instant, she knew. All day yesterday she had pictured Anatole at the crest of a barricade, a flag in his hand, defiant and daring. Now she hoped with all her heart that he had not found the courage to fight. That his neighbourhood had been swiftly defeated and that he had stayed safely in a cellar.

The entire city seemed under a grey pall. By this third day of fighting, fires were raging right across Paris. Zéphyrine's head roared, so she couldn't tell if the noise she heard was inside her or outside. Listing from street to street, unable to get her bearings, she began to wonder if she might even be weaving in circles.

Then hope came at last. A name – Balard – picked out in gold. It appeared ahead of her with a sign on either side – a snake coiled round a tree – and she knew where she was at last. Hope hiccupped in her chest as she read it for a second time. This was the pharmacy her grandmother had shown her. Just before she died, Zéphyrine had nearly sought it out. They used to pass here each week on their way to delivering the flowers to the milliners, and every time, without fail, Gran'mère would bob a curtsey at the open door, and smile, and nod her head. And then, as they turned the corner, she would remind Zéphyrine of the pharmacist's kindness in those dreadful weeks following her grandfather's fall. 'I know he did not tell the truth about the cost of the bandages and the medicines. Impossible, because each week, he charged less. Such a good man. Dear monsieur. How the world needs more like him.'

But the shopfront was shuttered. The place looked dead. Zéphyrine crossed the road anyway, and hurled herself at the glass-fronted door, which felt like ice against her burning forehead.

'Please. Oh please. Oh please,' she cried.

And then the blind whipped up in front of her, and there was Monsieur Balard, his elongated frame almost doubled over in the effort to identify her. Just behind the wavering glass, gold-rimmed spectacles magnified kindly eyes. At last he nodded recognition, then turned away and back, and nodded again. Thank God! He reached up to release the bolts and let her in.

Cool and consoling. Chemicals, camphor and cotton wool. As soon as the door shut tinkling behind her, and the blind was lowered once more, Zéphyrine found herself in a world of order. Rows of glass jars, each one identical, neatly labelled. Mahogany shelves. A polished counter. Columns of drawers with brass handles. Quietness. Everything was in the right place, except for her. Monsieur Balard kept talking; she didn't know what he was saying. He brought out a chair and sat her down, and then his wife came in from the back of the shop – a woman almost as tall as her scarecrow husband. She was talking too. They both asked questions, lots of questions, and her own mouth seemed to open and shut too, some sort of noise coming out of it.

She blinked, and shapes sharpened.

'Are you hurt? Is it your grandmother? How can we help?'

She shook her head. Her tongue started working better. No, she wasn't hurt, not much, she said. And though she had bad news about her grandmother, it was old news. She looked down. She had a bowl of coffee now in one hand, and a hunk of bread in the other. Zéphyrine ate and drank and gathered her strength and told her story. Madame Balard began to dress the graze on her leg. Then she led her to the back room, where the drugs were prepared, and she filled the sink with hot water so that Zéphyrine could wash the telltale blackness from her face and arms.

'You'll stay? A day or two?' Monsieur Balard put the question, but Zéphyrine glimpsed the horror in his wife's face, the tightening of her lips and the quick involuntary shake of her head.

'No . . . no . . . I must keep going. I – I have a friend . . .not so far from here . . . I must . . .' Jules would surely not be at the barricades. He would take her in, advise her. For Anatole's sake. She would be safe with him. He might even know where she could find Anatole.

'But if you cross the lines dressed like that . . .'

It was true. Round here was quite bad enough. When she reached the boulevards, she'd stand out like a crab in a barrel of herrings.

'I'll lend you a dress,' offered Madame Balard. 'You can return it when you can.'

'But . . .' Zéphyrine didn't want to seem ungrateful. Her eyes made the long journey from Madame Balard's high grey chignon to her narrow pointed shoes.

Luckily, the pharmacist understood immediately. 'My dear, supposing she has to run for her life?' Or fight again, thought Zéphyrine. 'She will trip over your long skirts. Much too long for little Zéphyrine. They'll be a hazard. I've a better idea.'

He only had to look at the white overall hanging on the door for his wife to understand. 'Of course. I'll wake Alphonse immediately. An excellent plan.'

Fifteen minutes later she was smartly dressed as the pharmacist's delivery boy, her new uniform complete with freshly starched white shirt and tie, the trousers just a little tight across her hips.

'There is a barber in the next street. Knock on the back door.'

He wrote a message for her, a kind of *laisser-passer* she supposed.

Zéphyrine gave her hair to the barber in payment. Well, it was no use to her any more. At least he could profit from it.

'It's lovely hair,' he told her, stroking it sadly. 'Thank you. And good luck. *Vive la Commune!*'

She straightened her tie in the mirror, took out her earrings and put them in her pocket, and stared. What a gaunt-eyed boy she made.

The day didn't want to get light. Redness, like dawn, persisted in the sky all morning, but the darkness never quite lifted. Marie didn't want to look. She kept the shutters bolted, and locked the door, and waited in her room, not even lighting the gas. She knew she should go to the cellar. It was stupid to stay here. But she hated to be underground. And what if her brother came?

She had run out of wool and did not know how else to pass the time, so she searched her drawers for a garment she could unpick. Anything would do. She was happy to start again. Pulling out a rose-pink muffler, she uncovered her tangled rosary. Silver and coral, carved Pater beads. To her fingertips, it felt like home.

She should never have put this away. She had cared too much for worldly success; she had wanted too much to be loved. Her ambitions had brought her down. It was her own fault that she was here alone, so tortured by uncertainty.

It was nearly noon now. Somewhere, surely, the Angelus bell would still be ringing. *Pray for us, O holy Mother of God.* The voice in her head made her continue aloud: 'That we may be made worthy of the promises of Christ.' She wanted to go out and find a real sanctuary, to confess her sins, to atone. But there was no knowing who you might find in a church these days.

'Pour forth, we beseech Thee, O Lord, Thy grace into our hearts, that we to whom the Incarnation of Christ, Thy Son, was made known by the message of an Angel, may by His Passion and Cross be brought to the glory of His Resurrection . . .'

She would just have to pray where she was, at the end of her bed, as she used to as a child. Very seriously, just as she'd been taught, but had forgotten. Bare knees on the coloured rug. God would protect her, wouldn't he? Wouldn't he tell her what to do?

Jules imagined Anatole creeping home wounded, unable to climb the stairs, even collapsing halfway home. He decided to risk a short foot patrol, a kind of reconnoitre. He'd check the whole building first, and then the neighbouring streets, just in case, staying well clear of the friends of order. He wasn't sure if they'd given up on him or not.

The maids had deserted the cellar. Jules realised he had the place entirely to himself now, which was a strange, chilling feeling. He inspected the inner courtyard before venturing out of the main door and onto the road, Holding his head high and trying to look satisfied with events, he immediately choked on the smoke. He decided to pay a visit to Monsieur Louvet's establishment to clear his throat, but also to find out if he had heard anything useful. When he got there, Jules quickly discovered a new word was ricocheting around the cafés and bars and pavements of Paris. Monsieur Louvet was surprised he'd not come across it already. Soon enough it would echo through newspapers around the world.

Pétroleuses, they called them.

'You need to take care,' Monsier Louvet warned. 'Keep your eyes peeled for these women. They're everywhere now, it seems. Unstoppable.'

Everyone was talking about the women incendiaries. The evil witches were setting fire to Paris, they said, pouring kerosene into basements and cellars. So cunning too – they disguised their weapons in milk bottles and shopping baskets. It was impossible to know where they might strike next. Just that morning, near the base of the broken column in the place Vendôme, thirteen shots rang out at once. Thirteen women fell to the ground. They were *pétroleuses*, it seemed. They deserved it of course, these monstrous women, maddened by resentment. Unnatural wives and mothers and daughters. Women who would destroy Paris before they surrendered the city. Of course the arsonists had to be destroyed. The whole Commune had to be exterminated, as fast as possible.

That's what everyone said.

Jules looked at the faces in the café, listening open-mouthed and terror-stricken, and he thought of Zéphyrine. Where was she now? What might Rose be saying to her next – mysterious Rose, always so busy that he and Anatole had still never set eyes on her? Was she half-crazed by now too, dispatching minions to do wicked deeds? But surely even they wouldn't . . . she couldn't . . . ?

Sometimes you could see the whole length of a street; at others a kiosk twenty metres away was blanketed in gritty fog. Zéphyrine's eyes itched and oozed, and her face was already filthy again, but she made herself walk at a measured pace.

270

She tried to look straight ahead: purposeful, the way a boy on business should be. She swung her free arm like a boy, and took long, deliberate strides. Her shoes were too big, and they flopped back at the heel with every step, in little gulps. If she needed to run, she'd kick them off, she decided. Her package of dressing, she carried like a talisman, wondering if there was a girl's way and a boy's way of carrying things.

It was hard to look purposeful when the front line was so uncertain. Distorted by hard stone walls, reverberating, whizzing and whining, echoing in strange ways, the noise of firing was hard to locate, and difficult to duck. Unless it was right in front of you, you could never tell where a shot was coming from. She had to rely on luck, and keep moving.

Once, but only once, she stopped to add a paving stone to a barricade: not to stop would have drawn attention she didn't need. Otherwise, she kept going, zigzagging her way out of trouble and towards Jules and Anatole's apartment. If she saw a soldier from either side, she kept her distance. Several times, she glimpsed a ragged band of National Guardsmen roped together, being led away. Some of the men had tried to rip the red stripe from their own trouser legs. There were catcalls from the pavement, well-dressed women jeering, bourgeois manners quite forgotten. 'Scum!' they always shouted. 'Communard scum!'

In her head, she rehearsed her story. A casualty of crossfire. Doctor's orders.

She was nearly there.

Out of the corner of her eye she noticed something strange. Masons at work, mixing cement. Hammering at knee and ankle level. They were blocking up the air vents for the cellars. But why? Didn't people need to breathe down there? Something was happening that she didn't understand at all, something that made her throat hammer too.

Faster, she urged herself. But not too fast. No, not too fast, not quite yet.

The final metres she couldn't help herself and ran. She pulled the bell knob. Behind the heavy outer door she could hear a hollow jangle, but there was no answering shuffle of a concierge's slippers, and no descending feet.

Perhaps they were in the cellar, Zéphyrine thought. She turned to check the street again. At the far end, another troop of soldiers was passing, with more prisoners. She rang the bell again, tapped her foot, feigned nonchalance. Nobody was looking. As soon as they were gone, she got back to her knees on the pavement, fists gripping the grating of the vent, still unblocked.

'Anatole?' she called, not too loud at first. 'Anatole? Are you in there?'

Her call was thrown back at her – stony, metallic. No other sound.

'Jules?'

Scrabbling on the pavement, she sat back and braced herself with both hands on the stones behind her, kicking at the bars across the vent with all her strength. Her body felt the impact, but the iron grating didn't move. Forward again, desperate now, she screamed into the cellar.

'Anatole! Jules! Are you down there? Help me. I need help! It's me, Zéphyrine. Please! Isn't anyone there? Jules!'

Like a cormorant, her hopes plunged. She slumped against the wall, struggling for air. All she could hear was her own harsh breathing. Where else could she go? Who would protect her in this part of town? Ten minutes' walk would take her to Marie's, fifteen or twenty if she kept to the side streets and avoided the arcades. She could keep going for fifteen more minutes, she decided. She had no choice, for she certainly couldn't stay where she was. Zéphyrine dragged herself upright again, and picked up the parcel. Marie would know what to do.

High above her head, a shutter quietly closed. In Babylon Jeremiah found palaces but no shelter.

A few seconds later, Jules opened the shutter again. He had to be quite certain, he told himself. He wasn't sure. But Zéphyrine was already gone.

Stupefied by terror and doubt, he had hesitated too long. It was hard to recognise a voice so thinned by despair, but Jules was suddenly convinced it really had been Zéphyrine calling. At the upper window, hardly able to hear or see her, he had just caught enough at first to know that someone was looking for Anatole. Of course it was her. But was she calling to check he wasn't there, so that she wouldn't set him alight too? And why was she dressed so strangely? What was that package she carried? Jules could have challenged her if he'd been quick enough. He should have stopped her, reasoned with her. He had taken too long to act when there had been no time to waste. Those few seconds of doubt and confusion could have put the whole building at risk.

Jules tore down the stairs, flight after flight, and pulled open the cellar door with a crash that brought down more plaster. Pausing on the threshold, he sniffed the air. As before, it was damp, slightly rodenty, dusty. Cool in his nostrils. But there was no smell of petrol. No flare of yellow or orange trickled towards him across the stone floor. Just a rectangle of natural light slanting from above into darkness, sliced by iron bars. A forest of unfashionable furniture, kept by the concierge, just in case. Shelves of cobwebbed bottles and a bin of coal. Nothing burning at all.

He walked across to check the ventilation shaft, and stood with head surrounded by floating backlit particles, wondering exactly what he'd witnessed.

He didn't seem able to think clearly any more. The previous day's unwanted visitors had removed his last whisper of reason along with the confiscated photograph. For those few crucial moments – as he had listened to the ringing, and the knocking and kicking and the cry of despair – he really had believed a monster was at the door, and that it was Zéphyrine.

Jules had tried to warn Anatole. He had always had a feeling that she would take things too far, that the revolution was all that mattered to her. Possessed, obsessed. But now that she was gone, and the cellar as cool and quiet as ever, he wondered if his own obsession was to blame, not hers, if this madness had taken over his senses too. What if Zéphyrine simply needed a safe place to hide, and he had sent her to her death?

But then again, what if Zéphyrine had simply been the advance guard, and she had left something behind her? Monsieur Louvet had warned him of this too. Just a scrap of paper the size of a postage stamp, a circle or a square pasted on the wall of the house as a small marker, and three letters that would condemn him: 'B.P.B.' – *bon pour brûler*. Good for burning. And even now, slinking along the wall, an uncombed hag with rough cheeks rouged by alcohol could be coming towards him, a milk can in her hand, petrol sloshing as she searched for that sign.

Blacker and thicker with every hour that passed, clouds of smoke unrolled from Notre-Dame's twin towers, and merged with those unfurling from Saint-Eustache. A vast crash signalled the collapse of the church's roof, crushing the pulpit from which so many women had raged these past few weeks. At the Théâtre Lyrique, the drama continued. The fire made no distinction between auditorium and stage. Scenery went up in flames. Silk and velvet, satin and furs, music stands and pianos and gilt-painted cherubs, all destroyed in a great roaring rush. Soon half the building was a smoking ruin.

Far below the curdled skies, something else was on the move: brown fur and scrabbling claws streaming through gutters, a screeching current of fear speeding away from the path of the flames. The rats were evacuating.

Behind the vast bulkhead of a new barricade, Anatole was probably safer than he'd been for days. A gigantic barracks building protected one flank, a huge department store the other. He felt his courage return, briefly, with the apparent success of their resistance. A boy had given him a kepi, and a woman had swapped his torn and ragged frock coat for a military jacket, in which he could move more easily – there was no mistaking now what he was. Anatole both looked and felt more like a soldier. He had even snatched some sleep the night before, huddled in the crowded square of the Hôtel de Ville, just before the building began to burn.

Word reached the diminished company that the Commune leaders had moved west and were now installed at a local town hall, not far away. That meant there would be proper orders soon, wouldn't there? Strategy, and the kind of plan that could be followed. A contagious spirit of elation flickered through what was left of the battalion, hope and hysteria mixed. The tactics that had got them here seemed to be working. An army couldn't penetrate burning buildings. And now they had arrived, and were dug in, they couldn't be outflanked again. Anatole caught the mood too.

'Here, give me that . . .' He reached for the red embroidered flag. Its wooden pole, polished from being passed from hand to hand for all these months, felt as right in his palm as his violin bow had done a week before. He hoisted himself up with a toe in the grating, keeping the flag low as he climbed, almost overbalancing when he reached the top.

A jolt of fear was checked by the cry from below.

'*Vive la Commune!*' Fumbling with one hand, feeling for a hole in the stones, Anatole found a place he could plant the flag. He hadn't shown himself to the enemy for more than a few seconds, but four bullets instantly screamed over his head. At least one thudded into the wood, knocking the flag into rakish submission. Anatole jumped away, landing on feet and hands, and they all laughed in terror.

Nobody there had heard yet that the Latin Quarter had fallen, the Panthéon with it, and seven hundred prisoners taken all at once. They had no idea that at the Opéra, the huntsmen's costumes, skulls and wolves' heads laid out ready for Monday night's grand performance had been seized by soldiers from Versailles, who were dressing up to watch executions in the courtyard. Nor that the Châtelet theatre was now a courtroom, where there were trials, but no justice. None of the men at this barricade, nor the women who were tending to the wounded, nor the children who ferried cartridges and water and wine back and forth, had seen the piles of corpses mounting on the streets of the Left Bank, or the gravediggers at work at the foot of the Tour Saint-Jacques. Anatole thought only of the wall of paving stones protecting him, and he felt grateful to every single citizen who had helped build it.

The grating rattle of the machine guns continued. Anatole imagined iron teeth, continually grinding, gnashing against each other like a troubled conscience interrupting sleep. This was the kind of noise you would surely meet in hell. But then he did hear news, or overheard it.

'It's not just the Hôtel de Ville, you know,' said a boy who had just arrived. He was wearing a National Guard kepi and what might have been his father's smock, both far too large for his gangly frame. 'They've set light to the theatres too, by the river. The Lyrique is blazing. Word is it's the women. They call them *pétroleuses*.'

'Good for them, and good riddance to the rest. That should hold 'em back a bit longer.'

Another man spat. 'Bourgeois baloney.'

Anatole's mouth opened and shut. So his own theatre was burning too. The knowledge chilled him. He pictured a blazing piano, a harp in flames, a golden inferno of contorted brass. Paint on a backdrop melting and sliding down canvas, wrinkling, blackening and finally turning to ash. He saw statues and mirrors shattering in the heat, while ironwork bent and buckled, flames licked up curtains and ropes, and rigging thundered through burning floorboards. He imagined the fire taking hold in the very loge where Zéphyrine had first dismayed him, remembered her theft and her flight, and in his mind heard the box itself crashing down in pieces into the orchestra pit. He began to doubt everything. Could Zéphyrine really care for him, if she believed destruction like this was worth it? If she thought this was the way to a better future? He wondered, for a moment, if she had bewitched him into throwing in his lot with savages.

Marie looked at Zéphyrine. She knew her by her voice as much as anything. Tears, unwiped, had formed pale rivulets on her grimy face, meandering channels in the layer of smoke particles. *Dust thou art and unto dust thou shalt return*, thought Marie. Sackcloth and ashes. Repentance time. But it was too late now for repentance. This was not Ash Wednesday.

'Is Anatole with you?' Zéphyrine asked.

'No, why should he be? What have you brought me?' She took the brown-paper parcel, wondering how Zéphyrine had even managed to slip up the stairs to this upper landing. And more importantly, who had seen her come. Then, without thinking, Marie reached out a hand to touch Zéphyrine's cropped and matted hair.

'Who did this to you?'

The fugitive grabbed at her, clamping hold of Marie's wrist so that it hurt.

'Let go!' said Marie, and Zéphyrine's brow creased as if she didn't understand.

'Are you hiding him?' she asked, still clutching at Marie. 'Is he here? You would do that, for him. I know you would.'

Marie shook her head. 'He's not here. I don't know where Anatole is. I've no idea.'

'Oh God,' said Zéphyrine simply. 'Oh God.' She began to shake, and her nails dug into Marie's white wrist.

'Stop!' Marie hissed, pulling back her arm, and Zéphyrine with it. She dropped the parcel and managed to free herself from Zéphyrine's clawing hands, for long enough to shake her by her skinny shoulders. 'You've got to stop this. Nobody must hear you.' She slapped her face, not hard, but enough to shock the girl briefly into focus. 'Just get inside as quickly as you can.'

At Versailles, Thiers made a speech to the National Assembly. 'Our valiant soldiers conduct themselves in such a manner as to inspire foreign countries with the highest esteem and admiration,' he said. Everybody cheered. In the heart of Paris, at the Lobau Barracks, behind high walls, out of sight but not out of hearing, the firing squads continued their work. People shuddered as they passed. All their lives they would be haunted by what they heard that week.

Rigault took matters into his own hands. An eye for an eye. No need now to make a show of consultation, and far too late anyway. For months already, Versailles had been executing prisoners. Now it was the Commune's turn to make good their threat. He gave the first command.

Meanwhile the fédérés made a final appeal to the soldiers of the line, the men who had turned their muskets upside down beside the cannon, up on the Montmartre hillside two months earlier.

'*Unite with the people – you are part of them. Soldiers, children, brothers! Listen, and let your conscience decide. When the order is unspeakable, disobedience is an obligation.*'

Babylon was burning. A burnished cloak of smoke smothered the city, its vast billows reddened or yellowed here and there by leaping flames, or briefly spotlit by the flash of artillery. Miniature volcanoes burst repeatedly from gunboats along the Seine. That afternoon, it was reported, the apocalyptic rush of sound reached a crescendo. Explosions rolled out in every direction, unorchestrated, and musketry fire came shrieking through the city like a demonic wind. As for the machine guns, their cartridges cranked out in a snarling rasp, an infernal stuttering. Ears whistled and sang. Bodies ached with waiting, and jerked with terror. Nostrils burned and throats retched. Watchers on rooftops thought of Nero's Rome, or a bonfire of vanities, and talked of the debauchery of the fallen empire. Paris had become a Gomorrah, they said, a city of lights and splendour and lechery and disgrace. It could never have lasted. It had to come to an end. Paris had sinned for years, they reminded each other: now she had to pay.

Blazing columns and pyramids of fire rose that night along the line of the river, breaking forth in staggered chorus. Walls collapsed like falling scenery. Gigantic furnaces showering sparks on neighbouring streets. There was no quenching this. The waters of the Seine threw back the flames, redoubling their glare so that the river itself seemed to be burning, like a winding path of molten lava. The sky turned from black to red. Unable to compete with so much unexpected light, the stars retreated.

31.

25th May

On Thursday ash fell like snow. Round the outskirts of Paris, on its ruined suburbs, and on the Prussian encampments that were closing in ever more firmly to the north and east, it settled in a dull grey coating on every horizontal surface. Everywhere you went, the air was harder to breathe: something seemed to block your lungs. Thousands had gone into hiding inside the city, but thousands more were beginning to venture out. The party of order strutted the streets with tricoloured armbands.

Early in the morning, a chimney sweep stood with his palms out. He was in no position to disobey. He was small and wiry, and the army captain looming in front of him was tall and armed.

'It's soot. Only soot,' he told him, looking up at the soldiers hopefully.

It was only soot, but these men didn't care.

'Sweeping chimneys at a time like this?'

'I do Madame Blanche's chimneys on the twenty-fifth of every month. Look!' He turned out his pocket. 'See . . . this is what she paid me.' His voice, barely broken, rose to a squeak, as they took his money.

'Take him away.'

Jules had never needed to fetch a horse himself before. There had always been someone around to send, but by Thursday the concierge had vanished entirely and he realised he didn't even know where the nearest livery stable was. For want of a beast, he dragged the small cart himself. His passport was in his pocket, along with a fair bit of money. He had fresh clothes hidden behind his equipment, for himself and for Anatole too, and the cat was shut in a box with a piece of sausage. At the last minute he ran back upstairs and came down with Anatole's violin, and hid that too.

Jules was an American, wasn't he? The Prussians would surely let him through if he could find a way to the eastern walls. They had no quarrel with America.

The streets were filling up again. People had come out to marvel at the devastation, and to watch the prisoners pass. Bare-headed and many bare-breasted, their clothes ripped by bayonets to show their sex, hands tied behind backs so they could do nothing to protect their modesty, women were marched with men west through Paris. A few children stumbled beside them. They passed by in their thousands, heading for Versailles, staggering and stupefied, bewildered or defiant. Men were forced to turn their jackets and coats inside out, to mark their shame. They were guarded by mounted hussars who kept them moving faster than most were able to walk, urging them along at the pace of their strutting horses, threatening any who fell behind. The animals looked better fed than most of the prisoners.

Jules kept his head down and his eyes protected by the brim of his top hat as his hesitant gaze raked over the captives. It was pitiful to watch. From time to time, a prisoner would shout out or wildly stare about for someone who might recognise them and prove their innocence before it was too late.

'It's a red cross!' a young man yelled, jabbing at his armband. 'I said the international Geneva Convention, not the International Workingmen's Association. I'm a medical student, for pity's sake. They've made a mistake. Can't anyone . . . ? I was just trying . . .' His protests were carried away.

A twisted logic beat circles in Jules's head. If he were to see Anatole here, alive, he would at least have a hope of rescuing him. But how? And perhaps, if he wasn't here, it meant he was free and safe. Or already slaughtered, or about to die. So better by far to see his face here, and know. And round again Jules went in his head, scanning the captives as he heaved his awkward load in the opposite direction. Like blowfly on a carcass, the onlookers were too busy spreading their poison to bother with Jules. 'Look!' they told their children, showing them what happened if you were bad, shaking heads in ribboned bonnets, and prodding with canes. Dogs yapped at the prisoners' heels, urged on by their owners.

The bars Jules dragged were made for horses, not human beings, and his strange little curtained vehicle was hard to pull alone. It made him too conspicuous, he thought, before he realised that it stood out less than the other wagons and handcarts passing by, with their grotesque freak shows of tangled, angled limbs. He wanted to turn away from them, to gag in privacy, but he had to check every face he could. He forced himself to meet blank open eyes, staring out from jumbles of boots and braids and banners, arms and legs and winding sheets.

All at once there was a string of explosions like firecrackers. It set off a panic-stricken race to escape, but running made matters worse. Fallen cartridges were firing spontaneously underfoot. As you fled, you set off more. Jules stopped, sheltering against his cart. He held his breath and his ground until the agitation was over. Then, more warily, he kept on walking east, towards the theatre, his heart beating a little higher and a little tighter in his chest.

'Are you hungry?' Marie whispered.

Zéphyrine shook her head without looking up. She sat on the floor, arms clutched round her knees, rocking gently without speaking. Sometimes she opened her mouth, but her tongue just paddled the air, and gave up.

'Are you sure?'

Marie crouched down in front of her, putting a hand on her raised knees and her face right in front of Zéphyrine's doll-dead eyes. Eventually they unglazed, surprised to see Marie there.

'What is it?' she asked, eyebrows twisting.

'Food. I'm going to get something to eat. I wanted to know what I could bring back for you.'

'Nothing. I don't want to put you to any trouble. I'm not hungry.'

Everything about Zéphyrine was dull now. She smelled of stale sweat. Really she needed to be washed as well as fed. At this rate, it wouldn't be long before someone would literally sniff her out. Marie wondered what Anatole would think if he saw her now, her skin coated, nothing about her shining like it used to.

'You really don't want anything at all?'

Zéphyrine just chewed her lip. 'Have you seen Anatole?' she said again.

'No. No, I haven't. Please, stop asking me that.'

What on earth was Marie to do with her? Zéphyrine was like a different person. Almost like a madwoman, so blank and lifeless. It was inhuman, this endless, mechanical rocking, and Marie didn't think she could stand much more. She had to get out, just for a short time, to eat, to breathe. She knew she would have to be quick, for Emile could turn up at any moment. Part of her wished he would. Her longing for him was intensifying all the time. Finally he felt so close. Soon she would embrace him, feel his living flesh, hear his voice, and know that all was well. But with Zéphyrine here, she had begun to dread his arrival. There was no knowing how he might react to her presence, or she to his. Marie took a basket from the hook behind the door.

'Don't let anyone in,' she said. 'Do you hear me?'

Tenderly she cupped the girl's face in her hand, searching it for understanding. It was cold as marble. She kissed her cheek, left, then right.

'On no account let anybody in while I'm gone. Understand?'

Zéphyrine's face contracted briefly in recognition, and she nodded. Then Marie sighed. The blank-eyed staring had returned. Safest to lock her in.

* * *

Of course Jules hadn't really expected to find Anatole at the theatre. But neither had he anticipated this smouldering hollow shell. The fire brigades were still at work, hoses in hand, enlisting anyone who passed to lend a hand with the pumping. Canvas snaked across wet ash, and a penetrating bitter smell of singed silk and fur and burnt horsehair hung in the air. Somebody had gone to the trouble of rescuing costumes: they were laid out on the ground in rows, like bodies awaiting identification. Here and there they sparkled silver and gold, as sunlight broke through and hit hidden spangles.

When he'd found a way round the abandoned broken barricade beside the Tour Saint-Jacques, another smell took over, which sent Jules reeling. It was a rotten stench with a sickly, perfumed undercurrent. The ground was all ploughed up, and at first he thought he was looking at logs, felled trees perhaps. A nearby boot gave the game away, then Jules noticed a triple-braided cuff still sheltering a wrist, and then another limb, protruding with an impossible twist. Though the square had been dug over, the graves were too shallow. Here and there lay smashed-up wicker baskets, filled with soil for barricades by market-women a few days earlier, now abandoned: mocking monuments in a makeshift cemetery. More bodies were arriving and in the distance a couple of army corporals were at work with buckets of lime, white powder clouding the air. Jules moved away, sickened, thinking of pestilence and plague pits, feeling dizzy with the effort to breathe less deeply.

Then he noticed something else that made his bile rise. At his feet crept lines of blood, sliding down the gutters towards the Seine, finding their way along the cracks between paving stones, dividing and reforming wherever they had to. He tried to step clear, but his wheels still left a track of crimson.

At this point, Jules considered abandoning his cart and his cameras, his clothes and his friend, and simply walking into the nearest bar and ordering an absinthe, and then another, and another. He felt almost ready to try oblivion. But if there was a chance of saving Anatole, Jules had to take it. He had to keep going. So he tied his silk handkerchief round his face against the smell, just below his eyes, which seemed to stretch them open. The back of his tongue rose instinctively in the roof of his mouth, barricading his nostrils from within.

In the café, Marie forced down a helping of mutton stew and pushed back her empty plate. She had chosen a place a few streets away, not one of her regular spots. Somewhere she wasn't known. Her pockets were stuffed with bread to take back for Zéphyrine, filled under the cover of her napkin. Marie wasn't going to risk carrying wine or milk back. As she had left her own building, the concierge had told her to abandon her basket. Women were being shot on the street for being caught with any kind of container. Things were worse even than she realised.

The proprietor came over with her bill. Standing at her elbow as she looked in her purse for the right coins, he kept his eyes on the window, watching the pavements, which were increasingly empty. People were beginning to walk in the middle of the road to advertise their safety. An idea came to her. It was obvious, in a way.

'Monsieur, do you have some paper? And a pen? I need to write something. I'm in a hurry.'

She wanted him to be quick because she didn't want to change her mind. Everything inside her started to thud at once, all her organs shifting. Her breath was forced out of her nostrils in such short quick bursts that she imagined the whole café must be alert to her fear. She was on the verge of doing a truly terrible thing. The worst she had done in her entire life. She would have to spend the rest of her life on her knees praying for forgiveness.

'Certainly, mademoiselle. Right away.'

Marie stared at his retreating back. She could still change her mind. No, she couldn't. This suddenly seemed the only answer.

An image was in her head and she couldn't dislodge it: Emile arriving, exhausted and armed, Zéphyrine in a huddle, rocking and rocking. How had Marie imagined there could possibly be time to explain, or a chance to intervene? What would she say? Emile was a soldier. He was trained to kill and the Commune was his enemy. It was obvious what he would have to do. At least Marie tried to persuade herself that this was the reason for her decision. She couldn't bear to witness, with her own eyes, whatever might happen next. The truth she pushed away was worse than that. The reason she was writing was that she wanted to be sure of her own safety.

'Here you are, mademoiselle. Thank you, mademoiselle. Very generous.' Sweeping the coins into the palm of his hand, he dropped them into the deep pocket of his white apron. A few moments later he had produced paper, pen and ink.

In a steady, looping hand, she began to write. 'To whom it may concern . . .'

* * *

Was disobedience really an obligation now? Anatole had no time to think. All too clearly, all too quickly, the enemy was advancing, and he was at the very centre of the storm. Every deafening crash and explosion seemed his last. But somehow it was still followed by yet another. He felt caught in the machinery of a giant boiler house, rolling and whistling and cracking and crushing, and he longed for the engine to spit him out. When the cry came for more ammunition, Anatole saw only screaming mouths and panic. All noise was one and nothing.

Running back to the temporary stores, dodging behind sandbags, a final blast made him turn his head. He fell headlong against a mess of stones that had once been the kerb of a pavement.

That evening, at about seven thirty, a man gave up hope. He was an old man, a brave man, a ravaged man. He had kept his nerve and his optimism all through the failed revolutions of 1830 and 1848, even surviving Devil's Island, the South American penal colony, though the consumption he contracted in Cayenne was slowly killing him. Military commander since April, Charles Delescluze had led the Commune with courage these last few weeks, but by Thursday he knew he could not save it.

Once again, he gave orders to evacuate. The wounded were to be sent on ahead: they couldn't be left to the vengeance of Versailles. The only safety left was the heights to the east, where Belleville and Père Lachaise still held firm. Delescluze wrote a letter to his sister, then pulled his broad red sash of office over his head, the only marker of his status. Black coat, grey trousers, silk hat, patent leather boots. He carried his habitual cane, but took no weapon.

It wasn't a long walk from the neighbourhood's town hall to the barricades on the place du Château d'Eau – perhaps twenty minutes – but the enemy fire never let up. As he walked, Delescluze greeted the men of the National Guard who had held firm all through this terrible week, and pressed their hands, foot soldiers as well as officers. He ignored their repeated warnings of the danger he was walking into, the screech of falling shells. When he reached the barricade, he turned, and looked at his comrades for the last time. The sun was setting. With difficulty – his joints resisted his command – he climbed to the top. Then he vanished, shot dead.

By midnight the remaining leaders of the Commune had moved for the last time. Holed up in Belleville, they resumed their arguments.

32.

Friday morning. In the chaos of that night, Anatole's dishevelled company followed orders, and began its final retreat. Thinking him dead, no doubt, or possibly drunk, they left him behind, knocked out among the rubble. He had lain unconscious while the Versailles troops swept through in the night and on up the hill. In the early hours of Friday morning, rain finally brought him round. A soup of mist was rewriting the city, distorting sight and sound, muffling the cannon's thunder and playing games with Anatole's mind. He remembered running through the rain with Zéphyrine in April. He imagined, though not for long, that he was with her again, hearing the storm cloud's thunder, soaked to the skin. She was urging him to take off his wet clothes, and he was laughing at her and making bargains. And of course, when he lifted his head, he found himself crumpled in the gutter, water rushing towards him, his sodden body damming a drain.

He raised himself up on his forearms, experimentally, and stared this way and that into unforgiving blackness. Screwing

292

up his eyes, he wiped his forehead uselessly with a drenched cuff, and ran a damp hand round a wool-chafed neck. He had lost his kepi. Anatole pressed gently on his skull. Everything felt dark and dripping and painful, and he could not tell if it was blood or rain on his fingers.

Shifting any part of his body was an effort. Movement, however small, awakened bruises, and the cold and wet came creeping into corners they hadn't reached before. But this was no place to stay. The hiatus couldn't last much longer. More people would be here soon, perhaps in uniforms, clearing away the dead, securing the buildings and searching for runaways like him. Anatole crawled forward on all fours, and his fingers brushed against cloth. With a small leap of hope at the thought of company, he grasped the bulky material firmly in both hands, thinking he might feel out a leg, or an arm, or even just a discarded coat. Any of these possibilities might offer a swig of brandy, and help get him through till daylight.

It was a leg, but it didn't move. Anatole shook it almost angrily. 'Come on,' he muttered. 'Don't let me down. Can't stay here.'

Then he realised that he had spent the night huddled close to a corpse, a corpse that presumably had kept him safe. Anatole drew back, and staggered, heaving, to his feet.

He recognised nothing and nowhere, barely knew which way he was moving. The city was in disguise: trees split as if by lighting, twisted ironwork and decapitated streetlamps confused him, and the onslaught had left buildings exposed and disfigured. Some were almost intact, except for a shutter dangling from a hinge. Others had become unrecognisable carcasses of brickwork and rafters and carpets, fog and smoke wandering into deserted drawing rooms through smashed-up walls, wreathing itself round banisters. Anatole imagined residents stirring in cellars beneath, thanking God they were still alive, not daring to emerge into the wreckage above their heads.

He didn't suppose any of them would knowingly take him in. He'd dumped his coat, despite the rain; the scattering of scorch marks on the shoulder of his jacket, tiny gunpowder-sprayed holes made by weapons fired immediately behind him, would betray him as fast as any uniform. Anatole shivered in filthy shirtsleeves, and while he looked for a temporary refuge his thoughts pendulumed from Zéphyrine to Jules and back again. He couldn't bear to think what might be happening in Montmartre now. He consoled himself with the thought that at least Jules must be safe. Jules was not a fool. He always knew what to do. Perhaps Anatole should have listened to him five days ago. He missed them both terribly.

The paving stones jolted vertically through the length of his body, heel to hip to head, chiselling his skull with every step he took. At last he found a likely-looking house. A shell must have hit it very recently. One window was smashed in completely, and every pane of glass on every floor had shattered. It was relatively easy for Anatole to climb inside, and there was still no one around to see him.

He checked the cellar first, which was empty, although some dirty cups, a blanket and mattress and a discarded cap and apron suggested it had been recently occupied, perhaps by a maid left to guard the house. Anatole thought she must have fled after the bombing, but he couldn't be quite sure. Nobody in the kitchen or scullery. There again were signs of hasty abandonment. Damp curtains flapped in the drawing room and dining room, where the furniture had been covered with dustsheets. Anatole continued his prowl upstairs. When he saw a single, canopied bed piled high with embroidered cushions, and skirted protectively with plenty of frills and lace, he plunged into the dustballs beneath it to hide.

If you have money, and good clothes, and if you talk nicely of course, doors will generally open. It's the way the world works. Jules had found a cheap travellers' hotel west of the canal and south of the station, paid in advance for his room and hot water, and even persuaded the proprietor to adopt the cat. It was harder for Jules to say goodbye to Minou than it was for Monsieur Valette to agree to take her in: with cats such a rarity in Paris, the mice were getting out of hand.

The following morning Jules recovered from a sleepless night with a coffee in the breakfast room. The table linen was a little stained, but crisply ironed, and the air carried only a faint hint of the previous night's food, or possibly the one before. He was not surprised to discover that there were no other guests. In a week with few customers, the hotelier seemed particularly anxious to please. He had carefully brilliantined his thinning hair and seemed quite determined to carry on as normal. So their conversation was studiedly neutral. The temperature of the bath was mentioned, and also the number of sugar lumps some guests required. Monsieur Valette had shut the windows against the rain, and both observed that an abnormal number of flies were now banging on the glass to escape.

The portable darkroom was safely locked up in the courtyard, and Jules had had quite enough of dragging the vehicle, so he asked Monsieur Valette to summon an ostler to negotiate the price of a horse for the day. Then he tried to prepare himself for whatever he might find outside. He rested his forehead on his fingertips, tilting it this way and that, as if it might channel his growing dread into something more useful.

He wasn't in a neighbourhood that he knew very well. When Jules first arrived in Paris, he'd drifted compulsively from boulevard to park to sidestreet, often tempted by the seedier parts of town. His wanderings had become more purposeful since he had discovered photography. He'd come to prefer the unexpected reflections and watery aquarium haze of those glass-covered arcades nearer home, where he'd first run into Anatole. An observer by nature, a watcher of crowds from within, Jules generally had an instinct for finding his way round the city. And he'd had a lifetime of staying out of trouble, of not being noticed when he didn't want to be. All he could do now, he decided, was simply keep on going. The important thing was to be systematic in his search, to stay as calm as he could – on the outside at least.

A bell rang, announcing the arrival of the livery boy, and Jules pushed back his chair. When he reached the dining-room door, he glanced behind him, suddenly overwhelmed by unspecified guilt, a feeling that he might have left something behind. The hotelier had cleared his tablecloth, and stood balanced on top of the table. He was reaching up with a rolled-up newspaper to swat at a gathering cloud of flies. Caught in the act, he shrugged apologetically.

'The dead,' he said. 'They are beginning to take their revenge.'

'Wait!' Marie wanted to say. 'We're not ready.' As if she ever could be.

They came so much earlier, so much more quickly than she'd imagined possible. A few minutes before, she'd woken to whimpering through the wall, and the crash and scrape of furniture violently thrown aside. An elderly schoolmistress had the room next door. Could she really be harbouring a rebel? Perhaps she taught at one of the new secular schools. That would be enough. Marie wondered what sort of person would betray an old woman like that. Then she realised exactly who might do such a thing. Someone with a grudge or a grievance. Someone frightened enough for their own life. Someone who didn't want to be caught themselves, who had never wanted to go along with any of this. Someone a bit like Marie. Seconds later they were hammering on her own door.

Zéphyrine had finally fallen asleep, her eyelids flickering against Marie's pillow, while Marie herself dozed, on and off, in the wickerwork chair. She sprang to her feet with unhinged knees, steadied herself and, remembering an old trick of her mother's, gently pinched Zéphyrine's empty earlobes. Her eyes duly opened without a sound. Marie shushed her with a finger on her lip.

The door handle was rattling. The old lady was weeping.

'Get in the trunk,' Marie said. She didn't know why. It was far too late to change her mind. She couldn't bear for Zéphyrine to see her face when the door opened. 'Quick.'

Zéphyrine leapt dizzily from the bed, and fell into the pile of clothes. Something tore as Marie whisked out a gown to make room for her, and Zéphyrine scrabbled for space, paddling like a mole. The trunk lid closed and the world went black. She lay with her face prickled against the twisting wire stems of flowers on a summer bonnet. She couldn't hear words: just a low rumble that told her these were men's voices. Then the reverberation of boots on the floorboards, followed by clinking metal. It wasn't a big room, but it seemed to take them no time at all to work out where she was. As quickly as she had hidden, she was exposed, left blinking at the light. An angry face thrust itself into hers.

'Out!' The spitting mouth flicked her with tobacco juice. It reeked with the stench of last night's brandy. She tried to bury herself further but the man simply reached in and dragged her out backwards by the elbows. She was only wearing a petticoat, one of Marie's, but he didn't care.

Horrified, Marie thrust a shawl at her. 'Take this.'

Marie wouldn't meet her eyes, and dropped to her knees on the floor. Zéphyrine felt her cool hands on her ankles, pushing her feet into shoes. She saw Marie's shoulders were shaking.

Zéphyrine's hands were roped behind her back. She was pushed down the stairs, bruising her shoulders as she lurched unevenly from wall to banister, and straight into a puddle outside. Now it was raining hard. The old schoolteacher from the next room and the young man she had been hiding – her nephew – were already soaked to the skin and shivering when they roped them all together, the weight of hemp doubled by wetness. Zéphyrine looked up, blinking, unable to shield her eyes from the falling rain. There were tricolour flags now damply hanging from almost every window in the street. No sign of Marie being pushed down the stairs to join her. Why not? What had they done with her? Would they shoot her on the spot? Zéphyrine came out of her stupor. She hadn't meant to put Marie's life in danger like this. She hadn't wanted this. She wondered how she would ever make amends. She almost wished she could pray for her, but what was the point?

As soon as they began to move, her shawl slid off her bare shoulders, tangling with the rope at her wrists, then dragging in the mud behind her until another prisoner stepped on it, nearly tripped, and tugged it free. Their little group joined others, and eventually there were twenty men and women all tied together, marching behind another twenty, in front of yet another twenty.

Blood raged under the skin of Zéphyrine's cheeks and left her face blazing. If her grandmother could see her now, she'd die again, for shame. She couldn't stand it. She wouldn't stand it. To be paraded like a whore, half-dressed, almost naked, hair shorn. It was indecent. Jeers and laughter roared like surf in her ears. The schoolteacher jerked and twisted her ancient neck, in contorted, failing circles, like a crazed pigeon courting, or a turkey begging to be beheaded. Her wet white hair flopped in snakes around her shoulders. Had she been driven mad? No, Zéphyrine realised. Someone had spat at her, right in her face, and she was trying to wipe off the insult on her shoulder.

Zéphyrine turned to confront the crowds on the pavement. Instantly she saw an expression she knew too well – not a face, but a look. Sneering, triumphant, despising. The look her stepfather had worn the day she had left home. When he knew, but she didn't, that she was not coming back. After that, Zéphyrine kept staring straight ahead, tilting her chin. It helped keep the tears from overflowing, and she didn't want to show tears. If it made her look arrogant, defiant, so much the better. It was the best kind of face to show the world.

She couldn't tell how much time passed, or how far they stumbled, before they were brought to a halt. The prisoners all knocked into each other, bodies taking too long to catch up with dulled minds. If one fell, all would, so they pushed and strained and jumbled together, trying to stay as one. A murmur passed through, quiet as a sigh. 'Stay on your feet. Don't die on your knees.' She locked her legs. She didn't want to die in any position.

Hot bodies, hot breath, rancid smells. But these strangers, all pressed up against each other, were strangely comforting. She felt a small hand brush against hers. It slid into her palm, and held on tight, too tight, gripping two of her fingers as though for life itself. When Zéphyrine twisted her head to see over her shoulder, her face and neck knotted with the effort, she realised it was just a little boy. When she tried to smile at him, to give him some comfort, her lips curled stiffly and it felt more like a snarl. The boy didn't speak, but he didn't let go.

Orders were shouted. Zéphyrine hardly knew what. Some men were picked out for further inspection. It wasn't clear how choices were made. They were looking for officers: possession of a watch was enough, it seemed, to mark out a man as a leader in the National Guard and condemn him. The captives stood waiting, surreptitiously rubbing their roped wrists, knowing this temporary release would most likely lead to something worse, but uncertain what that might be. A court martial? Were they to be tried, here and now, in this courtyard? Nobody knew.

Behind a wall, the machine guns began their dull clatter.

One National Guardsman's eyes kept measuring the distance between the gate and the huddle of prisoners. He was a paymaster, weighed down by his responsibility. Before it was too late, he grabbed a little pouch of coins from his breeches' pocket.

'Listen, comrades!' he said quickly. 'This is my unit's wages. I couldn't get it to the right people yesterday. God knows where they are now. Here – I want to give it to you – it won't do anyone any good if they shoot me.'

He threw the bag into the mass of prisoners, and somehow they passed the coins around. Zéphyrine shook her head. She had nowhere to keep a coin, and she didn't want to let go of the boy's fingers.

'Get in line! Closer! *Serrez les rangs!*'

Marching orders again, for those who remained. The taunting from the pavements continued, unending. 'Murderers! Thieves!' they shouted. 'Look what you've done, you bastard scum, you evil toads! Deport the lot of them, every last Communard. You're getting what you deserve now.'

There was still no sign of Marie.

Jules's camera hood gave him some protection, a place to hide his face, and somewhere to shelter his shock. Hidden by black velvet, through rain-spattered glass, he could scrutinise the streets almost without being seen, anonymous and invisible.

Mid-morning, a company of Versailles soldiers marched by, and his hands quivered on the lens cap, but they just glanced at him and nodded, clearly assuming he was on official business. Recording the crimes of the Commune, he supposed. Collecting evidence. The friends of order men who followed in their wake left him alone too, except for one enthusiastic officer who rushed back to tap him on the shoulder. He pointed out a place of execution Jules might otherwise have missed at the end of a long passage, where buildings rose high on either side: a dead end indeed.

Three or four times, Jules stopped at scenes so similar they merged in his mind: a wall, splashed and pockmarked with bullet holes, bodies slumped at its foot, or carelessly heaped, drenched in rain, dark with blood. Each time he fought his first impulse to vomit and flee. Each time he forced himself to confront these faces. Every one of these bodies was a person. Any one of them might be Anatole.

Some lay almost as if dreaming, concealing the secret of their death like a private joke with the ghost of a smile. Half-open milky eyes; lips curling back from tombstone teeth, tobacco-stained. All ages, all degrees of beauty, women alongside men, hair rat-tailed by the endless rain. He saw cheekbones hollow as poets' – the effect of a jaw, slackening in horror or relief, or the remains of hunger – lying in puddles. Greying temples, ragged beards, broken spectacles and sodden ripped banners. Jules looked at each face with proper care as he framed and focused, trying to commit its particular and specific features to memory, trying to make out detail through the distortions of raindrops and sometimes tears.

The horse stood and waited with drooping head, nostrils flaring.

Jules felt a responsibility to preserve each face he saw. These likenesses would be perfect – these eyes could not blink, these faces could not twitch. But he could only capture them in his memory; he had to fake his photography. Packed in sawdust at the back of the darkroom was a single collodion bottle, well-stoppered, containing the dregs of his last but one batch. Just enough, perhaps, to coat a single plate. He had to save it, because if he ever found the one face he was looking for, he needed to be able to keep its likeness. And if he didn't? If he never found that face again? Jules couldn't let himself believe this might happen. Surely, if Anatole was dead he would be able to feel it, he would somehow know?

Each time, as Jules and his camera and the darkroom on wheels moved on, leaving the bodies behind for others to stare at, he wondered who would pick them up, and when, and how anyone would ever know where they had gone. Also, how long he could continue this searching, which logic was beginning to tell him must be fruitless.

Anatole spent two hours lying in dust and darkness, waiting for a beam to give way, for voices or boots on the landing. It seemed implausible that he was still alive. When the house had remained silent for so long he felt his wits might turn, which was also when the ringing hum in his ears became too loud to bear, he backed out of his hiding place, and stood up and stretched, still listening. He wasn't quite sure what he was looking for. He opened a drawer, and shut it again quickly, flushing. Of course, this was a young girl's room. Vacant eyes stared at him from beneath carefully painted lashes and disdainful eyebrows: a doll with golden ringlets and pursed lips, fallen on the mantelpiece at a stiff diagonal.

He set her upright again. 'Don't move,' he told her, and tried the next room.

He hated prowling around like this, leaving streaks and scuffs as he slid against the wallpaper to keep out of sight. It was horrible, invasive, but absolutely necessary. Before long, he'd realised exactly what he needed and found it too. A rack of slightly musty coats and trousers in a man's dressing room – an elderly uncle or grandfather, he imagined. The cut of these clothes was a little old-fashioned, but the size wasn't impossible. He even found a ticket for the opera in the pocket of one, a frock coat with wide velvet lapels and cuffs. He held it against himself, and stood in front of a long oval looking glass, which pivoted in its frame. The glass was cracked in three, the bottom section missing, but Anatole saw at once that he would need to wash and shave before he went out again. To hide in plain sight, he would have to look the part.

Half an hour later, he thought he had come close enough, and left the building by the front door. He had even borrowed a silver-headed cane and a top hat, so that he could stride disapprovingly along what remained of the pavements, nodding to any passing policeman, if he dared. Luckily, he saw none. It was still pouring with rain, and hardly anybody was about. He tried to get some bearings. He supposed he should head home, that Jules would be waiting, as usual, in the apartment in the rue de Provence. Jules would be angry, very angry, but he would forgive him.

Then Anatole let himself hope, allowed fantasy free rein. Zéphyrine was always so resourceful. Surely she would be there too, waiting with Jules. Where else could she have taken shelter, after all? Where else would have been safer? Marie would be fine, he was sure. She was a survivor too. When he got back, the three of them would send her a message and then they could all have supper together. It would be . . . No, of course it wouldn't, it couldn't ever be like old times again.

Behind him, he heard the slow clippety-clop of a single horse's hooves, carriage wheels sloshing through the flooded road, and a harness jingling ever louder. It was the first vehicle that had approached since he had been walking. He urged himself to keep walking. No flinching, though every atom in his body begged him to turn and run. He continued to stroll, not too quickly, not too slowly, even humming a jaunty tune to complete the act. Oh, he looked like a bourgeois gentleman triumphant through and through, he persuaded himself. The masses were defeated. The madness was over. Order would soon return.

The vehicle drew up alongside him, and Anatole heard the hooves scuffle and stop, as the horse was reined in. He imagined the driver's head turning, a staring face. He kept looking straight ahead, kept smiling his stupid rigid smile, barely hitting one note in four as he hummed. His eyes flicked nervously towards the road, his view blocked by the brim of his hat.

'Anatole?' The voice wavered with disbelief.

At last Anatole looked up.

Jules jumped down from the high driver's seat with a cry like a sob, and splashed through the overflowing gutter. A second later he was crushing Anatole so hard that he struggled for breath. His knocked-off hat rolled back and forth on the pavement, his face lay pressed against a velvet lapel, and he heard Jules whisper, over and over again, 'My dear, my dear, oh my dear.'

They tied up the horse in a side street, and crouched in the dim orange light of the darkroom, rocking with relief, trying to work out the next step. In the heat of reunion, Jules kept grasping Anatole's hands, his dear familiar hands, the hands he thought he would never see again. Anatole returned his hot grip with equal strength.

'Oh Jules, I thought I'd never see you again,' said Anatole. He drew back to look at Jules, then reached out a hand to stroke his face and touch his shoulder. 'I can't believe you're here. I simply don't know how you found me. You're extraordinary. You cannot understand what this means to me.'

They were so close. Their lips could meet so easily. But just as Jules leaned forward, ready to declare his love out loud, unequivocally, once and for all, Anatole put a hand on his knee and asked him eagerly what news he had of Zéphyrine.

'Zéphyrine?' Jules choked and withdrew. He felt cold. His skin seemed to crawl, as if a spiderweb had floated onto his face.

'Yes, Zéphyrine. Of course Zéphyrine. What is it? What's happened? Haven't you seen her?'

'No. I'm sorry. I've no idea where she is.'

Anatole let out a groan.

'Shhh . . . someone will hear. Anyway, we can't stay. We have to get moving.'

'Wait! No! No idea? Oh Christ.'

'I'm sorry,' said Jules uneasily, hot with shame. 'It's been impossible. I don't know what you imagined. Montmartre fell so quickly. And I told you, I've been looking for you all this time. I had to find you before they did. I told you that.'

'Yes, yes, of course. I know. I understand. Thank you. I just thought, if she could, she would have . . .'

He didn't say, and Jules didn't want to hear.

'We can talk about it later. Right now, you must just stay here, in the back, out of sight, until I've sorted something out. Your clothes are absurd. You look like somebody's grandfather. And you've cut yourself shaving – didn't you notice? The fewer people that see you, the better.'

Anatole was still staring into nothingness, looking wilder than ever. 'What am I going to do?' he said almost inaudibly. 'I thought . . . I hoped . . .'

'Come on – we've got to hurry. It may be too late already to get out of Paris. The Prussians are closing their gates.'

'Get out? We can't leave now!'

'We can't stay. You can't. They're looking for you. They've been looking for you for days.'

Anatole looked bewildered.

'Do you really have no idea?' said Jules. 'The Commune can't last much longer. Hours. Days at the very most, but more likely just a few hours. And there are reprisals happening everywhere already.'

No reaction, but Anatole seemed a little calmer, so Jules jumped down to untie the horse. They had to get moving. As soon as they were out of danger, he wanted to find Anatole a doctor.

'Jules?' Anatole called softly.

'What is it?'

'Do we really have to leave Paris?'

'Yes, we do.'

'When can we come back?'

'I don't know. Look, you're going to have to be quiet now. We've got to start moving.'

'Yes. Sorry. But, Jules?'

'What?'

'My violin,' said Anatole. 'I don't suppose you brought my violin?'

Jules hesitated. He didn't want to tell Anatole about the missing photograph.

'Yes. Yes, I did. It's behind you, right behind the trunk. Don't worry. And Minou is safe too – no, not here. But I've found someone who'll take care of her, so you don't need to worry about her. Now, you mustn't talk any more.'

In Marie's doorway, a red-trousered soldier with a neatly trimmed blond moustache stood straight and tall, and very wet. His eyes were bloodshot and pouchy, his expression vacant. She opened her arms, ready to weep with happiness. When she told him what she had done, he would reassure her, even be proud of her. She could cast off the ghastly shame that dragged at her heart.

But Emile Le Gall had barely moved. He took a single sluggish step towards his sister and stopped. It hadn't been quite a year since they last saw each other, yet he seemed twenty years older.

'What's the matter?' she asked. He stared right through her. 'What are you looking at? What can you see? Say something, Emile . . . please. Tell me you're not hurt.'

He seemed to be making a vast effort to retrieve something, from some dark cellar in his mind.

'Why?' he said. Then he repeated the word, over and over again, until it lost all meaning. 'Why? Why? Why? Why?'

Marie heard a door bang. Anyone could be listening. She took Emile's arm, and pulled at it, but he just looked at her hand on his sleeve, as if it were unconnected to either of them.

'Come on, come inside,' she said. 'Sit down. Lie down, if you want to. You must be exhausted.'

She pushed him inside, and quickly turned the key in the lock. He swayed almost imperceptibly. Before she led him to the armchair, she reached up and gave him a quick kiss on the cheek, but he didn't return it. Just raised a hand, and cupped it over the place her lips had been, and went on staring. It was exactly the same empty stare she'd seen on Zéphyrine. A stare that took in everything, and nothing at all.

'Shhhh . . . Shhhhhhh . . . Give me your coat. You're soaking.' Marie started to unbutton it, and then stopped, and put her arms round him anyway, and tried to rock him like a baby. But he was stiff and resistant, more like a rigid corpse. 'It's over now. You've saved Paris. It's nearly over. We can celebrate. We're free.'

'Free?'

He jerked away from her, and she let out a cry. 'Emile! Stop it . . . Don't you know me? I'm your sister, remember?'

'You'll wish you weren't when you hear what I've done. You don't know what I've done.'

He just kept saying the same words.

'What?' she whispered, and at last he seemed to see her.

'Oh, Marie, I followed orders . . . I just followed orders. You know I've always done what I was told . . . but such orders . . . Oh God . . . How could this have been allowed? Why did I let myself? How did it happen? Why? Why? Why?'

Stuck on that single word again.

'Stop, stop, Emile.' She took him by the shoulders and shook him, and then tried to hold him up, to straighten his spine, as if she could physically resist his slouch of despair. The words on the poster came back to her. When the order is unspeakable, disobedience is an obligation. But that wasn't true. How could it be true? 'You have done your duty. What more could you ask of yourself? You're a hero. My brother, the hero of Paris – home at last!'

He shook his head. 'No. Oh no.'

There are always boys hanging around stations looking for errands to run. Jules quickly found a temporary guard for the darkroom. He told him that there were extremely dangerous chemicals in the back, and on no account should he go inside or allow anyone else to do so or he would risk an explosion. The boy looked impressed.

Jules hated leaving Anatole again, even for the short time he hoped it would take to buy two first-class tickets to

310

Geneva. Better to have some documentation than none at all, he reasoned. Something to keep inspectors happy. At the border, they would improvise. He had the trunk. He would work something out.

Part of the station had been cordoned off. They were setting up another execution post. Any big space with an open wall would do. A station was ideal. Policemen swaggered about the concourse in twos and threes, eyes everywhere, blue backs always ready to turn. Jules suddenly didn't know if he could carry this through. He had to hold on to a railing to steady himself. He remembered Marie and the breathing exercises she had given Zéphyrine to keep her still in front of the camera. He counted slowly to himself and walked purposefully towards the ticket office.

The queue was long and well dressed. He wanted to be calm and jovial, but didn't quite trust himself to speak. He ran through a few suitable pleasantries in his mind, and imagined himself exchanging them with the pair of middle-aged gentlemen that the snaking line had brought almost opposite him.

'Not the best day for travelling,' he said at last.

'Business is business. And time stops for no man.'

'Quite so. I hope they're keeping a good watch on these trains. Can't have those devils escaping, can we?'

'Certainly not. We'll need to keep our eyes peeled.'

'Well, at least the rain is easing off.'

Jules tried to shake off the conviction that they were staring at him oddly. He wished he knew where to get hold of one of those blue-white-and-red armbands. Then he prayed again that Anatole was keeping still and silent, that he wouldn't do anything stupid.

The line of passengers made steady progress. When the shooting began, out of sight at the back of the station, eyes blinked and jaws hardened, but nobody said a word.

Jules reached the glass window. There would be a train at midnight, he discovered. There were three first-class compartments left. He was lucky. He expressed surprise and relief that the trains were still running, and began a complicated story about the family wedding he was due to attend in —

The ticket seller cut him short. 'Oh they can afford to keep running the trains. It's easy to find someone on a train, if you know where to look.'

'Yes, I suppose it must be. Thank God for that.'

Outside the station, the boy who'd been minding the horse put out his hand for his coins. The rain had stopped completely. The horse stamped and swished its tail to be rid of the mobbing flies that had immediately returned.

'I've got one more job for you,' said Jules loudly enough for Anatole to hear. 'See the shop over there?' Then he shook his head. He didn't trust the boy with his shopping. 'No, on second thoughts, you wait here. I'll just be a few more minutes and then you'll get your money. If anyone comes, it's the same as before. If they won't go away, keep them talking until I get back. I don't advise you to get too close though.'

He bought the best pâté he could find and a good Bordeaux; it was a traveller's meal so irreproachably bourgeois that no revolutionary in flight could possibly consider it. More incongruously, he also bought a large sack of rice, which he asked the shop assistant to carry over to the waiting vehicle. The food was to show what fine, sensible, greedy gentlemen they were. The rice was to go in the trunk, to give it weight and realism when the porter slung it into the train carriage. A trunk heavy with a body would raise suspicion. Once they were on their way, each grain could be disposed of, bit by bit, leaving the hiding place vacant.

'Now will they shoot us?' The young boy asked the question as soon as the prisoners came to their next halt. There was angry shouting up ahead, and a call to clear the road.

'I hope so,' someone else said. 'Then it will be over.'

'One shot. That's all we need. That will be that,' said another.

'I don't know what will happen to us,' Zéphyrine told the boy. 'We'll see.'

Then she ducked her head, flinching. Something soft had fallen from the sky. She hunched her shoulders against attack, and another small object brushed gently against her face and landed in the mud at her feet. A flower. A rose. Flowers were raining down on them, bunches and loose stems of artificial flowers. Someone was throwing them down like alms from a balcony above, and the prisoners who caught them couldn't help kissing the dusty petals, and weeping at this sudden sign of sweetness and kindness and respect.

Anatole resisted the temptation to look out of the window. He kept expecting to see soldiers marching down the platform, ready to haul him off the train. His fingers picked so compulsively at the velvet buttons on the seat cushion that one came off in his hand. Every few seconds he glanced at the black silk blind.

'Very well. Pull it down if you insist. Perhaps it would be safer.'

'Nobody wants to walk into a first-class compartment, if they don't know who is inside,' argued Anatole.

'But we need to show we've got nothing to hide. Especially until the train leaves. They'll start searching when the train gets moving. Before the border. That's when you need to hide. Have some more pâté.'

'We could be asleep by now.'

'I said you could pull it down.'

Anatole pulled down the blind. A few minutes later Jules spoke again. 'You're my brother-in-law, remember? Your passport was burned. We couldn't wait.'

He was beginning to confuse himself. They had rehearsed and rejected so many different stories.

'I know. I know,' said Anatole. 'Our grandfather is on his deathbed, threatening to change his will. It is imperative that we reach Geneva with all speed. I understand. I'll remember.'

'Good.'

'Are you married to my sister or am I married to yours?' Anatole was beginning to panic.

'We said I was married to yours. Does that make sense? No. Make it the other way round. Her name is . . . Sophie.'

'And what time is it now? I thought we were meant to leave at midnight.'

Jules looked at his watch again.

'Still another two minutes to go,' he said.

314

'Two?'

Without warning, Anatole stood up, and pitched towards the corridor. He looked drunk. Before he could reach the door, Jules had jammed himself between the seats and luggage racks.

'No,' he insisted. 'No. Sit down. Now.'

'I can't.'

'You have to.'

'No, I can't do this, Jules. I can't leave Zéphyrine. I've got to try to find her. It's not too late. I know it isn't.'

'Don't make a scene,' hissed Jules. 'Let's not do this again. I won't let you. You can't help her now.'

'How can I leave Paris when I don't know if Zéphyrine is dead or alive?'

'You have to. Because I lied. I know. I know what's happened.'

Anatole stopped trying to push past him. Jules couldn't quite look at him. Lying now was the only way. Hadn't it been a kind of lie already, his failure to tell Anatole that the authorities already had Zéphyrine's photograph, that they would be looking for her now, if she wasn't dead already? It was time to go one step further. He coughed. He only had seconds left. He had to be convincing.

'I didn't want to tell you before. I knew how much it would upset you.'

'Tell me what? For God's sake. Tell me.'

A whistle shrieked.

'The day after you left, the morning after Montmartre had fallen, Zéphyrine came looking for you,' said Jules.

That much was true. The sudden joy on Anatole's face was agonising.

315

'She did come! Why didn't you say? I knew she would come!'

'She came because she wanted to make sure you weren't at the theatre. She had orders, you see. She had orders to burn down both the theatres by the river. They chose her because she knew the lie of the land better than anyone else. Zéphyrine was on her way to the Lyrique. I couldn't bear to tell you before. I wasn't even sure you would believe me. Zéphyrine was a *pétroleuse*, you see. She destroyed your theatre. And soon afterwards they caught her and shot her dead.'

The train began to move.

33.

27th May

Saturday. All through the night they slowly jolted through darkness, and a barely perceptible trickle of rice fell from the window to lie beside the track. Jules was methodical, releasing handful after handful of the dusty grains, while Anatole kept watch for ticket inspectors, or worse. Neither of them mentioned Zéphyrine again, but Jules quickly became haunted by the idea that Anatole might do something stupid, something operatic. He thought of all those stage lovers united in death. You couldn't see slaughter on the scale Jules had witnessed and have any faith in that. He prepared himself to act at the slightest warning sign from Anatole.

At Troyes the train suddenly filled with brocade and weaponry, and Anatole clambered into the trunk just in time. For several minutes, feet marched up and down the corridor, and they heard doors sliding open and shut. Then it was their turn for the compartment to be invaded.

Jules hated men like these, with their intrusive questions, their suspicious eyes. But he put on a brilliant act. He was the befuddled American tourist, too foolish to get out of Paris at the right time – it had all seemed an adventure, at first! – light-headed with relief that the city had been saved by the proper authorities. Now he was looking forward to joining his more sensible compatriots to recover on the shores of Lake Geneva. Just the thing after a fright like that. No, he agreed, Paris was not a pretty sight. And oh yes, he nodded, he was also sure that the city would soon be cleaned up, the boulevards blazing with light again, and the Americans back to do their shopping.

Sickened, Anatole listened, counting the seconds till the men left. When the door finally shut, he heard Jules sigh, long and deeply, and Anatole whispered his thanks like a prayer.

Marie sat in the armchair while Emile slept. From time to time she got up, lit a lamp and held feathers under his nose, to convince herself he was still breathing. There were lines in Emile's face she never expected to see, deep grooves round his mouth, and on his forehead. She hadn't thought a young man could change so much, in so short a time. It made her want to protect him. She never wanted to leave the room again, she felt. She would have been happy to stay within those four walls for the rest of her life, just her and Emile, nobody else ever again, if that were possible.

At last he woke. Marie jumped up, and began to fuss.

'What can I get you? Are you thirsty? What would you like me to do for you?' she said, trying to plump his pillow, desperate to make him comfortable, and also to make him talk. The funny thing was that once he started, there was almost no shushing him. Marie quickly gave up telling him everything would be fine, and her mouth hung open.

'We thought it would be easy when we first arrived. You should have seen how we marched straight through Passy – honestly, nobody even had to fire, though I can tell you I was ready to. We knew exactly how desperate – and how ruthless – the Communards were. We knew quite well they'd stop at nothing. Hadn't they always said they'd rather see Paris fall than give her up? Oh we knew exactly what we were dealing with. Animals. They kept telling us that. They'd been telling us for weeks.'

'And . . . ?'

'Well, it was extraordinary at first. Do you know, for all the talk of mines and counter-attacks, all the rumours – there was no resistance at all? We couldn't believe it. We laughed. Laughed! And you should have seen the crowds. It was the women I had to fight off, not the Communards. The women were all over us!'

Emile wiped at his eyes. Eyes are often watery when you first wake up, Marie told herself, and gave him her handkerchief.

'I'm not surprised . . . the relief they must have felt!' she said. But Emile's face had already darkened.

Marie encouraged him. 'So you came on Monday? Doesn't Monday seem years ago? I didn't dare go out, at first, and then, when I got your note, I didn't want to in case . . .' She squeezed his hand, and then couldn't stop herself from hugging him again. She wondered what he would say about Zéphyrine, and how she should tell him. 'I'd been waiting so long. I really had begun to think I'd never hear from you again. I didn't even know if they had sent you back yet from the prisoner-of-war camp.'

Later, she might tell him of her efforts to reach him, of what she had suffered in Rigault's office. But that could wait, she decided. Despite his reluctance to take the role, she really did want to give him a chance to be the hero, the saviour of Paris.

'I did write then, but God knows what happened to that letter. They told us nothing could get through to Paris. I hoped they were wrong.'

'Well, never mind . . . it's over now. You're here. We're together, at last.'

Emile tried to make the effort Marie needed. 'Yes, of course . . .' he began to say. 'That's the most important thing —'

But he couldn't do it. An unwanted vibrato had entered his voice: he was struggling to speak. Avoiding his eyes, Marie stared instead at the Adam's apple in his throat, frantically rising and falling and rising again in his effort to suppress his own sobs. Marie's skin iced over, and she began to breathe more quickly. She couldn't bear to know, but she couldn't wait any longer in ignorance.

'Tell me. Tell me what you've done.'

'I can't.'

His tears began to flow quite openly down now; he made no effort to wipe them away. His face had frozen into the grimace of a gargoyle, with stretched lips and bulging eyes, as if every part of his body was straining to contain the awfulness inside.

'Tell me. And afterwards I will tell you what I have done. And then you'll see. Your little sister is in no position to judge.'

It should have been no consolation. Two wrongs don't make a right. But something in Marie's grim expression seemed to release Emile's final words. And confession felt good.

'They told us we were fighting godless savages. They told us the workers hated us. They told us they were foreign infiltrators, not true French patriots. They told us we were fighting the enemies of the nation. They told us the Communards were crazed monsters, evil, inhuman . . . that the women were all —' he whispered the words as if saying them more quietly might somehow protect Marie — 'bitches and harpies and whores.'

'I know,' muttered Marie, who had from time to time told herself the same.

'We had a duty to restore public order. Of course we had to do our duty. That's what we kept telling ourselves.'

'You were right. It was your duty.'

'But then they brought them in. Lined them up. We saw them all . . . There were hundreds of them.'

'Arsonists and *pétroleuses*? Criminals?'

'No, no . . . I don't think they were . . . These were mothers with babies at their breasts, young boys, orphans, old men. National Guardsmen too of course. But just ordinary people, lots of them. Some were poor, some maybe getting by, not doing so badly, you know. Not so different from us, perhaps, if we'd been a bit less lucky. And now what will they do with them? What will they do with all the . . . ?'

He stopped. The thought was unspeakable. Marie put a hand on his, but he snatched it away, as if he didn't deserve her sympathy.

'I thought there would be court martials to find out the truth. I thought they would check, at least make sure they had the right people. I knew they couldn't all be guilty. Anyone could see that. How could they possibly all be guilty?'

'But surely they had a plan? The army . . . The government? They must have known what they were doing?' Marie had to persuade herself. 'They were looking for the ringleaders, weren't they?' That was what Anatole had told her. They would only execute the ringleaders.

'No, no, Marie, you don't understand. They wanted everyone. We didn't know what we were dealing with until it was too late. We didn't know there would be so many. That they would just keep on coming, and coming, and coming.'

Hatred. Vengeance.

'And then . . .' His voice faltered again, and Marie closed her eyes. 'They gave us the order to fire, and we had to obey.'

Anatole's head lay just above the train's thundering wheels. When it speeded up, the rhythm made him think of machine guns. When it slowed, he heard crackling flames. Anatole longed for silence. It was so long since there had been silence. He needed to be still to understand. All the power turning and sliding and pounding beneath him made him feel more powerless than ever. He was carried away from Paris despite himself. There was nothing he could do about Zéphyrine. At four in the morning, the train began to slow, long before it was near a station, and both Anatole and Jules almost lost their nerve.

'Chaumont! Chaumont! We will stop at Chaumont for fifteen minutes.'

The guard walked down the corridor shouting the announcement. Then the train fell silent, and they waited.

Anatole could just twist round enough to rap on the wooden

strut, like a rib over his back. 'What is it? Why aren't we moving? What's taking so long?'

'I don't know,' muttered Jules, getting stiffly to his feet.

Through a crack in the blind, he saw men getting on and off the train. Jules wasn't sure if he was imagining the click of rifles being cocked. One bolt, two. Noise. Noise. How many more times did they have to go through this? He didn't think he could stand it again. And at last the train began to move again.

Anatole's eyelids kept sliding shut. Each time he felt himself floating and falling, he thought of death, and twitched his eyes back open. His portion of air might not last him. He mustn't breathe it in too fast. He'd almost been buried alive once. He couldn't suffocate now. From time to time, Jules reached a hand under the banquette and opened the lid a fraction, to let in the air and reassure him that they were nearly there.

Just as it was getting light, they pulled into another station, and it felt like a miracle. Jules slid back the window and put his head into the steam, wanting to be absolutely sure it was safe for Anatole to emerge. From the next carriage, a nun leapt onto the platform. *'Vive la Commune!'* came her triumphant cry, as she threw back her headdress.

There was nothing anyone could do. Perhaps nothing anyone here wanted to do. Anatole and Jules were safely in Switzerland, and like this Communarde, finally out of reach of arrest.

Anatole was stiff and shivering when Jules helped him out of the trunk: he leaned on his friend like an old man. They embraced each other, and then they wept. Anatole screwed up his eyes against the sun, and looked at the wonder of a blue sky and white clouds, and gulped down all the sweet air he could, before heaving himself back onto the train to continue the journey to Geneva. Jules opened the blind.

For some time they sat opposite each other in silence. Anatole stared at the carriage floor between his feet and thought of Zéphyrine's naked body, golden under the flickering candlelight of her draughty attic, but pale next to his own. He remembered how they had tangled their limbs together, and how it had felt to love her entirely, skin to skin. All that burning energy. It couldn't simply be gone, as easily as that, like a snuffed-out flame. He couldn't believe it.

'Jules?' he said at last.

'Yes?'

'Do you think it's not true then? I always imagined . . . Don't they always say . . . that people know, somehow, you know, when someone you love has died? That you can feel it.'

Jules looked out of the window. The pastures were very green, and clean, and normal. There were daisies and brown cows in them, and hay barns and sometimes orchards.

'I – I don't know.'

Anatole persisted. 'I know it sounds ridiculous . . . but I just don't feel that Zéphyrine can be dead. It's not that I don't believe you. I'm not accusing you of anything of course. But could you tell me again, just tell me exactly how you know, how you can be so certain?'

Jules couldn't do it again. His lips began to twitch; his whole face seemed almost to disintegrate.

'Anatole, I'm sorry. I can't. I can't be certain. I don't know where Zéphyrine is, or what has happened to her. But I couldn't let you go back, not when we were so close to getting out of

Paris, so close to freedom. I couldn't let you risk your life again when there was so little hope that it would do any good. And that's why I lied to you. Forgive me. Please.'

Anatole nodded, trying to take it in. Jules took both his hands, and looked straight at him, determined that Anatole would believe him this time. 'When we get to Geneva, we will start trying to find out. I'll help you. There will be a way. Someone must know. Maybe Marie can help us too. We won't give up. We'll do it together.'

'Yes, and of course I've got my photograph of Zéphyrine, thank God. Perhaps that will help our search.'

Jules steeled himself. Better to get this over with, he decided.

'Anatole. I'm so sorry. They searched our apartment. They've taken the photograph.'

The rain came back, more relentless than before. When it finally stopped, the flat plain around the prison was a sea of mud. Journalists came to stare. Their carriages sank up to their axles as they approached, and they were greeted by soldiers booted to the thigh in mud. Just outside the walls of the barrack yard, a group of disused tents lay collapsed in the mud, as if in surrender.

Cannon pointed into the yard, through rough holes knocked into the walls, either side of a closely guarded gate. Artillerymen stood behind them at all times, prepared for mutiny. Inside the yard, thousands of men were crammed into vast open sheds, a line of guards in front of each, and thousands more lay on sodden straw in the open, blue with cold and misery. The only building there housed the interrogation room, and above that, the women and children.

At least Zéphyrine was under shelter now. The shoes Marie had given her so carefully – her strongest shoes – had just about held together through the long march, but caked in ooze they refused to dry. There wasn't room here to lie down, and barely enough to sit but Zéphyrine preferred to stand. She wanted to be upright. They had been ordered to their knees so many times on the journey here – before every church they passed, and in front of the palace at Versailles, the cry '*À genoux! À genoux!*' was always repeated. Anyway, even with the layer of straw, the room's only furniture, the closer you were to the floorboards, the harder it was to ignore the low rumbling of questioning taking place, hour after hour, immediately below. But whether your hands were clamped over your ears, or a borrowed shawl covered your head, you couldn't help but hear the sound of picks and shovels outside, grunts and sighs of effort and despair, followed by the now-familiar volleys of shots.

All day the soldiers tramped down and up the bare board stairs. At night they arrived too, with lanterns swinging and always a list in their hands. When their heads appeared, the whole room seemed to catch its breath at once. Zéphyrine felt a fluttering ripple pass through her: the barely perceptible movement of several hundred heads, shifting at just the same time, in hope or in terror.

'I wish they would say my name,' murmured the schoolteacher eventually.

Zéphyrine shifted her weight, and rubbed the front of one calf against the back of another. A crust of mud crumbled onto the floor and disintegrated into powder. She shook her head. She knew that she wasn't ready to die without knowing what she was accused of, without a fight, without a trial. And if they said her name now, she could never find out where Anatole was. Even now he might be sprawled somewhere in the mud outside, just a short distance away. If they said her name now, she might never be able to find Rose's family, and thank them for all they had done for her, and tell them how brave Rose was when she died. If they said her name now, she would never see her own family again, never put fresh flowers on her grandparents' grave. Until they said her name, there was a chance. Until then, they could not destroy her.

34.

28th May

Seventy-two days. That was how long it lasted. And when on Sunday the curtain fell on the Commune, everything was left on show.

Victors and reporters came out to applaud and to condemn, holding handkerchiefs before their faces and treading carefully over pavements white-powdered with lime. Bodies were still warm in the cemetery of Père Lachaise when they arrived to inspect the battle scene, the boot-trampled flowers, funeral wreaths tattered to shreds, and sepulchres cracked open by shells. A journalist recorded fingerprints smeared in blood on a white marble slab, and imagined some wounded creature briefly clinging on in hope, dragging himself along the tomb before collapsing, or being dragged away for execution. Over the brow of the hill, he noted the blood-spattered wall and the burial ditch. There was no doubting that this city would never be allowed to rise in revolution again.

'*Inhabitants of Paris,*' read the placards on Sunday afternoon, '*the army of France has come to save you. Paris is delivered. At four o'clock our soldiers carried the last position occupied by the insurgents. Today the struggle is over. Order, work and security will now return.'*

The city was left a stinking, smoking ruin, the smouldering skeleton of the Tuileries Palace at its heart. Omnibuses were turned into hearses, and as the ashes of buildings cooled, a more reluctant fuel burned and festered. Complicated and foul, the stench intensified.

1880

Nine years later.

Zéphyrine is at sea again. Shackled below deck, but going home. Months and years of campaigns and petitions in Europe have come to fruition: every surviving Communard has been pardoned. The amnesty is complete. The last boatload has left the islands, and they are sailing towards Europe. Lying once more on planks, lulled by creaking wood and breaking foam, Zéphyrine tries hard to keep her mind on the future. Just one day ahead. One day, and then the next.

She's good at this now, practised. How else could you survive the uncertainty of life in a Pacific penal colony, the elasticity of years turning into yet more years, the distances of time and space colliding, with too many opportunities to see exactly what happens to those who lived in the past? It killed them, she saw. It broke their hearts.

But it never stops being difficult. Now that Zéphyrine is going home, it's harder than ever. Going home without knowing where home is, the nearer she gets, the more she can't help but look back. The swell of the waves, the stink of the hold, too much time doing nothing when she's used to working so hard: everything reminds her of the voyage out, when she slowly came to learn such tricks of thinking.

On that journey too, leaving France after the trial, her mind had drifted continually to the past. She had been in prison for two years already, brooding on all that had taken her there. On the boat, when they first set off into exile, everything seemed to take her backwards, even to a time before the Commune. One thing turned into another. Her skin, blistered from brief exposure to the burning sun, reminded her of her grandmother. At the end of a day's work, when the room was bright with flowers that had no smell, Zéphyrine used to peel the glue off her fingertips. Gran'mère would chide her, telling her to hurry, to get along. But glue dries like fish scales, translucent. You have to get it off, bit by bit. They get everywhere, fish scales. They stick to your hands and arms without you noticing. Then Zéphyrine went back further, right back to Brittany, to evenings by the fire tenderly picking stray fish scales from her mother's skin, when it was still just the two of them.

When they left, the exiles thought they were sailing towards coral seas and cannibals. That's what she'd heard one man say, the journalist with the high forehead who suffered from seasickness. The captain was wary, but the crew were not cruel. They hadn't heard the judges' speeches. Godless demons, moral monstrosities, the authorities pronounced, over and over again. The Communards were savages, said Versailles: France must be purged of their corrupting presence. The criminals must themselves be purged. So they'd been sent to civilise other so-called savages. It made no sense at all to Zéphyrine.

Ninety-four cages had been lined up on the gun deck of a frigate, opposite ninety-four more. Towards the stern were another forty cages, for the women deportees, a small cannon threatening every one. Even below decks, salt in the air dried stickily on Zéphyrine's face and coated her throat. It gave her a retching, intolerable kind of thirst, such as she'd never known before. Her tongue crept out involuntarily, sweeping across lips so cracked and dry that she could taste blood.

Memories like tides reconfigured her thoughts over and over again, drawing and redrawing everything she could remember. It seemed the only way to keep hold of herself. So she tried to remember everything she could about everything, and everyone. Anatole, hungry for her, always. Anatole, who made her feel precious. When she tried to remember their first meeting, it was overlaid with their last parting. She tried to remember Rose too: all spirit forever now. And Jules, so distant and unfathomable. Would he have saved her if he could? Was it possible he was there and had heard her calling him? And then there was Marie. Bitterly Zéphyrine remembered the old schoolteacher's words that afternoon at the prison, when Marie had appeared from nowhere, and vanished again. 'A kind girl, that one. She lived next door to me once.'

Every day people used to come there to sneer and point and triumph over the defeated Communards, to celebrate their degradation. Week after week, like visitors to a zoo or freak show, crowds of them appeared. A few days after the trial, Marie was suddenly there among them, her face white and shimmering like a ghost's, smeared in Zéphyrine's uncertain vision, as if she'd moved too fast before a lens. Zéphyrine flared to her feet. Pushing aside other prisoners, she ploughed towards the fence, fingers curling round metal.

They were face to face, breath to breath.

'Here,' Marie had whispered, pushing a package through the wire, through a space so small that the paper caught and tore. White cotton spilled out, streaked with rust. Marie had brought Zéphyrine what every woman in the prison yard most longed for – clean, fresh undergarments. For the first time in months, Zéphyrine's eyes overflowed.

Marie nodded at the parcel and turned to go, but a drowning cry stopped her:

'No. Not yet. You can't go yet. Come back.'

Reluctantly, Marie returned to the fence. 'I'm sorry . . .' she said. 'I'm sorry . . .'

Eyes wide, Marie watched silently, and made sure that Zéphyrine found what she had hidden. Tucked inside the underwear was an article torn from a newspaper. A list of names: all the Communards who had been condemned to death in their absence the previous week. Anatole's was near the top, shakily underlined. He is alive, Marie had written in the margin. And soon he will know that you are too.

Alive. They were both alive.

'You told him?'

Marie seemed about to choke. But she gathered herself together. 'He wrote to me,' she said. 'For news of you.'

Zéphyrine's joints loosened, weakening her fingers, and the clothing and paper fell from her hands to the mud at her feet. She gripped the fence again, thrusting her face against the metal so that it dug into her skin. She wanted it to hurt. She wanted to see if she could feel.

'What did you say? How did you know what to tell him?'

'I went to the Prefecture last week. I asked. They told me you were here, that you were still waiting for your trial. Anatole didn't say much, just that Jules had helped him to escape to Geneva. He only agreed to leave Paris because he thought you were dead.'

Geneva . . . not so far. Zéphyrine's hopes briefly rose, and then fell. It made no difference how far it was when returning to France meant execution for Anatole.

A trio of middle-aged women appeared, cackling and crowing and laughing about the pitiful state of the prisoners. They jostled Marie, pushing her along a few steps to the left, and Zéphyrine had to scrabble along the fence on the other side to keep her in sight. She was determined not to lose eye-contact. She was afraid Marie would drift away, disappear. She had to keep her in earshot.

'Do you have an address?' Zéphyrine begged, trampling her new clothes in the mud. 'Can you send a message?'

Marie didn't exactly answer. 'They were moving on, to London. He gave me a forwarding address and I've written to him there. Thousands are waiting in London already, waiting for news, waiting to see if it will ever be safe to return. But I will try to come back, don't worry. I'll let you know.'

She dissolved into the crowd, and there was nothing Zéphyrine could do. Maybe she really did mean to come back.

The trial, so long in coming, was over almost before it began. The charge was arson, the evidence cursory. Zéphyrine decided to confess. What did the truth matter by then? She would have built a wall of flame across Paris to protect her friends from slaughter. She wished she had. The Commune had looked after her when she had nothing and taught her how to hope. It had offered her everything: she owed it everything.

In the courtroom, the judge waved a photograph from the files. Her stomach turned in recognition of her own stern face. For the briefest of moments, she believed the worse. It was Anatole's picture. Anatole must have betrayed her. How else could they have that card? Where had they found it? Or had they stolen it? Then the judge held up another piece of paper, and read aloud the denunciation, which was signed in ink. Quite a rarity, he remarked. They had thousands of such notes, but most were anonymous. 'There is a *pétroleuse* from Montmartre hiding in my room. Her name is Zéphyrine. You will find her in Room 31, Staircase 10, cité Bergère, Paris.' Then he read the name: Marie Le Gall. Zéphyrine was still trying to breathe when the next prisoner was shoved forward, and she was pushed away.

Her sentence was transportation.

A few days later the prisoners shuffled on board the *Virginie*, destined for New Caledonia.

On board a ship, in any prison, time telescopes.

In the middle of nowhere, Zéphyrine lay in her cage, throat rasping.

'Citizen!'

At the sound of a woman's voice, a man dropped down from the upper deck. He was a Breton sailor whose songs had kept them warm a few weeks earlier as they sailed into the dark frozen air and polar seas south of Africa. White snow dissolving into blackness. The songs made Zéphyrine think of Concarneau, its fishermen and its clifftops, and the scent of yellow gorse blossom. And later still, the strange white fruit of the coconut palm would make her think of those songs again.

'Citizen!' It was the prisoner they called the Red Virgin, the woman who had found her a job when she was destitute. 'This young woman needs some water. Can you help?'

The sailor nodded, and went for the barrel.

The Red Virgin never gave up hope, thought Zéphyrine. Nobody had courage like her. Better to be in exile, she whispered, than stay in Paris and see the collapse of all their dreams. She was the kind of woman who saw diamonds flash in the rushing wake of the ship, and heard organ music in the roar of the wind in its sails. She refused to give up looking to the future, yet she also knew how to hold on to the past. She told them to remember Delescluze: he returned from exile, coming back half-broken from Devil's Island, and yet he took to the barricades a third and final time for the Commune. You had to keep fighting, she said, even if you die fighting in the end.

The Red Virgin wrote letters and scribbled messages, and the comforting words she passed through the bars to other prisoners were smuggled from cage to cage. One day Zéphyrine received a poem she had written about the albatrosses, those huge white birds whose wings beat against the sides of ships long after sailors have hung them by their beaks to die. Angry and loud they swish and drum at first, then ever more forlorn, they fall silent. The men refuse to cut their throats for fear a drop of blood might stain their feathers.

Zéphyrine took the scoop of fresh water in both hands, and let it trickle slowly down her throat. It was warm and stale, and tasted of wood and iron. Then the last mouthful was gone. She handed back the wooden scoop, and ducked her head. 'Thank you,' she said. 'You're very kind.'

He shrugged, and went to see if any of the other Communards were thirsty.

Zéphyrine stood up then, and searched for the Red Virgin's eyes to thank her for the water and smile. She was right. Better to live fighting, she thought. And she knew then that she wanted to stay alive.

She still does. For nine years now, she has stayed alive.

Colville Place, London. November.

A hansom cab and a couple of four-wheelers are waiting at the end of the pavement when Anatole comes home. He tips his dripping hat to a trio of departing ladies, wishing he'd timed his return slightly better. Jules's last portraiture session has clearly overrun. Now that these young women have seen Anatole, they seem to be taking even longer to leave, fussing about with coats and muffs and umbrellas, and upsetting the landlady, Mrs Barton, who is doing her very best to see them out with all haste. Chorus girls, Anatole decides, as he presses himself against the wall of the narrow hall and their giggles fade. He can imagine exactly the kind of photograph they wanted on their visiting cards, and the mood Jules will now be in: this is his least favourite type of work. But it all helps make ends meet. It might even fund a visit to Savile Row. Jules hasn't once mentioned his father since his disinheritance, but giving up the regular services of a good tailor has possibly been the hardest thing for him to bear.

At last the terraced house is silent and the hooks in the hallway are bare except for Jules's coat. Anatole puts down his violin and hangs up his mac. He's already had an entire day's worth of sidelong looks from young ladies, having spent the morning giving private lessons in various Marylebone music rooms under the scrutiny of a succession of governesses, and the afternoon taking choir practice at a new girls' school in Camden. Which had been even more exhausting – all those dark tunics and serious faces. All he wants now is simply to sit down by the fire, dry off his shoes and trousers and do absolutely nothing for the rest of the evening.

'Cup of tea?' says the landlady. 'I'm just making a pot for Mr Crowfield and his visitor. Another French visitor, he's got.'

'Oh. Then, yes please, Mrs Barton. No milk, if you don't mind. They're in the studio, are they?'

'That's right, dear. I'll be along in a mo. I expect you'd like a crumpet, too, would you?'

'Splendid stuff,' agrees Anatole.

Mrs Barton disappears into the kitchen and Anatole heads up the stairs to join Jules in the glass room built on top of the first-floor rear extension. It's considerably smaller and colder than the old Paris studio, and has no view at all, but the light isn't bad, and the location certainly suits Anatole: just off Charlotte Street they are completely surrounded by fellow exiles from France. At least they were until very recently. Anatole braces himself for another conversation about 'going home', perhaps even another fond farewell. He needs to talk to Jules about his own return. His family has come to visit a few times, but not recently, and it's been over ten years now since Anatole left Limoges. He has to make a decision.

The voices stop. Anatole is greeted at the threshold by silence, and the sight of Marie. He closes his eyes. The last time he saw her was in the Tuileries Garden that Sunday evening in May, nine years earlier. After she wrote back to him, confessing her part in Zéphyrine's arrest and conviction, he broke off all communication with her. Something about the way both she and Jules stare at him now, their identical expressions, makes him think that perhaps Jules didn't do the same.

'Hello, Marie,' says Anatole. 'I saw you were in town, but I wasn't expecting this.'

Marie's name is often on the posters outside the Opera House these days, and just as often in the gossip columns. She made a career for herself outside France at first, and now flits regularly between Paris, Rome and London, clearly well looked-after wherever she goes. She looks odd here, like a peacock in a pigeon's nest. Anatole's coldness doesn't disconcert her. She stands up to offer him a hand, which he duly kisses. It feels plumper than he remembers, and it's decorated with plenty of jewels. She still smells of jasmine. That unsteadies him more than the changes.

'I wanted to make sure you knew, that you both knew.'

She looks to Jules for reassurance, who looks at his feet.

Anatole can't stop himself. 'I really don't want you here. I'd like you to leave now.'

'Please stop being angry with me,' says Marie. 'Please.'

Jules stands up, nods at Marie, and walks across to Anatole. He takes his arm, and leads him to an armchair, as if Anatole is an old man. 'I hope you won't be angry with me either,' he says.

'What? What's the matter with you both?' Anatole shakes him off, resisting his efforts to soothe him. He thinks someone must be dead. He fears the worst. 'For God's sake, tell me what's going on. Why should I be angry with you, Jules?'

Again they look at each other.

'You tell him,' says Marie. 'But this time you have to tell him everything.'

'I know.' Jules nods. 'I was going to. I was always going to. I've made too many excuses already.'

Anatole feels sick. 'What about?' he says.

'I'll start at the end,' says Jules.

'Just start,' whispers Marie.

'Yes. Of course,' Jules says. 'Listen. First of all, Marie has some very good news. It's not completely certain yet, mind you, and perhaps we shouldn't get our hopes up – but there's a boat coming from Sydney, and —'

'Zéphyrine? You think Zéphyrine is on it?' Anatole is on his feet again. He can't possibly sit down. He's been waiting so long. Over the years, he's tried to write, but it was hard to keep going forever, not knowing if a letter would actually arrive, how many months or years it might take, or if he would even still be living at the same address by the time any reply could make it back. Zéphyrine did not write with confidence, he knew. Once a letter reached him, just once, four years earlier, but it didn't say much. It didn't sound like Zéphyrine. Ever since the official pardon, announced in July, Anatole has been paralysed by uncertainty, waiting for a reason to act, unwilling to leave the only address he knew she could possibly have for him. 'They've released her? My God, my God. I must get to Paris. Will they let me go now? Must I get a passport first? Tell me quickly, I don't know what to do. I'll need to go quickly, won't I? I can't risk missing her.'

He keeps turning from Jules to Marie, grabbing at them as if he could shake the information out of them, as if he's quite forgotten why he has not seen Marie for so many years. Looking at Marie more closely, he realises that she must know things, and that she has ways of finding things out. He doesn't want to know what these are. 'What must I do?'

'Calm down, first of all. Because the boat is apparently due to dock here, in London —' says Jules. Anatole is almost out of the door already. 'Wait! It's not due till the morning. Just listen. There's more.'

Anatole is almost incapable of listening. He lets them sit him down again, but his fists keep drumming on his knees, and his feet drum the floor. Tap, tap, tap, tap.

'I must get ready. I can't miss it. What if she's not expecting me? What if I'm not there on time?' The worse possibility he pushes away, but it comes back of course. What if she doesn't want me now?

'You will be,' says Marie. 'But surely you can't wait at the docks all night. It's not safe. And I have to warn you again, my information is very good —' (her blush is almost unnoticeable) '— and I'm sure this boat is coming. But I don't know exactly who is on it. I can't promise.'

'Of course you must go,' says Jules.

'I can wait all night. I'll go and get ready now. I'll change my trousers. Are you coming?'

'No, I think you should go by yourself,' Jules says very slowly, and Anatole remembers.

'What else? What else were you going to tell me?'

At just this moment Mrs Barton bustles back with a rattling

tea tray and her sing-song announcements. 'Butter! Milk – not for you, dear! Sugar! Strainer! Think it's all here! And I'll be off . . . I've laid a cold supper in the sitting room, as I'm out tonight.'

'Mrs Barton,' says Marie with enormous charm in her delightful English, looking her straight in the eye. 'I wonder if you could show me the way to . . .'

'Oh yes, certainly . . . Do follow me, madame.'

Then Jules and Anatole are alone. Neither speaks immediately and Anatole's dread quickly gathers. Several times Jules walks the short distance from one end of the studio to the other. Finally, he pulls up a footstool next to Anatole's armchair.

'Now, I don't know how to say this. It's about Marie. You've blamed Marie for everything all these years, I know. Ever since you wrote to her from Geneva, and she had the guts and the honesty to write back and tell you what she'd done.'

'I'd have found out eventually,' points out Anatole. 'Almost certainly.'

'Perhaps. But she had the courage to admit it to you. She wasn't proud of it. She's always regretted it. But at least she was prepared to be honest.'

It's true. And as the exiles have discovered, Marie was hardly the only person that terrible week to save her own skin with such a betrayal. How many years of secret notes had burned with the Palace of Justice, and how many more were written while it still blazed? It was not surprising, perhaps. Born and bred into a police state, Parisians had been trained for years to react like that. Anatole thinks of Marie, and her brother Emile, and their own desperation. He feels he has nurtured his anger for quite long enough. Everything is about to change, after all. There's a relief in letting go.

'Yes, you're right,' he says. 'When she comes back, I must say something. And I will. A complete amnesty – that's the idea now, after all. All sins forgotten and forgiven. A fresh start for everyone, I hope.'

'Yes,' says Jules quietly. 'Forgotten and forgiven indeed. But I haven't finished.'

Anatole's cold dread returns. 'Go on,' he says.

'You wouldn't be needing to forgive Marie if it weren't for me. She'd never have had the chance to betray Zéphyrine. On the train to Geneva, do you remember that I told you I'd lied about her execution, to try to stop you going after her, to save your life?'

'Of course I remember,' Anatole says. His voice is slow and uncertain. 'Keep going.'

'It wasn't all a lie. She did come looking for you, to our apartment. I heard her. I even saw her. She was dressed strangely, and she . . . she was carrying something. It sounds so stupid now, but I was frightened. Terribly confused and uncertain. You don't know what it was like there then. Everyone was talking about the *pétroleuses*. Everyone was terrified, infected by a kind of madness. And she had something in her hands, but I couldn't see what it was from upstairs. I just didn't know. I should have checked. I should have gone down right away to make sure. I shouldn't have jumped to conclusions. I should have been quicker about everything.'

By this time, Jules is leaning on Anatole's damp knee and weeping. Anatole strokes his hair, and notices a few grey strands. 'Shhhh . . . shhhhh . . .' he says.

'I should have let her in. I betrayed you both.'

346

'Yes.'

'I'm sorry,' says Jules. 'It really was my fault. You can't know how sorry I am, how many times I've tried to tell you.'

The idea has dawned on Anatole slowly over the years. He's gone back over their conversations too many times. He knows Jules far too well not to have already begun to guess where truth shaded into fabrication. He hasn't made it easy for Jules to tell him before now. He could pinpoint the times he had let a conversation swerve. Part of Anatole hadn't wanted to know.

'Well. You've told me now. I'm glad of that. We can draw a line. And now I'm going to change these blasted trousers. Can I take your thick coat? It's going to be cold tonight. I can't wait until the morning. I want to go right now.'

Marie waits for him to get ready, and then they hail a four-wheeler and she accompanies Anatole to the docks. Just before she drives off – he doesn't ask where she's going next – she presses his hand, and wishes him luck.

'Ask for the *John Helder*, coming from Sydney,' she reminds him, and then says, 'So will I see you now in Paris? Soon, perhaps?'

'Perhaps,' he replies. 'We'll see.'

The rain is beginning to turn to mist, flattening the big square warehouse buildings into a kind of stage set. Anatole walks alone down to the quayside, and gazes out at the forest of masts on the water. How will he ever find the right ship? How does it all work here? A prostitute comes out of the shadows, calling something he doesn't quite understand, and he turns briskly away, out of the heavily spiced air that makes him think of gingerbread and into the nearest pub, warm and yeasty with ale and tobacco smoke and sawdust.

When the roar of voices begins to separate itself out, Anatole realises that there are other French speakers among them. He sees faces he recognises from meetings around Charlotte Street and Fitzroy Square and Saffron Hill, and one or two from Paris itself. Others have come to meet this ship too, old Communards in exile, and they talk about who might be aboard – the Red Virgin, someone thinks, though others argue – and they invite Anatole to join their party. They've already chartered a pleasure launch, and others are arranging fishing boats to meet the deportees.

They share memories and swap stories all night, and by the morning the mist has turned to fog, a thick white fog that smothers everything and is so dense that some of the pilot boats refuse to leave port. Muffled foghorns sound from the stranded vessels in the middle of the Thames. Warehouse owners fret, and dockers stand idle with nothing yet to unload. But the easy-going captain of their own launch is undaunted – he doesn't want to give back shillings already in his pocket – and off they pitch into the whiteness with lanterns lit, straining their ears and calling out to warn of their presence. Anatole begins to sing. Soon he hears voices joining in from all the other small boats that are bravely heading out with them.

'*Quand nous chanterons le temps des cerises . . .*'

While tiny droplets of water cling to their hair and glisten on their eyebrows, as they tighten the mufflers round their necks, the exiles sing again of the cherry season, and of love, and nightingales and sorrow. Before they reach the end of the third verse, they can make out new voices, still unseen, coming from down the river, singing the same words. Anatole falls silent, and listens, hope rising, for that one familiar voice.

Historical Afterword

Aftermath

Figures for the number of Communards (and suspects) killed during Bloody Week and in the reprisals that followed remain a matter of significant debate, but most historians agree on a figure between 20,000 and 35,000. About 43,000 captives were taken to Versailles, resulting in over 100 death sentences, 13,000 prison sentences and 4,000 deportations to New Caledonia. In the final week of its existence, 55 hostages of the Commune were executed, including the archbishop of Paris, while in the Versailles army 877 were left dead and 6,454 wounded. Paris was under martial law until early 1876. Thousands of French men and women returned from imprisonment and exile after a complete amnesty for Communards in July 1880.

The existence of organised *pétroleuses* has never been proven.

Ruins

Thomas Cook began organising trips to see the ruins of Paris within weeks of the Commune's destruction. Within a few years, Paris had been completely rebuilt – including the Vendôme Column, Thiers's house, the Hôtel de Ville and the

Théâtre Lyrique, largely with identical reconstructions – and the Sacré-Coeur de Montmartre was erected on the site of the artillery park where the revolution broke out on 18th March in 'expiation' for the crimes of the Commune.

Only the ruins of the Tuileries Palace – much photographed – were kept, as a warning against revolution. These were controversially demolished and cleared in 1883. Pilgrimages to the cemetery of Père Lachaise (where Oscar Wilde is also buried) began in 1880. They reached a peak in 1936, when 600,000 demonstrators gathered at the Mur de Fédérés where 147 Communards were gunned down and buried on the last day of the Commune. The wall was only classified a historical monument in 1983.

Connections

The Paris Commune was of huge symbolic significance to the International Brigades during the Spanish Civil War (1936–9), as I discovered while writing *A World Between Us*. The song that united Republicans and foreign volunteers was 'The Internationale', which was written by Eugène Pottier at the fall of the Commune. At least four French battalions were named after either the Commune or significant Communards.

These included Louise Michel, known as the Red Virgin, who never gave up her revolutionary activities and ran an anarchist school in London when she came to Britain in 1890 to escape police harassment in France. *Liberty's Fire* began to take shape in my head after I came across Michel's extraordinary story through my great-great grandmother, N. F. Dryhurst (an anarchist herself and translator of Kropotkin's

The Great French Revolution) who volunteered at this school alongside her lover, the war journalist Henry Nevinson. You can read more about all three in Angela V. John's *War, Journalism and the Shaping of the Twentieth Century: The Life and Times of Henry W. Nevinson* (2006).

Find out more about the history behind *Liberty's Fire* at
www.lydiasyson.com

Acknowledgements

You wouldn't be reading this book if I hadn't received a grant to write it from Arts Council England, for which I am profoundly grateful. Public investment in arts and culture is currently under serious threat in this country and I hope this won't be the case for much longer.

I have also benefited hugely from expertise embodied in the following libraries, archives and museums: the British Library; the London Library; the Eugene W Schulkind Paris Commune Collection at The Keep (University of Sussex Special Collections); the Liddell Hart Centre for Military Archives, King's College London; the Bibliothèque Historique de la Ville de Paris; the Musée Carnavalet; the Musée d'Art et d'Histoire de Saint Denis; the Musée Montmartre; the Musée de l'Opera and the Musée de l'Armée (Paris) and I'm particularly grateful to Laura Gaudenzi and her colleagues at the Musée de l'Histoire Vivante in Montreuil. Les Amies et Amis de la Commune de Paris have also been a superb source of information. My ideas were very much shaped by Delphine Mordey's invaluable PhD research on music during the siege of Paris and the Paris Commune, and she was generous in sharing this, while Marshall Mateer first alerted me to the significance of photography during and immediately after the Commune.

As always, vast quantities of thanks are also owed to the regular suspects: to Natasha Lehrer, both for putting me up in Paris and putting up with my endless requests for translations, explanations, directions, readers . . . (pedants of the world unite, and that includes you, Raphael Vock); to Catherine Clarke, always there; to the brilliant Hot Key team, especially Sarah Odedina for believing in *Liberty's Fire* in the first place and Naomi Colthurst for taking over the editorial reins with such grace; all my Finsbury Group; Tig Thomas, ever incisive; and finally my whole family (partner, parents, siblings, children), every one of whom has played a vital part. What would I do without you?

Lydia Syson

Lydia Syson is a fifth-generation Londoner who lives in Camberwell. She spent much of her early working life as a World Service radio producer, leaving the BBC after the birth of the first of her four children. She went on to write a PhD about explorers, poets and Timbuktu and then a biography of the eighteenth-century 'electric' doctor, James Graham, *Doctor of Love*, before turning to fiction. Lydia's first novel, *A World Between Us*, was longlisted for the Guardian Children's Fiction Prize and shortlisted for the Branford Boase Award, with a special 'Highly Commended' mention from the judges.

Find out more about Lydia at: www.lydiasyson.com or on Twitter: @LydiaSyson

Thank you for choosing a Hot Key book.

If you want to know more about our authors and what we publish, you can find us online.

You can start at our website

www.hotkeybooks.com

And you can also find us on:

We hope to see you soon!